THE BRAMBLE BUSH

is the powerful and disturbing novel which has provoked a huge storm of moral and literary controversy from coast to coast. Some of the widely differing comments follow:

YES "Extraordinary novel . . . a matter for controversy . . . destined to be a best seller. Don't miss it!"

BOSTON HERALD

NO "You will be hearing a lot about THE BRAMBLE BUSH. The author makes a feint at mercy-killing as a theme, but his book is not about that sore and baffling subject. Its chief concern is the equally complex matter of S-E-X!"

RALEIGH NEWS AND OBSERVER

YES "Soul-searching, thought-provoking . . ."

FORT WAYNE NEWS-SENTINEL

NO "Bound to become controversial, THE BRAMBLE BUSH is a 'sexsational' book, involving major and minor characters in sex of one kind or another; name it, it's probably here—frankly, in detail and spelled out."

HE PILOT

YES "A big novel about people in a small town who have much to hide."

LOS ANGELES HERALD-EXPRESS

NO "A lurid novel . . . THE BRAMBLE BUSH is a sex-steeped story of a small town."

NEW HAVEN REGISTER

YES "A mixture of the best elements of **Peyton Place and Anatomy of a Murder!**"

LOS ANGELES MIRROR-NEWS

NO "Why must it be published? Why does Hollywood buy such tripe?"

AUSTIN STATESMAN

YES "Deals with big sins and big problems . . ."

ANNISTON STAR

THE BRAMBLE BUSH

CHARLES MERGENDAHL

*This low-priced Bantam Book
has been completely reset in a type face
designed for easy reading, and was printed
from new plates. It contains the complete
text of the original hard-cover edition.*
NOT ONE WORD HAS BEEN OMITTED.

THE BRAMBLE BUSH
*A Bantam Book / published by arrangement with
G. P. Putnam's Sons*

PRINTING HISTORY
Putnam's Sons edition published August 1958
2nd printing ...... August 1958
3rd printing ... September 1958
4th printing ... November 1958

Bantam edition published June 1959
2nd printing .... June 1959
3rd printing .... June 1959
4th printing .... June 1959
5th printing .... June 1959
6th printing .... June 1959
7th printing .... June 1959
8th printing .... July 1959
9th printing ... February 1960
10th printing ... February 1960
11th printing ..... March 1960
12th printing ..... March 1960
13th printing ..... March 1960
14th printing ..... March 1960
15th printing ..... March 1960
16th printing ...... April 1960
17th printing .... May 1960
18th printing .... July 1960
19th printing .. September 1960
20th printing .. September 1960
21st printing .... May 1961
22nd printing .... May 1962
23rd printing .. November 1962
24th printing .... July 1965

Published simultaneously in the United States and Canada.

---

*Bantam Books are published by Bantam Books, Inc., a subsidiary
of Grosset & Dunlap, Inc. Its trade-mark, consisting of the words
"Bantam Books" and the portrayal of a bantam, is registered in the
United States Patent Office and in other countries. Marca Registrada.
Bantam Books, Inc., 271 Madison Avenue, New York, N. Y. 10016.*

PRINTED IN THE UNITED STATES OF AMERICA

In memory of Katherine,
who is still helping.

There was a man in our town,
And he was wondrous wise.
He jumped into a bramble bush,
And scratched out both his eyes;
But when he saw his eyes were out,
With all his might and main,
He jumped into another bush,
And scratched 'em in again.

—Nursery Rhyme

PART ONE

CHAPTER ONE

He lay quiet a moment, groping for the nightmare that had left him shaky. Caesar whined, then barked. The phone continued ringing. He shook his head violently, pulled up from the bed, stumbled down the narrow "ship's stairs" to the hallway, through the small living room with its huge brick fireplace and Dutch oven and beamed ceiling, on to his office—white and clinical and modern, in direct contrast to the rest of the house.

He jerked the receiver from the wall phone, said, "Doctor Montford," and listened to the woman's excited voice rattling on about a crushed finger in the Portuguese section along the lower water front. He said, "I'll be right there," returned upstairs to the bathroom, doused cold water in his face, and stared at his own tired eyes in the mirror above the basin. The beginnings of permanent circles were impressed like molded half-moons above his cheekbones. Lines ran out from his mouth along the square shape of his jaw, and the tip of his nose was a reddish purple left over from a bad sunburn during the early summer months. He decided he was working too hard, he should go sailing more often, then pulled on his clothes and went down the stairs again, through his office and the waiting room beyond, out to the gentle black rain that left a shine on the streets and sidewalks.

The fisherman swore Portuguese oaths while his finger was being bandaged. His wife hovered nearby in a flowered kimono, worrying, "How we gonna pay you, Doctor Montford? How? . . . How, with the last baby not paid for yet?"

"Now that's my worry. All you've got to do is keep right on having them." He smiled at her dark face, closed his bag, said, "Just don't let your husband fool around with outboard motors at four thirty in the morning," then waved good-by, returned to his house, and made himself a large breakfast of fried eggs, Canadian bacon, toast, and black coffee.

It was still only twenty after six. He looked out the kitchen window at the falling rain and murmured, "Larry comes today." His own voice startled him and, washing the dishes, he forced his mind to grasp at other thoughts—other hands washing other dishes—the Indian woman from Mashpee who'd been his mother's cook. She'd spoken beautiful English and made quahog pies for Friday suppers. That was quite a time ago, back when he'd lived among three-ply carpets and horsehair sofas and a corner cupboard littered with sea shells and strange bits of coral that his seafaring grandfather had brought back from some round the world voyage.

The phone rang again, and he rose wearily, thinking that perhaps he should hire a housekeeper. He was too disorganized. He needed someone to turn his eggs and dispose of the outdated magazines in his waiting room, pay his neglected bills and get him permanently settled into the orderly routine of a young widower.

He picked up the receiver. "Doctor Montford," while he leaned an elbow against the white plaster wall.

The answering voice was gruff, even harsh, and directly to the point. "Guy . . . Kelsey here. . . . There's been a fire out on that Falmouth cutoff. Bolls is tied up, and I can't leave the hospital myself. So if you'd get out there pronto—"

"The cutoff?"

"The Robins Nest Motel. You'll see the police cars."

"Sure, all right." And then, "Isn't Larry due about now?"

"Don't worry about it."

"But Sam's expecting me to be on hand when the plane arrives."

"To hell with Sam! People are dying out there, so will you please get off your ass and get going!"

The receiver was slammed down from the other end.

Guy swore and shrugged into his raincoat. He picked up his black bag, spoke an "O.K." to the brown mongrel dog that waited by the door, then went out to the garage and drove his car down the winding hill through the softly falling rain, past Pat's Bar and Grill and the barbershop and the liquor store, past the tearoom and the cut-rate drugstore and Castner's Drygoods and a souvenir shop with pink shells in the window, past an antique shop and the office of the *Chronicle* and East Norton's new supermarket that boasted meats wrapped in cellophane and wire baskets on wheels.

The streets of town were deserted now in the early morning light of mid-September. All still, cool, no sounds at all, until he heard the erratic sputtering of an engine in the field behind the hospital. Then, swinging onto the Falmouth Road, he saw the helicopter. It had just landed, and the propeller stopped turning as he slowed the car and stopped. The door was flung open and the pilot leaped out while the silent crowd edged forward, opening their collective mouths, shuffling their collective feet.

Among the watchers he recognized Chet Belknap from the boatyard; Nancy Messner from the *Chronicle;* Bill Watts, the milkman; the sheriff, Larson Whitt, and Stewed Schaeffer, the town drunk, whose first name, Stewart, had not been used by anyone for more than twenty years. Doctor Kelsey was there, too, his white hair matted by the rain. And Sam McFie was there, striding nervously back and forth between Saul Kelsey and one of the two nurses who waited beside him.

Guy sat motionless, wetting his lips, waiting. The pilot reached up and helped a woman leap lightly to the ground. She was dark, wearing a gray gabardine suit and a transparent plastic raincoat. Her hair glistened black in the rain. She turned to Doctor Kelsey and Sam McFie. Sam flapped his arms like the wings of a hurt bird, and then Sam and Doctor Kelsey and the pilot climbed back into the plane. They emerged a moment later carrying a white stretcher. A man lay on the stretcher. Sam held his raincoat protectively over the man's face. The crowd edged in closer, still silent, leaning forward, too. His elbow brushed the horn rim, and the sudden blast was an explosion in the still morning.

The crowd started as one, turned as one, and looked directly at him. Chet Belknap and Bill Watts, Nancy Messner and Larson Whitt, and even Stewed Schaeffer, who staggered with the effort. The dark woman turned with them. Even at this distance he could see that her eyes were black without expression. He wondered if he should wave, call out that there'd been a fire at the Robins Nest. "Cut it out," he said aloud. "People are dying, so get off your ass and get going!" His foot jammed down on the accelerator. The tires squealed on the wet pavement. Through the rear-view mirror he saw the crowd turn back toward the man on the white stretcher. The stretcher moved fast across the field and into the hospital. Sam McFie ran stumbling beside it, still holding his coat over the patient's face. The dark woman walked behind him, slow, her feet dragging in the rain-soaked grass.

". . . Mr. and Mrs. Robert Briskin."
"You sure?"
"It's on the register. Couple in Number 6."
"Lucky."

"Yeah, she's coming around now. Doctor'll be here in a minute, soon as he gets through with that crowd in Number 5."

"Four of 'em."

"And now there are two. Both girls burned beyond recognition. And if *that* ain't bad enough on their families—well, being here at *all,* you know. Eighteen years old, burned up drunk in a crumby bed with a couple of bums who picked 'em up in a bar in Falmouth."

The voices talked in Fran Walker's darkness. They could not be talking about her, though, because there had been only herself and Bert, and they'd been in Number 6, not Number 5, so she could not have been burned beyond recognition. She was hearing the voices, wasn't she? Except perhaps she could still hear—burned beyond recognition, only her ears still alive, all the rest of her charred and dead, with only her ears left . . . two naked ears . . . listening . . . listening . . .

She screamed and opened her eyes.

A state trooper was bending over her. He was young, tanned, wearing a brown western hat. "You're all right, Mrs. Briskin."

"Bert . . . Bert . . ."

"Bob? Your husband? He's all right, too. There . . . See, right there beside you."

Fran turned her head slowly to the side. She was lying on a twin bed in another room, not Number 6, but much like Number 6, and on the bed next to her Bert sat motionless, his head bent forward into his hands. He wore only his pants, and despite his broad shoulders and the big muscles in his naked back, he looked very pathetic, a small, pathetic boy with his strong hands trembling against his face.

The trooper had moved back to the doorway, where he spoke in low tones to an older, heavier state policeman. Then suddenly he turned back to her. "O.K. now," and he stepped aside to let Guy Montford through the doorway.

In that moment Fran Walker died a second time. She tried to sit up, but could not. She closed her eyes tight and heard the trooper say, "Mr. and Mrs. Briskin, Doctor. The husband's all right, I think, but Mrs. Briskin was moaning about her side a while back, so if you could take a look—"

"Fine," Guy Montford said.

Fran opened her eyes again. She watched Guy's tall frame bend over as he spoke to Bert. "You all right, Mr. Briskin?" Bert stammered something low and horrified as he recognized the doctor, and Guy said, "All right then, if you're well enough to drive, why don't you go along to the hospital in

East Norton? It's straight on down the road. Can't miss it. They'll give you a check-up there, and in the meantime I'll have a look at your wife, then drive her back with me."

The two troopers left the room. Guy put a hand under Bert's bare elbow. His professional voice abruptly personal. "Come on, Bert, come on, fella. You're all right. Everything's all right."

Bert shook his head and laughed a strange, crazy laugh that meant nothing at all. "Listen, Guy . . . Understand, Guy . . ."

"For God's sake, Bert, don't go worrying about your wounded dignity at a time like this." He helped Bert on with his shirt and coat, his socks and shoes. He slapped his shoulder, said, "Come on, fella," and Bert said, "O.K., O.K." But he was still laughing foolishly as he turned toward her and started to speak, couldn't, waved his hands, then moved wearily out the doorway.

Guy closed the door. She watched him turn casually and look down at her. "How do you feel, Fran?"

"Guy . . . Listen, Guy . . ."

"Now I've already told Bert—stop the nonsense."

"Please, Guy—"

"Understand you fell—hurt your side."

She nodded dumbly, her eyes fixed on his face. But she found no accusation there. He was a doctor trying to help her, a friend trying to comfort her. She watched his tanned face come closer, felt his carefully impersonal hand slide gently, probing against her ribs. "Does that hurt, Fran? . . . That? . . . There?"

"No," and "Yes, a little."

He patted her shoulder when she started to cry, then turned away and preoccupied himself with closing his bag.

She sat up. "My underclothes . . . my shoes and stockings . . ."

"Can you manage by yourself?"

"Yes, I think so."

"We'll have that rib X-rayed back at the hospital." He had turned toward the window, where he stood motionless, his back to her as she took off her dress, put it on again over her bra and panties, then pulled on her shoes and stockings.

The long silence became unbearable. "People," she said finally, squirming her foot into a shoe, "other people . . . they were hurt . . ."

"Two girls. The fire started in Number 5. They were drunk and dropped a cigarette on the bed."

"It's terrible."

"Yes."

"An awful thing," thinking about herself as well as the two girls in Number 5. "All right now." She moved toward the doorway, wavered.

He caught her arm, looked directly into her eyes, and his voice was very soft and warm and sympathetic. "Fran . . . I realize how you feel about this. But you're lucky. You're both very lucky, and that's all you should think about now."

"I guess so."

"And the police report has you listed as Mr. and Mrs. Robert Briskin. So will mine."

"Guy . . ."

"Now just forget about it." He swung away, opened the door, and led her out to the gravel drive.

The rain was still falling gently. She was aware of the two police cars and the single, old-fashioned fire engine, tended by volunteer firemen busily pumping water through a window of the long, rectangular building. Now, in daylight, in the rain, the motel looked ugly, shabby, dirty, so that she felt sick and wanted to get out of here and never come back again. She turned blindly toward Guy's car and saw the two dazed men, grimy, wild-looking, standing stupidly by the covered bodies of the two dead girls. The girls' legs stuck out from beneath the blankets. One of them had lost a shoe from her left foot. The other had no feet at all.

"Where'n the hell's the ambulance? Where'n the hell?" one of the grimy men kept repeating, until finally the older trooper touched his arm (roughly, Fran thought) and said, "What difference does it make anyway? What the hell difference?"

Guy opened the door and helped her into the car. He went around the front, got in on the driver's side, and had just started the engine when the green sedan screamed into the drive, slammed to a stop, and Parker Welk stared across at them through his open window.

Parker was unshaven, his fringe of hair uncombed, his white mustache a dirty gray; and, always, his eyes probed into her and through her, so she wondered if he knew what she was really doing here—and if so, how he would use it to his own advantage.

She looked aside, out the opposite window. She heard Parker say, "Some fire, eh, Guy?" and, "How'd you get here so fast anyway?"

Guy said he'd received a call from the hospital. He'd met Fran walking back from the bus stop, and had brought her along to help out. "Nothing like a good nurse at a time like this."

"Yeah," Parker said. And a pause, and, "Visiting in Falmouth, Fran?"

She forced her head in his direction, forced her eyes to remain steady on his. "Yes. . . . A nurse at the hospital there. I'd just gotten off the bus when Doctor Montford saw me."

"Yeah," Parker said, half acknowledgment, half question. "A lucky thing."

"A lucky thing," Guy said. Then he nodded and swung the car out to the highway.

For a while they drove in silence. Fran stole an occasional glance at Guy's face in the mirror. He looked worried, preoccupied. She stared ahead at the slippery road. There were scrub pines on either side. Occasionally they passed a pond, a tiny orchard, a stand of summer corn, once an oddly shaped windmill. A rabbit darted out before them, ran ahead for a few yards, then jumped off into the brush. The tires hummed and Guy looked straight ahead and she wanted to scream into the unspeaking silence.

"Fran," he said finally, "there's absolutely no reason for this to go on anybody's official record. And I lied to Parker Welk because if you know Parker, he'll print anything in the *Chronicle,* no matter what it is or whom it hurts."

"He likes it better when it hurts."

"But he won't even know, so don't you worry about it." He handed her a cigarette, held the lighter for her. She had to hold his hand to steady her own, and she liked its big warmth and the way he squeezed her fingers to comfort her. There was something she had to say, some way to make him understand why she had been there at the Robins Nest with Bert Mosley, why she had been with Bert on other nights in other places. It was extremely important, because then, if he knew . . . if he really knew what went on inside her . . .

Funny, though, she started talking about her childhood instead. "I was born in Indiana, you know. A town called Sagamore. It was even smaller than East Norton, but I left it when I was eighteen, you see, to become a nurse. I remember it so clearly, though. . . . Of course eight years ago isn't such a long time really, but I remember *so* clearly . . . going to Sunday school in a pink dress, and a dog, a big Irish setter—even bigger than Caesar here—and his name was Alfred. And my first boy friend . . . I was only fourteen at the time, and he was such a baby . . . Such a child, even though he was two years older than I was . . . I mean I had to treat him gently, and I liked him, but I didn't *want* to treat him gently, you see . . . And it's like that with Bert, too, you know. He's such a smart lawyer, and so ambitious, too, and he's good-looking, and strong as a bull, but still he's almost a child about some things, and—" And there she was, going on and on, faster and faster, the words tumbling out all together, explaining how she felt almost motherly toward Bert, almost sorry for Bert—exposing Bert and herself, too, saying all the things that she had never said and should never say to anyone.

"I'll bet you miss that pretty town sometimes."

The tires hummed. The windshield wipers clicked. And she thought how considerate he was—how good and strong and attractive and considerate.

A helicopter rose up beyond the rim of trees. It hung there, sputtering, like a huge dragonfly above them.

"Larry McFie?" she asked.

Guy nodded, and they drove on in silence through the rain.

CHAPTER TWO

The Mills Memorial Hospital stood next to the library by the single stop light at the fork where Main Street branched off from the macadam road that ran on eight miles east to Hyannis, thirteen miles west to Falmouth. Its name was derived from the widow of a New York millionaire, a Mrs. Cyrus Mills, who'd left most of her money for the purpose of converting her monstrous summer home into a badly needed hospital. And though her bequest had been used wisely, the hospital was still inadequate for the town's needs. Gray and awkward and Victorian, it rose high over the library, its dormers looking out on all sides, its chimneys poking their red snouts above the slate roof. A portico projected over the curved gravel drive; black fire escapes ran up and down all sides; and rhododendron bushes leaned wearily against the framed walls, struggling to stay alive in the sandy soil.

With only thirty-eight beds, the hospital was still badly under-staffed. The nine permanent nurses lived in the made-over stable, and though elevators had been installed, the operating and X-ray rooms were poorly located. East Norton, however, was grateful to have any hospital at all. Accordingly, the citizens had entrusted it to the care of their oldest, most experienced physician, Doctor Saul Kelsey, who laid down the rules and ran everything in a firm, if slightly offhand manner.

Now, in the growing morning of this wet September day, Sam McFie paced nervously around the green linoleum floor of Room 2B, located on the hospital's second floor, with a window that looked out across the bay. It was the largest, finest private room (only one other had a bath), and had been scrubbed, painted, polished and redecorated under the efficient direction of nurse Fran Walker.

Sam plucked a petal from a huge American Beauty rose that stood among many in one of a half-dozen vases of flowers. He read the inscription on a tiny white card. "Get well, Larry, from the class of '38." There were other "Get well" cards, from the Congregational Church, the Rotary, the "Boys down at Pat's," from the volunteer firemen and the high school faculty and the staff of the hospital. Sam read all the cards. He turned toward his son. "Everyone remembers you," he said. "Everyone says to get well." He swung abruptly to the window, looked down at the gravel drive below. "Where's Guy? . . . Where the hell is Guy? . . . Promised to be here, and then some goddamned fire, and—"

He moved away, sat close to the bed in a folding metal chair. Sam was a nervous, almost boyish-looking man, despite his thin reddish hair, the weary slope of his shoulders. He wore hairy sport coats, gray flannels, and loafers—never a complete suit except on special occasions and church on Sundays. His hands twitched constantly, touching each other, his own haunted face, his sun-bleached eyebrows, the sheets of the bed. He trembled all through his body, swore violently, rose again, paused again, then stopped abruptly as Guy Montford came through the doorway.

"Guy— Where the hell—what the hell—"

"Sorry, Sam. An emergency."

"Isn't *this* an emergency?"

Guy did not answer. He moved slowly toward the figure in the white iron bed, looked down at Larry McFie, who had disappeared somewhere in sickness, leaving a strange man under the fresh white sheets. His face was old and wasted, so he looked much like an unhealthy version of his father, and nearly as old. His naturally light hair was mottled and grayed; his cheeks had sunken, and the lines of pain were etched permanently above his eyes. He was thirty-six and he looked fifty. He'd been a drinker, a lover, a soldier, an athlete, and was now too weak to raise his head from the pillow. But he managed a smile as Guy edged closer. His bony hand jerked painfully upward. "Hello, Guy. Hello, fellow."

Guy took the clawlike hand and squeezed it gently. "Good to have you back, Larry."

"Good to be here."
"Tired after the trip?"
"Got a shot before the plane ride, and I just woke up."
"Well, fella, you look like hell." It was the best way. Casual, out in the open, the lies hidden behind the informal frankness. "First thing, have to fatten you up." He sat in the folding chair, said "Fatten you up" again, and added, "Have you up and around in no time."
"Cut the crap," Larry said, then turned his head away. "The room's nice. Fixed up nice." His eyes moved over the prints along the wall, over the gay monk's-cloth curtains and the table radio and the portable television and the case of books and magazines.
"Well, you're special, you know. Even a good view of the harbor." Guy rose and cranked the bed up slowly until Larry's eyes could see above the window sill. "The white Friendship out there. She's mine. Remember?"
"Yeah—the last time I came home. You and Julia had just named her—some ridiculous name."
"*Tinker Bell.* But I changed it to *Julia* six years ago."
"Sure." And then, after a pause, "I'm sorry, Guy. I wrote you at the time. But what can you write?"
"Nothing. Sometimes things happen, and you can't say anything at all." He moved to the window and stared out across the bay. He picked out the light at Keever's Point and the roof of Sam's cannery, the gold cross on St. Joseph's, and the jagged line of rocks where Julia's car had gone off the road those six years ago. He'd been on a call in Pirate's Cove at the time, and when he'd stopped in at the hospital on his way home to dinner, he'd noticed Doctor Kelsey and two nurses in the Emergency Room, and he'd said, "What's this?" and stepped through the doorway and seen her lying there with a great gash between her wonderful breasts. She had never regained consciousness, and had died only twenty minutes later.
Behind him Sam complained, "Well, if you're not going to *do* anything, Guy—"
"An old hen," Larry said, "and he hasn't eaten yet either."
Guy said, "Why don't you eat something, Sam?"
"Well, I don't know—"
"Go on, Dad. Please. Go eat something."
Sam's voice croaked good-by. His loafers shuffled toward the door, then stopped as he apologized, "I'll only be a minute. Just a minute." Then the hard-soled shoes once more, thumping out to the corridor, where the sound was muffled on the rubber carpet.
"How's Dad been?" Larry asked.

"All right. Fine."

"No more trouble? None of that old business?"

"No."

"That's good."

"Yes." He rested his forehead against the cold grass. Before him was the present: the bay, his house on the hill, a small house with gray weather-beaten shingles and sixteen-paned windows and a unique and unsightly widow's walk that jutted from the room—an old house, built in the late eighteenth century by men from the South of England with memories of Cornish cottages against a hill. And there was *Julia* at her mooring—white, graceful in her chubbiness—a thirty-two-foot Friendship from Casco Bay, never converted from the fishing boat for which she was designed, because like all Muscongus Bay sloops, she could not take the docking of her main boom and the shortening of her bowsprit.

"With a smaller sail area," he said aloud, "she'd be slower, wouldn't tack so easily."

"What?" Larry said.

"Julia."

"A good boat."

"Yes, a good boat." A good boat and a good house, all in a good present before his eyes, while in the room behind him a good part of the past lay dead and shriveled with pained eyes that looked backwards now because they would never see a future beyond the walls of this very room. For Larry was talking of old times now, reminiscing over the fishing excursions in open dories, the duck shoots at dawn with the gray clouds above the Cape Cod marshes and the shotguns held loose in the crooks of their arms. "God, those were the days! . . . Remember that time we swam to Keever's Point?"

"I remember."

"Only I didn't make it so you had to tow me in. Actually saved my life. And remember those boats we used to race across the bay? Not much, but it seemed they'd go like hell in those days . . . And the time we decided to smoke cigarettes, and the time we had one drink apiece and thought we were drunk as hoots; and those two summer girls—sisters—both of them virgins, and so were we, for that matter—in the beginning anyway—and you went to confession afterwards, twice in the same morning . . ." talking on about this time and that time, with his voice rising in enthusiasm while Guy listened and nodded and marveled at the bald courage of the man.

"They were sure the days," he agreed. And then, somehow, hearing the enthusiasm in Larry's voice, he could not stand to hear it, and he remembered that back then, back in those days that were "sure the days," Larry had been dependent upon him for every piece of boyhood adventure. He'd been the older of the two, the unofficial leader who planned each escapade, while Larry had trusted his judgment in all things, no questions asked.

Now Larry remembered. And now again Larry trusted, because Guy Montford was leader, and Guy Montford made no mistakes. He placed his fist against the window and noticed the white of his own knuckles and wanted to smash the fist against the glass.

Behind him the voice had changed. It was serious now. "Hear me, Guy . . . Hear me . . ."

"Sure, I remember," turning slowly from the window.

"You weren't listening."

"That time with the two sisters."

"Yeah . . . that time and other times." Larry laughed jerkily, winced suddenly in pain, and when the spasm had passed, he spoke more deliberately, more urgently than before. "Margreth—my wife, Guy. Went out for breakfast so I could see Dad alone for a minute. Wish you'd sort of—look out for her. She's a fine person, Guy. Done everything for me. Stayed up night after night. Everything . . . and all tired out now . . . and you know what Dad's like . . . So it'll be tough on her, and—" The pain returned. He grimaced and lay quiet.

Guy looked at the pain-racked face. "I'll get you a sedative."

"Promise you'll—"

"Anything, Larry . . . *Anything!*"

"Take her sailing. She'd love sailing."

"Of course I will. Of course." He rose, rang for the nurse, and sent her quickly for morphine. Giving the injection he thought how far down the road Larry had come. Past the codeine and aspirin. Past the demerol to the quarter grains of morphine. He sat and waited with perspiration running in trickles down his back. He did not feel cool again until the pain lines had gone and Larry slept.

He was still watching the final calm on Larry's face when the slight rustle of cloth sounded close behind him. He turned slowly and his eyes found the woman standing there in the center of the room. She wore the gray gabardine suit and plastic raincoat he'd seen before across a field. She was slender, nearly fragile, and rather tall, with shiny black hair that was pulled back straight and smooth, tied in a knot behind her head. Her face was oval and white and delicate, her eyes black, her mouth a gently curved line of red. She was a tired woman, but one who stood proudly with no expression on her face, with only the sadness of her long suffering there in the reflected light of her eyes. She smiled with the corners of her mouth. "Hello—I'm Margreth."

"Hello." He pulled up from the chair. "Hello, Margreth." He touched the white extended hand, looked into her eyes for a moment, then back to Larry's peaceful face. "I gave him a sedative. He'll sleep for a while."

"Did you—talk to him?"

"Yes."

"He was all right? Cheerful? All right?" The accent was Southern without being a drawl—a soft voice, a trifle husky, so the words were clear and seemed to echo in the room, though she scarcely spoke above a whisper.

"All right," he said.

"Well then—" She stopped, and he understood why and felt the same himself. There should be a great deal to discuss. Yet here in the room with Larry sleeping only a few feet away, the words could not be found. There was too much antiseptic in the air and their voices were too low and the shoes of a passing nurse made too soft a sound in the hall outside.

"No sense in waiting," he said finally. "I'll drive you out to Sam's if you like. Show you the town along the way."

"Larry—"

"He'll be asleep for quite a while."

She turned and started for the doorway, paused, and swung back into the room. She approached the bed, looked down at the white, sunken face, then bent and touched Larry's forehead with her lips. "Go to sleep," she whispered. "Go to sleep." She straightened and moved out through the doorway.

Guy walked behind her. He noticed the way she carried herself, tall and straight, though she must be aching with weariness. Her slender legs moved out firmly, and the sound of her high heels was rhythmical, like a steady heartbeat on the matting along the hall. He watched the black knot of her hair, and noticed how perfectly groomed she was despite the travel and confusion and lack of sleep.

Fran Walker stepped out of the elevator as they approached. She wore a stiff white uniform, neat and clean. But her eyes were tired, her forced smile weak and embarrassed.

Guy touched her arm. "Fran . . . This is Mrs. McFie . . ." Then to Margreth, "Fran Walker, our prize nurse. She'll be seeing a lot of Larry. In fact, Fran's responsible for having made his room so livable."

Margreth nodded and said, "I appreciate it, Miss Walker. You've been very helpful."

"Anything I can do, Mrs. McFie."

"How's the ribs?" Guy asked. "Get them X-rayed?"
"Yes, and it's just a bruise."
"Sure you feel like going on duty?"
"Yes, I want to."
"Well, that's fine." He turned back to Margreth. "The reason I wasn't here when Larry arrived—a fire down the road, and Fran went along with me. She had a small accident tending the victims." He guided Margreth to the elevator, hoping he had said everything just right. Not too much, not laying it on, but exactly right.

Sam came hurrying toward them as they crossed the gravel drive. "You're leaving? . . . Where you going? . . . Shouldn't somebody be up there?"
"He's asleep," Guy said.
"All the same—"
"He'll sleep for quite a while, Sam."
"All the same, I'd—I'd like to go up again. Just sit there, you know. Just sit." He looked at Margreth. "But I guess you're tired. You want to get unpacked, get some rest."
Guy said, "I'll drop her off myself."
"Well, if you don't mind." Then to Margreth, "And the housekeeper's there—Mrs. O'Hara—she'll take care of you." He hesitated. His mouth worked. Then he turned abruptly and strode away.

Guy looked after him. "He's had a rough time. All his life. But you'd be surprised. He's a good businessman. Tough. Smart. He built that cannery out of nothing. Survived the crash, got through the depression." He led her quickly through the drizzle to his car. And then Caesar was slobbering on her raincoat and she laughed and said, "Hello, boy, hello, fellow," and he said, "All right, leave her alone, Caesar," and, "He goes everywhere with me, wouldn't miss one of my calls." Then they were inside the car, out of the rain, and he tried to relax. But the windshield wipers clicked out of rhythm and the cigarette tasted too dry and the blue smoke was suffocating as it swirled about his head.
"Want to look at the town?" he asked.
"All right."
"If you'd rather go straight to Sam's—"
"No, I'd like to just sit and ride for a little."
He drove slowly through the town. "There," he explained as they moved on over the wet pavements, "that's the courthouse, the green, the Civil War cannon, monument of the Civil War dead, and down there the railroad station . . . only two trains a day, though, stopping off between Falmouth and Provincetown . . . And all the stores are right along here on Main Street . . . Quite a few of them, you see, but most

of them are closed up now after Labor Day . . . We're a summer town now, though when I was a kid, nobody'd really 'discovered' East Norton, and we had only a small scattering of summer people, and no 'foreigners' at all during the winter . . . Now we have quite a few, though . . . artists, a couple of retired businessmen . . . Bert Mosley, one of our two lawyers . . . He was from Boston originally, came here sort of by chance, set up a practice, and now he'd like to go back, I think, but he's sort of stuck here . . . Oh, and there, down the side street—that's part of the original section of town . . . That sailmaker's shop is supposed to date back to 1660 . . . A lot of fishing back then, though the first settlers were farmers mostly. Not much farming now, but there's still plenty of fishing, only the fishermen are mostly Portuguese now . . . And over to your right, that's the office of the *Chronicle* . . . Owned by Parker Welk . . . You'll probably meet Parker soon . . . The *Chronicle's* a weekly, because our population in winter is less than a thousand . . . Five times that in the summer, though, so there's another paper during July and August, put out by a group of the cottage owners—social news mostly . . . And there's the yacht club and Sam's cannery, and up there, above us, that's my house . . ."

"It's nice," Margreth said. "It's lovely."

"After you've lived somewhere long enough, you stop knowing whether a house is beautiful or not." He drove on, talking as they went. He showed her the Congregational Church, the Presbyterian Church, the Lutheran Church, the Methodist Church. "Even the churches are closed in the wintertime, except for the Congregational and St. Joseph's up ahead there. About sixty per cent of the town is Congregationalist, about thirty per cent Catholic, including all the Portuguese, of course, and the other ten per cent don't go to church at all."

"Which are you?"

"The minority," he said. Then he slowed and waved at Stewed Schaeffer, who was moving dazedly down the road toward Pat's. As always, Stewed wore those flashy, outdated clothes of thirty years ago—a bright vest, a gold watch chain, a stiff collar and string tie, narrow trousers and spats. The clothes were clean, though worn and patched, and there was a strange, sick dignity in Stewed's face as he turned his bleary eyes toward the car.

"How goes it?" Guy said, forcing the words from his throat, hoping that someday he would get over this awkwardness with Stewed. Someday he and Stewed would both forget the wall between them.

They drove on into the small Portuguese fishing section, and he became conscious of Margreth's dark eyes watching him in the mirror. "Well, that's about all, I guess."

"You're very popular, aren't you?"

"I know everyone, if that's what you mean."

"No, that isn't what I mean. The special way you seemed to feel about that drunken old man—as though you'd once been friends or something."

"We were never friends." He laughed. "That's very funny."

"Is it?"

"Yes, it's very funny." They were passing St. Joseph's then. Father Serrano, the Italian priest, was moving slowly from his house to the church next door. Guy called out to him, and the old man turned and moved toward them, limping slightly, leaning heavily on a twisted cane, his hair almost pure white against his black coat.

"Guy," he said. "Guy . . ."

"Hello, Father." He introduced Margreth, and the priest's bright smiling eyes studied her candidly, then swung back to Guy again. "We've completely redecorated," he said.

"Yes, I noticed the windows. They're new."

"Imported from Italy. But you should see inside."

"Maybe I will." Guy grinned, embarrassed. "You never can tell, Father."

"No, you never can tell." He nodded and limped away.

Guy drove on again. He felt uncomfortable, having seen Stewed Schaeffer and Father Serrano all within minutes. There were things he did not want to remember, and he pushed them from his mind, conscious that Margreth still watched him in the mirror. He knew they'd been avoiding everything, driving around and talking and avoiding everything. "What are you thinking?" he asked finally.

"That once you were a Catholic, and still are really, but you don't go to church any more."

"Something like that."

"I was a Presbyterian before I met Larry. Then, after we were married, I became a Congregationalist."

"Did you?" And then, after a moment, "Well, that's about it. East Norton in a clamshell."

"What's that big place up there?"

"Oh, that's the old Lincoln Hotel. Stays open all year, but does a pretty slow business after Labor Day. A few rooms, dining room, bar." She was staring at the old building, and he guessed what she was thinking. "Would you like to go in? . . . Something to eat? . . . Coffee?"

"No, I—"

"Name it."
"Well, I—frankly I could stand a martini. But I promise you, I don't generally drink in the morning. My nerves are terribly on edge, though. But if it's not proper. I mean—"
"We don't have to worry about what's proper," although of course he did, or had, and would again when everything returned to normal. He parked before the hotel and walked beside her across the wooden porch and into the tiny cocktail lounge. He hadn't been in the Lincoln himself for a long time now. He preferred the meals at Pat's, and since he seldom drank anything but coffee and Coca-Cola, there was no reason to enter the Lincoln outside of those occasions when he spoke at the Rotary meetings.
The cocktail lounge had been repainted since he'd last been here some months before. A nickelodeon had been added, and the old cross-legged tables had been replaced by metal ones with formica tops. The walls were covered with imitation knotty pine, and the ash trays were made from painted clamshells. It was an ugly, untasteful place. But Margreth paid no attention to the room. She sat in a plastic-covered booth, laid both hands on the table, and accepted the cigarette from his crumpled pack.
"I suppose I'm keeping you from your patients," tapping the cigarette on the table between them.
"No."
"You're trying very hard to be nice."
"No, I—naturally I want to help Larry's wife all I can."
"You think I need help?"
"I think it's only normal for you to be depressed."
"You're trying very hard to be a doctor—just a doctor."
"Does it show?"
"Very much."
"I'm sorry." He could not explain, and was relieved when Betsy came and he ordered a dry martini for Margreth and a bottle of beer for himself. Betsy eyed Margreth curiously while she took the order. She was dark herself, thin, as close to being a prostitute as any woman in East Norton. She'd gone to school with Guy, and once, long ago, he had slept with her. It had been a meaningless, almost repulsive experience, yet he still felt awkward in her presence.
Betsy left, and he said, "I've promised to take you sailing, let you get some salt air against your face."
"He's going to die, isn't he?"
"Everybody's going to die."
"Doctors are always so terribly vague. Please don't be a doctor. Please don't be vague."

"Margreth—it's Hodgkin's disease, and of course it's serious, and sometimes doctors give up hope. That's something I've never done."

"Oh, it was explained to me very clearly once. A lump in the neck, fever, disease of lymph nodes. They grow big, then more and more grow big. You treat it with X-ray and nitrogen mustard— You see, I know all about it."

"Nobody knows all about it." And he waited with his fist knotted once more until Betsy brought the drinks and he relaxed his fist and poured the beer into the glass, tipping it carefully to avoid too large a head. He did not really want it, but knew Margreth would be more at ease if he drank something too. He put down the bottle and said, "Here's the go," and raised his glass. She raised hers, carefully, trying not to spill it. But her hand was shaking, and a few drops of liquid ran down the stem and dribbled on the table. Her fingers were long and her nails red, and her lips were smooth and red when they touched the glass.

"There!" she said. "There—now let me hold the glass. You see, that's the important thing. Just to hold something. And now tell me very carefully and very clearly. When is he going to die?"

"Please, Margreth . . . Please . . ."

"I want to know. When is he going to die?"

"Margreth . . . you've seen other doctors, and I'm sure you've already been told everything there is to know."

"When will it happen?"

"When he's ninety-five."

"You're as vague as the others, aren't you?"

"Look, there's just no sense in talking about it."

She took another large swallow. Her eyes were black and wide above the rim of the glass. "I'm trying to be glad that Larry came here. I'm trying to believe it's the best thing for him."

"It's a nice town. It's Larry's."

"And yours. Larry's and yours. Not mine at all."

He was not quite certain what she meant, and did not give her a direct answer. He said, "You won't find Larry's father an easy man to live with."

"We will have something in common though—all three of us—we all love the same person." She finished the martini, snubbed her cigarette carefully in the green-painted clamshell, then stood and walked stiffly to the doorway. She did not speak again as they drove through the wet town, turned left, then right again on Elm Street, which ran parallel to Main.

Sam McFie's house was a large white two-story Georgian,

with a hip roof, two huge chimneys and a beautiful old door boasting Corinthian pilasters, front and side fanlights, and hand-carved woodwork. Set back from the road, it was now, one hundred and fifty years after a rich sea captain had built it, nearly obscured by the elm trees and high rhododendrons, Norway spruce and forsythia and lilacs and rose bushes that huddled against its front and sides.

Guy pulled into the drive and switched off the motor. "There's a terrace out back," he said. "You can still enjoy it for a few weeks more."

"A few weeks?"

"Indian summer," he said carefully. *"Please* . . . I was talking about the weather."

"I know. I'm sorry." She stared through the window at the great white house. "So this is where Larry was born . . . lived twenty years of his life."

"Yes." He paused. "Your bags?"

"They were sent ahead by taxi."

"Well, Mrs. O'Hara will take care of everything."

"Yes—I'll take a bath and get some sleep."

"You need sleep."

"I know." He watched her step out to the drive, pause, then turn back and pat Caesar as a drop of water rolled along her forehead and her eyes became dark and faraway, looking at something he could not see. "You don't know how long?"

"Until after the leaves fall."

"Larry? How long it will be?" He did not answer. She said, "I know anyway," and forced a quick smile, turned sharply, and walked to the doorway with her black hair glistening in the rain.

CHAPTER THREE

The dream was strange and almost terrifying.

A horse appeared without warning from around the corner of the hospital. Guy slammed on the brakes. But it was too late then. The horse reared. The small boy on its back fell crying to the ground, and the horse's forelegs crashed down through the windshield. Guy said, "Are you all right?" She nodded dumbly. Guy got out of the car, picked up the small boy, brushed him off and comforted him until he stopped crying. He looked at the horse. The horse was screaming. There was a great gaping hole in its side. Guy went back to the car, drew a revolver from the glove compartment, and deliberately shot the horse in the center of its forehead. She saw the brown, pain-racked eyes, heard the explosion, saw the sudden round hole as the horse's eyes glazed over. Then she screamed, again and again. She turned and ran stumbling, falling, picking herself up, running on up the little hill past Guy's odd-looking house, which was right next door to the hospital. Guy shouted after her and she kept on running. He kept on shouting and she kept running. But the house got no closer because she was not really moving at all, and finally she fell exhausted at the side of the road . . .

Margreth opened her eyes. She closed them again, then opened them very slowly. She was lying in a strange high-canopied bed in a strange large bedroom, furnished with colonial furniture and hand-hooked rugs. Darkness fell outside the window. Rain fell with the darkness. The horse still screamed and Guy still shouted and she still lay there at the side of the road.

She shook her head violently, sat up, noticed that she wore only a slip, and fell back once more against the pillow. She touched the slip and remembered that she had bought it at Bergfeld's in Atlanta only a few days before she and Larry had left for a town called East Norton, somewhere on the south shore of Cape Cod. So now everything was all right, because she'd been having a nightmare, of course, and she was lying now in an upstairs bedroom in the house of Mr. Samuel McFie. A Portuguese housekeeper with the ridiculous name of Mrs. O'Hara had shown her to her room, where she'd taken off her dress and lain down in utter exhaustion. That had been some time in the late morning. Now it was after seven at night.

She lay still, caressing the silk slip. She would sleep many nights in this bed, have many feverish dreams in this bed. Many nights and many dreams, or a few nights and a few dreams, until it was all over, ended, *kaput,* until "Death do us part," and she could think about that now, squarely, without horror any longer, simply because she could not quite believe her own forced resignation.

She must never think of the future again. She must not think, "Next summer," or "When you are well," or "When we are old"—not about that trip to Italy they'd been planning for five years now—not about that baby they'd been planning for fourteen. She must not wonder what Larry would look like when he was sixty, or whether or not he would ever become a vice-president at Dekker and Lobe or finish that do-it-yourself bookcase he had started in the cellar. She must think only in the past, remember only what had been, what *was*, good and bad alike—Larry's bright, boyish face when they'd first met at that U.S.O. dance back those fourteen years ago, the quick, crazy courtship, and the marriage itself over the protests of her mother who believed that good Southerners never married anyone from north of Washington . . . The year without Larry, absorbing herself in gardening and Red Cross work and Presbyterian church activities, until he'd come back one bleak February day, when it had been snowing even in Georgia, slush in the gutter, and he'd made wild love to her again—a funny, almost immoral event, because it had happened in the very proper guest room of her mother's proper house.

Twelve years ago now, with ten good years that followed after, before the sickness had come from nowhere—before the laughter had given way to pain on twisted lips, the love-making to exhaustion—before the eager, still young, still bright-eyed man had turned slowly to a ghost, and the rich feeling between them had vanished with him. Not love that had gone, for she loved him more than ever now, with the ache gnawing ever deeper into her heart and bones, but their oneness rather, so she could no longer reach out and touch the very soul of him. If he were well—if she were sick—then perhaps they would make contact again—in the same way, a different way, some way that was not this—the crying inside, the blind groping toward him as he dropped ever closer toward that place to which she could not follow.

She sat up, pushed to her feet, and looked out the window at the night and the rain falling gently on the brick terrace.

Mr. McFie's car was in the drive. Dinner would be served in a few minutes now. She selected a dark, conservative dress from the clothes that Mrs. O'Hara had hung neatly in the closet, slipped it over her head, then sat at the vanity and ran lipstick along her upper lip. She wondered at a woman's vanity table in an impersonal guest room. A young girl with bobbed hair, wearing a dress of the twenties, smiled at her from a photograph in a gold frame. Larry's mother probably, who had died in childbirth. She was pretty and looked a great deal as Larry had looked in the long months ago.

A knock on the door and Mrs. O'Hara's voice calling, "Mrs. McFie?"

"Yes, I'm awake."

"Dinner'll be served in a few minutes now."

"Thank you, I'll be right down." She pressed her lips together, spreading the make-up evenly, then stared intently at her own face in the mirror. Larry maintained it was a beautiful face. Larry's face, too, had once been beautiful.

"Now stop that!" She rose abruptly, brushed out her hair, pulled on her stockings, and slipped into her shoes. She glanced out at the rain once more, then opened the door and stepped into the upper hallway. From below she could hear the hard, erratic click of Mr. McFie's loafers as he walked between the braided rugs on the old pine floor of the living room. If he didn't stop that, she would scream. If she screamed, then he'd probably become hysterical. Larry had warned her of his changing moods, his deep depressions. Once, years ago, he'd spent some months in a sanitarium. But he was completely well now. He would stay well, so long as he didn't drink—so long as he kept himself under control.

"Don't you worry, Mr. McFie." She spoke aloud, then straightened her shoulders and walked stiffly down the stairs.

The living room was large, with white paneling beneath the windows and around the fireplace. The furniture, like the fittings, was simple colonial. But among the English china and Revere silver were a black-and-gold lacquer box from China, a huge Japanese silk on the far wall, rare shells along the mantel, bits of ivory and alabaster, and two great pink matching sea shells from the West Indies. A green poll parrot sat on a perch by the window. His name was Peter, Mrs. O'Hara had said. Peter had been a gift from Mr. McFie's secretary. Everything else in the room, though, had belonged to Mr. McFie's relatives, handed down through many generations of sea captains and cabinetmakers, fishermen and farmers, ending here with Mr. Samuel McFie, who applied modern methods to can the same fish his forefathers had caught in the years ago.

Sam turned from an old dry sink converted into a bar. In his hand was a highball. "Have a drink?" he said.

"No . . . thank you." She stared at the drink, at his trembling hands, his thin body coiled like a steel spring.

"Dinner'll be ready in a minute."

"Fine," she said. "I'm hungry."

The phone rang in the hall. Mrs. O'Hara's dark face appeared in the doorway. "It's Mr. Parker Welk at the *Chronicle*."

Sam went into the hall. Mrs. O'Hara glanced at the open bar and frowned darkly. She started to speak, then changed her mind and went back to the kitchen. Sam's voice said yes, Larry was fine, and yes, Mrs. McFie was here now, and yes, Guy had already seen Larry, and was extremely optimistic.

The phone clicked down and he appeared in the doorway. "The local paper," he said, and moved back to the bar.

Margreth watched his shaking hands as they mixed another drink. She thought he had no business drinking anything, and he had no business telling the local paper that Doctor Montford was optimistic.

"We'll go up to the hospital again tonight," Sam said. "Guy'll be there, and maybe he'll have some new ideas."

"Ideas?"

"What to do."

"Mr. McFie—Larry's already been in two other hospitals. Doctor Montford has all the records. He already knows what to do."

Sam turned away and took a long pull at his drink. "All the same," he murmured. And then, "He's a good doctor, Guy is," as though trying to convince himself more than her. "And a damn nice fellow too."

"I know that."

"Lot of people around town think I have something against him. But that's not true. I try to be a fair man, business and social both. Guy was Larry's best friend—all through school together, and I never tried to break them up."

"What are you trying to say, Mr. McFie?"

"Saying I don't go along with this 'Like father, like son' business."

Mar watched him curiously. Larry had told her that Guy's father had been a very successful, very popular doctor in East Norton. He'd started to say more. But then suddenly he'd stopped and changed the subject.

Now Sam was changing the subject too. "Go to church with me on Sunday. Meet the minister—Doctor Treleaven—and some of the ladies. They'll invite you around, give you something to do—"

"Yes . . . That will be fine."

Sam looked out the window at the rain, started to speak, stopped, then said it flatly. "Guy—he doesn't go to any church."

"I know."

"Oh?"

"He told me."

"I see." He pulled at his drink once more. "Well," he said, slowly, bitterly, almost fiercely, "well, his father did. He was a Catholic . . . He was a Catholic, and he killed my wife."

Then Mrs. O'Hara announced dinner, and Sam put down his empty glass and turned and walked into the dining room.

Parker Welk sat at the roll-top desk in his cluttered office at the rear of the printing shop. He sat in shirt sleeves, writing laboriously in longhand. ". . . Mrs. McFie, the former Margreth Sloane of Atlanta, Georgia, accompanied her husband on his return to East Norton . . ." His meaty hand moved slowly across the paper, made the final period with a heavy stab.

He was through for the night. But it had been a rough day, almost as bad as those eighteen-hour days during the height of the summer season. Two large events at once were almost more than the *Chronicle* could handle. But Jean Messner had done a good feature story on the landing of the helicopter, and he'd covered that fire at the Robins Nest himself. "The two survivors, Mr. and Mrs. Robert Briskin . . ." He drew the story from under a sheaf of proofs and stared at it intently, unblinking, for a long, silent moment. He smiled. Finally he laughed outright. "Jesus!" he said, "a sitting duck!" He was still laughing when he reached for the phone on the small table beside his desk.

"Mills Memorial Hospital . . . Nurses' quarters."

"Hello, this is Parker Welk at the *Chronicle*."

"Oh, hello, Mr. Welk. This is Ida Primmer."

"Just wondering, Miss Primmer . . . Fran Walker wouldn't happen to be there, would she?"

"Why, yes, she is, Mr. Welk. Would you like to speak to her?"

"Please," he said, then added, "About that fire at the Robins Nest. I understand she was there with Doctor Montford. I thought she might fill me in on a few details."

"I'm sure she'd love to. If you'll hang on a minute." Miss Primmer's voice faded on the last few words.

Parker sat motionless. He felt a quick dampness on his shirt. His hands was sweating, too, ruining the helicopter story. He swore and pushed the story aside, drew out a handkerchief and mopped his face. He cleared his throat, twice, then three times, and kept his voice low, sure, almost flat when Fran finally answered. "Hello," he said. "Fran . . . this is Parker. You remember I saw you at the fire this morning, and I thought you might give me an eyewitness account."

"Well, I—" Fran's voice sounded nervous. "Perhaps if you asked Doctor Montford—"

"I'd rather ask you."

"But I'm sure Doctor Montford—"

"I'm sure *you'd* like to tell me about it, wouldn't you, Fran?"

A long pause. She was a sitting duck and he knew it. But just to make certain, he added, "I wanted to ask you about that Robert Briskin couple. I talked to the state police about them, you see, and they sounded like quite an interesting pair.

Wife about twenty-five, wearing a white cotton dress . . . Man about thirty-eight, big, curly blond hair . . . You know . . . They sounded interesting."

Fran did not answer.

"Did you hear me, Fran?"

"Yes, I heard."

"Shall I say any more? I'm a thorough reporter, you know."

"No, don't say any more."

"Sunday night then?"

"Sunday?"

"Here at my office. We'll talk about it." There was a long silence, and for a moment he was afraid. The sweat turned cold on his hand, and he moved his mouth closer to the phone. "Fran . . . Fran . . . I won't touch you . . . I promise that . . . I won't lay a finger on you . . ."

"I believe you." There was contempt in her voice. The receiver slammed down at the other end of the wire, and Parker said, "Bitch! Goddamned bitch! You'd think I was going to rape her or something!" He stood up, angry, hating her. Then, thinking about Sunday, the hatred melted and he began to feel rather pleased with himself. He hummed a little tune as he put on his coat, switched off the light, and walked through the big ink-smelling room with the presses black and idle under the single naked bulb. He closed the outer door, locked it, turned up his coat, and walked off slowly into the night.

Years ago, as a young man, Parker had been laughing and loud, a boisterous big fellow, full of dirty jokes and large ambitions. He had made time with nearly every available girl in town, and eventually would have gone off to New Haven or Hartford or Boston, or perhaps even New York, carrying those good memories with him—if it had not been for Polly Werner. He had raped Polly Werner, or it had amounted to nearly the same thing. Then Polly had become pregnant, and after the bitter threats, the hysterical accusations, he had married Polly exactly six and a half months before Alice was born.

Parker spent his wedding night drinking 3.2 beer alone in a Hyannis bar. The next morning he told Polly that he'd done it deliberately and would deliberately avoid her for the rest of their married life. He had kept that promise, too. For not once in marriage did Parker ever sleep with his own wife. And though he prided himself on this accomplishment, actually, after the first two or three months, it had become an easy self-denial. First Polly had been very pregnant and very unattractive. Then, after the birth of Alice, she had become inordinately fat, and had remained that way, until now, at the age of fifty-one, she weighed a monstrous three hundred and twenty pounds, and could not move up and down stairs without holding tight to the banister.

Parker lived without her. In the same house, without her. She refused to give him a divorce, and though at first he had taken up with occasional other women, he had never again found any satisfaction in the sexual act. It had made a fool of him in the eyes of the town. It had ruined his ambitions in the eyes of himself. He hated the town and Polly and Alice and himself and God. Eventually he learned to hate sex, too, so that he lived completely without it except in his own half-romantic, half-perverted way.

Now, walking home in the rain, Parker thought about Fran Walker. There'd been others before Fran—summer girls mostly—some amused, some shocked, some even excited and willing, like the waitress Betsy at the Lincoln Hotel. Fran, though, was very special. He'd approached her two years ago. She'd understood him immediately, and she'd laughed contemptuously in his face. Now she was not laughing. *He* was laughing—inside, all through him—laughing as he moved down Elm Street past Sam McFie's house, four houses down to his ugly Victorian place on the corner.

Polly was in the living room when he entered. She said, "Wipe your feet, Parker."

"Go to hell," Parker said. He looked at her mammoth body and thought how he hated fat women. Suddenly he laughed aloud.

"What's the matter with you?" Polly said.

"Wouldn't you like to know!"

"No, I don't think I would."

He looked at her with open revulsion. Ever since Alice had grown up and married and moved off to Pittsburgh, he had found no reason to even pretend politeness. He sat in a chair across the room and stared out the window at the night. Polly asked if he were hungry. He said no. She said they'd been invited to a buffet supper Sunday night at Judge Manning's house. He said he'd be busy Sunday night, and smiled secretly into the dark rain.

CHAPTER FOUR

Bert Mosley caught up with Fran Walker on the corner by the drugstore. He touched her arm, but she kept on walking. "Fran," he pleaded. "For God's sake, Fran!"

She stopped then. She looked beautiful, Bert thought, in the girlish pink suit and the flowered hat she'd worn to church this morning, her lips a moist red in the noon sunlight, her blond hair soft about her ears. He remembered only days ago, when she had not looked quite so young nor quite so innocent, and of course she was remembering too, and there had to be something he could say. "If we could just talk, Fran. Go somewhere and talk."

Fran shrugged and turned into the drugstore. She sat in a booth at the rear. Bert sat across from her. "Coffee?" he said.

"Please . . ." She took off her white gloves, smoothed them out, laid them together on the marble-top table. "Look, Bert —" She spoke carefully. "It wasn't your fault . . . All summer on the dunes . . . all the other times in all the other places . . . I was as much to blame as you were."

Bert had a square, handsome face. His hair was blond and curly, his shoulders broad, his arms long and muscular, his veined hands strong and restless. They moved constantly about the table, touching the sugar bowl, the jar of cream, the mustard and the catsup and rack of paper napkins. The coffee came and he stirred the black liquid round and round, though he took neither cream nor sugar. "Guy," he said finally, "he drove you back, didn't he?"

"Yes. He was very nice."

"He didn't say anything?"

"What would he say?"

"I don't know. Something."

"He said it was none of his business. He'd keep our names off his official report, and we should just forget about it."

"So nobody knows."

"No . . ." She picked up her gloves, put them down again. "Except Parker Welk drove up as we were leaving. Guy told him I'd come along with him to help out."

"Parker didn't think anything was fishy?"

"No."

"Because if he did—well, the man's a sonovabitch. You know that. A real sonovabitch."

"I know that."

"Well—" Bert sipped at his coffee. Fran was acting strange, aloof, faraway, thinking about other things. "You're sure," he persisted. "You're sure Guy didn't say anything—or you didn't say the wrong thing to him?"

"What would *I* say to *him?*"

"Well—considering how you feel about him."

"Now what does that mean?"

"Come off it, Fran! Just come off it!"

"No, I want to know what you mean."

"Well, I don't know." And he didn't. But the way Fran looked at Guy sometimes, and some of the little things she'd said about him. Guy was easy and sure, and once he'd taken Fran sailing. She'd sworn nothing had come of it. And he'd believed her, too. But all the same— "All right," he said. "All right, you're off tonight, aren't you? I'll pick you up around eight."

"No, I'm sorry, Bert."

"But you're off, aren't you?"

"Yes, but—" She lifted her coffee cup. He noticed her hand was shaking. He said, "It's got something to do with the other night, doesn't it? You feel dirty about it. You wouldn't if there hadn't been a fire. But there *was* a fire and Guy *did* show up, and somehow that makes everything different. Almost as if it's my fault. As if I *set* the fire, and you don't see me in the same way any more."

"No, Bert, that's not true."

"It is true."

"No, it isn't! So will you leave it alone now! Will you please just leave it alone!" She dropped the cup into the saucer. Coffee spilled and ran along the white marble. "I'm sorry . . . I'm sorry, Bert . . . sorry." She was almost crying. She dabbed at her eyes and rose quickly and walked off toward the doorway.

Bert watched her go, then paid the check, went out to the street, and walked toward his small apartment over an antique store at the edge of town. Passing an alley that led down to the water front, he caught sight of Guy's boat moving slowly across the bay. He stared at it for a long moment, his lips puckered, a finger scratching absently at his ear. He'd always liked Guy Montford. Everybody liked Guy. You couldn't help but like him. All the same, though, Fran was his, Bert Mosley's property, and not Guy Montford's or anybody else's either. A girl like Fran—so abandoned, so eager, so willing to please—was a rare commodity in East Norton. He'd found Fran and he'd keep Fran. The fact was, he *needed* Fran. Someday—if he still felt this way—if he got more than these petty legal cases—made some decent money and saw a way to get back to Boston again—someday he might even marry her.

It was warm after the rain. Margreth left her jacket in the cabin and sat in brown woolen slacks and a checkered sport shirt with her legs stretched before her in the cockpit, her elbows resting on the gunwale. The shirt collar flopped about her neck, and drops of spray glistened in her smooth black hair. She said little, and there were moments when Guy forgot her presence entirely. Then, glancing at her face lifted to the wind, he understood her silence. For even now on her first day of sailing, she felt the thrill a veteran sailor finds in the endless water ahead and the white sail above. Though she was completely relaxed, still she was sailing the boat herself, leaning with it, straining with the taut sheet, a part of this boat and this September day.

"I used to ride horses a great deal," she said once. "Tennessee Walkers, and it was almost the same, really."

"I've heard that."

"A boat is slower, but seems even faster. The wind, I guess."

"Yes, against your face."

"And the trail never ends. You don't have to slow down to a walk or ease around holes or look out for passing cars."

"No . . ."

"You give the boat her head from the very first." Then she was silent again until they'd reached the open sea past Keever's Light, until they'd rounded the point and the town was lost from view. "It's gone," she said then. "You can't see it any more."

"What?"

"The hospital. I could see it all the way until now."

"Yes, I've noticed."

"Even Larry's window."

"I've noticed that too."

She relaxed a little, and after a while he said, "I'm afraid I really don't know very much about you."

"I was born outside Atlanta, and my father was quite a successful insurance man, and I went to school at Sweet Briar."

"Thumbnail sketch."

"Once upon a time I was quite a different person. But that was once upon a time."

"Your family's still living?"

"A sister and my mother. My father's dead."
"So is mine."
"I know."
"Oh?" He glanced up sharply.
"Larry told me. Both your father and mother." She paused, squinting out at a tiny sail on the horizon. "Perhaps if Larry and I had a child—perhaps there might be some design to all this." She laughed briefly and was silent then while the boat came about and he guided it through a narrow channel between the sand bars. He lowered the sail and started the small auxiliary engine. He swore because it was slow in starting, because it was an engine, and someday he would remove it and depend entirely on the wind and his own abilities.
"For perspective," he said as they putted along the winding waterway that came down through the marshes to the sea. "After sailing in the open it's good to move along close to shore. It reminds you of where you're not." He cut off the engine and dropped the anchor into the shallow water. They were in a small pool then at a spot where the river widened some quarter mile from the sea. Close on either side were the dunes and the high grass of the marsh with the gulls wheeling above them, and in the distance a scraggly pine and the gold cross on the steeple of St. Joseph's.
"Here," she said, "it's a marsh. In the South it's a swamp. Your marsh is colder, but not so frightening." She rose and went down the ladder to the tiny cabin. He followed and lit the stove, sat in the bunk where Caesar slept and snored, and watched Margreth drop the frankfurters into the black iron skillet. Her graceful fingers looked rather ludicrous touching frankfurters. Her body seemed too slim and young for a woman in her thirties. She turned the frankfurters with a stainless steel fork and spoke down to the spitting grease. "What was she like?"
"Julia?"
"Yes, Julia."
"Oh, she was small—freckled, with reddish hair—and she laughed a great deal and loved sailing and fishing, and just—living. Her family owned a cottage around the point. We met in the summer—quite a few years ago now. We were married for two."
"Very much in love."
"Yes. Afterwards—after the accident—her family sold the cottage."
"But you stayed on."
"It's my town, you see. I like it here—I'm needed here.

And you'd be surprised how gratifying it is to be a small-town doctor."

"You mean how gratifying it *was*. Until now, with me here. I mean everything would be a lot simpler for you if I weren't here at all—if Larry had never married and you could talk about old times together without my getting in the way."

"No, that's not true." He lit a cigarette and wanted to explain why. But he did not know himself. So he avoided her eyes and was glad when the frankfurters were done and they sat across from each other in the narrow bunks, munching hot dogs and drinking black coffee poured steaming from the enameled pot.

"You know," Margreth said, feeding Caesar a frankfurter, tasting the coffee with the tip of a red tongue, "you know, I'm afraid I don't really understand you very well."

"I'm a simple fellow."

"Living alone in that house. Where do you eat? Who takes care of the housework?"

"A woman comes in three times a week to clean up, and I do my own cooking, or I eat at Pat's Grill or in the drugstore sometimes. I do need a housekeeper, though, and I've been thinking of getting one." He laughed. "You see, I am a simple fellow."

"Now, perhaps."

"Meaning?"

"I think there used to be a lot of violent emotion in you. I think you've squelched it on purpose."

"Maybe."

"I think, in some strange way, Larry's coming back is sort of—digging it up again."

"Maybe you're right."

"Or I'm just talking nonsense. Someone says something, so you make up new questions and new answers. You don't mean them at all until you say them."

"All right." He laughed again. "Stop fencing?"

"Right."

"Shake on it?"

"Right."

They shook hands solemnly, and Margreth said, "I'm trying to like this town. And *Julia* too." She patted the bunk, and in the awkward silence that followed, she stood abruptly to set her plate in the tiny metal sink. Guy rose at the same moment, so they were wedged for a second between the bunks, each balancing a china plate in one hand, a tin coffee mug in the other. They were quite close, and he saw into her eyes then for the first time of all. He saw darkness and pain, and he saw the woman of her down there in the darkness. It was warm and Southern. It could freeze very easily in a New England winter.

She side-stepped past him. Her arm brushed against his own and the plate dropped from her hand and smashed against the deck. Caesar leaped off the bunk. Margreth bent to pick up the pieces. Guy leaned down beside her and, reaching for a splinter of china, their fingers touched. When they straightened together they were close again, so he smelled the salt spray in her hair and saw that thwarted warmth of womanhood once more behind her eyes. He thought that this was Larry's wife, and she was quite beautiful because Larry loved beauty and Larry had married her. So there must be something magic inside her that only Larry had ever touched.

"I'm sorry," she said quietly. "About the plate."

He started, laughed nervously. "It doesn't matter."

"Perhaps *Julia* won't like me for it."

"I think she already loves you. I know Caesar does. As for me, may I start calling you Mar instead of Margreth?" He turned abruptly, climbed the ladder and stood smoking with one foot on the rail, his eyes looking out across the marsh, his ears filled with the sound of water running into the metal sink below.

The sun was dropping when they chugged out from the inlet and hoisted canvas and sailed back around the rocks of Keever's Point. Then suddenly the hospital came into view, and they were both conscious of unseen eyes watching them from the window of Room 2B.

"Next time," Guy said, "we may understand each other better."

"First of all we'd better understand ourselves."

"I think I—"

"I think you do, too. And maybe that's why I resent you a little. Because you realize it's almost impossible to be both, when Larry needs a friend as much as a doctor."

"And a wife more than he needs a friend."

"Now we're fencing again." She leaned far back across the coaming with her hair dropping down behind and her throat red in the sunlight and her breasts drawn up sharply against the checkered shirt. She started to sing, "Sailing, sailing home again," and Caesar whined and she laughed and it was not until they'd reached the breakwater that her voice died and her head came up level with his own. She saw his admiring eyes watching the curve of her throat and the slim length of her body, and she said, "Cold, isn't it? Getting cold," and went below for her jacket. When she returned the jacket was buttoned high about her neck. "It's better," she said.

Guy maneuvered in toward the buoy and watched the surefooted way that Mar clambered forward and caught the mooring line. He made everything shipshape, climbed down to the dinghy, called to Caesar, then held Mar's arm while she leaped in beside him. It was a slender arm, but firm too, and he felt the strength in the tightened muscle as she braced herself in the rocking boat. She fastened the knot in her hair and sat in the stern with her feet together on the floorboards that slopped in the inch of water beneath.

"I'm sorry," she said as he rowed back to the dock.

"About what?"

"The broken dish."

"I told you it didn't matter."

"And about what I said. I guess it's because I don't trust myself. I know you're bursting inside, but you can still control yourself. Someday I may have to lean on you, and I guess that's what I really resent—my own weakness."

"Lean all you want."

"Next time I'll be careful not to break anything at all." She laughed jerkily, ignored his hand, and climbed up to the pier without assistance. And once on land again she said, "I know how a sailor feels. The whole world is rocking."

There was no point, Fran decided, in wearing her best lingerie. In fact, it would show a kind of casual contempt if she wore her shabbiest cotton everyday things, with no perfume, only the barest of make-up. She was not the least bit morally ashamed, not even disgusted really, except by the thought of Parker himself—the ugly, unhealthy personality of the man. She wished, though, that she were not afraid. There was nothing to fear, of course, because she was quite sure that Parker was not a sadist or sex maniac or anything like that—just a twisted, dirty old man, who probably had a great many reasons for being the way he was. And considering that fat slob of a wife of his—

Well, she would try not to think about it. She would think about other, more pleasant things—now, and walking through the dark, and later still—and going home, too, she would think about other things.

Ida Primmer said, "You got a date, Fran?"

"Yes."

"With Bert?"

"No, not with Bert."

"He's nice, Bert is. Easygoing and fun, and the way I

hear, he's a real good lawyer, too. Only he doesn't get much chance to prove it. Now if he could only win a case against Colin Eustis—make the District Attorney look like a fool, you know, in some real bloody murder case—if we only had a *murder* case around here—"

"Only we won't," Fran said, and smiled and walked out into the night. A car swung past her as she moved across the gravel drive. The car stopped and Guy Montford stepped out on one side, Mrs. McFie on the other. They were dressed in casual sailing clothes.

Guy nodded. "Evening, Fran."

"Hello, Doctor . . . Good evening, Mrs. McFie."

"Larry all right?" Guy asked.

"Fine . . . When I went off duty."

"Well, then—" He spoke to Mrs. McFie, and they walked off together toward the hospital.

Fran walked on slowly toward the center of town. She scuffled the dead leaves as she went, and remembered scuffling other leaves in another town far west of here. She wondered why it was that when you were open and good, friendly and warm, and you honestly meant everything you did and said—why was it that you got into trouble, and no one really understood you at all? Guy Montford, though—he would understand her, if she only had the opportunity to express herself. But Guy hardly knew she existed except as "nurse" Fran Walker, efficient, patient, a favorite among children and old people, a rather silly girl who was sleeping with Bert Mosley, and what did Guy care what she did with her time off?

Oh, she'd been sailing with Guy once. Last summer it was. She'd begged him to take her. And finally he'd given in, and Lord knows, she'd done everything possible to make him aware of her. She'd tried to be very gay and witty, and she'd left her blouse unbuttoned almost to the waist because she did have marvelous high breasts, and Guy was not indifferent—he *couldn't* be indifferent. But he'd paid no attention all the same, just as he'd paid no attention while examining her ribs at that awful Robins Nest Motel. He'd even managed to reject her, somehow—without her knowing how—helping her to keep her dignity, so that she was more embarrassed in rebuttoning the blouse than she'd been in unbuttoning it.

Well, poor Guy . . . poor Guy . . . with his oldest friend dying up there in the hospital, having to placate that hysterical Sam McFie, tell all kinds of lies to Larry's wife, who looked like a nice enough woman—a little thin, Southern—none of that soft openness that she had herself. She felt terribly sorry for Guy. Give her half a chance, though, and she could be terribly good for him—give him a lot of warmth and understanding and honest-to-God "womanism" that he'd never get from anyone else.

There was no point in thinking about that. She kicked at the leaves and noticed she was only two blocks away now. Her feet slowed, and for a moment she stopped dead on the pavement as a touch of fear ran up her spine. She forced it away, reminding herself that there was nothing about Parker Welk she could not handle. But then, moving on again, she wished suddenly that she'd told Bert all about this business, because Bert would have gone half crazy with rage, and she wouldn't be here now, moving ever closer to the office of the *Chronicle*.

She hadn't told Bert, though, and for that very reason. He'd have made a scene with no real evidence to go on. He'd have accused Parker, beaten him up probably, and afterwards Parker would print the story about the Robert Briskins, using the correct names, and there'd be nothing they could do about it. Absolutely nothing. So it was better this way. In a sense, she was being a kind of martyr, protecting Bert as well as herself. And thinking about it now, she began to feel warm and motherly toward Bert, the way she always felt, even in bed with him, and she thought perhaps she might even marry Bert someday, help him along with his career, perhaps even help him get over whatever the problem was that prevented him from enjoying sex in an absolutely free and unashamed way. It was a comforting thought, and she kept it with her all the way through the empty streets of Sunday night.

The shades were drawn over the glass front office of the *Chronicle*. The door was locked. Fran drew a deep breath, then knocked lightly. A moment passed before the door opened and Parker stood there in his shirt sleeves. He held the door wide as she went in, then closed the door behind her.

"Fran . . . I'm glad you came, Fran . . ." He was nervous, guilty, trying to pretend she had come voluntarily.

She said, "Cut it out, Parker," and he stopped and his voice became suddenly harsh.

"Whore!" he said. "Lousy whore!"

She laughed, and he stepped forward with his hand raised as though to strike her. The hand hung in mid-air. Sweat glistened on his bald head and his mustache worked and his little eyes were those of a pig. He lowered the hand slowly and turned away toward the dim light in his office across the room. "Shacking up with that Bert Mosley," he mumbled. "He's a big man—a bi-ig man."

"A better man than you are."

Parker did not answer. And she knew for certain now that he could never hurt her. Parker was a sick old man at the age of fifty-three. She'd seen many like him in the psychiatric wards and the alcoholic wards—in the general day-by-day routine of a nurse's life.

She felt almost sorry for him as she climbed the steep flight of wooden stairs, and went through the open trap door to the loft above the shop. She felt, in a strange way, something close to pleasure about the whole filthy business.

CHAPTER FIVE

. . . Leaves crackling dry against the window . . . the bay very blue in the October sun . . . because it was October . . . Mar had said it was October . . . And the pain greater now than a month ago . . . a pain all through him, too much for X-rays or nitrogen mustard, too much for quarter grains of morphine . . . the pain of slow death . . . creeping in, a "fog on cat's feet" . . . so there were moments, hours with nothing but the pain . . . faces only blurred through the pain, vaguely familiar shapes that hovered anxiously above the bed . . . faces from other times and other places . . . Keep low till they're in close, then rise fast and shoot fast . . . Ducks over the marsh . . . men in helmets like the women's hats of the nineteen twenties . . . Shrapnel in my ass, Lieutenant . . . No joke, because it hurts like hell . . . So stop your goddamned laughing . . . Stop laughing, Mar . . . It's according to plan . . . three shelves . . . twelve-inch, ten-inch, eight-inch . . . Do-it-yourself, and when will I finish the bookcase? . . . When? . . . And when will I finish pruning the roses or planting the tulips or painting the bathroom? . . . And when will we go to bed again? . . . Your cool legs and your cool breasts and cool fingers and cool lips, all cool, and then suddenly warm, a fire burning inside . . . then cool again, slowly cool again . . . like the early mornings on the marsh . . . the first plunge into the summer bay . . . not cool, but cold, really, freezing cold in the black water . . . Christ, it's cold! . . . Christ, Guy, it's cold as hell . . . They're not so cold, fella, not those two, the way they've been eying us all afternoon . . . You take the short one and I'll take the tall one, and I'll be in clover before you . . . virgins no more, no more . . . But you think I'd tell anyone? . . . *Anyone?* . . . And you're telling Father Serrano? . . . A *priest?* . . . Walking right up to a booth and telling that priest man . . . What's it like in there, Guy? . . . Scary? . . . It must be scary . . . No, I'm not scared . . . Let's face it . . . Hodgkins' disease . . . a very bad business, worse than mumps or impetigo or pinkeye or measles . . . Go home and rest . . . Dad come to visit . . . good old miserable Dad, who never cared a damn when I was living—even tried to kill a man, partly because I *was* alive . . . two years in a sanitarium . . . Didn't care a damn about me then . . . but cares like hell now, when I'm dying and it's too late for any of that father and son crap . . . too late for most everything but the pain and the lying here . . . turning my head slightly, inch by inch, eyes opened wide to the sun and the dry falling leaves and the white boat across the bay . . . You'll like him, Mar . . . oldest friend . . . hope you like him . . . many a sail, over the bounding main . . . and maybe someday, after all the long sails, after the pain is all over and done with . . . maybe you won't have to go back to Atlanta and that Yankee-hating, proper-thinking, little gray-haired old mother of yours . . . won't have to go back, because maybe you and Guy . . . maybe . . . And why not? . . . And maybe even children . . . too late for our children . . . my child . . . your child . . . Guy's child . . . your child . . . All God's chillun . . . God help me . . . God help Mar and Dad and Guy . . . God have mercy on my soul . . . "Now I lay me down to sleep, I pray the Lord my soul to keep. If I should die before I wake . . ."

"He's waking up now," Mar said.

"Yes." Guy glanced at the fluttering eyelids on Larry's masklike face, then turned back to the window again. The trees were completely bare. The last leaves of all were being swept up and burned in small fires along the green. Smoke rose high in the cold air, nearly obscuring the far-off cottages along the water front, the tiny figurines of fishermen in flannel shirts and windbreakers as they put out to the choppy sea.

"No more sailing?" Larry croaked behind him, the voice hoarse now, a throaty whisper.

"*Julia's* being hauled tomorrow. Putting her in Chet Belknap's big shed."

"No sailing today?"

"Well—I do have a few calls to make, and it's a little cold," though the sun was already warm through the window. He turned into the room once more. Mar sat staring at the floor. Larry's voice croaked on. "Mar's got a long winter ahead, and just one more sail before you haul her."

"All right, if Mar wants to go." He turned and walked swiftly to the elevator. Mar followed, saying nothing.

But once in the car she laughed shortly. "You don't really want to go."

"I am a little busy."

"You're not really busy."

"No."

"We don't have to go."

"Larry'll be watching."

"He thinks he can force pleasure on someone."

"Can't he?"

"Not that way."

What way? he wanted to say. What way then? But instead he said, "No time to change clothes. Have to go as we are." And he parked at the dock and walked beside her, unspeaking, down the creaking planks, while Caesar trotted close behind.

The sun was high as they cleared the breakwater. Mar wore a brown woolen dress the color of her brown legs beneath the wind-whirled skirt. Her face became pink with cold, and she said nothing, but only looked into the wind, while behind her Guy sucked on his pipe and watched her and remembered being very young and remembered a visit to a cousin's house in Dennis, and his mother saying, "Now go play with Kathy," pushing him after the little girl to the garden, where they'd sat together and stared at each other, disliking each other simply because others had told them how well they'd get along. He remembered other sails in the weeks before. On some of them Mar had laughed genuine laughter. On some her slim body had been warm in a soft sweater and slacks or shorts. Now she did not laugh at all, and she wore a street dress beneath her coat, and somehow this last sail seemed completely pointless.

They stayed out less than two hours. They did not anchor, and spent the entire time in the open cockpit. Once Mar went below to warm up, and once she took the wheel while he went down to light his pipe away from the wind. The cabin was cold and desolate. He looked at the bunk and saw where Mar had once sat drinking coffee, staring into the brown liquid with her black eyes half closed and her long lashes clear against the brown of her face.

He went back to the cockpit. He took the wheel and said, "Funny, we never really got to know each other."

"It isn't really so strange at all."

"No, I suppose it isn't." He brought the boat about and

tacked back through the breakwater and tied up at the pier. He walked beside Mar down the dock, opened the car door, and said, "I'll take you home."

"Thank you. I'll walk. It's a beautiful day, and—"

"And you'd rather walk."

"Yes."

"Well," he said, and shut the door. He looked at the permanent sadness in her face. "Next spring perhaps things may be easier."

"Perhaps."

"I've enjoyed having you sail with me."

"If it weren't for Larry, you'd have gone alone."

"Mar—listen, Mar," with a fierceness that burst from nowhere. "I know how much good these sails—these escapes—have done you. But now you'll have to find other things—get involved with the church—the Women's Club—anything. But you can't go to pieces, because then Larry'd have nothing. You see—you see? As long as you're all right, cheerful, affectionate, he'll be all right, too. So you've got to hold onto yourself. You've got to because—"

"It won't be long. That's what you mean, isn't it? That's what you mean." The sun behind her gave a haunted look to Mar's oval face. There were circles beneath her eyes; thin, wearing lines along her mouth. She laughed in her throat. "I wanted to lean on you, Guy. And I always resented you. Because you're not hard enough—too human to hold us all up at once—doctor, friend, nurse, everything—and you're too human to keep yourself detached from all of it—and all of us—"

"Mar—listen, Mar—"

"Next spring," she said. And, "Good-by, Caesar. I love you, Caesar." She waited a second, then waved her hand quickly and moved off along the rutted street. She walked with her head bent forward against the wind.

CHAPTER SIX

The Sunday night suppers of the Congregational Church of East Norton, Massachusetts, were attended with pleasure by the ladies of the town, and with sullen acceptance by their husbands. They were held in the church basement—

a large, bare, low-ceilinged room with plank tables set in a U shape, so that everyone could "get to know each other better." Everyone knew each other already, and knew *about* each other, too, so that any "light conversation" was merely disguised gossip, and outside of the weather and raising funds for a new steeple, there was nothing to talk about anyway—except each other.

The minister's wife, Mrs. Frances Treleaven, was the official receptionist. Over the years, however, Clara Coffin had gradually usurped the honor, so that it was Clara who took Mar in hand that first evening, while Frances Treleaven was a wounded, fluttering bird, dancing behind Clara's bulk, chirping her how-do-you-dos over Clara's loud, hearty greetings.

"I've been *so* anxious to become really acquainted with Larry's wife. I mean, after all, I did know Larry when he was just a growing boy, you know. I'll never forget how he and Guy Montford used to beg—literally beg my husband to take them riding on his boat."

"Mr. Coffin is a fisherman," Judge Manning's wife explained sweetly. And Mar nodded and Clara glared at Mrs. Manning.

Then Mrs. Maidie Bolls said that her husband, *Doctor* Bolls, had the greatest respect and admiration for Guy, the very greatest respect—and Doctor Kelsey's wife gave Mrs. Bolls a sardonic smile and commented that Guy would probably be the next head of the hospital, which prompted Maidie Bolls to turn away for another tuna fish sandwich.

There was an awkward silence. Polly Welk pulled at the girdle round her massive frame and remarked that Parker couldn't come tonight because he was busy at the office. "Every other Sunday night or so—all this research he's doing—working away in that little musty office."

Nancy Messner said, "He doesn't make me work at night."

"You're just a child, dear, and Parker wouldn't take advantage of a child."

"Two Sundays ago," Frances Treleaven said, "I noticed a light on the second floor."

"The loft," Polly explained. "He stores things up there. But don't ask me. All I know is he's telephoned Philadelphia twice in the last three weeks, and yesterday he received a letter from some newspaper there. He just won't talk about it. But I suppose some old friend is very sick—or maybe even *dying*." She stopped, glanced at Mar, embarrassed, said, "Well—that cheese is very good, even if I did bring it myself—" and waddled off across the room, leaning on Nancy's arm.

Ida Primmer filled the pause. She said that Fran Walker

used to come to all the suppers. But now that Fran was going around steady with Bert Mosley— Ida was only twenty, with a long nose and protruding teeth, and lacking a steady boy friend of her own, she got some vicarious pleasure from talking about Fran's. "After all, we *room* together in the nurses' quarters, and believe me, if she doesn't marry Bert Mosley soon, then I miss my guess, that's all." Ida popped an olive between her prominent teeth and joined Maidie Bolls at the coffee urn.

"Nurses!" Clara said. "I can't stand them. How nurses and doctors could both be in sort of the same profession—how a doctor could ever *marry* a nurse! Maidie Bolls was a nurse, you know."

"No," Mar said, "I didn't know."

"Although it's different with judges. Being involved in politics, you know, they have to marry for money and social position."

"Now, Clara—" Frances Treleaven laughed in her chirping way.

"She *is* rich," Clara said. "Don't tell *me* she isn't rich. Her grandfather owned just about half the property around here, and when the 'foreigners' started buying up land for their summer cottages—"

"I don't mean she isn't rich," Frances Treleaven persisted. "I mean that's not the reason Judge Manning married her."

"Hah! He thought she could help him become County Court Judge. But he never made it, did he? All he ever did or ever will do, is fine some teen-ager for speeding or put Stewed Schaeffer in jail for the night, while Crawford Strike over in Harpswell—he gets all the *big* cases—and he doesn't even live right here in the County Seat."

Mar said, "I think Judge and Mrs. Manning are both very sweet," and Mrs. Coffin said, "Well, anyway, Guy Montford didn't marry a nurse—and he didn't marry for money either."

"She was lovely," Frances Treleaven said. "Julia—her name was Julia—tiny, you know, and always laughing, with that freckled nose and that short reddish hair. She was a church member, too, though Guy wasn't, and still isn't, of course. So she came to the suppers alone—and well, it brightened everything up, I can tell you. Everything!"

"Until the accident," Clara said.

"Yes."

"I saw it."

"Now, Clara—"

"I did. And I'll never forget Larson Whitt lifting her body out of that car."

"Please, Clara, you can spare us the details."

"He put her down on the grass, and there was blood all over her white dress. It was ripped wide open, and you could see this great jagged hole right in the middle of her chest, and—"

Mrs. Treleaven left.

Clara laughed. "She could never stand to hear about anything unpleasant. Not anything at all."

Mar suggested that perhaps it was time for her to go along. If she could pull Sam away from that knot of men in the corner.

"Don't try, dear." Mrs. Coffin smiled faintly. "He hasn't been drinking, has he?"

"No, he—"

"Oh, everybody in town knows Sam McFie takes a little nip now and then, though of course he shouldn't—not a drop—because he used to drink something terrible until he went off his head and got sent away for a while. It all started after his wife died, you know, because—" She stopped, hesitated for the first time that evening.

"Yes?" Mar said. "Yes, Mrs. Coffin?"

Mrs. Coffin hedged, then let it out slowly, savoring every word of it. "Guy's father—Paul Montford—he was a doctor, you know."

"Yes . . ."

"And Sam's closest friend besides. They grew up in this town together, just like Guy and Larry."

"Yes."

"Well, Guy's father was a Catholic, you see. And he delivered Sam's baby—Larry. Well, it was a breach birth, you see, and Larry wasn't breathing, and Sam's wife was hemorrhaging, so—well, that was nearly forty years ago, but Sam never got over it."

"She died," Mar said. "Larry told me."

"And Sam never forgave Paul Montford."

"But why?"

"Because Paul was a Catholic. And Sam was convinced he let his wife die in order to save the baby. 'Murder,' he called it."

"But that's silly, Mrs. Coffin. She probably would have died anyway. And besides, there isn't any real choice a doctor has to make in a situation like that. I mean *any* doctor tries to save both the mother and child, and—well, everybody knows that sort of thing is just completely ridiculous—just an old wives' tale."

"Yes . . ." Mrs. Coffin agreed. "Yes, it was ridiculous, of course. But Sam believed it all the same, and he began getting drunk and carrying on about it, until finally he got very drunk one night, in a terrible paranoiac rage, and he got a gun and went up to Paul Montford's house and shot out all the windows and tried to kill the doctor until George Potts—he was the sheriff then—he came and took him away, and they sent him to a sanitarium because Doctor Montford wouldn't prefer criminal charges. And well, after he got out—then Ruth Kiley became his secretary, and she helped him more than anyone else on earth—kept him under control, you know—because he *could* go off again, get violent again, even now—and he's never, *ever* forgiven Paul Montford."

Mar said nothing. She thought of Sam in the living room, holding his single drink or his two carefully poured drinks, building toward something—something.

"Oh, I suppose I shouldn't have said all this. I am sorry, and—"

"No, it's all right . . . It's all right." The low-ceilinged room was too warm. Steam crackled in the radiators and the knot of men laughed and the women's voices rose and fell, and Mrs. Coffin apologized again because it was not really a proper subject for a church supper, and "Of course I shouldn't have told you," and "How about one of my nice tuna sandwiches?"

Mar said, "Yes." Mrs. Coffin turned away toward the long tables and Mar thought of tuna fish and felt sick in her stomach. Behind her a swinging door led to a coatroom and an outer basement door. She backed a step toward it, then turned and went through, grabbed at her coat, and rushed up the stairs to the October night.

The stars were bright. A cold breeze blew in from the bay. She breathed deep, then turned quickly and strode off through the town. Behind her a woman's voice called her name. But she did not turn. She strode on fast, not thinking about anything at all except that it was good to walk in the air . . . it was good to be out of there and be alone, and it would be good to walk this way forever.

A car pulled up beside her. Guy looked out through the open window. "Hello, there."

"Hello." She stopped, patted Caesar, who leaned out from the rear seat.

"Give you a lift?" Guy said.

"No . . . No, thanks."

"I'm going to the hospital. Sunday night rounds."

"No, I—not tonight. Tell Larry I'll—I'll see him tomorrow."

"Something wrong, Mar?"

"No, nothing wrong."

"Well, then—" He started to say more. Mar looked into his face and saw deep sorrow, deep pain hidden there behind his eyes. She had never noticed it before. "Well—" he said again, and drove off down the dark street. The taillights disappeared around a corner.

She walked on to Sam's house, where she told Mrs. O'Hara that she hadn't felt well, so she'd left the church early and was going straight to bed. No, there was nothing Mrs. O'Hara could do for her. Thanks all the same, but there was nothing.

Peter began squawking on his perch. "Goddammit, goddammit!"

"He's terrible," Mrs. O'Hara said.

Mar went up to her room and undressed. She slipped into pajamas, went into the bathroom, and brought a full glass of water back to the bedside table. Sam's car drove up outside. She lay back on the bed, breathing ever slower, waiting. Finally the knock came, followed by Sam's voice from the hallway. "You all right, Mar?"

"Yes, I'm fine."

"Sorry you didn't wait for me."

"I wanted to walk. The fresh air was good for me."

"Well—good night then."

"Good night."

Sam's footsteps sounded on the stairs. He'd be in the living room now, mixing a drink probably. He'd have one or two before he called the hospital to inquire after Larry. Then he'd come upstairs to bed and think about thirty-six years ago when he'd blamed a doctor for sacrificing his wife for a child he did not want, think about going crazy that time, trying to kill Doctor Montford in a paranoiac rage. Larry had never told her about that. But it must have hurt Larry terribly—being resented—almost blamed—all through childhood, all through adolescence, right up until this moment when he was dying. And now when it was too late, Sam expected Guy Montford to save Larry in the same emotional, unreasoning, uncompromising way that he'd expected Paul Montford to save his wife.

She sat up, opened the window. The cold air blew in and chilled her body beneath the thin pajamas. She shivered and slipped under the covers and lay there quiet a moment, thinking she would never go to a church supper again.

There was a small bottle of pills in the night-table drawer. She took three with a glass of water. Perhaps tonight she would not have that recurring dream . . . the horse's hoofs crashing down through the car's windshield . . . the small boy crying in the dust . . . and the horse screaming on until

Guy fired the revolver and the round hole appeared in the center of its forehead . . . She would not run, perhaps—screaming and stumbling while Guy followed, shouting after—and though she made no progress in her running . . . he never caught her either.

Fran Walker was at the duty nurse's desk when Guy stepped out of the elevator on the second floor. "Hello, Fran." He nodded and smiled into her eyes. "How's things tonight?"

"Fine, Doctor."

"Well, let's have a look, shall we?" He walked on down the rubber-matted corridor, stepping briskly through the open doorways as he moved along. He inspected the temperature chart of the small girl with whooping cough. He checked the stitches of a freshly sewn incision on the hairy belly of a Portuguese clam digger. He nodded and smiled while he touched a hand here, patted a forehead there, talking all the time in that warm, reassuring voice that had gained him the love and confidence of every patient he had ever tended.

Fran walked behind him as he made the rounds. She spoke soft, praising words as they moved between the rooms. "Doctor Kelsey said Mrs. Trigvie would have died if you hadn't recognized that lockjaw. There hasn't been a case here for so long that—"

"I saw a little during the war." He felt sorry for Fran, understood the embarrassment behind her words of praise. He wished, for no reason, that nurses' shoes were not rubber-soled, would make some sound on the rubber matting behind him.

He turned into the next room and noticed that the bed was empty. He crossed to the window, looked out at the night. "Well, I see Mrs. McTyre has gone."

"Yes, the baby was fine and she's nursing him beautifully."

"She was a difficult patient, Fran, and you were wonderful with her." He turned and looked at the iron hospital bed. It was cold, as the room was cold with those monotonous green walls and those horrible calendar pictures. A vase of wilting roses stood on the bedside table. He lifted one from the stale water, sniffed at it, and returned it carefully to the hospital vase. "Everything dies."

"Guy . . ."

"You know, Fran, I wish we could afford to fix up every room the way you did Larry McFie's."

"He was special."

"No, Fran, nobody's ever special. Just more sick or less sick." He touched her arm, smiled with honest affection. "I guess that covers it for tonight. Sorry I kept you overtime."

"The relief nurse is late anyway."

"All the same—" He moved out to the hallway. "Good night, Fran."

"Aren't you going to check Larry McFie?"

"Yes, but—if you don't mind, I'd—rather see him alone tonight."

"All right, Doctor." Her voice floated between the green plaster walls. "I've increased the morphine injections to every eight hours like you said. Shall I keep it that way?"

"Yes."

"He's having a lot of pain."

"I know."

She was waiting behind him. He said, "Keep it at eight, and I'll write it up for you later."

"He's been bleeding at the nose. And the nitrogen mustard makes him sick."

"I know, Fran . . . God, I know . . ." He leaned against the green wall, and Fran touched his arm and moved off down the corridor. He looked after her and thought that for all her girlish confusion, she was a warmer, more honestly real person than most nurses—than most people he had known.

Larry's eyes were black holes in a Halloween mask. He wheezed as he breathed, and his wasted body was a skin-covered skeleton like that first cadaver in medical school. It had been an old man, shriveled to nothing, even his genitals nothing but loose skin. Someone had named him "Jocko" and Guy had become angry, then sick on that first day, so it had taken great will power to start dissecting the body on the following morning. Not because the old man was dead or ugly, but because somehow he looked wise and peaceful—even beautiful in naked death. And touching him with the cold steel of a fine scalpel—it was like waking him to die all over again.

"Cut it out! Now cut that out!" He turned back to the doorway. Larry wheezed behind him. He said, "God is with you, Larry," and went out to the hall and walked fast toward the elevator, more certain than ever now that God was not with anyone at all.

The night was cold. It cleared his mind of unwanted thoughts as he quickened his pace toward the parking space behind the building. He had to get hold of himself. He was a doctor, wasn't he? He'd seen death before, hadn't he? His own wife, his own father. Men dying violently under a black rain in Germany . . . Children dying slow and wide-eyed in antiseptic rooms, believing to the end that there was nothing but life through all eternity. "So just because you *know* him," he told himself. "Simply because he's an old close friend, a part of yourself dying with him—even so—even so—"

He opened the car door. A cigarette glowed in the dark, and Fran said, "Guy, I want to talk to you—I have to talk to you."

"Fran . . ." He hesitated. "Don't say anything, Fran. Don't hurt yourself. I'm not a priest or a minister, not even a psychiatrist. I'm just an ordinary doctor, Fran, and I told you before . . . You're a good person, Fran, and you don't measure a person's goodness in terms of his emotional life."

"Please," she said. "Please, Guy . . ."

"All right." He slipped in behind the wheel and closed the door. He leaned back against the seat, and felt an odd closeness to Fran, a kind of empathy that made no sense at all.

Fran said, "It wasn't about that night at the Robins Nest. I know you understand about that. I've been going with Bert for nearly two years now. So of course you understand that."

"Yes, Fran . . . Yes, I do."

"It was about—about us."

"Us?"

"I'm in love with you."

"Fran . . . Fran . . ."

"I can't help it. I dream about you, I can't wait for you to come to the hospital . . . I know you were just being kind, but still I was so jealous when you used to take Mrs. McFie sailing, and—I don't know—I just wanted you to know—I wanted to tell you."

"Fran, I'm sorry, Fran."

"And you don't have to be sorry, either. I just want you to know. I'm not a very nice girl . . . Much worse than you even know . . . But all the same—what I'm trying to say—I understand how you feel about Larry McFie, how it's eating inside you, and—well, I know you don't drink very much or take drugs or anything, and you don't have any girl—I mean not any *particular* girl, do you?"

"No . . ."

"Because if you did, then I wouldn't be saying all this, and—I just wanted to say—"

"Yes, Fran?" He closed his eyes and waited. He did not want her to say the words, but they came out anyway because there was nothing he could do to stop them.

"If you ever need anything—comfort, understanding—if you want to cry—if it would help for you to sleep with somebody—you see, I love you, so I have no shame, and if it would help—if you want me—"

She stopped and the sudden silence was deep, almost

audible. Then finally he heard her crying softly, and he put an arm around her shoulder and held her close against him. She cried into his chest and he patted her shoulder and felt that he was comforting a child, until her hands groped beneath his shirt, and suddenly then she was a woman, saying, "Please, Guy, look at me, Guy," while she straightened, and he turned his head and watched her unbutton her uniform, drop it over her shoulders, unfasten her bra and drop that too, until she was naked to the waist, still half-crying, saying, "Don't you want me, Guy? Don't you even want me?"

"Of course, of course," with the words thick in his throat. "But I don't want to hurt you, Fran. And I don't want to hate myself for pretending it wouldn't hurt you."

"It wouldn't hurt me . . . It wouldn't . . ."

"Fran," he said, "Fran," and could not keep his eyes from her body, could not stop his hands from reaching out to caress the wonderfully firm breasts, and when she moved toward him, could not keep his mouth from the soft moisture of her parted lips, while her tongue explored his own and her soft body squirmed in his arms and her restless hands exposed his passion, until suddenly Caesar barked from the back seat and he said, "Oh, Jesus God, Fran! . . . No, Fran! . . . No, Fran!" And he pulled back, breathing heavily, and laughed and lit a cigarette and forced himself under control once more.

"So you know how attractive you are . . . You know that, don't you?" He kissed her lightly and buttoned her dress with care, laughing all the time, saying he'd take her sailing in the spring, and by then she'd realize she wasn't in love with him at all. Maybe a little concerned for him—and close, because they did work together—but not in love with him. And she'd realize that. She was a beautiful, attractive, wonderful girl, and he was awed—honored—that she even thought she felt this way—even for a little while.

Fran did not answer. She sat motionless, a full, passionate woman turned suddenly to a child again, waiting patiently while her dress was buttoned. Then she opened the door and stepped out to the gravel. "I'm sorry," she said.

"Fran . . ."

"I'm sorry." She started to run. Guy called after her, but she kept on running.

". . . Fran?" Parker looked down at the phone as though he might actually see her through the mouthpiece. The letter was on the desk before him. He rubbed it with a fat damp finger, leaving an inky smear. "Fran . . ." He chuckled. "Haven't seen you lately, Fran."

"Why should you?"

"Now, Fran—"

"The last time was the last time, and it was a fair agreement."

"Yes, Fran, it was." He was a fair man. He fought dirty, but was honest within his code. "Trouble is, Fran, something's come up . . . a letter I got from Philadelphia."

"Philadelphia?" Fran said.

"A little epistle, you might say, from a friend of mine on one of the newspapers."

"Go on, Parker."

"One of those little items that big papers get hold of, then don't print, you know, because some organization puts pressure on them. You know—the police, schools—maybe a hospital." There was silence on Fran's end of the wire. He could imagine her standing there with her lips parted, maybe breathing heavily so her breasts moved up and down under the starched uniform. He said, "All about a nurse who got bounced from a hospital because she got caught in bed with one of the patients—by the man's wife, no less." He laughed. "Was the bed cranked up, Fran, or was it lying flat?"

Silence.

"We're starting fresh—all over again. Can't make it next Sunday myself. So a week from Sunday, all right?" And then, when there was still no answer, he hung up and sat there motionless, thinking it *could* be next Sunday, except he couldn't put off Mrs. Manning's buffet chicken à la king much longer, and the waiting would make it better anyway, give him something to look forward to. And he looked forward to it now, and thought about Fran, not naked, but almost naked, in bed with that patient in Philadelphia—the bed cranked all the way up, too, he bet, and then the wife walking in, and Jesus! . . . Jesus!

He stood up and put out the lights. He'd walk fast on his way home. He'd think hard about something else—Polly stuffing herself with bread and processed cheese at the church supper. That should stop this feeling. That would stop it.

CHAPTER SEVEN

Doctor Saul Kelsey sat behind the desk in his private office off the hospital's waiting room. He chewed the end off a cigar, stood up, strode to the door, and flung it open. "Isn't he free yet?" he said to the nurse who sat outside.

"He's in the delivery room, Doctor."

"Well, as soon as the baby decides to come out and give the world a try—" He closed the door and sat behind the desk again. He lit the cigar, puffed on it, and thought this Larry McFie business was beginning to undermine the entire hospital. What it was doing to Guy alone— Goddammit, a thing like this could ruin the best of doctors. And Guy was the best. He had everything a doctor needed—skill, compassion, dedication—including a strange awe of death, so that he hated death and fought death, and died a little inside himself each time a patient died.

Some doctors would argue for a cold-blooded, clinical approach to their work—Bolls, for instance, who was damn near a repressed sadist with his eagerness to perform operations on a case that required little more than aspirin. Well, to hell with Bolls! He knew about Bolls, knew him as well as he knew Guy and had known Guy's father, too. Now there was a good man. Back in the "Tin Lizzie" days. Not even a hospital then. Made most deliveries with a lot of hot water in an upstairs bedroom. Delivered Larry in an upstairs bedroom and, God, the way Sam had carried on—the way he was carrying on right now, in fact, starting it all over again. All that crap over his wife's death—all that religious crap, and then all that violence—and now all this crap about Larry. If Sam didn't get hold of himself—and fast—he could get drunk again, violent again, maybe hurt someone, even kill someone. Larry was going to die, and the sooner Sam realized it, the better off he'd be. As a matter of fact, take it for all in all, the sooner Larry did die, the better for everyone concerned. Not a noble thought for a doctor. But when an incurable sickness spread itself around—infecting everyone like some form of cancer—eating away at everyone—

There was a knock at the door. "Come in!" his voice boomed.

The door opened and Guy came into the room. "You want to see me, Saul?"

Saul looked up over the heavy pouches beneath his eyes. He tipped the ash from his cigar, half rose, and said, "Damn it, Guy, I thought you were looking after this McFie business."

"I am—everything possible." Guy sat in the leather chair that faced Saul's desk. He crossed his legs, took out his pipe, changed his mind and lit a cigarette. "What's the matter, Saul?"

"Plenty the matter." The big man puffed on the cigar, made a wry face, and swung his swivel chair toward the window. The back of his head was silver beneath the light of the desk lamp. His huge shoulders sagged forward as he peered at something in the yard. "Mrs. McFie better take a vacation or something."

"Mrs. McFie?"

"I've been giving her sedatives for two weeks now."

"Mar?"

"Said she couldn't sleep, so I started her on tranquilizers. She's allergic to some of them, gets no help from others. So I switched her to Nembutal. I could see it all over her face. She throws off drugs like water. Increased it to three-quarter grains, and finally refused her any more unless she had a thorough physical. Won't take a physical because she doesn't *want* anything to be the matter with her. Enough sickness around here already. But she's still not sleeping."

"I see," Guy said. "I see."

"Wakes up at night feeling hot, restless. Says it's nerves, and she's probably right. I told her to take a vacation. Go down to Atlanta for a week or so. Visit her mother. She's got a sister somewhere, too. The point is, Sam's not doing her any good—not doing himself any good either—and she's heading for her own breakdown if this keeps up."

"I'll talk to her," Guy said.

"It's a rotten business. It stinks!"

"I'll see what I can do." Guy started for the door.

"Guy . . ." Saul leaned forward across his desk. "You too."

"Me?"

"Take a vacation."

"Now, Saul—"

"Not right away. A couple of weeks. Next month. There's a medical convention in Boston. One of us ought to go. Let Bolls take over your patients and—"

"Look, Saul—"

"I said next month, Guy. And Pastene'll be there."

"Pastene?"

"He's God on this sort of thing."

"I know. But even so—"

"Next month. By then this whole business—it could be over before Christmas."

It was hot in the phone booth. Guy left the door open until the phone buzzed. Mrs. O'Hara said "Hello," and then finally he heard Mar's voice. It sounded huskier than ever. It trembled when she spoke.

He tried making a joke of it. "What's this I've been hearing about you? Not sleeping. Taking sedatives."

"You wanted me to lean on you, and I guess I leaned too far and toppled over."

"So you tried leaning on someone else."

There was a pause at the other end of the wire. He opened the booth door, then closed it again and said, "Mar . . ."

"After you hauled the boat, I—I felt like I couldn't get hold of you any more."

"I've been in town the whole time."

"I know, but—I knew you'd refuse me any sedatives—and anyway, I didn't want you to know."

"Why not?"

"You've got enough troubles."

"For Christ's sake, Mar!" He was angry. She'd been avoiding him. She'd gone to Saul behind his back. She didn't trust him, and somehow, desperately, he wanted her to trust him all the way.

The cigarette he'd lit in Saul's office had burned down to his fingers. He opened the booth door again, dropped the butt on the wooden floor, and ground it beneath his heel. He was smoking too many cigarettes these days. Too nervous for a pipe, so he'd become a chain smoker. "Damn it!" He slammed the door. "You need a vacation, Mar." He was talking fast now, still angry both with Mar and with himself. "Come up to the hospital at seven. I'll be here and we'll talk about your going back to Atlanta for a few days."

"I'm not going anywhere, Guy."

"Seven o'clock and we'll talk about it." He hung up quickly. It was stifling hot inside the booth. Perspiration ran down beneath his shirt. He stepped out quickly, looked at the receptionist, muttered, "Hot in there," and strode out to the afternoon.

Mar sat close against the bed. She held Larry's hand as she spoke quietly about what she'd been doing, whom she'd seen on the street today and what Sam had said at breakfast this morning. She looked up as Guy entered, said, "Here's Guy, Larry—here's Guy," and moved away.

"Hello," Larry managed. And then, "Mar needs you," whispering in his throat. "I can tell. Needs those sails—something—needs something—"

"Yes, I—I think she ought to go back to Atlanta for a few days. It would do her a lot of good."

"Won't go . . . tried to make her . . . won't go."

"Well, something else . . . somewhere else. But don't you worry about it. I'll see that Mar's all right."

"Know you will." Larry's bony face contorted in quick pain before his words came again, stronger now, urgently as his fingers closed tightly on Guy's arm. "Not stupid, Guy—noticed the morphine—every eight hours now—know what that means, Guy—"

"Listen, Larry—"

"Want to tell you—when it's over—" He grimaced again and his eyes rolled and his nails made a deep scratch along the back of Guy's hand. Guy looked at the red line and the small trickle of blood. He heard Larry say, "When will it be over? . . . Wish it would . . . When? . . . Wish it would . . ." before the voice died away and his eyes closed and his breathing became regular again.

Mar jerked from the wall where she'd been standing with her hands pressed flat against the plaster. She moved toward the bed, and now for the first time Guy saw the haunted look in her black eyes, the nervous twitch of her hands, the uncertain way in which she moved. He watched her kneel and lay her face against Larry's withered body. He heard her sobs and watched her body tremble. It was no time to discuss Atlanta or anything else. Mar wanted to be alone now, and he knew and left the hospital and drove back to his house in a light November snow that melted as it touched the pavements.

. . . There was no use in trying to share his suffering . . . no good in still trying to make contact, still trying to break through the layer of dark between them. Back in the beginning; then contact had been easy, and the good, pain-free months had been heightened so that sometimes they laughed together, and sometimes, back then, she had made love to him, kissing his body all over, tenderly, caressing him until that final moment when he'd sighed deep and said, "It makes me feel so goddamned unmanly. Here *I've* always been the one who couldn't have children—a goddamned impotent mess

—and now this, lying here, can't even sleep with my wife any more. She has to make love to me like some perverted woman playing with a small boy . . ."

She'd hushed him and kissed him. She'd known these moments of intimacy would be gone soon enough, so if they brought them closer in any way at all, then they were good moments to have. Like the times back in Atlanta, when he'd been able to sit up, and she'd wheeled him about in a big garden of azaleas outside the hospital. Or sometimes they had sat together in the sun on a concrete terrace, and she'd read to him and talked about tomorrow and next month, and even next year, and even children and growing old. Sometimes, in his room, he had grown passionate, and she'd sat beside him on the bed while he touched her. Once he'd tried to sleep with her. But the effort had been too great, and he'd cried like a child. It was the only time he had ever cried, and afterwards he had laughed, embarrassed, and said, "Well, I guess that's the last thing a man likes to lose . . . next to life, I guess . . ." And she thought about that now. "Next to life, I guess." And a poem by A. E. Housman—"Life, to be sure, is nothing much to lose . . . But young men think it is . . . And we were young."

They were both still young, still in their thirties, and life, to be sure, was a great deal to lose, and she should understand that now, and accept it, too, so she should not cry like this . . . not kneel here like this with her face pressed into the blanket against his body . . . She should get some sleep . . . She should go to Atlanta . . . She should stop feeling the insides of her pulling and tearing, her mind whirling and breaking, stopping and starting, everything out of kilter, out of focus, so that someday it would all go at once and she would snap apart . . . burst into a million pieces that could never be put right again.

She pulled to her feet. She murmured, "Good night, darling, I love you, darling," and moved out the door, down the rubber matting to the elevator. The duty nurse was Miss Ida Primmer. Ida nodded. "Good night, Mrs. McFie," and Mar said, "Good night, Miss Primmer," and rode down in the elevator and walked slowly across the drive.

It was snowing now in large, soft flakes that covered her hair and shoulders as she moved on through the town, not seeing anything or anyone, merely walking through the falling snow, going nowhere except away somewhere . . . into some piece of memory, some moment of ease or laughter . . .

The boatyard was dark, silent. The water slapped against the shore and the snow fell silently against her face. A door banged open in a gust of wind, banged shut again. She turned toward the door and saw all the boats inside the wooden shed. Guy's boat was there toward the rear, a dim white shape in the darkness. She moved into the shed, found her way to the chunky sloop, and slid her hand along the smooth hull. She patted it gently, whispered, "Hello, *Julia,* hello, *Julia,*" and remembered the days of sailing, the moments of freedom then, when she'd still had some control over her emotions . . . Now, at this moment, if she could go sailing again, feel the chill wind watering her eyes, reach down and touch the cold rushing water, look up at the full-blown sail and the wind-blown clouds and the bright sun shining . . . But this, too, this too had passed away.

She pressed her face against the cold hull. She started to cry softly, then pulled away and climbed the ladder to the cockpit. She sat in the stern and heard the water against the rocks and the wind through an open skylight. She slipped down into the cabin. A swinging lantern bumped her shoulder and she groped for matches, lit the kerosene lamp, then sat on a bunk and felt that she was alone now . . . away from everything . . . The snow melted in her hair and on her face . . . the lantern swung gently . . . the yellow light made patterns on familiar objects . . . and this, now, was as far away as she could ever go.

The house was quiet. Even the phone was silent, and the old pine boards creaked under Guy's feet as he climbed the narrow stairs to the bedroom. He removed his clothes and took a shower. He ran the water hot, then cold, and rubbed himself briskly with a towel. He wrapped the towel about his waist, returned to the bedroom, sat on the bed, then lay back and smoked a cigarette, staring up at the small round hole, still there in the cracked plaster ceiling. The stairs creaked by themselves; the wind rattled the window. And he remembered way back when he was eight years old, lying in this same bed, and suddenly that window had been shattered by a great explosion, and outside a man had screamed drunken hatred in the night. "Killed her! . . . You killed her!" while the rifle went on firing, five more explosions, five more shattering windows. He'd lain here in terror until finally his mother had come up to see if he was all right. Then he'd looked out the broken window and seen Mr. Potts, the sheriff, leading Larry's father away to his car. Mr. McFie had still been screaming when the car rolled off down the hill.

"He's crazy," his mother had said. "It'll be all right now. So go to sleep and it'll be all right now."

But he had not slept. He'd kept staring at the round bullet

hole in the plaster ceiling. He could not sleep now either. Not even relax. He got up and dressed in his old sailing clothes and went down to the tiny living room and smoked his pipe and skimmed through a medical journal. The stairs creaked and the windowpanes snapped in the cold air. He opened the front door and looked out at the early night and felt the cold against his face. The snow was sticking, but he knew it would not last—only lie there like spilled sugar during the night, then disappear bit by bit until all that remained was a round wet spot in the shade behind the garage.

Larry was everywhere—a part of the dark and the silence and the falling snow. Caesar whined and Guy shuddered and forced his attention to the boathouse, a black shape out there, black and very cold out there with all the boats sitting quiet in the cold of the shed. Long ago, when his boat had been called *Tinker Bell,* he and Julia had worked on her during the long winter nights. They'd make a fire in the kerosene stove and start painting forward in the sail locker, working gradually aft, taking all winter to finish the job because there were always so many interruptions—so many breaks for coffee and kisses, so much love-making in the warm bunks—that afterwards it was better to lie there motionless together, saying, "Love you," and "To hell with any more painting tonight!"

The boat had been their private hideaway—a child's cave—a young lover's secret spot in some wooden glen. Sometimes, when he'd had to make a house call, he'd come back at night and Julia would be gone. There'd be no note, because communication was not necessary. He knew where she'd be waiting, and he'd put on his leather jacket and walk down to the boathouse through the snow. He'd find her there, sitting on a bunk, waiting, and he'd laugh and say, "A lot of work you're doing," and Julia would only smile a little with her child's mouth beneath the freckled nose, and perhaps, that night, they would not paint the boat at all.

He turned back into the room. Outside the snow was falling. Here, inside the room, Caesar whined again, and he thought that Julia was waiting in the boathouse, and he had not thought this way for months now. In the beginning, after the accident, he had found her everywhere. He'd come home a dozen times and called out her name, then stopped abruptly, because of course she was waiting in the boathouse. Once he had actually gone down to see, half expecting to find her there—her ghost—some feeling that she'd left behind, bottled and saved inside the boat's tiny cabin.

He felt that way tonight—a chill along his spine that was not cold really, but the feeling that Julia was waiting in the dark and he had known it all the time—taking the shower, changing his clothes, skimming the magazines, looking into the snow-filled night—he had known it all the time.

He moved, restless, to the phonograph, switched it on, heard an unknown record drop, a faint scratching, then recognized the mysterious opening bars of Schelling's "Victory Ball"—the discordant echoes of a deserted battlefield, the slow change to a polonaise, a suggested tango, the gay music of a gay crowd making merry after the battle, laughing and dancing in a great ballroom, until the sudden hush, the trumpet call, the roll of drums, and from far away, moving ever closer, the steady measured footsteps of the approaching dead.

The dancers whirled into a waltz, trying to stamp out the marching ghosts. They danced and they drank and they made love. But it was no good, because the dead feet marched closer and the drum rolled loud before it slowly died away, leaving only the far-off sound of a trumpet playing taps.

The phonograph clicked off. Silence again, and that same feeling again, that Julia waited in the dark. He murmured her name, "Julia . . . Julia . . ." then put on his leather jacket and went out through his office and waiting room, down the hill in the snow. The boathouse door was open. He looked in at the dim shapes and saw a light inside the shed—two round dots of light from *Julia*'s portholes. He stood motionless in the sawdust, staring at the circles of light, then moved carefully toward the sloop, stepping around the loose boards and the kegs of nails and the pots of hardened paint. There was no sound from inside the boat. But the light in the porthole flickered gently as though the kerosene lamp were swinging inside the cabin.

He touched the board rungs of the homemade ladder. He climbed the ladder soundlessly, until he stood in the cockpit looking down through the open hatch to the lighted cabin, where Mar sat huddled in a bunk with her arms clasped tight about her knees.

She looked up slowly, her eyes expressionless. She wore a red woolen blouse and black slacks. She shivered, and he said, "I'll light the stove. It'll warm up in a minute." He came down into the cabin and lit the small kerosene stove. "It sucks up the air. Not very healthy, but better than being cold."

"What did Larry mean about the morphine?"

"Why should he mean anything?"

"You ordered the shots increased to every eight hours instead of twelve."

"He's feeling more pain. A man gets tolerant to a certain amount of morphine."

"So it's increased to once every eight hours, then six, then four—"

"It takes a long time, Mar."

"But finally it kills him."

"Look—look—" He stood above her, stared down at the way her black hair shone in the yellow light. "You'd better go away for a while. Back to Atlanta. Somewhere away from here."

"So I won't talk any more? So you won't have to bother with an emotional woman when you can hardly control your own emotions? So you don't have to tell me or even admit to yourself what I already know anyway? He's going to die very soon now, and I'll tell you why if you like. Because it won't be long before something gets unbalanced in his body. There'll be too much or too little of one thing or another, and finally he'll die. Morphine might weaken his resistance so he dies of pneumonia or any number of other things. All anybody knows is that drugs will keep him from having so much pain. But it takes more and more to relieve him, so he gets more and more. And finally he dies of it." She laughed hysterically. "Doctor Margreth McFie speaking," and she let the laughter go and shivered a moment longer before she relaxed slowly as the cabin became warmer. "I'm sorry," she said finally.

"It's all right."

"Even God couldn't do anything."

"Go away, Mar. Go away for a while."

"About what Larry said—about *wanting* to die."

"Leave it alone, will you? Will you please just leave it alone?" He was shouting then. But the words only aroused her more, so she pulled up sharply from the bunk and stood with her fists clenched while she threw her own words into his face.

"You're a doctor, aren't you? You're supposed to admit things, accept things for what they are! But instead you've been increasing the morphine at the same time you've been telling me how everything's going to be all right! And you know why? Because you don't trust me, and you don't trust yourself either!"

"Mar . . ."

"Oh, I know how hard this is on you. But what about me? I'm his *wife*. But as far as you're concerned, I'm just a nuisance. So you resent me. You've resented me from the beginning."

"That's not true, Mar!" Emotion had left him. There was

ice, near hatred inside him when he spoke again. "You're all shot, Mar, and it's not doing Larry any good to—"

"I won't go away! I won't, I won't!" screaming at him as she pushed her face close to his, so he saw the wild light in her black eyes and knew she was hysterical and would explode and then be nothing. He raised a hand to slap her. But she gripped at his arms, dug her fingers into his flesh. "Please, Guy—help me, Guy—"

"Away, Mar. Somewhere, Mar . . ."

"Somewhere," with her wild face still close to his, whispering in that hoarse, pleading way while he looked down into her eyes, watched her trembling mouth until finally something exploded in himself, too, and his mouth crushed down on hers and he felt her body arch crazily against him and saw red lights behind his eyes—until after a long time, breathing more easily now with the kerosene lamp still flickering and the air dry from the stove and the smell of fresh paint in the air around him, her voice came back from far away, saying, "I've gone away—gone away—" And she was crying again, but like a child now, huddled close in his arms with her naked body smooth under his comforting hands and her face in his shoulder and the world outside.

"I'm sorry," he said finally, talking dumbly to himself. "You were hysterical, you see, and I—I only planned to slap your face."

CHAPTER EIGHT

The snow did not last. Nothing was left by morning except scattered damp spots about the town. But it snowed again before a week had passed, and this time it clutched at the frozen ground and took life from the cold winds that blew in across the bay.

"Earliest snow I seen in forty years," Chet Belknap remarked to anyone who passed the boathouse doorway. "Usually warmer along a shore than in further. But not this year. No, sir!" And he flapped his paint-splattered arms and went in and shut the creaking door behind him.

But East Norton had seen much snow in its time, and though it talked of each change in the weather as though it forecast the end of the world, still it accepted all weather with philosophy and pride. Fishermen cleared the decks of blanketed craft, while their wives swept doorsteps and complained of the frozen clothes that hung grotesque and stiff on the back-yard clotheslines. The smaller children scooped tiny pyramids of snow from the cannon balls on the village green, and their older brothers worried because Thanksgiving was only a short time off, and the Turkey Day Classic with Harpswell promised to be a bitter, freezing battle, with scarcely anyone there to cheer the home team on to victory.

The rear door of Pat's Bar and Grill was closed tight for the winter, the cracks sealed with weatherproofing. The iron stove was lighted, and the big men stamped their boots as they came in from the snow-filled streets and laughed and warmed their hands before taking up their beer and smacking their lips and saying, "God, it's cold! Earliest snow I ever seen. And usually it's warmer along the coast than inland a ways."

Stewed Schaeffer had gone indoors for the winter. Every afternoon he could be found seated on a stool in Pat's, his threadbare elbows on the counter, his shaking hands lifting one glass of beer after another toward his bloated face that had once been handsome. Stewed was accepted because he came from one of the town's older families. Though he'd always been a heavy drinker, many years ago he'd been an easygoing, likable young fellow, and had never let himself become a bum in the sense that he cadged drinks or slept in gutters. He looked like an elegant man who had completely deteriorated, carrying the past along with him in his clothes and manner of speech. The speech was blurred because he was perpetually drunk. But the stammered words were those of a literate man who had once had something to say. Also, Stewed was dependent on no one. He lived in his own paid-up room over the grocery store on money his father had made at the glassworks. And most important, he had, in his time, contributed to a town scandal and a resulting tragedy that was remembered with awe by some, revulsion by others—and even now, some twenty-eight years later, was not entirely understood by anyone.

Bert Mosley knew only the haziest rumors about Stewed's past. He cared less. He sat next to Stewed at Pat's Bar, his powerful body hunched over the counter, and complained sourly of the rotten weather and the inevitable dullness that settled over East Norton after the summer people had gone.

"What you ought to do," Pat said, "is run for District Attorney, and kick that wiseacre Colin Eustis right out of office."

"And don't think I couldn't," Bert agreed, and thought that was a part of his restlessness, but not so immediate as the problem of Fran Walker, who'd been avoiding him like the plague lately, without giving him one good reason why. She'd stated flatly that it had nothing to do with that affair at the Robins Nest. He'd believed her, too. So maybe it still had something to do with Guy Montford. If you asked him, Guy had been acting a little moody lately. And he wasn't the only one who thought so either.

Mrs. Clara Coffin agreed with Bert, though she attributed Guy's moodiness to his concern over Larry McFie. She thought Margreth was unusually depressed, too, and invited her to an afternoon tea, where she tried to console her, got nowhere, and ended where she'd started—thinking that Guy was depressed and Mrs. McFie was depressed, and Sam McFie was more depressed than either of them, drinking a great deal more than he should, and doing more to upset his daughter-in-law than to console her.

Actually, though, Sam saw very little of Margreth. They lived under the same roof together. But Mar was quiet and withdrawn. And since Sam spent most of his days hovering around Larry's hospital room, most of his evenings catching up on his paper work at the office, they had few opportunities to be together anyway. In the heart of him he resented Mar, as he'd always resented and mistrusted Guy. If Guy weren't Larry's closest friend, he'd have insisted on a different doctor a long time before this. If it weren't for an occasional drink when his nerves were most on edge, he'd have shown his feelings outright to both of them. He didn't like them and he didn't understand them. He was also vaguely aware that he had never understood himself.

Nancy Messner did not understand Parker Welk. Nancy was eighteen. She was energetic, ambitious, and rather pretty in a girlish, enthusiastic way. She'd started working for Parker when she was sixteen, hoping someday to become a full-fledged reporter on a big paper. Parker taught her to write. He was constructive with his criticisms. He paid her faithfully. And sometimes he looked at her with those little eyes of his in a way that sent an odd shiver along her spine. Sort of undressing her, she thought, though he'd never so much as touched her hand in all the months she'd worked for him.

Lately, though, Parker had not looked at her in quite the same way. There was a new kind of secret contempt behind his eyes. She could not explain it exactly, except that it was as though he used to think she was attractive, but he didn't think so any more. Sort of the way an old boy friend used to look at her—detached, aloof—after he'd thrown her over.

As winter rushed on toward East Norton, Maidie Bolls invited Mrs. Kelsey to dinner twice in a week in a last desperate stand to get her husband in line for Doctor Kelsey's position when the old man retired. After eight years of patient tutoring, Mrs. O'Hara finally persuaded Peter to say "Let us pray," so that Peter now said, "Let us pray, goddammit!" And Bill Watts, the milkman, got a new truck, with no hood at all, and started delivering eggs and butter along with milk in what might lead to an actual milk company, including an entire herd of cows, two more trucks, and a position for himself in which he did not rise in the morning until well after eight o'clock.

Ruth Kiley found a half-empty bottle of whiskey in the bottom drawer of Sam's office desk, and Larson Whitt captured an automobile thief on the Hyannis road. Ida Primmer had a blind date with a boy from Harpswell, who paid no attention to her at all, and Betsy, in the Lincoln Hotel, caught the attention of a rare overnight guest—a lingerie salesman—who tried to pay for her services, and received a slap in the face for his innocent generosity.

The snow fell and the snow melted. But it would come again, and next time it would stick.

The November moon reached down into the room, and as Guy moved around the screen toward the unconscious figure, he made out the woman on the chair between the bed and screen. It was Mar, sitting quietly in the dark, her feet together, her hands clasped tightly in her lap. Her head came up slowly, and after a long time she rose and moved soundlessly around the bed. The moon touched her face. It was calm, almost mystic in its sadness. "Hello," she said quietly. "Hello, Doctor Montford."

"Hello, Mar—" He stood uncertain, then moved to the window, touched the frosted pane with his fingers.

"The nurse said I could stay awhile. I was just sitting—just—sitting."

"How are you, Mar? It's been over a week."

"Nine days."

"Yes—exactly nine days."

"I—" She stopped, ran a hand very carefully over the bed's white footrail, and finally the whisper came. "The morphine. It's every six hours now."

"Yes." And watching her through the dark, he groped for something to say about these past nine days—something about this strange calm that had descended over him, something about *Julia* and their time together in her cabin. It seemed odd, this meeting, full of the awkwardness of people who did not know each other, as though that night in the cabin were yet to come, though actually of course it was over, and except for his own awesome memories, almost a sweetness that had never happened at all.

"What are you thinking?" Her face was half-lighted over the flame of a quick-burning match, so he saw only her lips on the cigarette and the shadows on her high cheekbones. "You were thinking how odd it is—everything—how terribly sad and strange it is."

"I was thinking how strange that such things can happen and leave nothing behind at all."

"Nothing?"

"Nothing I can say. Nothing you'd want to hear. 'Forget it,' you told me, and there's nothing you want to hear."

She dragged deep on the cigarette, snubbed it carefully in a tray on the bed table. She lifted a glass and sipped and put the glass down again. "I've been drinking ginger ale all evening through a glass straw. Why do hospitals always have ginger ale?"

"Good for the stomach."

"Remember the first day I came—you took me to the Lincoln Hotel?"

"I remember."

"I've wanted to go again. Sometimes I think about just one martini—just picking it up and feeling how cold it is in my hand—and just looking at it."

"We could go again."

"No, it's New England and cold, and you can't even go back to the Lincoln Hotel." She let the words trail away, then sat once more in the chair beside the bed. She folded her hands and her head dropped forward so she was staring at Larry's face. She did not move. She did not speak. After a long time Guy left the room and drove back to his house in the freezing night.

He parked in the open garage, then entered the house, took off his coat, and put it on again. He climbed the stairs to the second floor, on up the tiny ladder to the widow's walk. The trap door was frozen tight, and he put his shoulder to it before it gave with the cracking of ice, sending powdered snow about his neck. He heaved up to the roof and stood there leaning against the rail, looking down at the rocks below and the boathouse beyond with the snow lying heavy on its roof. And leaning far across the rail, it seemed that he could still see himself beneath that shingled roof and beneath the canvas-covered deck of the sloop. A week—nine days ago. Yet he could still hear Mar's queer little laugh as he'd helped her down the ladder from *Julia*'s deck. It had been all dark then with the light no longer shining through the portholes. They'd stumbled often in the sawdust as they groped for the doorway. He had held tight to her hand as they'd moved along, and he'd wondered if she would keep their secret, and wondered if it was a secret after all in the sense that it was all wrong and could never be made right again.

"I don't know why it happened." She'd been painfully frank standing there in the cold air outside the boathouse with that first wet snow of the year dotting her face and her voice calm for the first time in many days. "Larry, of course. You wouldn't understand. But it was thinking of Larry, of course—"

"Blame me, if you like, I told you before. I only intended to slap your face."

"Things happen. They get over with."

"It's been happening a long time, and I didn't know it."

"Guy . . ." She'd been near, but also far away, and he'd had the disturbing feeling that if this night had never happened, then perhaps someday everything would have worked out and she would not be putting out her hand and saying, "I'd rather you didn't try to justify anything. I'd rather you think what you like and let it go—just let it go." She would not have licked the wet from her lips with the tip of a red tongue, drawn her hand from his and said, "Good night, Guy," and walked away into the snow that was already turning to rain.

He leaned farther across the rail, said, "I should have known this all along," then dropped his eyes to the rocks below and remembered twenty-eight years ago—another man standing here in this same spot on this same widow's walk. He'd seen the man from a long way off—from a secret place along the dunes. The man had looked very much like Charlie Chaplin, and—

He pulled back from the rail. He was shivering, remembering twenty-eight years ago—nine days ago—or it was simply the cold, he argued, and descended quickly to the warmth of the living room. But the shivering would not stop. He was still shivering when the phone rang.

It was Margreth. She was half sobbing as she talked. Something about Sam. He'd gotten terribly drunk after dinner. He'd accused her of not paying enough attention to Larry, of not caring about Larry, simply because she was trying so hard to control her emotions. She'd tried to calm him down. But he'd only become more abusive. "And he threatened me—physically—he actually threatened me."

"Where is he now?" Guy asked.

"Gone to the cannery, and it's Mrs. O'Hara's night out—so at least she didn't hear, and—I don't know—being alone here—with Peter squawking away—and the things Sam said —about your father—"

"He hated my father."

"No—a lot of horrible lies about how your father died, and why, and—"

"They're not lies, Mar. It's all true."

"Guy . . . Guy . . ."

"It was a long time ago, and we were talking about you."

"I'm frightened, Guy. I don't know why. But ever since I came back from the hospital and found him drunk—I'm frightened."

"Go to bed. Try to go to sleep."

"I thought you might come over until Sam gets back. He'll be sobered up by then. Terribly repentant, and—"

"Mar—I can't come over."

"I thought we could play chess or something. You play chess, don't you?"

"Yes, but I can't come over."

"Why? I'm frightened, Guy, and I'm terribly depressed, and—"

"I can't come over!" He shouted the words, then hung up and sat down and patted Caesar, and thought he'd shouted at Mar. He'd been cruel to her. She needed help, but he could not give it because Sam was not home and Mrs. O'Hara was not home, and he knew what would happen to him once he saw her and heard her voice and looked into the black of her eyes.

"All right," he told himself. "All right. You're the doctor, old boy. Somebody needs you, you go. That's all. And Sam could be dangerous. So think about that. She needs you, so you go, and that's all you think about."

He was still shivering as he slipped into his coat and went out to the night, still shivering as he drove to Elm Street and pulled into the gravel drive. The big house was dark except for a single light in an upstairs bedroom window. He stared at the light, clenched his fists hard on the steering wheel.

"Go home," he told himself. "Get out of here. She'll go to sleep finally. She'll be all right, so get the hell out of here!" But it was empty talk. And he knew as he climbed out of the car and moved up the steps to the big front door—he knew what had made him calm these past nine days. He knew also that he would not go home . . .

. . . Mar lay quiet, propped up on the big canopied bed. She wore cotton pajamas, and her hair was down, long and black across her shoulders. She held a book in her hands. But she was not reading. The house was deathly still. Occasionally Peter squawked something unintelligible from his perch in the living room. Her heart began pounding heavily for no reason, and she thought that Sam had not lied about the death of Guy's father. It was all horribly true, and she thought that Guy had refused to come tonight, but there was still nothing to be afraid of. Sam would not return until he was sober, so there was nothing to make her heart pound up this way, cause this tingling all through her body.

A car pulled into the driveway. She listened, tensing in fright. A long wait, and then a door slammed. But it would not be Sam, because Sam's car had a different sound.

She waited. The bell rang downstairs and she started violently, sat up and shook her head, put trembling hands across her face. "Answer it, answer it." She pulled to her feet, threw a flowered robe over her shoulders, put on her slippers, and went out to the hall. The man's figure was a dark silhouette through the panels of glass against the doorframe. She flicked on the hall light, moved slowly down the stairs, supporting herself on the banister. Peter squawked and she said, "All right, Peter, all right, Peter," and recognized Guy Montford. She opened the door and laughed and said, "I thought you weren't coming. You don't care. You keep thinking about the other night—nine days ago—and you feel nothing for me now except contempt."

"Listen, Mar—"

"I told you then—I told you we'd forget about it. And I don't need you now. I'm all right now." She tried to close the door. Guy's body blocked the doorway. He took the door from her hands, closed it, snapped the lock. *"I told you we'd forget about it."*

"Have you forgotten about it?"

"Yes, I've forgotten." She hissed the words at him, then turned away and moved off into the living room, seeking escape among the sea shells and the hooked rugs and the litter of bric-a-brac from foreign lands. "I've forgotten, Guy. Forgotten." The blood was in her head, pounding at her temples. She sensed him moving toward her, felt his arms about her waist, and pulled away sharply so the flowered robe fell open and his hands were cool on her skin beneath the pajama top, rising slowly along her ribs, trembling along her stiffening body, while she could not move, but only whisper "Stop it, stop it," with the words grown fierce and husky in her throat. She clawed at his groping hands, until suddenly the tension left her and she turned in to him wildly and felt her body lifted into his arms, saw his eyes on her naked breasts as he carried her up the creaking stairs. She closed her eyes tight. She said, "Please, Guy, please, Guy," as her body sank into the feather bed. And then his hands again, caressing now, undressing her gently, gently, and then the wet tears in her own eyes, and that terrible wonderful sinking —that hated wanted drifting away—until she was gone from this house and this world, and somehow now—in some strange way—she was almost a little child again.

"No . . ." She spoke softly. "No . . ." stretched full-length on the embroidered spread with her black hair like a cover across her tiny breasts. "That isn't why I wanted you . . . It was Sam and I was frightened, and after he told me about your father's death, then I felt terribly sorry for you, and I just thought we could play chess, you see, and—" She laughed a little and said, "Doctor's taking care of me. Called my doctor, you see . . . needed my doctor."

"Shut up, Mar!"

"Can't happen again."

"I know it. That's why I wouldn't come." His voice broke. He said, "You wanted to play chess. Shall we play chess? I'm very good at chess."

"All right." She giggled. She could not stop giggling. "Red or black? . . . First move or second move?" He had turned away while she pulled the robe about her shoulders.

He preceded her down the stairs and set up the chessboard and pulled up two folding chairs to the card table. All the time he did not look at her.

They played two games and he won them both.

Sam came home, nearly sober, very much ashamed. "How's it going?" he asked.

"He's good," Mar said. "I'm checkmated."

CHAPTER NINE

Bert Mosley was fourteen when he enjoyed his first sexual experience. At that time, during the depression, he lived with his mother, father, and three sisters in Belmont, a suburb of Boston, where his father owned a small corner drugstore with wire chairs and a tile floor and a big overhead fan that turned slowly and uselessly on summer nights.

The object of Bert's sexual initiation was his middle sister, Joanie, aged twelve. Joanie slept alone in a second-floor room in their old gray house on a shaded side street. Bert slept in the attic directly above her. Coiled neatly beneath the window of his room was a homemade fire escape—a long heavy rope with an attached bosun's chair—which was never to be used except in an extreme emergency. The emergency never arose. But one night in summer, bored, restless, full of adventurous dreams, Bert decided to try out his fire escape, despite his father's strict orders. He lowered the rope to the ground, eased into the wooden chair, and lowered himself until he was abreast of Joanie's window, looking straight at her through the screening. Joanie was standing naked before the mirror, admiring her own twelve-year-old figure. She saw Bert's reflection in the glass, gasped, and leaped into her pajamas.

Bert laughed. "Caught you," he joked. But there was a strange lump in his throat and his mouth felt very dry when he spoke.

Joanie said he shouldn't spy on her like that, and Bert said he wasn't spying, just trying out the fire escape. He raised the screen and swung into the room. Then for a while they sat on the bed and talked about what their father would say if he found out Bert had disobeyed orders, until Joanie got to giggling over Bert's prank and Bert got to tickling Joanie, first on the back of her pajamas and then on her skin beneath. She told him to stop. She pushed at his hand, still giggling, and then in a moment they were wrestling on the bed and Joanie's pajama top had become unbuttoned, and as they wrestled and laughed in controlled whispers, Bert's hand brushed against her child's breasts. The excitement surged all through him. He remembered how she had looked through the screening, naked before the mirror, and from then on the wrestling had a single purpose—to touch Joanie—to expose her breasts—to touch them and see them without her realizing it was in any way deliberate.

Bert came down his fire escape on the next night, and again on the night after. Joanie laughed again. And if she understood his excited purpose, she never let on. Night after night they talked, tickled, they wrestled. He taught her to stand on her head, waiting each time for her pajama top to fall loose around her shoulders, exposing her breasts to the dim light. Then he would help her balance herself, and his hands would move over her body and he would say meaningless words like "Keep your feet together," or "Don't wobble so much," or "Don't worry, I've got you . . . I've got you."

Eventually his mother found out about it. Then the game became more difficult and more exciting too. His mother never faced him outright with her knowledge. But he could tell she knew by the way she checked on him every night exactly ten minutes after he'd gone to bed. Then he would wait till her footsteps retreated once more to the living room, and then once more he would lower the rope over the window sill.

He knew it was all wrong—wicked, sinful. He hated the awful guilt inside him, and eventually he found a way to control himself. He wrote notes, swearing on his deepest honor that he would never touch Joanie again. He sealed the notes shut with his junior high school ring pressed into the soft candle wax, and hid the written vows behind picture frames, under the rug, beneath the newspapers in his bureau drawers. Then he sat on the bed, aching all through him, feeling like doing what he knew the other fellows did—what his father had warned him would make him weak and imbecilic—not daring to do it, and yet determined not ever to touch Joanie again.

He broke his promise twice. Once when he was fifteen, and it happened all by itself on a slushy winter afternoon when Joanie was showing him her first evening dress; again on a hot summer night when he was sixteen, and took her for a moonlight swim. He dared her to go in naked, and she took the dare. For a while they just swam, and he talked fast, away from her, laughing and joking to keep her from guessing. But then, back in his father's car, getting dressed again, he suddenly touched her without quite intending to, and then he kissed her and pulled her hard against his naked body. She was fully developed then at fourteen, and her body was cold, covered with goose-pimples. Her mouth was damp under his own, and she fought him playfully, laughing, calling him silly, until finally he pulled away and dressed behind the car. She chatted all the way home. But he did not speak a word because he knew that next time he would not stop himself at all. And that sin could never be forgiven—not by her or himself or God.

There never was a next time. Bert finished Belmont High, went on to Boston University, where he was president of the Debating Club and fullback on the junior varsity football team, then on to the Gilberts and Marshalls and Manila Bay, and back to Boston University for his law degree. During all that time, despite numerous dates, numerous sexual adventures of one kind or another, he never experienced any real physical satisfaction. Sometimes he thought about Joanie. Sometimes he dreamed about her. He wondered who had found those hidden notes. He wondered what Joanie remembered and what she had felt and what she thought, now that she was married with two children and a good husband who slept with her twice a week. He never found out.

In 1950, fresh out of law school, he took a minor position with a law firm in Boston, had one unsatisfactory affair, quit both the firm and the girl, and went on a summer vacation to East Norton. He liked it there. During the summer he could do a pretty fair business, and in time he might become district attorney or even county court judge. He decided to stay. He set up a practice, then became impatient with the slow pace of a small town. It did not suit his restless ambitions. He decided to return to Boston, then changed his mind again when he met Fran Walker.

On their second date, Fran Walker made all the advances. She helped undress him. She said his muscular body was beautiful. She helped him and comforted him, and seemed almost to understand him. It was the first really satisfying experience he had ever known. He stayed on in East Norton.

"Why in the hell do they have to turn the heat off on Sunday?" Bert flung down the pen, stuffed the legal papers into the top drawer of the desk with numb fingers. He'd been sitting here in his tiny, cluttered office above the hardware store since three o'clock, trying to get some work done, trying to keep his mind occupied. But what could a man do when there was no heat and he had to work in an overcoat? He swore again, decided Mrs. Pinkney had no grounds anyway. It was an old problem, always a hassle in court, always Judge Manning deciding for the defendant. So what was the good of it? Mr. Thomas Jones had dug a well on his own property, on lower ground than Mrs. Pinkney's well next door. So this fall Mrs. Pinkney's well had gone dry while Jones' was overflowing. "The water under the ground . . . anything *under* a person's property . . . running off to another person's property . . ." To hell with all that!

Bert stared into the crooked mirror beside the hatrack. His face was reddening from the cold. His eyes were gray, large, in a square, handsome face. His hair was blond, curly, and because a hat tended to flatten the curls, he refused to wear one in even the coldest weather. He straightened his solid black tie, pulled down his French cuffs, worn only to display his Boston University cuff links, locked up his office, and walked along the oiled floor of the hallway, down the narrow steps to the street.

It was warmer out here in the November sun. Pat's didn't open until five. So if he could kill the next hour or so by riding aimlessly around the town, then a couple of more hours drinking beer in Pat's—then it would be time to call Fran, and maybe tonight she would not be "tied up." She'd avoided him again in church this morning, the same way she'd avoided him last week and the week before that. He was goddamned sore about it, and who did she think she was anyway? He'd practically *stayed* in this town because of her. He'd realized two years ago that this place was a dead end. Colin Eustis had the D.A. job tied up tighter than a Pullman window, and old Judge Strike would stay county court judge forever. Even Judge Manning couldn't break through that twosome. So there was no point in staying here, and if he wanted to get out tomorrow, he could—go up to Boston and get into something more exciting than the water in people's wells and income tax reports and bank closings and the wills of people who had nothing to leave anyway. Yes, he could. Only he didn't know where he'd go exactly, and of course he'd be leaving Fran. Not that he needed her. Hell, no! He *might* have married her. He might still, if she cut this coy business of putting him off all the time.

He got into his car and began driving. "I don't need you," he said into the windshield. "I don't need you, Fran Walker!"

Only three days ago he'd gone out with Betsy at the Lincoln Hotel. They'd had a few drinks in a roadhouse in Harpswell, and afterward he'd gone into Betsy's room—a small place off the kitchen at the rear of the hotel. Betsy was thirty-five and a little thin, but not bad-looking really, and God she'd been willing enough. But nothing had happened.

"What's the matter?" she'd said. "You go limp when you drink too much?"

"No, it's not that."

"You a pansy or something?"

"No . . . No . . ."

"Then what the hell *is* the matter?"

He'd found it impossible to explain, like he could never explain to any of the whores he'd visited in Hawaii during the war. Betsy, like the whores, just lay there waiting, and he could not bring himself to actually *take* a woman, even when she wanted him to. Over and over, he'd thought that this indifferent kind of woman would be the easiest for him, and that eventually he'd be able to actually force his attentions on a really nice, resisting girl. But it had never worked out that way. He still felt guilty whenever he was supposed to make the advances by himself. He still felt like writing notes and sealing them in wax and hiding them about his room. Except he'd never felt that way with Fran, because Fran always took the guilt on herself somehow, and—

"To hell with you! I don't need you, Fran Walker. I don't need you!"

The streets were quiet, nearly deserted. The melting snow had frozen again, leaving stretches of ice along the road. He cruised around slowly, looking for something or someone, not sure exactly what, until after a while he drove past the Catholic cemetery on the edge of town. He slowed down and looked at the rows of monuments, some old and grayed, dating back two hundred years or more, some new and white and rather dignified. "God, imagine being buried there. In this hick cemetery in this hick town." He snorted and started off again when he spied the figure of Stewed Schaeffer, lying flat on a patch of ice before a tombstone.

Bert stopped the car. He got out and walked through the cemetery under the black branches of the frozen trees. He called out, "Stewed! . . . You all right, Stewed?"

Stewed pulled staggering to his feet. He stumbled and shouted something, then fell again against a withered wreath.

"Stewed!" Bert was close now. He could see that Stewed was really plastered, practically passed out cold. The old man tried to crawl along the grave and touch the tombstone. All the time he kept addressing it. "Lishen . . . lishen . . . Don't keep blamin' me . . . not all my fault . . . so lishen you . . . lishen . . ."

He fought as Bert pulled him upright. His eyes were red, wild. His uncut hair flopped about his face. His worn but fancy clothes were wet and muddy. "Lishen . . . lishen . . ."

"Come on," Bert said. "Let's go, Stewed, let's go." He got the man's arm around his neck and started off for the car. Passing the tombstone he noticed the name: *Paul Montford . . . Beloved Doctor . . . 1881–1929*. Beside it was a twin stone: *Esther Montford . . . 1894–1943*.

Stewed's room over the grocery store was a shambles of empty bottles, dirty dishes, filth all over everything. His bed was unmade, the sheets gray and torn. Only his few outdated clothes were clean, hung neatly on a hook.

Bert had never been here before, and would never come again. He'd heard that Stewed had once been a witty, charming, and handsome man. It was all still there, buried deep behind the red eyes and the loose-hanging flesh and the mumbling words. He felt sick to his stomach as he lowered the man to the cot and pulled the covers over him. "Go to sleep," he said. "Take a good nap, Stewed." And then, in sudden pity for the old man, he said, "Stewart . . . Take a nap, Stewart."

"Have a drink," Stewart mumbled.

"No, thanks."

"Lishen . . . Lishen . . ." He was still mumbling when Bert

left the room and went down the stairs to the clean air. He felt depressed. He wondered what the hell was wrong with the old man, making a drunken slobbering commotion over the graves of Doctor Paul Montford and his wife. Guy's parents, they were. But hell, they'd both been dead for years now. So what was all the fuss about?

It was five o'clock. He drove to Pat's, went in and sat at the bar and drank a cold beer. Pat asked if he'd like a whiskey, and he thought of Stewed and said no. Larson Whitt came in. He said some kid in the Portuguese section had just knifed his own brother. "Over a girl," Larson explained. "Jealousy. That old black jealousy. I had to lock him up, but there'll be no charges, so—" He shrugged, drank his beer.

That old black jealousy. Bert could not get the phrase out of his mind. At six o'clock it was stamped there even deeper. At six thirty he ate some fried clams smothered in tartar sauce, greasy French fries, wilted lettuce, and a soggy slice of tomato. He complained that the food got worse every day. He'd been eating here twice a day for a long time now, but beginning tomorrow he'd take his business to the Lincoln Hotel.

"You can afford it?" Pat said.

"Balls!" Bert said. That old black jealousy.

Chet Belknap sat down beside him. Chet mumbled on about the door to the boathouse. It needed new hinges, a new lock. The kids were breaking in at night. They'd wrecked the door and it kept blowing open in the wind. "You catch those damn kids," he said to Larson Whitt.

"It's your boatyard."

"You're the sheriff, ain't you?"

"I'll look into it," Larson said.

That old black jealousy. Bert drank another beer, then went to the wall phone and called Fran at the hospital. Ida Primmer answered and said Fran was in the shower.

"Tell her I want to talk to her."

"She's in the shower."

"I don't care if she's on the pot."

Ida gasped in indignation. She said to wait a minute. Then Fran's voice sounded low, placating, "I'm sorry, Bert, really I am, and next week we have a date, just like we used to. I promise you. Next week."

"What's the matter with tonight?"

"Now please, Bert—"

"I want to know what's the matter with tonight."

Fran's voice was almost crying. "Next week, Bert . . . . I promise . . . Next week . . ." The receiver clicked down.

Bert had two more beers. He was not drunk. But he was

plenty mad, boiling, jealous of whatever it was that had gotten between them. Guy Montford. Always so goddamned pleasant, so goddamned popular. Everybody liked old Guy Montford. A great guy . . . a nice guy . . . a sweet guy . . . Guy is a good guy . . . a good guy Guy . . . probably laying Fran and every other nurse in the hospital, too. Not that he blamed him, not that he didn't secretly envy him. But Fran was *his*, and—

He swore aloud. Larson stared at him. "What's the matter, Bert?"

"Nothing."

"Having trouble with Fran?"

"No, I'm not having trouble with Fran." Some fishermen laughed, and Bill Watts came in and said, "What's this about Fran? I just saw her. Just this minute, ten seconds ago."

"Oh?" Bert said. "Where?"

"Walkin' down the street in the dark. Saw her face under a street light. Looked back through the mirror of my new truck—got one of those double mirrors, you know—flip it to a different angle and it takes the glare off the headlights behind."

"Where?" Bert said again.

"Course I couldn't make her out too good all the same. But enough to see she ducked in the office of the *Chronicle*."

Larson said, "Giving Parker some dirt on you, Bert?"

Everyone laughed.

Bert said, "That's right. Parker's doing an editorial on accidents and safety, you know, and she's giving him some facts. Like that time she went out to the fire at the Robins Nest—" He stopped. His beer was half gone. He drank it very slowly, thinking, trying to make sense out of his own words. Finally he paid and nodded. "G'night, Pat . . . Larson . . . Chet . . . Bill . . ." He went out to the street.

It was dark now. The yellow street lamps cast huge dark shadows along the store fronts. A cold wind had come in across the bay. It whipped at Bert's curly hair, and he thought that next summer he'd get a crew-cut. Like Guy Montford. Guy Montford had a crew-cut.

The office of the *Chronicle* was dark. But a light leaked through shutters in the loft above. Bert tried the door. It was locked. He moved slowly around the building, testing each window. They were all locked. One had been broken though, and was covered with black tar paper. He sliced the paper with a bit of broken glass, then carefully tore a hole wide enough to crawl through. Inside he stood motionless a long moment, letting his eyes become accustomed to the darkness.

The stairs to the loft were only a few feet away. He moved cautiously, bumped into a pail of oily rags, swore under his breath, stopped, listening. There was no sound from above. No words, no movement. Nothing. He inched painfully toward the open stairs, grasped them with his hands, and climbed upward step by step, crawling on his knees to make less sound. The trap door was closed, but unlocked. It was heavy and should be raised wth a single violent shove. But he raised it slowly. His arms ached. His big shoulders trembled beneath the weight. Gradually, though, it moved upward, and gradually the scene came into view and he did not feel the weight any longer, but stood upright instead, staring dumbly at the naked bulb that hung from the cobwebbed rafter, at Fran beneath the bulb, naked, too, posing like a photographer's model on an old army blanket.

Fran looked cold. Her nipples were hard, erect, her skin very tight, almost bluish, as she leaned backwards, bracing herself on both arms. Her eyes were closed, not tight in fear or horror, but rather in calm resignation, as though she were thinking of other times and other places.

Bert wet his lips. He closed his own eyes tight, and there, in a fleeting second, he saw Joanie standing naked before a mirror, admiring her still-undeveloped body while he hung suspended, gaping, on a rope outside her window. He jerked his eyes open, and now it was not Joanie, but Fran again, full-bodied, with high, incredibly firm breasts and rather large rounded thighs. He saw this, and then finally he heard the breathing—slow, heavy, wheezing—his own breathing—then, back then—before the notes sealed in wax, stamped with his junior high ring—the guilt eating inside him while he laughed and chatted, trying to cover the signs of his own roaring passions. He was there. Bert Mosley was there in the dark corner, hidden, breathing heavily, ashamed and guilty, acting in a way that would make him weak and imbecilic. He'd been warned by his father, and he had never done it—never—

"You sonovabitch!" He leaped toward the surprised figure in the corner. He pounded the man's face with his big fist. He tripped him, then kicked him hard in the groin. The man screamed. Bert's hand found a chair leg in the clutter of broken furniture. He struck the man's face and felt the nose crunch beneath the blow. He struck the bald head and heard a low moan. He struck again and then again. "Sonovabitch, you sonovabitch!" And then hands pulled at his shoulder and Fran's voice said, "Bert . . . Bert!" rising almost to a scream.

He stood up, trembling all through him. Fran took the chair leg from his hand and dropped it to the floor. She was still naked, whimpering, "Bert . . . Bert . . ." until finally awareness returned and he understood and said, "God . . . Get dressed . . . My God . . . my God!"

Fran dressed quickly under the yellow bulb. Parker was still unconscious. His face was covered with blood. Dead, Bert thought, dead, except he was still breathing. He jerked away, said, "Come on . . . come on . . ." and pushed Fran down the stairs to the shop below. He held tight to her hand as he climbed out the window and turned to help her down. After glancing quickly up and down the street, he pulled Fran out to the sidewalk and began walking fast toward his car three blocks away in front of Pat's.

"Do you want a drink?" he said finally.

"No . . . No . . . And we've got to go back. You've hurt him, Bert—"

"To hell with him!"

"You can't just *leave* the man."

"I'll send someone else. Right now you ought to have a drink."

"All right. But not in Pat's. And you've got to send someone back there right away."

"We'll go to the Lincoln."

Larson Whitt came out of Pat's as Bert opened the car door. "See you found her," Larson said.

"Yeah." He remembered Bill Watts looking through the double mirror of his new milk truck. "You were right, Larson." He laughed. "She was giving Parker all the dirt about me."

Larson laughed with him. Then Bert got into the car, started the engine, and drove off toward the Lincoln. He remembered that Betsy would be there, and he hadn't seen Betsy since that night when he'd planned to lay her, then chickened out and left her laughing at him. But Betsy was unimportant now. He switched his mind to Parker Welk. "Sonovabitch!" he said.

"Bert . . ." Fran was crying now. "He didn't even touch me. Never. He never touched me. He knew about us being at the Robins Nest, you see, and he threatened to put it in the paper, and—but he never touched me, Bert."

"Sure," Bert said. "Sure."

"Understand, Bert. Please try to understand."

"I understand, sure, I understand," adding, "the perverted bastard," though he felt rather uncomfortable in saying it.

CHAPTER TEN

The knock sounded twice before Sam pulled out of his reverie, quickly hid the whiskey bottle in the bottom drawer, then heaved up from behind his desk and opened the frosted glass door. Miss Kiley stood in the doorway. She was a few years younger than Sam, gray-haired, wearing steel-rimmed glasses, and as self-conscious now as she'd been many years ago when he'd first hired her as his secretary.

"I saw your light," Miss Kiley said, "and seeing how it's Sunday night and all, I thought if you had an especial lot of work to do—"

"No," Sam said, "I was just finishing up."

"Well, then—" She hesitated, started to move off.

"I'll drive you home," he said.

"No sense going out of your way."

"It's not out of my way." He put out the lights and walked behind Miss Kiley through a narrow fish-smelling corridor, out to his car on the pier beside the cannery. He opened the door for her, and she said, "Thank you, Mr. McFie," and then he got in and drove slowly toward her rooming house.

She sat motionless against the door as he steered through the winding streets. They had little to say to each other now, though some thirty years ago, he'd had a violent love affair with Miss Ruth Kiley. He had just been released from the sanitarium then, and had decided to forget his lost wife and all the past entirely by trying to put the cannery back on its feet again. He'd hired Miss Kiley to work for him as a personal secretary, though at that time he could not afford a personal secretary and had no use for one anyway. But Miss Kiley (he'd called her Ruth back then) had seemed to have some glimmer of understanding of the torture that sometimes ate inside him. She'd been attractive and cheerful. She'd helped keep him from drinking, even stood by him during the crash and the following depression, holding him up while the cannery gasped and struggled and finally breathed easily again.

Those six or seven years of hard work had been as productive and happy as any Sam could remember outside of his three brief years of marriage, before that Catholic Doctor

Montford had decided to sacrifice his wife for a child he had not really wanted anyway. He'd worked hard during the day, with Ruth always there at a desk beside him. Then, at night they'd drive to a cottage overlooking the bay, where they made love and he'd felt some peace, some contentment, some faint belief that life was worth living after all.

But something had happened to end all that. He never knew exactly what, or why, or how it had come out. Gradually, though, he'd begun to feel that he ought to marry Ruth. Yet every time he thought seriously of marriage, he remembered his wife again, and despite all the satisfaction he found in Ruth, despite all she had done for him, somehow she could never take his dead wife's place.

Ruth understood this. Sam understood that she understood. Neither of them ever spoke of it. But the trips to the cottage became less frequent, until finally they stopped altogether. Over the years "Ruth" became "Miss Kiley." "Sam" became "Mr. McFie." She became the faithful secretary, he the sympathetic boss. They acted now as though there'd never been anything personal between them at all.

"How's Larry?" Miss Kiley spoke away, out the window.

"About the same," though Larry was worse, and everyone knew it.

"Well, as long as he's not getting worse."

Sam pulled up at the rooming house where Miss Kiley had lived nearly all her life. He used to drive her back here from the cottage in a Graham Page. He said, "Here we are," and she said, "Yes," and got out and said, "Mr. McFie—"

"Yes?"

"I shouldn't mention this, I know. But I was clearing your desk the other day, and I—"

"Yes, Miss Kiley?"

"I found a bottle, Sam." It was the first time she'd used that name in years. She hesitated, said it again. "Sam . . . Don't be angry . . . But remember the last time . . . Don't let it happen again."

"I won't," he said.

"You're not angry?"

"No, I'm not angry."

"If there's anything I can do."

"No, thanks, Ruth." He smiled at her. "Ruth—no, thanks." Then, "Good night," he said, and drove away down the street. Through the rear-view mirror he could see her standing there on the sidewalk, plump, past middle age, staring after him for a moment before she turned and wearily climbed the wooden stairs.

It was nine o'clock now, too early for bed, and he was

restless with nowhere to go. He was passing the Lincoln Hotel, and decided to go in for a drink. He'd had two in the office, but they were wearing off now, and he was thirsty, and Miss Kiley was not entirely justified in worrying about him. Sure, since Larry's return he'd been drinking a little more than he should. In fact one night he'd had a lot too much and said things to Margreth that shouldn't have been said to anyone. He'd learned his lesson that night, though, and the next day he hadn't touched a drop, so of course it wasn't going to happen again. No more of those bad alcoholic bouts of the years ago. Not for him. No more crazy stuff like almost killing Paul Montford that time. And then those long months sitting stupidly behind bars with crazy men, when he was not really crazy himself—waiting numbly for visiting days, when Mrs. O'Hara brought Larry up to see him. He'd had nothing to say to the boy, and sometimes, looking at him, he'd thought that if Larry had never been born, then he wouldn't be here at all.

The Lincoln's cocktail lounge was nearly empty now on Sunday night. Bert Mosley and Fran Walker sat together in a corner booth. They both seemed upset, nervous, wary. Bert looked acutely embarrassed each time Betsy passed their booth. Sam nodded to them and sat at a single table in the opposite corner. He ordered a scotch on the rocks and tried to concentrate on taking the drink very slowly—keeping his mind away from tonight and tomorrow and the day after that.

Bert Mosley rose abruptly. He leaned over, said something quick and hard to Fran, then strode to the nickelodeon and put in a coin. Then he went into the phone booth. The nickelodeon started. The song was "Stardust," a very old song. "Sometimes I wonder why I spend these lonely nights . . ." It drowned out any possibility of hearing what Bert said into the telephone. It must have been an important call, though, for when Bert returned to his table a moment later, he seemed to relax, as though making the call had involved some big decision, and now that it was done and over with, he felt enormously relieved.

". . . But that was long ago, and now my inspiration is in the stardust of a song . . ." Sam had another drink. He thought about Miss Kiley, calling him "Sam" like that, and then his suddenly calling her "Ruth" after all these years. He thought about all these years, but they merged together into one long stretch of time that had been broken only on rare occasions by events which had always seemed to be unpleasant.

Once the cannery had caught fire, almost burned to the ground. Then Larry had gone off to college, leaving him alone with only Peter and Mrs. O'Hara. Larry had come back from college. They'd tried to make contact with each other. Yet still, as in Larry's boyhood days, they'd been little more than strangers. He'd bought a power cruiser and smashed it on the rocks only two months later. Larry had gone off to war, and written letters only once every three or four months. The letters were empty gestures of a son's duty to his father. His own answering notes were just as impersonal. One of Larry's letters had mentioned a quick marriage to a Margreth Sloane in Atlanta. He'd sent them his best wishes and a fine Sheffield silver service that had belonged to his grandmother. Margreth had written a thank-you note, and after Larry's return from overseas, she'd invited him to visit them for the summer. He'd gone, stayed in their house and eaten their food and known, all the time, that he was in the way. It was terribly hot that summer, and there was nothing for him to do, nothing to say to either of them. They were very much in love, and he envied them. When he left, he resented them. Once Larry came home to visit—alone—staying only the weekend. Occasional letters from Atlanta. Then, two years ago, a letter informing him that Larry was sick. Other letters, avoiding the real issue, but implying Larry was getting worse. He'd decided to fly down and see for himself. Margreth telephoned. "No, he's getting along all right, and I'll keep you informed if there's any change." Then suddenly a change. Larry was much worse. Nothing could be done. He was returning to his home town, where he wanted to be treated by his oldest friend.

Suddenly, in that moment, while reading that letter, Sam had felt that Larry was really his own son. It was the first time he'd felt that way in thirty-six long years.

"No . . . No, thanks." He did not want another drink. He put a bill on the table, nodded good night to Betsy, then to Bert and Fran, and went out to his car. Driving home in the dark, he realized that he'd be very late for dinner. They were having one of Mrs. O'Hara's very special Cape Cod "turkeys" tonight, and he wondered if Margreth had already eaten. He wondered why nothing good had ever happened in his life. He thought about Ruth Kiley, and wondered if perhaps something good might once have happened—only he'd paid no attention, and now it was too late for anything.

Dinner began with frozen shrimp cocktail. Mrs. O'Hara explained that fresh shrimp were much better, of course, but since they were out of season, and there weren't any shrimp around here when they *were* in season—anyway, a shrimp cocktail made a nice start for a good old Cape Cod fish dinner, even though shrimp were not native to these parts.

Everything else was, though, and sitting across the table from Sam, staring down at the Portuguese soup that followed the shrimp, the heavy mixture of red beans and kale and linguica sausage and potatoes, Mar wondered if she would ever, after leaving here, *ever* want to eat fish again. Mrs. O'Hara prided herself on her Cape Cod cooking, and Sam, having been brought up on it, felt that everyone should have fish at least three nights a week. So far, in the weeks Mar had been here, they'd had steamed clams, clam chowder, clam stew and clam cakes; fried scallops, creamed scallops, boiled lobster and broiled lobster; cod tongues and cheeks, codfish balls, and broiled scrod; spawn and haddock, and fried eels twice, though she had not eaten them either time.

This Sunday night Mrs. O'Hara had settled on a main course of Cape Cod "turkey" with savory sauce. All afternoon, while Mar had sat alone, reading in the living room, Mrs. O'Hara had popped in regularly from the kitchen to keep her informed on the exact progress of the recipe. "You take a four-pound cod, leave the head and tail on, and clean it just like you would for baking. Wipe it good with a damp cloth, and rub it all over with seasoning. After you put in the savory stuffing, you make a few gashes on top of the fish and place strips of salt pork in the gashes."

Mar had nodded politely, inadvertently encouraging Mrs. O'Hara to go into further detail, so on her next trip from the kitchen, she explained that savory stuffing was made by mixing one cup of bread crumbs, a half cup melted butter, a half cup of hot water, a quarter teaspoon salt, half teaspoon sage, a half onion minced, and an eighth teaspoon of pepper.

Now, as Mrs. O'Hara removed the soup plates and proudly brought forth her creation, garnished with parsley and wedges of lemon, she complained, "If you hadn't been late, Mr. McFie—supposed to bake about nine minutes a pound at 400 degrees. But you didn't come, so I had to lower it to 300, and you should never overcook fish. You know that, Mr. McFie?"

"I know that," Sam said. His eyes were bleary. His hand trembled when he lifted the fork. Mar wondered if the reason he liked to work at night was not so much to have his days free at the hospital as to have his nights free, alone, locked in his office with a bottle.

"You like it?" Mrs. O'Hara's dark eyes watched her from the kitchen doorway.

"Yes, it's very good." She took a small bite, felt sudden nausea, and used all her will power to smile and swallow. "It's wonderful."

Mrs. O'Hara grunted and went back to the kitchen. Sam said "Sorry I was late," and Mar said, "You couldn't help it." She felt sick again. The fisheye was open. It stared up at her from the white platter. It was cold and dead, like the black branches of the dead trees and the brown grass along the dunes—like the dead past of so many people she had known, like the dead future of so many others. She remembered corn bread and spoon bread and fried chicken and turnip greens, scrambled eggs with lettuce and fresh strawberries, and magnolia trees and azaleas in bloom, and the water cress growing thick in a cold stream on a summer's day. A lot of the South was dead, too, of course. But not quite so cold in death, not quite so starkly real, so there was always the feeling that life might come again—the horses might prance before the polished carriages, the musicians might play in the great ballrooms while the young girls whirled again in their crinoline dresses. And there was other music, too—banjos and whippoorwills and tree frogs and bobwhites, and Negroes singing in the Southern night. The ghosts still lived in the moss-covered mansions, whereas here, in the severity of a New England winter, the ghosts were dead—cold stone dead—and they would never rise again.

"You feeling all right?" Sam asked.

"I'm—afraid I'm not very hungry."

"Blueberry pie for dessert. Frozen blueberries, of course. But good."

"Thank you, no."

Sam went on eating. "Something's wrong," he said finally. "I've been noticing. You've been thinking about going back to Atlanta."

"No . . ."

"Somewhere."

"Yes, I— New Haven, as a matter of fact. I have a friend there. We were roommates at Sweet Briar, and she's been urging me to visit her for a long time now."

"I don't know."

"I'd only be gone a day or two, and I'd call the hospital every day, of course, and—"

"You tell Guy yet?"

"No, but I spoke to Doctor Kelsey. He thought I ought to take a few days away."

"Huh." Sam grunted, pulled a fishbone from between his teeth. "I thought everyone *wanted* you to go and you wouldn't. So now you changed your mind."

"That's right—I changed my mind." She pushed back her chair. "Excuse me—I don't feel well. If I'm going to New Haven, I'll want to leave Friday, but right now I feel like I'm coming down with a cold, and I'll want to be over it, you see, and—" She murmured another apology, then turned and climbed the stairs to her room. She undressed, put out the light, and crept into bed, where she lay quiet, thinking idly that she'd been unfair in condemning Cape Cod as always cold, always severe and dead. Perhaps, if she could sail forever with the wind in her face—if she could sit close in *Julia's* cabin, lie warm in this bed— She moved her hands slowly, gently across the embroidered spread and remembered the hard warmth of Guy's body, then shut her eyes and thought that it was becoming impossible to face Larry—even when he was unconscious—impossible to sit there by his bed, knowing what she'd done, feeling as she still felt—disloyal, unfaithful, the contemptible bitch who waited until her husband was too sick to fight back, too weak to be told—unable to ever learn the truth—the whole truth—nothing but the truth—

She was going to New Haven next Friday. Her old roommate knew of a doctor there, who, for a reasonable fee, would do something about this new life that grew inside her. Bitch, she thought. Whore, she thought. Then, Murderer, she thought, and opened her eyes and stared once more into the unspeaking dark.

CHAPTER ELEVEN

Guy's office phone rang at five minutes after nine. The urgent voice was deliberately disguised. "Doctor Montford . . . You better get down to the *Chronicle* right away . . . Parker Welk's just had an accident." The receiver was clicked down.

Guy telephoned Larson Whitt. Mrs. Whitt said that Larson was out somewhere. Guy told her to send him over to the *Chronicle* as soon as she got in touch with him. Then he grabbed up his bag, put on his coat, and drove to the closed front of the newspaper office. The door was locked. He pounded on it, got no answer, and circled the building until he found the ripped tar paper. He crawled through the window, located a light switch, then searched the pressroom and Parker's private office. He found nothing. But the trap door to the loft was open.

Parker lay motionless, his battered face covered with drying blood. His nose was broken, his head severely bruised—concussion—a possible fracture. There was an old brown army blanket spread out neatly beneath a single light bulb. A Polaroid Land Camera lay on its side near Parker's body, and in the dust by his hip was a gold cuff link bearing the seal of Boston University.

Guy put the cuff link in his pocket. Parker moaned, and a car pulled up outside. Parker moaned again as Guy opened the camera and removed the automatically developed photograph of Fran Walker, naked, posing on the army blanket. He put the picture in his pocket along with the cuff link. It was the last picture in a roll of eight. He groped in Parker's pockets and found the other seven—all like the first—various poses of a naked Fran Walker.

"Guy! . . . You up there?" It was Larson from the room below.

"Up here, Larson!"

Larson's head appeared through the trap door. "What the hell!" he said. "What happened?"

"Somebody beat him up."

"They sure did." Larson bent over the moaning body. "He going to be all right?"

"You better call an ambulance."

Larson went down the stairs. His voice echoed up from Parker's office as he called the hospital. Guy administered what little first aid was possible before the ambulance arrived. Looking at Parker's battered face, he remembered it from weeks ago, leering at him from the window of his car in front of the Robins Nest Motel. Fran had been with him then. Parker had not fully believed that she'd accompanied him to the fire in the capacity of a nurse. He remembered that Bert Mosley had gone to Boston University.

Larson returned and inspected the loft in his best professional manner. He found the bloody chair leg. "The weapon," he called it. He looked at the empty camera. "Parker's about the only one in town with one of these Polaroid things. Uses it in his work. Develops the picture right inside the camera."

"That's right."

"What'd he have it up here for?"

"You'll have to ask Parker."

"Yeah . . . Well, there's a motive to point at every person in town. Nothing Parker liked better than digging up a lot of dirt, then printing those moralizing editorials, when if you know anything about Parker—he's no goddamned saint himself."

The ambulance arrived. They carried Parker down the steep

flight of stairs and drove off to the hospital with the siren going.

Guy followed in his car, and Larson followed Guy. At the hospital, Parker's head was X-rayed, his nose taped. He came to long enough to mumble that he'd surprised a vandal in the loft. The vandal had attacked him with a broken chair leg. He didn't know what the fellow could be looking for, and he'd never seen him before in his life.

Guy sent Larson from the room. He moved about, looked out the window, heard Parker whispering behind him. "Who found me? . . . Who found me?"

"I did."

"Guy . . . Listen, Guy . . ."

"O.K., Parker. I found the camera, too. I'll burn the pictures."

"Why?" Even in pain, even semiconscious, he could not believe that everyone else was not as lousy as himself. "Why? . . . Why?"

"Not for your sake, Parker."

"You been laying Fran Walker?"

"No."

"Then why?"

"Because she was a victim, Parker. I'll cover for the victim any day."

"You covered for her before—out at the Robins Nest."

"But I'll never have to again—not for her or anybody else, so far as you're concerned." He bent down over the bed and saw the smashed ugly face and hated it. "I'll tell you something, Parker. I'm not going to burn those pictures after all. I'm going to keep them around. With a sonovabitch like you in town, with Fran and Bert and myself to testify, they might come in handy someday."

Ida Primmer was at the desk as he left. "It's awful," she said. "Imagine someone beating up poor old Mr. Welk!"

"Yes," Guy said, "it's terrible." He went down in the elevator, stepped into the lobby as Polly Welk came huffing in. She said poor Parker wouldn't hurt a soul. Poor Parker had been working Sunday nights for quite a while now, even gave up the church suppers to do it, and, "Poor Parker . . . Poor Parker . . ." She started to cry. Guy led her to a chair, where she lowered herself and sobbed uncontrollably.

Doctor Kelsey stepped out of his office and nodded Guy inside. "All right," he said. "What happened?"

"Didn't the sheriff tell you?"

"I'm asking you."

"Look, Saul, it's one of those things. Parker's going to be all right. He'll tell his own story—if anyone else gets involved, then he may tell a different story. If things get bad enough, then I'll have to tell mine. Only they won't get that bad."

"You know that?"

"I know that."

"All right." Saul lit a cigar, leaned back wearily in his leather chair. "A doctor's confidence—ethics— Jesus Christ, Guy, there's a limit to everything!" He paused, puffed long and slowly on the cigar so the end turned to white ash. "Would it make it any easier if you happened to be out of town for a few days? Parker gets better and does his explaining, whatever it is. Maybe somebody else does some explaining, too. But at least you won't get involved. And by the time you get back, it'll be all blown over—or rather the story will be reasonable anyway. And you know how anxious everyone around here is to keep a story reasonable. Everyone's got his own little skeleton in the closet. Dig deep enough, open too many closet doors, and the whole damn town's involved."

"I know. Or don't you remember?"

"Guy—that was a long time ago."

"Even so—you see why I hate this kind of thing. You see why I cover for people when sometimes maybe I shouldn't."

"You look tired, Guy."

"I'm tired."

"More than tired."

"All right, Saul, all right!" He was angry. He moved about, finally stopped, said, "But I can't leave town and you know it. Sam would never forgive me."

"To hell with Sam!"

"And Margreth—"

"She's leaving town herself."

Guy turned and studied him carefully. "That's a fact, Saul?"

"Told me herself. Going to New Haven on Friday to visit a college roommate. We both prescribed a vacation for her. So now she's taking one."

"I see."

"I told Sam I wanted you at that medical convention next week. He raised hell at first—drinking, if you ask me—and I told him Pastene would be there, and Bolls would look after Larry personally while you were gone. He raised hell about that, too, so I said all right, I'd look after Larry myself." Saul stood up and moved around the desk. "Guy—not for the convention, not for this Parker Welk business, whatever it is—not even for Pastene—for yourself, Guy. Get away from Larry—this town—get a few days off or you'll end up a patient yourself."

"No extra beds."

"I'm reserving one in the state asylum."

Guy sat and lit a cigarette. He said, "Does it show that much, Saul?"

"It shows."

"All right, I'll—think about it."

"*Do* it, Guy. And you can leave Caesar with me."

"I'll think about it." He moved to the doorway, turned, smiled, said, "Thanks, Saul."

"I'm a good vet, too."

"For not asking questions—about anything."

Mrs. Welk had gone from the reception room as he went out the glass door and crossed the parking lot. Bert Mosley's car was parked close to his own, and when he neared it, Bert rolled down the window and called out to him.

He said, "Hello, Bert."

"Understand Parker got beat up. Vandals or something?"

"Yes." He noticed Fran sitting huddled against the door. He said, "Hello, Fran." But she did not answer.

"How is he?" Bert asked.

"Smashed up, but he'll recover."

"That's good. He see who did it?"

"Didn't you say he surprised a vandal or something?"

"Well, that's what Larson said anyway. You see, Fran was there herself earlier tonight. She was helping Parker with one of those crusading editorials of his—a nurse's views on accidents—safety—you know—and well, Bill Watts saw her going in, and I picked her up outside myself. About quarter past eight, that was, and—" He kept on talking. But the words began stumbling over each other, until finally they stopped altogether, and he said, "Guy . . . Listen, Guy . . ."

Guy took the cuff link from his pocket. He dropped it in Bert's hand. Bert held it still between his fingers, then fastened it carefully to his cuff. "There was a reason," he said finally.

"I know."

"He had a camera," Fran said suddenly. "Oh, God, I just remembered!"

"I found it. I'm going to burn the pictures. But Parker doesn't know that."

Silence then. In the corner Fran began to cry silently. Guy wanted to say something in comfort or understanding. But there was nothing he could say. He nodded good night and drove home in the dark.

He sat motionless in the living room. The grandfather clock struck eleven in the hallway. He drew the photographs of Fran Walker from his pocket and studied them one by one. She was a luscious girl, all right, but somehow, after all this, he felt sick inside his stomach. He burned the pictures in the fireplace. They made a crackling, disgusting smell as they dissolved into ashes.

He sat in the chair once more. He wondered what Mar was doing—now—right this minute—what she would do next weekend in New Haven. He thought it was a good idea for them to be far apart for a few days. Caesar brushed against his legs and he patted the brown head and said, "Good boy, good boy." He remembered an old saying, "The quickest way to make an enemy is to do someone a favor."

He had made a lot of enemies tonight.

CHAPTER TWELVE

Boston was gray and damp, the streets wet with a mush-like slush. The medical convention, held in a ballroom of the Statler Hotel, was a three-day affair, lasting from Thursday through Saturday morning. Papers were read in long, detailed length. Speeches gave scientific accounts of long experimentations with new drugs, new techniques in surgery, new approaches to the cure of old diseases. The room was large. The amplifier did not work properly. Guy's seat was toward the rear, and he could hear little of what was said. He was hot; cigar smoke watered his eyes; time dragged. Even the special round-table discussions brought out little that he had not read before in various medical journals, or heard in loud, oath-filled terms from Saul Kelsey, who knew as much about sickness and health as any man here. Most of these men were specialists. Saul was a general practitioner. But Saul specialized in everything. He was a "doctor" in the true old sense—the complete, all-covering sense—Saul was a "doctor."

Back in Harvard Medical School, only a mile or two away across the Charles River, Guy had felt a great awe toward all "doctors." They were different from other people—closer to death—closer to life. Even before medical school, as a very young child, he had felt this same way each time he heard his father coming home late at night in the rattling old Dodge touring car, talking to his mother in the living room while he drank coffee before coming up to bed. "Well—Mrs. Potter had a girl," or "That Scopes boy's going to be crippled for life," or "Old man Steward is dying, and there's nothing to be done about it." A child was born; a boy remained crippled; an old man died—all under the direction of Doctor Paul Montford. Guy had been awed then—and the awe had only increased in medical school. Then, during the war, suddenly there had been no time to see the profession as such a sacred thing. Men were wounded and men screamed and men moaned and men died, and he had learned about death in those days—in the same childlike way that any soldier learns of death. Yet the more he'd seen of death, the more he'd lost that awe of medicine; though in a strange way, he'd gained even more respect for the men who practiced it. The reason, he knew, was because he'd finally realized that doctors were only men. They had learned what other men did not learn. They dealt with the fundamentals of life and death. Yet they were still men—ordinary, sometimes good, sometimes bad, amusing or dull, simple or pompous, adjusted or maladjusted—they were men. And in the final analysis, though they saw children born and watched old people die, they knew as little about the mysteries behind it all as the very simplest of their patients.

Now, at this convention, though he learned little of practical interest, Guy felt a new kinship with his colleagues, along with new doubts and a strange new confidence in himself. He sought out Doctor Pastene, who talked very technically—this and that—this success, that failure. He used the word "arrested" over and over. Hodgkin's could occasionally be "arrested." A year, two years. In some cases, as long as six years. If the patient were in extreme pain, subject to long comas, that state could not be relieved—but sometimes it could still be arrested.

"So you keep a patient alive as long as possible?" Guy said. "You make him suffer as long as you possibly can?"

"What else would you suggest?" Doctor Pastene looked at him narrowly through bright, rimless glasses. "It's a step, isn't it? What else can you do?"

Guy had no answer. Doctor Pastene, too, was only a man. And sometimes there were no answers.

On Friday he called Saul Kelsey. Saul said that Larry was about the same. Caesar was eating him out of house and home. Margreth had left for New Haven early this morning. He said not to worry. Bolls was taking care of all emergencies, and he was ready to step in himself whenever necessary. If Larry showed any change, he would call Guy immediately.

"I've been talking to Pastene," Guy told him.

"Yes . . ."

"He said he's had some luck in arresting it in certain cases."

"Yes?"

"Nothing." He hung up and paced nervously in his room. In the years after Julia's death he had enjoyed these infrequent escapes from East Norton. He'd made it a deliberate point to let himself go, indulge himself with liquor and women, purposely saturate himself with the physical pleasures he carefully avoided in his own home town. He told himself that nothing was any different than it had ever been. It was Friday night. Tomorrow, Saturday, after a few closing speeches, the convention would end. "Get away," Saul told him. "Blow off steam. Relax."

He honestly tried. Cocktails and dinner at Locke Obers with a Mike Heggen, whom he'd known in medical school. Then the floor show at the Latin Quarter, followed by drinks in the Top Hat Bar in Scollay Square. Mike got very drunk and began talking about his wife. He hated her. He'd divorce her tomorrow, except he had three children and a good practice in Manchester. "And you know these small New England towns, Guy—keep your nose clean—clean nose, good nose—everything's fine. Pick your nose, blow your nose—nobody trusts you any more—don't come around for those old pills any more. And my wife's like a popsickle—hasn't let me sleep with her in a month. Why?—Who knows?—So there I am, and Christ, a doctor's not any different than anybody else!"

"I've been thinking that."

"I'd divorce her in a minute. Tell you what, fella, there's girls in this old Scollay Square . . . You remember in med school—pick 'em up in any bar—right in this bar—see that one over there in the black dress. Now she's been eying us . . ."

Guy took Mike back to the Statler in a cab. He got the man to bed, wondered why he had not felt all the drinks himself, decided they'd been watered, and went down to the hotel bar for a nightcap. It was noisy. He could not think. He bought a fifth of bourbon and took it back to his room, where he sat on the bed in his pajama bottoms and drank slowly and felt his mind slipping, shifting gears—automatically, beyond his control. It had happened before. He drank little because when he lost touch with reality, then it always happened, like a great delusion, though it had been real at the time, and it was real now while he was drunk, sitting here in the lonely room—it was a very real scene.

He tried to fight it, put it down, replace it with a picture of Mar lying naked beside him on an embroidered spread. But even that memory faded, and finally, with another long drink, the scene was all there again, and he had to live it again, lying flat on his stomach now, his head spinning, the scene spinning, his face buried in the pillow, the scene slowing down now, coming into focus until finally it was clear . . . and would only fade in heavy sleep . . .

. . . St. Joseph's had only one confessional booth, and the wait was quite long that day, so there was plenty of time to think over his sins, except he was not sure exactly where his own sin lay in the sins of others.

He'd come home from grammar school early on the afternoon before, because there'd been a teachers' meeting at two o'clock. He'd gone into the house through the back door, on through the kitchen to the living room. There'd been no sound in the house at all. He'd looked out the window because sometimes his mother was in the yard emptying the garbage or hanging up the clothes. But she was nowhere in sight. So he'd decided she must have gone to visit a neighbor, and had climbed the stairs to change his good school trousers for after-school knickers. Then, on the landing, he'd heard his mother's voice from her bedroom. She was laughing gently to herself, the way she laughed a great deal in those days, and he'd knocked lightly on her door, then pushed it open and stepped into the doorway.

His mother had sat up quickly, pulling the sheet over her naked breast. The man beside her had said nothing at all. His jaw dropped open; his mouth worked; his hands groped automatically for the clothes on the floor beside the bed.

The silence had been interminable. "You should have knocked . . . Why didn't you knock?" That was all his mother had said. The words had come broken, crying, gasping from her throat, meaning something else entirely, meaning, "Oh, God, this never would have happened . . . You'd never have found us here . . . If only you'd knocked a little louder . . . If only we'd locked the door . . . If only you hadn't come home at all." She said it again, stupidly, "Guy, why didn't you knock?" and again in a long piercing scream. But he'd been moving away then, down the stairs, out into the afternoon—moving on and on and going nowhere at all.

He had come back for supper. His mother had laughed as usual. They'd had swordfish, a Friday night treat. His father had said, "Why don't you eat, Guy?" And his mother had smiled at him and cut the swordfish into three equal shares.

"Where have you been all afternoon, Guy?"

"Just—out." He'd kept his eyes on his plate. His mother had always been beautiful, he'd thought, with a black bun of hair and bright dark laughing eyes, and a voice that tinkled in laughter. Now, though, she was ugly, and he had not wanted to look at her.

His father had said, "Guy, your mother asked you a question."

"It's all right," his mother had said. "Guy's upset today, and after dinner we're going to have a long talk, aren't we,

Guy?" She'd touched his head and a chill had run down his back. She'd turned to his father, bent and kissed his father on the cheek. His father had touched her hand affectionately. And then—abruptly—he'd been terribly sick, and he'd left the table.

Now, entering the dark booth in St. Joseph's, he was not sure of his own sin, though he knew that he'd sinned in some way that was very deep, very wrong, and he was still not sure during the prayer and the confession of minor sins . . . "I accuse myself of having taken the Lord's name in vain . . . of lying, and of unchristian thoughts toward many people of my acquaintance . . ." the words all jumbled together until he remembered the little *Catechism of Christian Doctrine*, Lesson Twentieth, page 42, where it said, "We must speak clearly and truthfully." So he spoke clearly then, but could still not find the exact truth within himself. Father Serrano was talking, but he did not hear the Father's words. The book said also to tell one of several past sins. He said, "I also accuse myself of all the sins of my past life. I stole a fountain pen," a very good old sin, way back two years ago in the fourth grade. And old sins were the easiest to tell because after a while they were not really sins at all, but experiences instead.

Father Serrano gave absolution.

Then, rising, he remembered the Act of Contrition. The book said, "We should from our heart renew the Act of Contrition." And suddenly, in that moment, he found his sin, and he said, "I hate my mother . . . I *hate* my mother . . . I *hate* my mother . . ." over and over because he finally knew, and it was almost as great as that sin of hers, which was dark and evil—though he did not quite, not fully understand it.

At lunch that same day, they had quahog pie, cooked by the Indian woman from Mashpee. He was not hungry. His father said, "Why don't you eat, Guy?" and his mother smiled at him and cut the pie into three equal shares.

"Did you go to confession, Guy?"

"I went." Again he kept his eyes on his plate. Until yesterday his mother had always been beautiful, he thought, with that black bun of hair and those bright dark laughing eyes, and a voice that tinkled in laughter. Only now she was ugly, and he still did not want to look at her.

His father said, "Guy, can't you be civil to your mother?"

"It's all right," his mother said. "Guy's upset today. We were going to have a long talk after dinner last night, only Guy wasn't feeling well, so we're going to have that talk this afternoon, aren't we, Guy?" Again she touched his head and a chill ran down his back, and again she turned to his father and bent and kissed his cheek and again his father touched her hand with great affection. Again he felt terribly sick. He said, "Yes, I went to confession . . . And you know what I said?"

"Guy . . ." His mother's back stiffened. She jerked upright from the table. "Guy . . . Guy . . ."

"I said I hated my mother . . . I hate my mother . . . *You* . . . I hate *you!*"

His father's hand made a hard sharp smack against his face. But he did not feel it. He laughed. He kept on laughing, crying at the same time, "I saw her . . . yesterday . . . I saw her . . . Right in the bedroom . . . I *saw!*" He screamed the last of it. His father had a small mustache. Suddenly it looked just like Charlie Chaplin's in the movies. His eyes became wide—just like Charlie Chaplin's. His voice stammered, saying, "Who? . . . What? . . . Who? . . . What? . . ."

"Stewart Schaeffer! They were in bed together without any clothes on . . . her and Stewart Schaeffer!" He rushed out of the dining room and slammed the door behind him. He leaned back against the door, breathing hard. His father's voice was muffled, weary, almost crying, saying, "Esther . . . Esther . . . You promised me . . . you swore to me . . . Ten years ago . . . You asked my forgiveness and I gave it. And I even married you because I loved you, and all this time I've treated him like—"

The rest was lost in his own gasping sobs as he ran all the way to his private cave beneath the dunes. The water pounded up along the shore. It was big and almost comforting. And strangely then, sobbing into the wet sand, he wondered what she'd been doing with Stewart Schaeffer anyway, and why it was Stewart Schaeffer instead of his own father. Because Stewart was younger than his father? Because Stewart's father had owned the glassworks? Because Stewart was good-looking and drank a lot and laughed a lot and dressed up more and drove his Buick touring car faster than anyone else in town? Why Stewart Schaeffer? . . . Why anyone? . . . Why anyone at all?

The sobbing stopped. He crawled from the cave and peered over the high grass across the dune. He could see the cross on St. Joseph's and the widow's walk on his own house. A man appeared slowly through the trap door to the widow's walk. He stood there a moment, looking out to sea. Then he turned and looked at the sunlit cross on the steeple of St. Joseph's. He took off his coat, folded it, and laid it carefully on the wooden railing. It was the way Charlie Chaplin would do it. He raised his arms straight over his head—a tiny figure in the far distance. And he still looked like Charlie Chaplin as he dove headfirst over the rail, down below the line of waving grass to the rocks below the house.

CHAPTER THIRTEEN

The light tapping became a heavy knock. Guy struggled up from sleep. "Coming . . . coming," groggy, stumbling, as he made his way across the hotel room, unlocked the door, and swung it inward.

"You look awful, Doctor Montford." Mar smiled at his bare chest and his drooping pajama bottoms, then moved past him into the room and walked about slowly, frowning at the near-empty bottle of bourbon, the cigarette butts piled four deep in the glass ash tray. Her black woolen suit was rumpled. She moved mechanically as though completely exhausted, as though she'd used up all her emotions, all her energy, so that nothing seemed important any longer.

Guy closed the door behind her. He shook his head violently, grabbed at the sleep in his bleary eyes. "Mar," he stammered, "what the hell, Mar!" And he went into the bathroom, where he doused cold water in his face and told himself Mar was here in Boston—here in this room—right here in the Statler Hotel in Park Square, Boston, Massachusetts. He returned to the bedroom, where Mar stood by the window. She tapped a finger on the pane of glass. She laughed and said, "Visiting hours haven't begun? Too early? Not receiving patients?"

"Mar . . ."

"Terrible when a woman can't rely on her own doctor. Especially when she's in such a delicate condition."

"How did you find me?"

"Only one medical convention going on. Not very hard. Had to find my doctor, you see. Such a terribly delicate condition. Went to another doctor in New Haven first. Yesterday, that was. I have a college friend in New Haven. Stayed with her and found this very fine doctor. But he was a terribly busy man and I had to sit a long time in the waiting room. Just yesterday that was, and I read four *National Geographics* in all, and you know what I found out?"

"No . . . What?" Guy sat dumbly on the bed. His head was splitting; his throat was dry. He frowned and watched Mar's weary body slumped against the sill and watched her tapping fingers as she talked on against the glass.

"Well, I learned that some African tribes deface their wives so that other men won't want them. But the point is, you see, do they want them any longer themselves?" She laughed briefly, turned into the room and walked slowly up and down, touching everything—the bed, the lamps, the handkerchiefs on the dresser as she passed.

"The doctor," Guy said.

"Oh, a very expensive man. Five hundred dollars, he wanted. 'Very delicate,' he said. 'And you have a very fine pelvis, Mrs. McFie.' "

"Mar! . . . For God's sake, Mar!" He jerked up from the bed, then sat again as she ignored him completely and kept on pacing and kept on talking. "So my wonderful pelvis was supposed to make it easier for both of us, because the doctor had four children of his own, and maybe his wife had a terrible pelvis or something. Anyway, there was a nurse, and she took me into the operating room and told me it would only take a little while. The operating room was terribly white and clean and it smelled funny too. So I sat there and thought how funny it smelled and how the doctor had a scraggly mustache and four children, and how the nurse had thick legs, and she probably had a terrible pelvis too. And then I thought how Larry and I had been trying to have a child for years and years and how doctors had told us we probably never could, and then how this little doctor with the children and the mustache said that after this little operation, then maybe I never could again, and—well, suddenly I just walked out of the operating room into the doctor's office. He was talking to the nurse about how I ought to have a thorough physical before the operation, and I said, 'Good-by, Doctor, good-by, Nurse, and thank you very much.' And then I wanted to see my own doctor, so I took the night train and here I am."

"A baby," Guy said absently. "A baby." He ran a hand along the sheets of the bed and thought of the bed as an operating table like the one in that clean, odd-smelling room in New Haven. He snatched his hand away. He laughed for no reason, stood, and walked in tight circles around the room and could not seem to bring anything into focus, could not seem to make himself understand the implications of what had happened.

Mar slumped wearily in a chair by the window. "I did right, didn't I, Guy? This is what you'd have wanted?"

He shook his head, took the handkerchief from the top of the dresser and wiped his forehead. He looked at the rumpled white of the bed linen. "Need a drink." He laughed and placed the handkerchief back on the dresser. He went into the bathroom, rinsed out a tumbler, and poured a straight shot into the glass.

"I'm tired, Guy." Her voice echoed through the open doorway. "Took the milk train and sat up all the way. Had to see you and I'm awfully tired."

"Don't worry." The liquor had cleared his head. He coughed and went back to the room and saw Mar clearly now, and understood now what had happened. Mar was nodding as exhaustion came in to take her. She was still mumbling, saying, "Going to have my baby . . . Can't ever face Larry again . . . tired, Guy . . . help me, Guy . . ." while her head fell forward and she dropped into sleep like a runner who can stride far and fight the whole way until the last second when the race is over and he collapses all at once.

Guy lifted her from the chair. He laid her gently on the bed and carefully removed her suit, her slip, her shoes and stockings. He moved to a chair by the window and sat there watching her as she dropped quickly into sleep. He looked at the stretch of bare skin between her bra and panties. Beneath it something stirred and grew. It was partly his and partly Mar's. It had nothing to do with Larry McFie.

Mar opened her eyes on the late morning. For a long moment she stared straight up at the ceiling. Then she dropped her eyes until they found Guy, still dressed in his pajama bottoms, watching her from a chair by the window. He looked very serious and worried—very nice, she thought, and very attractive, too, with that lean, hard body and that short wiry hair and straight mouth that could turn so easily to a smile.

"Hello," he said.

"Hi there."

"How you feeling?"

"I'm all right now. I'm fine."

"I knew you would be."

"I suppose you've been thinking."

"Yes."

"About my growing bigger until finally I show and even Larry sees it."

"No," he said, "I wasn't thinking that."

"What then?"

"I was thinking I'm in love with you."

"Guy . . . Guy . . ." She sat up and dressed slowly, avoiding his eyes until she was completely groomed with fresh make-up on her mouth, her hair rolled in a black knot behind her head. His words turned over in her mind, but she could not quite absorb them now—or answer them at all. She turned and faced him. "Of course I can't go back to Larry. For a week or a month, perhaps. But not much longer. Not even till

I start to show. You see, I'm being quite objective, aren't I? I know how long it will take me to crack, how long before I can't bear to face him at all."

"Don't think about it now."

"Because I love him, you see. I loved him terribly from the beginning, and then he became sick and the sickness wedged itself between us and tried to smother us. But the love stayed, and it always will."

"I believe you."

"I know—after what we've done—it sounds ridiculous."

"I said I believe you."

"You're terribly quiet."

"I was thinking."

"What?"

"How good it must feel to be the person you love."

"Guy . . . Wonderful guy, Guy." She went to him and knelt and laid her head in his lap, put her arms about his bare waist. "You're so beautifully strong, and sometime, I think, I'm going to love you very much."

His hand touched her hair, and she liked the touch of his fingers, and knew what he was thinking, for the thought had been there eating in her own mind, too. "Sometime," she had said.

"Look—Mar—you're not expected back until tomorrow."

"No . . ."

"I called the hospital while you were asleep. Everything's the same, and Boston's a wonderful town."

"My bag's checked in the South Station."

"I'll pick it up for you."

"I won't sleep here. Not right here."

"I don't want you to. I'll get you a room."

"All right." She stood and laughed. "Sometime, Guy."

"Sometime." He laughed, too, and went into the bathroom to shave and dress. She heard the shooshing sound as he brushed his teeth. It was an odd, pleasant, intimate sound, and she was sorry when it ended.

They walked through the melting snow on Boston Common. They fed the shivering pigeons and strode around the corner of Tremont and Boylston, the coldest corner in New England—on to Stewart Street and Jake Wirth's, where they ate liverwurst on rye and drank black German beer in the big glass steins brought by bald-headed waiters in white shirts and black pants with towels hung over their hairy arms.

Then, after lunch, Guy brought his car down the winding ramps of the Motor Mart Garage, and they drove through the crooked streets that had once been cowpaths, over to Beacon Hill, past the gold-domed Capitol, along the Charles River to Cambridge. He showed her the dormitory where he'd spent the years of study, the boathouse where they'd stored the sculls he'd rowed on Sunday afternoons. He showed her the corner where McBride's Bar had once stood, and the Washington Elm, then swung out to Lexington and Fitch's Tavern, where the Minute Men had gathered on that April night in '75. ". . . If they mean to have war, let it begin here," on to Concord and the bridge where they'd fired the shot heard round the world.

They had tea in the Concord Inn, drove back to Charlestown and Bunker Hill. ". . . Don't fire till you see the whites of their eyes," on to the Old North Church, where the lanterns had been hung for Paul Revere. "One if by land, and two if by sea . . ."

"Did you know," Guy said, "Paul Revere forgot his spurs?"

She laughed.

"No, it's true. He had to send his dog back home with a note around its neck, and his wife sent the spurs back to him tied to the dog's collar. Then he got in the boat with two other men and found the oars made too much noise and had to be muffled. One of the fellows had a girl friend who lived nearby. So they all walked back to her house, and they threw pebbles at her bedroom window, and she opened the window and threw down a petticoat. It was still warm."

"I don't believe any of it."

"It's all true. And then, when they finally got to the other shore, he had to steal a horse to go warn everybody that the Redcoats were coming. But the horse—it was a mare, by the way—belonged to a deacon, and I guess it got returned eventually."

"You're making it all up."

"No, it's all true. Except in grammar school I did make up a poem about the Boston Tea Party. I forget most of it now, except it had a wonderful last line. You see, the Rebels all dressed up like Indians and dumped the tea overboard, and then, in my own immortal words:

"Away they flew as fast as a flea,
And that was the Boston Tea Par-ty."

"It scans beautifully." And Mar was still laughing when they returned to the Statler. He took a room for her down the hall from his own. She went to her room and dressed for the evening, thinking nothing at all except what a lovely day it had been. And Guy showered and shaved again and thought of her there down the hall, and thought how much he loved her and nothing beyond that.

They ate pheasant and wild rice in the dining room of the Ritz Carleton, then went to a very bad play and loved every minute of it. Two long nightcaps in the Statler Bar before he went up with her in the elevator, down the corridor to her room. He opened the door for her. He said, "I won't come in."

"No . . ."

"I'm very New England, you know. I'm a very moral man."

"I think you are."

"And I love you very much." He kissed her lightly and walked back to his room and slept deep and well and knew she slept the same.

They had breakfast in the hotel coffee shop before starting the drive back to the Cape.

"Still all right?" he asked her over the scrambled eggs.

"Still fine. Having a lovely time. Glad you're here."

"I'll let you off in Falmouth. You'd better take a train from there."

"Yes, but don't talk about it now. It makes me feel secret and dirty, and I'm going to feel that way soon enough. But not now. Not till it's absolutely necessary."

The sky was a low ceiling of gray clouds as they drove south on Route 128. Guy turned on the radio and they listened to music and said very little to each other. The silence was good between them. They'd had a day out of space and time. But now each mile brought them closer to reality. For that precious yesterday had been made of glass, and would shatter into jagged hurting pieces before this day was through.

They stopped for lunch at a huge roadside Chinese restaurant: THE DRAGON'S LAIR—AUTHENTIC CANTONESE DISHES.

Mar said she'd never had anything Chinese except chop suey, and Guy told her what an interesting man he was because he was full of so many bits of useless information. "Like chop suey, for instance. You know where that name came from? Well, there was a Chinese viceroy who was eating a Chinese meal in Washington, and a lot of reporters were watching him and bothering him. Finally one of them asked what he was eating, and the viceroy got annoyed and said, 'Chop suey.' "

"Do you know any other interesting stories?"

"No, the point is—the literal translation of 'chop suey' is 'dirty mixed fragments.' But the reporters didn't know that, and the word got into the papers and stuck. And the Chinese restaurant owners saw no reason to destroy the Americans' illusion, so they adopted the word themselves."

"That's fascinating," Mar said.

"I'm a fascinating man." He parked behind the restaurant. "Very fascinating, and very much in love with you."

"And very moral."

"And sometime you'll be in love with me."

She smiled at him as they got out and went into the huge, near-empty restaurant. They drank two martinis each and ordered from the Family Dinner for Two. Won Ton Soup and Egg Rolls; and from Column A, Don Jun Arp, steamed duck, stuffed with lotus nuts and white nuts and bamboo shoots and herbs and mushrooms; and from Column B, Chow Yong Yook Si, fried slices of mutton with Chinese vegetables. Guy insisted they have a side order of pork with sweet and sour sauce, and he would not let Mar put sugar in her tea, and made her try the chopsticks that came wrapped like straws in Chinese paper.

"You see," he said, "there's quite a Chinatown in Boston, and I used to go there a lot in medical school."

"I like ordering the Family Dinner. There's something very intimate about it." And then a pause and, "Did you ever sleep with a Chinese girl?"

"Now that's a very rude question."

"Did you ever sleep with any other girl at all? Not counting Julia, of course."

"Not counting Julia?" He thought very hard and said, "I can't remember them all, of course, but there was an Ubangi girl once, when I was in Africa during the war. She had a neck three feet long, covered with brass rings, and she had to take these wooden discs out of her mouth to kiss me. It was like being kissed by a St. Bernard."

"Did you ever have a baby with anyone else but me?"

"No . . ." He looked at her soberly across the table. "Not with anyone else but you." Then he laughed and spoke very quickly, saying, "I'm sorry they don't have dogmeat on the menu, because it's really quite a delicacy, you know. In Canton, they feed dogs a special diet, you see, and—" He stopped.

The glass was broken. It lay around them in jagged pieces. They were no longer hungry. They said, "It was good," and "Yes," and "They always serve you too much," and "It wears off, though, so you're starving again in an hour."

They drove on to Falmouth, planning to meet the 3:18 train for East Norton. They were fifteen minutes early, the train fifteen minutes late. They drank coffee in a shop across the street, and when the train arrived, he helped her up the steps as though she were already eight months pregnant.

"Sometime," he said, and kissed her.

She was crying then. He turned and left the train and watched it puff away down the tracks.

"You take the high road and I'll take the low road . . ." And he drove on slowly toward East Norton.

CHAPTER FOURTEEN

"Let us pray, goddammit, let us pray, goddammit!"

"Shut up! Will you please shut up!"

"Let us pray, goddammit!"

Someday he would kill that parrot, strangle it with his bare hands. The only reason he had the bird at all was because Ruth Kiley had given it to him as a birthday gift, years and years ago when there'd been a lot between them. "Perfect for your living room," she'd said. "The old sea captains used to bring them home from long voyages. And besides that, maybe Peter'll be good company."

Peter had never been good company.

Sam picked up the whiskey bottle from the dry sink and poured himself another shot. Mrs. O'Hara came in from the kitchen. She looked at the drink in his hand. "Mr. McFie . . ."

"You spying on me?"

"About dinner. It's four o'clock now, and—"

"To hell with dinner!"

"You'll have to eat something," said Mrs. O'Hara.

"I don't *have* to eat anything."

"But Mrs. McFie—"

"If she's hungry when she gets back from the hospital, she can fix something for herself." He finished the drink, said, "Why don't you go visit that cousin in Harpswell?"

Mrs. O'Hara pursed her brown lips and went back to the kitchen.

He should not have spoken to her that way. He should not be pouring another drink. But there'd been something strange about these last two days since Margreth had returned from New Haven. Something queer and secretive. Something she knew that he didn't. Like that time some thirty-five years ago, when Doctor Paul Montford had tried to explain about his wife's condition. He'd sensed something wrong then, too, way before that moment when Paul had put a hand on his arm and said, "It's a boy, Sam, but—I'm sorry, Sam."

Yes, he'd been sorry, all right. Probably planned the whole thing for days. Couldn't save both mother and child, so he wouldn't even *ask* the husband about it—not even give him a choice. Just take the mother's life because Paul was a Catholic, and Catholics had their little rules, and nobody was going to give him any of this crap about how there'd never been any choice involved, or how it had never been a Catholic issue in the first place.

Well, he'd sensed something then. And he sensed something now, too. Guy just back from Boston. Margreth acting strange, upset, but in a different, almost calm way now—the kind of calm hysteria a person gets before he blows wide open—the calm before the storm.

"Let us pray, goddammit!"

"I told you to shut up!" He strode into the hall and called Guy's office. The line was busy. He had another drink, thinking about it carefully now, wondering if any of Guy's childhood religion still slept inside the man. Not that it made any difference really, because in Larry's particular case, the more deeply religious a doctor was, the better it might possibly be. He called Guy again. The line was still busy. He swore and Peter swore, and then Sam went out to his car and drove through the dusk toward Guy's little house on the hill. Passing Pat's Bar and Grill he considered going in for a quick one. But he could see Stewed Schaeffer at the bar, and remembering what had put Stewed where he was today, remembering where the last long drunk had put himself, he decided against it, and decided, too, that beginning tomorrow he would taper off gradually until he stopped drinking altogether.

Going up the walk between the boxwood hedges, he paused, swaying, and looked down at the sloping ground of jagged rocks, where violets bloomed in the springtime—feeding on the blood of Paul Montford, dead these many years. His skull had cracked wide open against the rocks. His wife, Esther, had become hysterical, and Father Serrano had given him last rites before he'd even realized it was suicide and the man had been dead for a good twenty minutes. "Served him right," Sam muttered, then wished he had not said it, because he, too, was looking at loss and death, and if he, now, were on that square shape of widow's walk—right now—right this minute—

The door to Guy's inner office was closed. Muffled voices seeped out beneath the door. Sam sat in a wicker chair and looked through a copy of *Life* magazine. It was an old issue. He flung it down and stared at his own hands and his own feet, and thought his loafers needed a good polishing. For that matter, he needed a new pair of loafers. Black next time, with those little tassels on them.

Mrs. Columbo, Guy's Portuguese cleaning woman, came in from the living room. She straightened the magazines, took her old coat from the waiting-room hatrack, and left through the outer door. Sam wondered why Guy didn't get someone permanent like Mrs. O'Hara. Or why didn't he get married again? Hell, it was six years now since Julia had died. But that was a hot one, that was! In his own case, it was already thirty-six.

Guy came out of the office. A high-school boy was with him, limping as he came. "Maybe a month," Guy was saying. "Maybe more. You've torn a ligament there, Frankie, and it's just going to take some time."

"No more basketball?" said Frankie.

"I'm sorry, Frankie."

"Baseball?"

"Well, we'll see. That's the best I can do."

"I get all the breaks," Frankie complained, and went out the door.

Sam lurched to his feet. "Called you, Guy . . . Line was busy . . . Called you again."

"Yes, Sam?"

"About Margreth. Something screwy and I didn't know what. But I've got it figured now."

"Oh?"

"Yeah . . . At that medical convention. You must have asked questions, heard reports."

"Yes, I did."

"Found out something about Larry."

"Well, I did speak to a Doctor Pastene."

"And he told you something, and you told Margreth, but you're not telling me."

"Pastene said—he said in many cases the disease could be arrested."

"Arrested?"

"That was his word."

"You arresting it?"

"Everything possible, Sam. You know that. There's nothing I or anybody else can do."

"Except pray," Sam said.

"Yes, Sam . . . Pray."

"That's a good one, that is. You haven't been to any church in twenty years."

Guy did not answer. He turned away, then back again slowly, and said, "Sam . . . You're pretty shot, Sam. If you'd let me give you some pills, take it easy for a few days."

"I don't need the pills. It's Margreth needs the pills. Since the minute she got back from New Haven . . . Something going on . . . Something . . . Something . . ." He stumbled toward the door, stopped, said, "All right, we'll pray. The whole goddamned town. I'll talk to John Treleaven, get the whole church in on it—next Sunday—one of those big prayer things you hear about." He laughed ironically. "You'll be there, won't you?"

"Sam . . ."

"No reason you *can't* be there, is there? I mean I know Catholics aren't supposed to go to other churches. But you're not a real Catholic now, or anything else either, so there's no reason you *can't* be there, is there?"

"I'll be there," Guy said. He turned away, picked up his black bag, put on his hat and overcoat.

"You going to the hospital?"

"Yes."

"You see Margreth there, you tell her about next Sunday."

"I'll tell her."

"Well—" He watched Guy button the overcoat. There was still something strange and terrifying about all this, and he still didn't know exactly what it was. He went out to his car and drove down the hill past Pat's Bar and Grill. Stewed Schaeffer was still there. He remembered that he'd sent Mrs. O'Hara away and there'd be no dinner at home tonight. He decided on a seafood platter in Pat's. And since he wasn't going on the wagon until tomorrow—maybe another drink or two tonight.

A white screen had been placed between the bed and doorway. The room was dark. She knelt there in the darkness with her face pressed into the white sheet. She held the clawlike hand and kissed the bony fingers, and the words came out low and run-together, though he was in a coma now, and could not hear them. But it was better than not saying the words at all, because if he could hear them, perhaps then she would not have the courage—it would not be wise—it would not even be right to say the words at all.

". . . Nothing to do with loving you, darling. And I tried to stop myself, but I couldn't, and it only happened twice, and both times I couldn't help it, you see. And then when I *could* help it, then it didn't happen, and— Please, darling, please, darling! I'm not leaving you. I don't ever want to leave you. And what I did—it was wrong, but I can't have you that way any more, and I wanted you that way so badly—except when it happened it wasn't like it used to be with you . . . not like with you, darling . . . Years ago, you remember, darling, how very abandoned we were, and how we teased each other and took hours, long hours, long, long hours, just listening to music and touching each other, and that was making love, you see, really making love, while this thing—it happened all at once, in a minute of time, and not like us at all. And please forgive me, darling, please forgive me, please . . . please . . ."

She cried into the white sheet. The tears fell onto his hand and she brushed them away, carefully, with her handkerchief before she dried her own eyes and pulled to her feet and looked down at his face in the light of the moon outside the window, remembering other moons across his face when she'd lain awake beside him, watching him in sleep, putting out a finger to run it along his cheek and nose and mouth, so that he half awakened, slow, groping toward her, smiling in sleep, an all-in-one-togetherness in the melting snows of yesteryear.

"Good night . . . Good night, darling, good night." She kissed the skeleton's face, then moved dumbly around the screen, and there was Fran Walker, standing silent in the doorway.

Fran cleared her throat. "It's time for his injection."

"All right."

"Doctor Montford's here, and he said it was time now." She seemed embarrassed. She paused. "Are you all right, Mrs. McFie?"

"Yes, I'm all right." She moved out to the corridor, leaned wearily against the doorframe. From a room down the hall she heard a rising voice, "Ah, shut up, will you!"

"Parker Welk," said Fran. "He's leaving tomorrow, and he's being very difficult."

"Yes, I heard—he was attacked or something."

"A vandal, but they never caught him."

"Oh . . ." She sucked in her breath and thought she had to pull herself together. Things happened, and the world moved on, and you rode with it, like it or not, right or wrong, you rode along and never asked where you were heading.

Polly Welk's voice said, "You're going to stay in bed a few days, and I'll move the television so you can see it from the bed, and I'll read to you whenever you want."

"Oh, God," Parker said, "why don't you go home and have a sandwich or something? Why don't you please just get the hell out of here?"

"I'd be angry with you, Parker, but after the hard time you've had—well, swear at me all you like. But a little Christian charity—"

"A little Christian crap," Parker said. And Polly gasped and appeared waddling in the hallway. She started to cry, then choked the sobs down into her throat and said, "He's upset," speaking to Fran. "He never could stand to be inactive. It gets on his nerves something terrible. But really he's a lamb . . . a perfect lamb."

Fran said, "I know."

Polly heaved on down the hallway and Mar walked slowly behind her.

Guy came out of a room at the end of the corridor. He smiled at Polly. "Well, Parker's getting back to his old self again."

Polly said, "Yes," as though it were the greatest tragedy of all, and stepped into the elevator and pushed the button. She rode alone, for there was scarcely room for another.

Guy said he'd finished his rounds. He gave Fran some instructions concerning a woman with pneumonia in 6B, then turned to Mar. "I'll give you a lift," he said.

"Thank you." She thought he looked as near the breaking point as herself or Sam. She remembered only two days before. They had laughed then. She wondered if they would ever laugh again.

As they drove off into the dark, Guy spoke away from her into the windshield. "Want to see how *Julia*'s cabin is coming along? I did some painting last night."

"Guy . . ."

"We have to talk about things."

"All right." She was silent as he drove to the boathouse, opened the creaking door, took her hand and led her through the darkened shed, up the ladder, down to *Julia*'s cabin. She remembered the last time, but this was not the same at all. She sat on the narrow bunk and smoked and watched Guy light the stove and the kerosene lamp, and watched the shadows across his face. She knew they were safe this night—from themselves and from each other. For now, with his child inside her, she felt more tenderness than passion—and knew he felt the same.

"Things to talk about?" she said finally.

"No plans, Mar. All I know is you've got to stick this out. Something will happen. I'll think of something."

"If I didn't love him—"

"I know."

"If I didn't want this baby—if there were any hope for Larry—if—if—if— And you won't think of anything because there *is* no way out. None at all. And now I can't face him any more. Not when he's conscious. I talk to him. I tell him everything. But only when he can't hear me, you see. And soon now I won't be able to stand it, because we've always been honest with each other, and—and he's getting worse, isn't he?"

"Mar . . ."

"And you've increased the morphine again."

"Mar—Sam came to see me today. He went to Doctor Treleaven. There's going to be a prayer for Larry in church next Sunday."

"Medicine fails, so now we call on God. I don't know—what can God do? Whot does He care?"

"He cares."

"You don't even believe that yourself. You care and I care and Sam cares. But God—what does God care?"

"If you pray hard enough—"

"When was the last time *you* ever prayed for anything?" She felt the hysteria rising inside her, and she began laughing, saying, "You of all people, you of all people!" laughing on until the hysteria was gone and he drove her home under the clear black sky and a million pricks of light.

"Give Him a chance," Guy said, walking beside her to the door.

"Him?"

"God."

"How many chances—"

"We'll both pray—Sunday. Both of us. So will everyone in town."

"Guy," she said, "Guy, did you ever think—if God can help Larry—he can also send us both to Hell." She laughed again and went into the empty house. She switched on the light. Peter stirred on his perch. She said, "Let us pray, Peter, let us pray."

But Peter was asleep and did not answer.

The prayer for Larry McFie came early in the service, after the Reverend John Treleaven had paused and wiped his glasses and surveyed his congregation with the tired eyes of a man who will pray again and again for miracles that he secretly suspects may never come about. He waited until the last rustle, the last nervous whisper had died away among the wooden rafters. Then he raised his robe-covered arms and lowered his head so his glasses caught the light and reflected blue and red from the stained-glass window. "Let us pray," he said.

Guy rested his chin on a hand against the pew before him. He pushed his knuckles into his eyes until he saw red and his eyeballs ached. He wet his lips and listened to John Treleaven's words: "Heavenly Father . . . we are gathered here to ask that Your eternal kindness be bestowed upon one whom we all love—one who needs his Saviour in his time of trouble . . . Larry McFie . . . sick beyond the understanding of common man . . . wrapped in an illness that only Thou, oh, Father, can fathom . . . or cure . . . we beseech Thee, Oh, Father . . . give back to us . . . to his wife, his father, his friends . . . we beseech Thee, oh, Father . . ." And the voice went on, the prayer went on, while Guy's knuckles dug harder into his eyes and he tried very hard to pray until the sweat was on his forehead and in his hands, and it seemed, after a while, that he was really praying, honestly praying as he never had before in all these years since childhood, entranced by the quiet around him and the singsong voice and the sincerity of the repetitious words—praying, actually praying, until finally his lips moved and the prayer came out in a whisper for his own disbelieving ears. "Please let him die, oh, God. Please let Larry die."

When the prayer ended, Guy's forehead still rested against his white hand that clutched at the back of a wooden pew. The word "Amen" fell away among the bowed heads, and the heads came up amid the shuffling of feet and the renewed wheezing of the organ. Doctor Treleaven sighed audibly and announced that now they would sing Hymn Number 237. The congregation stood, while Guy sat motionless as before with the sweat running cold along his clenched fists, starting in drops along his forehead. A man next to him, a clerk in the hardware store, bent low and whispered, "You all right, Doc?" And Guy heard in the corner of his brain. He pushed blindly to his feet and accepted the hymn-book thrust before him. He sang in a monotone, then sat down again while his wandering eyes found the stained-glass window, and he thought that Father Serrano had put new windows in St. Joseph's, but this was the Congregational Church. And he kept his eyes on the windows with the angels there, blowing their golden trumpets in the reddish light of God's December sky as Doctor Treleaven preached on about the meaning of Faith and the recessional hymn was sung and the choir moved back down the aisle.

It was over then. The parishioners rose in knots and groups. They wedged into the aisle and pushed on toward the rear pew, where Guy sat motionless, a fixed smile on his lips as he nodded to those who passed.

Clara Coffin wore a new hat with yellow flowers. She leaned over, beaming happily. "It was real nice, wasn't it?"

Bert Mosley passed, walking with Fran, a protective hand beneath her elbow. Maidie and Doctor Bolls; Judge Manning and his rich wife; Frances Treleaven, Nancy Messner; Ruth Kiley, Polly Welk. Ida Primmer and four other nurses from the hospital; Chet Belknap with a knot of fishermen from the Portuguese section. They all looked at him and into him as they passed, pinning him there in the pew, this man who never went to church, this fellow they all knew and liked, this warm, easygoing man, who sat here now with the dampness still on his forehead, his hands still clutched tight to the hymnbook.

Doctor Kelsey passed toward the end. He looked down at Guy quizzically, started to speak, then changed his mind. Behind him was Sam McFie. And behind Sam was Mar.

Guy rose as she came abreast of him. He looked at her white face, and there in her trembling lips and bottomless eyes, he saw the inner being of a woman who has looked into the horror of her own soul, into the face of the screaming devil within herself. He found his voice. "Mar . . . Margreth . . ." Then he stopped as Sam's eyes turned upon him. He said "Mar" again, still looking straight into her eyes, down into that black depth of terror. She did not blink; she did not speak. But a tremble seemed to run shivering through her entire body before she turned and followed Sam down the aisle and out of sight.

Guy pushed to his feet. The church was empty now. John Treleaven returned from greeting his congregation at the doorway. He peered at Guy through his rimless glasses. "How'd you like it, Guy?"

"Fine. It was all right."

"Like the prayer?"

"Yes, it was fine."

"Don't believe in prayers, do you?"

"It depends, I guess."

"Depends?"

"On what you pray for."

The minister's eyes narrowed slightly, then widened again as he studied Guy carefully in the dim light of the church. He started to speak, but Guy moved dumbly past him, out to the churchyard that was empty now. He strode fast down the hill. Behind him the minister watched with puckered lips.

CHAPTER FIFTEEN

"She's leaving! The train's coming in right now, and they just called me from the station to say good-by! I'm at the cannery—no car here—I walked over, so—"

"All right, Sam!" Guy slammed the receiver back on the hook, grabbed at his coat, and drove fast from his house toward the village depot. He could hear the train whistling on a curve only a mile away, and realized suddenly that it was already beyond the town. He swore, swung out to the highway, and drove the thirteen miles to Falmouth with his foot jamming the accelerator to the floor.

They were unloading packages from the mail car when he

pulled up at the Falmouth station. The old engine stood wheezing, shooting steam and coal dust into the late afternoon, and the coaches had already been lighted, though darkness had not yet fallen. He raced down the platform, shouted to a conductor to hold up for a minute, and boarded the last car. He strode forward, his head swinging from side to side as he moved down the aisles until finally, in the fourth car from the rear, he saw the familiar knot of hair, ebony-black in the light from the dusty yellow lamps.

Mar looked up slowly. Her face was dead. She showed no surprise, as though all emotion had been drained completely. She said, "Why don't you leave me alone?"

"Where are you going?"

"Taking a ride. Just going."

"To kill yourself—and everybody else." He lifted the bag from the rack above her head. "Come on," he said and walked back down the aisle. He knew she followed by the clicking of her heels. But he did not turn around until he'd reached the car and had stored her suitcase in the rear beside his own black physician's bag. Then he opened the door and helped her in. She wore a brown woolen coat. She shivered as she slumped into the seat and looked out dumbly at the train that was gathering steam now, jerking its way out of Falmouth until finally it was rolling free and the last car disappeared around a curve.

He swung in a U turn, heading back toward East Norton. Mar looked out through the windshield at the passing countryside. He watched her in the mirror. They passed a cranberry bog, and he said, "They're made by filling a marsh or pond with sand. Then they cut trenches and build dikes and turn a brook to flood the bog."

"Oh . . ."

"Yes, and those birdhouses along the edge—they're trying to encourage birds to live near and keep away the insects."

Mar nodded, her eyes fixed absently on the solid mat of yellow vines across the bog. The air was cold, and now, though the season was officially over, a few Portuguese in gaily colored clothes were still kneeling along the muddy rows, picking the last of the berries with the scoops held firm in their brown-gloved hands. "Cotton," she murmured, after a while. "In the southern heat, it's the cotton and the Negroes—in the cold, the Portuguese and cranberries."

"At one time the cranberry picking was a kind of community project. Before so many Portuguese arrived."

"The difference between us, really. In the South, you see, we never did community work. Somehow the help was always there." She was silent as they swung back into town, where Guy stopped the car before the rambling old hotel with the name LINCOLN painted in black letters on a weather-beaten sign above the porch.

"I'm going to buy you a drink," he said. "And dinner." He touched her elbow as they moved up the walk, then drew his hand away and followed her up the wooden stairs and into the tasteless bar. He sat across from her in the same booth where they'd sat before when summer was ending and winter had not yet blown in sight. He ordered martinis, waited until Betsy had gone, then touched his glass to Mar's. "To your child," he said, thinking he'd had a reluctant beer with her those months ago, thinking this was his first martini since that Chinese restaurant on the road from Boston, thinking he had not said, "Our child," but "Your child," because already, despite her tortured emotions, Mar was accepting everything as her own responsibility. She was asking nothing of him at all except a little understanding.

"I suppose," she said quietly, "I suppose we'd better be very clear about all this."

"You were going back to New Haven. You had a doctor's appointment."

"Yes, I—I went to church yesterday, and I prayed just like you said I should. I was praying for Larry, but—but not for him to live. I mean—"

"I know what you mean."

"Do you really?"

"Yes—really. You started to pray for his life. Then suddenly you caught yourself thinking how much simpler, easier it would be for everyone—him, you, the baby—how much better for everyone if he should die."

She looked at him slowly. "You thought that too?"

"I've thought that for weeks. Almost from the beginning, when I knew he'd die, regardless of what anyone did for him. I didn't want to think it, so I fought it, smothered it inside. Then, in church, I found myself actually praying for his death—and I realized I'd been trying to avoid the truth—lying to you—lying to myself. Larry's going to die, Mar, and if God had any understanding, he'd have let him die months ago, saved him all this pain—saved you this horrible waiting, with no way out for anyone."

"I found a way," she said. "I was going to New Haven."

"You'd never have stopped hating yourself. Other women maybe, but not you."

"So I'll have to tell Larry everything. When he's clear and conscious. You see, I—I can't live like this, and I can't pray for his death again, no matter how much I want my child." She sipped at her martini, then set it down carefully with a trembling hand. "You see, I'm going to have to tell him."

"No, Mar."

"Either that or get another doctor's appointment." Her eyes raised to his and her mouth twitched and she swallowed the olive and twirled the glass between her fingers. "Yes, he should have died two months ago—or yesterday—or tomorrow. . . . Even tomorrow. I don't know. Why doesn't he have the right to die quickly, decently? And what's the price of sin? Destroying someone you love? . . . Destroying yourself? . . . An unborn child?"

Guy watched her fingers curled on the twirling glass. He watched her mouth and her bowed head, and understood that she was dangling at the end of the rope. Her fingers were slipping fast. "Larry," he said after a long time. "He's expecting you tonight."

"Yes."

"You'll go, of course."

"Yes, tonight I'll go."

"And if he's conscious, then you'll tell him?"

"Yes, I'll tell him because I love him and I'm weak, and if I don't, I can't ever face him or myself again—and after the baby's born, I won't be able to face that either." She raised her eyes to his, and they clung there for a long time while Betsy came and he ordered lobster and coffee, and another cocktail before they ate. And even when the lobster came, even then they did not speak except in meaningless circles.

"Until I came here," she said, poking at the white meat of the lobster with her fork, "I'd never eaten much lobster. Soft-shelled crabs and those Florida lobsters—crayfish, really, without any claws at all—and shrimp—"

"They're better in Maine."

"Lobster, of course."

"Shrimp too. They're smaller in Maine."

"I've never been to Maine. The farthest I've ever been is Boston, and that was only for a day and a night with a charming young doctor—and New Haven, of course, where I saw this other doctor who was older and had four children and the scraggliest mustache. He said I had a very wonderful pelvis, you see, but afterwards I might never have any more children—"

"Mar!"

"The nurse had very thick legs, you see, so I was just thinking about that, and—"

"I'm in love with you, Mar."

"And I would have gone back. If it hadn't been for you,

I'd have gone through with it." She laid down the fork and placed her hand flat on the table. "Yes, you've told me. But *are* you in love with me? Really, honest-to-God in love with me?"

"Yes."

"I'm not in love with you."

"I know that."

"I told you—sometime, when I can let myself."

"Don't think about it. Just let me be in love with you and let me take care of everything." He moved his own hand so that it covered hers. He felt the cold of her fingers, and knew suddenly that it was a useless gesture. He loved her and she was going to have his child. Yet there was nothing he could do to help.

He was still sitting like that, his hand covering Mar's, when he sensed the person behind him. He drew his hand away, turned slowly, and looked up into the watching eyes of Fran Walker. Her face was white, her full lips pulled into a thin white line. She said nothing. But a slow blush of red passed quickly across her cheeks before she turned away to join Ida Primmer at a corner table.

Mar looked after her. "That was Miss Walker."

"Yes."

"She's in love with you. I can tell."

"Perhaps she thought she was."

"And now she hates you."

"I don't know."

"Do you know her well?"

"She's a mixed-up girl. But a nice girl."

"Will she be the mother of your child?"

"No."

"Then you don't know her very well." She placed both hands about the martini glass, cupping it gently while she looked down into the white liquid as into a crystal ball. "I've been having a dream, you know—for a long time now. It means something, of course, but I never knew exactly what. Now—perhaps I do."

"Yes?"

"There's a horse with a child on its back. The horse rears and its legs smash through the windshield of your car. It's badly hurt, but the child is all right. You shoot the horse."

"Do I?"

"Yes. And I think now that the horse is supposed to be Larry."

He did not answer. His throat felt dry as she went on talking, still staring into her glass. "The boy is my baby—our baby. And in the end you always chase after me. You didn't used to catch me. But lately you've caught me every time." For a moment she was silent. Her hands tightened on the glass, then relaxed slowly and she laughed and said, "It's silly to believe in dreams," and rose and walked before him to the coming night.

A warm breeze had come in from the southwest. The melting snow shone yellow beneath the street lights. Rivulets of water ran black along the gutters, and there was steam on the lighted window of Pat's Bar and Castner's Drygoods. Frozen chunks of snow dropped from beneath the fenders of the car. They plopped in the street, dirty with oil and mud.

Guy pulled up before the hospital, stopped, then changed his mind and drove to the parking lot behind the building. He cut the motor and switched off the headlights. He slumped in the seat, tapped a finger on the wheel and looked up at the lighted windows. "Are you all right, Mar?"

"Yes."

"I want you to promise me something. Don't tell Larry anything tonight."

"When?"

"Not tonight."

"I don't know. If he's conscious and I put it off any longer, then I'll start praying backwards again like in the church, and then I'll go back to New Haven or go out of my mind. I have to be honest now, no matter whom it hurts. I have to be honest. I have to, I have to, I *have* to—" Her voice rose and touched hysteria, dropped once more as she gripped the door handle, then twisted her body and looked at him oddly through the darkness. "You think I'm already crazy, don't you?"

"I'm in love with you, Mar." He reached out an arm and she slipped trembling back against him. He waited until her body relaxed, then turned her face to his with his hand cupped firmly beneath her chin. He kissed her, tasting the bitter lipstick and the moistness of her parted lips. He said, "I love you, Mar, and I want you to see Larry alone. But don't say anything tonight. Not anything."

"I'll try. Really I will." She touched his arm, then opened the door, stepped out, and walked slowly across the melting snow in the gravel drive.

Guy waited until Mar's figure had gone from sight. Then he started the engine once more and drove down the Hyannis road with his foot pressed hard on the accelerator. Three miles out of town he stopped at a roadhouse and drank a scotch highball with his eyes focused on his own tense face in the mirror above the rows of bottles. Not a very handsome face. Square, almost rough, with the circles growing even deeper beneath his eyes. The scotch was good, though drinking it was merely a passing of time. He could drink twenty scotches and feel nothing—not even relaxation.

During the next three hours Guy Montford drove close to seventy-five miles and drank three more scotch and sodas. He was fighting something, but was not sure exactly whom or what. God, he supposed. Or man, or his own uncertain loyalties, his own confused emotions. He tried to be clear about this business—logical, the way he'd been during those courses in semantics and logic and ethics and metaphysics back in college days. This point here: Larry was his oldest friend, and Larry was dying. This point there: Mar was having a child, his child, and he was in love with Mar, which was not a logical point at all, of course, but a purely emotional point that must be completely disregarded. Somebody loses, somebody wins . . .

It was twelve o'clock. He was two miles from East Norton, but still had no plans, understood nothing. He drove slowly, pushing everything from his mind because the circumstances were so overwhelming now that they could finally be ignored completely. Then memories flooded in, and they were memories of himself and Larry in those years before. Hunting for ambergris and the buried treasures of romantic pirates along the dunes; driving to that chain of fresh-water lakes around Harwich, where they'd hired rowboats and fished indolently for bass and perch and the wily pickerel in the weeds. And duck hunting, too. Together they had scorned the standard Cape Cod method of hunting ducks—that bloodthirsty arrangement in which live decoys and a drake were tethered before a shanty, and other live trained decoys were sent out to bring the approaching flock in close to the low shanties, where many men with many guns could rise and kill fifteen or twenty at a crack.

No, he and Larry had hunted in their own way—ducks and whistles, coot and geese, and sheldrakes too, with no more than a temporary blind of seaweed and a few wooden decoys. They always shot birds on the wing, getting no game at all sometimes. But then, it was the sporting way, and—

"On the wing," he said aloud. "I taught you that. Always on the wing, Larry." And he shook his head sharply as he swung into the hospital drive, parked in the vacant lot, stepped out as he'd done a thousand times before, and walked with firm steps across the drive. All the lights were out. Yet still, up there in the night, he could see the hole that was Larry's window. He could feel the pain of Larry's breathing, hear Larry's prayers for peaceful death. He swung back to the car, reminded himself to return Mar's suitcase in the morning, then lifted his own black bag from the rear seat and carried it with him across the drive.

The tiny reception room was empty. The elevator sighed as it rose two stories. The doors slid open, and there was Fran Walker, seated behind the tiny desk. A dim light burned in the gooseneck lamp, and her face was shadowed when she raised her head. "Yes, Doctor?" her voice cold, almost hateful.

"Larry?"

"Still in a coma."

"Has he been conscious this evening? At any time? When Mrs. McFie was here?"

"I didn't come on till eleven."

"Any other visitors?"

"Mr. McFie."

"He wasn't conscious then?"

"No."

"Thank you." He avoided her accusing eyes. He listened to the creaking walls of the old building, then turned and walked down the corridor to Larry's room. His shoes squeaked on the rubber matting. His mouth was dry from the alcohol.

Larry lay still—a corpse—dead in every part except his slow-beating heart and his rasping breath. Guy switched on the dim light beside the bed. He sat in a straight metal chair, set his black bag beside the bed, and looked down at the ghostly face. For a long time he did not move. He thought of the flying ducks and the long sails and that pickerel they'd caught that had been the fourth largest ever seen around these parts. He looked out the window at the winking light at Keever's Point and thought of that crazy swim and thought how he'd once saved Larry's life. He noticed the clouded sky and thought a storm was brewing. Then finally he pulled his eyes back to the white, immobile face, and his voice was a low, rasping whisper.

"Larry . . . Listen, Larry, she's going to have a baby, Larry. Please try to understand. It's not your baby. But that doesn't mean she's stopped loving you. She's a woman, Larry. You understand that. A fine woman, a very brave and very kind one who loves you very much and would kill herself before she'd hurt you. I know she sinned against you . . . both of us did. But it was a healthy thing for her to do. I know how that sounds, but it's true all the same. And I know it hurts you to hear all this. But she's dying, Larry. And she wants this child that she can love as much as she's always loved you. She doesn't love another man . . . Not me, Larry . . . Just her child . . . just her baby . . . So please don't be hurt, Larry. Please just understand and let the baby live and let Mar live. I know you would if you were able to do anything about it yourself. If you could—if you could—if you could—" And he kept saying the words over and over, until finally he rose and stumbled out to the corridor once more and back toward the desk. It was deserted now. But Fran's voice echoed from an open doorway down the hall, and in a moment she appeared and walked quickly to the phone. She lifted the receiver and asked for Doctor Bolls in Harpswell.

"It's Mrs. Roscoe," she said into the phone. "The pains are fifteen minutes apart now, and she's quite hysterical about it. All right, Doctor. I understand." She hung up, turned, and looked full into Guy's face as he stood waiting by the elevator. "I'll have to get a relief nurse. There'll be a delivery very soon."

"I'll take care of it." He was surprised at the hoarseness of his own voice.

"But it's Doctor Bolls' patient. He's in Harpswell now, but he's already on his way."

"Getting the relief nurse, I mean." He paused, listening to the first wails of the woman down the hall. "Better go in with her. Stay until Doctor Bolls gets here."

"Why?" She looked at him, puzzled. "Why should you worry about getting the relief?"

"I don't know. I—" And he didn't know. The offer had been spontaneous. He could not understand his own motives. "Anyway," he said, and sat heavily in the wooden chair behind the desk, setting the black bag on the floor beside him. Fran looked at him closely, then shrugged, picked up a key from the desk, and hurried to the utility room down the hall. She returned in a moment with a cotton mask and a small bottle of ether. She placed the key on the desk, then changed her mind and slipped it in the small front drawer. She was close to him then, bending down so her white starched uniform bloused out and he could see the soft beginnings of her breasts. She stood motionless a moment, watching his face. Then suddenly she jerked upright. Her own face was stone with bright coals for eyes. "That was some joke, wasn't it? . . . That night in the car."

"Fran . . ."

"And those pictures you burned. I bet you got a real big laugh out of them." She laughed herself and swung and walked off to the room where the woman moaned in agony.

Guy wet his dry lips. He looked at the green blotter before him and thought that he was thirsty. He could drink a gallon of ice water. He listened to the screams of the strange pregnant woman—not her screams at all really, but the screams of wild ducks in the long ago, the screams of Larry and the screams of Mar—crying because the baby would not be born, crying for her child and crying for her life and crying for God to please do something, do something, *do something!* He placed his hands over his ears. But the screams continued inside his head. He forced his attention to the green blotter, and his eyes saw the tiny drawer, open a half inch, with the key to the utility room shining yellow in the lamplight.

"If you could," he murmured. "If you could, Larry, if you could." His stiff fingers touched the key. His hand gripped it as he pushed to his feet. He stumbled against the black medicine bag, paused, then opened it and took out a syringe, holding it gingerly as he walked slowly down the hall. He passed the room where Fran Walker sat with the moaning woman, reached the utility room, slipped the key in the lock, and opened the door. He moved silently without knowing it, knowing nothing really except that the morphine was here on the second shelf, in tablet form requiring a solution. He touched the bottle, then drew his hand away and groped along the shelf until he found the liquid morphine. He took the bottle down, stared at the rubber cap for a long moment, poised the syringe, and started to push the needle through. But he'd forgotten to sterilize it. He set the bottle on a table and wiped the needle carefully with cotton soaked in alcohol. It was very dangerous not to sterilize a needle.

The sterile needle slid easily through the rubber. He released the plunger, watched the morphine suck into the syringe, then pulled the needle free, dropped the bottle in his pocket, and left the room. He locked the door behind him, walked past the room where Fran still sat and the woman still screamed at intervals now, back to the desk, where he placed the key in the drawer from which he'd taken it.

Then he telephoned the nurses' quarters. "This is Doctor Montford. Miss Walker is busy with an emergency maternity, so we need someone on the floor right away." He hung up and walked straight on to Larry's room. The syringe was held carefully before him like a weapon. He did not look at it. He looked at nothing but the white screen and the white bed and Larry's white arm. "It won't hurt," he said. "Won't hurt, Larry. And you remember I taught you the sporting way. You shoot them on the wing. And you're drowning, Larry, and I—I'm going to save you again. I'm going to save you—" The words choked in his throat. He dropped his eyes to the needle, a sliver of light in the darkened room. He wet his dry lips, forced his stiffened fingers to relax, then plunged the needle into the flesh, shot in the morphine, straightened, and walked slowly back down the hallway. The syringe was still in his hand. He thrust it in his pocket as Doctor Bolls and Ida Primmer stepped out of the elevator.

Doctor Bolls nodded. "Evening, Guy." He blinked sleepily and hurried on to attend his patient.

Guy looked after him. Ida Primmer stood waiting by the desk, the sleep still clinging to her eyes. He smiled at her. "Sorry you had to come over."

"That's all right, Doctor."

"Well, I—I guess I can go along now."

"Yes. Good night, Doctor."

"Miss Walker will bring you up to date."

"Yes—good night."

"Good night." He nodded and stepped into the open elevator, then remembered his black bag and returned to the desk. He picked up the bag, walked back to the elevator, and as the door slid shut, he noticed that the woman had finally stopped her screaming, so the screaming had also stopped inside himself.

Walking out to his car he felt the syringe and empty bottle in his pocket. He took them out and looked at the needle in the moonlight. He opened the bag, dropped in the bottle, then the syringe. He closed the bag and wondered dumbly why, using one hundred milligrams of morphine, he'd bothered to sterilize the needle.

PART TWO

CHAPTER SIXTEEN

Whenever she spoke of it aloud or recalled it nostalgically in her more secure moments, Fran Walker always remembered childhood in terms of pink dresses and large dogs, of stone collections and swims in a flooded granite quarry, of occasional picnics and frequent games of "king-of-the-mountain" and "beckon" and "duck-on-the-rock." At night, though, alone, sitting between rounds behind the duty desk on the second floor of the Mills Memorial Hospital, then childhood often returned as it had existed in reality—bewildering, lonely, and frustrating.

Mr. Walker had owned a small lumber business in Sagamore, one of Indiana's numerous smaller towns, where Fran had lived in a large frame house on six acres of unused pasture land. The first Mrs. Walker had died when Fran was still a baby, so she did not remember her real mother at all. She remembered her stepmother, though—small, tight-lipped, thin-faced, extremely possessive of her new husband and the new house which had suddenly become her own. Fran had adored her father, tried desperately to please him. And since he desired nothing more than a good relationship between his daughter and his second wife, she'd made endless attempts to win over her new mother. But her displays of affection had not been reciprocated. Her stepmother had remained constantly jealous, resentful, without the slightest understanding of the small girl's motives and emotions.

Fran had felt herself losing out, slipping away into an inferior position. She began to exaggerate—often lie—about friends, feelings, grades at school, anything possible to keep herself high in her father's esteem, and at the same time gain some small bit of admiration from her mother. The exaggerations, though, had constantly turned back on her, until eventually a disgusted Mrs. Walker had insisted she be sent away to a nearby summer camp. "They award a badge of honor there," she had said, "and if you win it—not a single untruth all summer—then we'll know you've stopped lying and we'll do something very special for you."

"We'll give you a pony," her father had promised.

Fran wanted the pony. More than the pony, she wanted to prove herself. After two months of near-painful honesty, she finally won the badge of honor, and brought it home clutched tight in her fist, hidden in her pocket while she waited, waited, all the way from the station, all during the iced tea in the living room, for the exact proper moment to make her announcement of glorious victory.

"Well?" her mother had said finally over the dregs of her iced tea. "Well, Fran?"

"Well—" with the excitement building higher and higher as she drew in her breath, thought of exactly how to say it.

"You can't hide it any longer, Fran." Her mother had sighed in hopeless resignation. "We know you didn't win it, so there's simply no point in lying about it now."

Fran had closed her mouth. She'd stared at her mother, then stood and gone out to the yard and looked across the green meadow where the pony was going to graze. She'd taken the green felt badge from her pocket, fingered it tenderly, then buried it beneath a rock in the garden. She'd gone back into the house and said, "No, I didn't win it," and her mother had said, "Well, at least you didn't lie *this* time," and her father had held her while she'd cried and known finally that there was no further use in trying.

Her father bought her an Irish setter as a consolation prize. She loved Alfred and loved to watch him race across the meadow, jumping high every few yards or so to get his bearings over the tall grass. She was twelve then. Two years later Alfred was killed by a mail truck, and she loved a high-school boy instead. They explored each other in the hay of the very stall where the pony might have slept, and a few weeks later she eagerly helped the boy make love to her, though she began crying at the last, when it hurt so very much.

At eighteen Fran had gone to nurses' school in Des Moines. There'd been an intern there—a dark, intense young fellow who'd liked her desperate, freely given favors. After that came Philadelphia and the passionate patient and the irate wife who had stood screaming in the doorway with her eyes like great white moons. A few months alone in a New York rooming house, and then East Norton and Bert Mosley—East Norton and Parker Welk and Guy Montford, and this slow understanding of herself as she sat at the duty desk during the long winter nights and carefully examined her trembling emotions: Desire to love and be loved; hatred for the mean; compassion for the hurt. She supposed that was why she'd chosen a nursing career. In his own way, each patient felt close to his nurse; each patient demanded something personal to give him confidence or assuage his pain. She was entirely appreciated, and it was quite easy to love the small, hurt, whimpering child, the old lady dying half-crazy in the dark, the young mother giving birth to her first child, bravely worrying about her husband in the hall.

"I suppose," Fran said aloud. "I suppose." She lit a cigarette and glanced at the tiny leather traveling clock on the green blotter. It was ten minutes to six. Doctor Bolls had gone and Ida Primmer had gone, and Mrs. Roscoe was sleeping peacefully, her new son sleeping too in the incubator on the floor below. Daylight was coming slowly outside the windows, and in a moment now, the patients would wake and the day would begin.

The buzzer sounded, and a light on the signal board showed that Parker Welk was already awake. Fran rose and walked slowly toward his room. Parker was supposed to have left the hospital four days ago. She wondered why he hadn't. She wondered how much longer she would have to talk to him, nurse him, run errands for him, be kind to him, while nothing of what had brought him here was ever spoken between them.

Parker wanted the bedpan.

"You can get up," she told him. "You know where the bathroom is."

"I don't feel good," said Parker.

"You can get up, Parker."

"I'm paying to urinate in bed, and I'm entitled to do so."

"All right," she said, and got the pan. She slipped it under the sheet, careful not to touch him in any way. "I'll be back," she said. But he told her to wait, and she heard the tinkling sound as she stared out at the coming dawn and wondered why she'd ever bothered to try to understand Parker Welk at all. He did not even disgust her any longer. Instead she felt nothing but a weary tolerance of an ugly, beaten, rather pathetic man who had to go to the bathroom. She removed the pan, keeping the white cloth carefully over the opening. She said, "Breakfast will be ready in a few minutes."

"Tomato juice," said Parker. "I'm sick of orange juice, and I'm leaving this morning."

"I'll remember."

"Fran . . ."

"Tomato juice."

"We never talked about the other night, Fran. Guy, you know . . ."

"He burned the pictures," Fran said.

Parker squinted at her. His pig eyes were almost shut on either side of the tape across his nose as he shifted his gaze to the warm metal pan held gingerly between her hands. He seemed to shrink away with unexpected revulsion. "Get that the hell out of here!" And then, as she moved toward the door, "You're sure?"

"I'm sure. So forget it, Parker. Please forget it, and just *leave me alone!*" She went down the corridor to the bathroom, where she emptied the pan with her face averted.

It was six o'clock when she returned to the desk. Outside the light had crept in a shade or two more, and she remembered that Larry got his morphine now, just before she went off duty. She went to the utility room, took down the morphine, carefully filled a syringe with a quarter-grain dosage, and held the syringe in front of her as she walked back down the green linoleum to room 2B.

Larry was sleeping soundly. She found his wasted arm and held it gently as she poised the needle. Then very slowly she let the arm go and thought idly that it was cold. She slid her fingers to his pulse. There was nothing. She stood quiet a moment, staring at his face, slipped her hand under his nightshirt and placed it on his sunken chest, then turned abruptly and walked back stiffly to the telephone.

Doctor Kelsey said he'd be right over. Fran waited at the desk, staring absently at the green blotter. She thought that it was all for the best really. She remembered Guy's wild, red-eyed, sleepless face when he'd come up to check on Larry only hours before. She'd been cruel to him then. It had been wrong, and now she was dreadfully sorry. Of course he'd had a right to touch Mrs. McFie's hand in the Lincoln Hotel. God knows what he must have gone through with that woman, consoling her, pampering her—while all the time he'd known that Larry would die. Yes, she'd been completely unfair. She should have realized the man had no time, no emotions, no energy for love—for her or anyone else, for that matter. She'd offered to sleep with him—her own idea, not prompted by Guy in any way—and she was sorry now that she'd done it, yet glad too, even though it had shamed her at the time.

"I don't know," she thought. "I just don't *know.*" She put her head into her hands, her elbows on the blotter. Everything had become confused and a little unreal—starting back at the Robins Nest Motel—yes, back then, with Guy discovering her with Bert, and then Bert finding her with Parker and Guy's knowledge of all that, too—all mixed up, so that she was tossed back and forth, trying to be fair, honest, good to those who deserved goodness, hard on those who didn't. But the hardness was difficult to come by. "I don't know. I just don't *know.*" She wanted to cry. Larry was dead, and that, for some reason, made her very sad in her personal self, completely detached from the relief she felt as an objective nurse. She sobbed into her hands and was still crying when Doctor Kelsey stepped out of the elevator.

"For God's sake," he said brusquely. "You're a *nurse,*" he scolded.

"Yes, sir." She brushed at her eyes and followed his huge bulk down the corridor to Larry's room, where he jerked back the sheet, exposing the thin, half-naked body in the hospital gown. "Cold skin . . . no heartbeat . . . no pulse . . . no corneal reflex . . ." He worked methodically, speaking sharply to the green walls of the room. "All right," he said finally, and pulled the sheet over the ghostly face. "Have you called Doctor Montford?"

"No, I—I thought you ought to know about it first."

"Why should—" He stopped, looked at her closely, then nodded his bushy head. "You're a smart girl, Fran. Smart. But call him now, and let me do the talking."

Fran went back to the phone at the tiny desk. She called Guy's number and tried to picture his face, his eyes, his hands, the weary stoop of his body as he moved through his house toward the office phone. The ringing went on for a long time, and she was about to hang up when the receiver finally clicked and his blurred voice said, "Hello . . . Doctor Montford."

"Guy, this is Fran."

"Oh, hello, Fran." She could hear his breathing as he waited. "Something wrong?"

"It's Mr. McFie," she said. "Larry." And somehow, now that Larry was dead, she was using his given name for the first time. "Doctor Kelsey's here, and he wants you to come down right away."

"Thank you," Guy said. Then a pause and, "Fran . . . ?"

"Yes?"

"Nothing. Thank you."

She hung up and sat waiting at the desk. She remembered the last words she had spoken to Guy. "It must have been a big joke—out in the car—a big joke." God, if she had never said them!

The relief nurse arrived and said that Fran could leave now if she liked. There were only a few minutes to go till seven o'clock. Fran said she'd wait anyway. She gave the nurse instructions, and the nurse picked up the syringe from the desk and said, "What's this for?" She was fat and old and the syringe was buried in the flesh of her hand.

"Larry McFie . . . But he doesn't need it now."

"Oh . . . *C'est la vie* . . . or *C'est le mort,* rather. Or is *mort* feminine or what?"

"I don't know," said Fran.

"You checked the drugs?"

"In a minute."

"Something wrong?"

"No."

"What's been done?"

"Doctor Kelsey's still down there. Doctor Montford's on his way."

"Too bad," the old nurse said. Then the buzzer began to sound and the light blinked on and off, and she said, "That goddamn baby! That goddamn Parker Welk!"

Then minutes later Guy stepped out of the elevator. He looked terrible. Eyes all red, deep circles underneath, a stubble of beard, and he moved like an old man. He said, "Fran . . ." then looked away and moved off down the corridor. She heard voices rise and fall from that 2B room of merciful death. She heard Mrs. Roscoe say, "You mean we get our choice—bacon or sausage?" She heard Parker say, "You deaf or something? I told Miss Walker—tomato juice, and for Christ's sake, is *everybody* deaf around here?" She shook her head sharply, then rose and carried the syringe with the unused morphine back to the utility room. She unlocked the door, put away the morphine, and began automatically checking off the drugs. She was thinking of something else then—a brown dog in a summer field, a smooth-skinned boy in a pony stall—so it was not until she'd put the list away and started to close the door that she realized something was wrong. She snapped herself awake and checked again. Missing—one hundred milligrams of liquid morphine.

Guy and Doctor Kelsey came back down the corridor. The old doctor's arm was thrown over Guy's shoulder. He was talking in a low, sympathetic voice. The check list was still in Fran's hand, the ball-point pen poised just above it. She hesitated, looked up at the two men as they stopped by the elevator. Guy turned slowly toward her. His face showed no expression. For a long moment she stared into those haunted eyes. And then very slowly she turned away, made a notation in the book, put it back on the shelf, then closed and locked the door.

The elevator came. She said good night to the old nurse, got into the elevator, and stood there silent between Guy and

Doctor Kelsey. Stepping out, Guy said, "No, I'll tell them myself," and Doctor Kelsey said, "Take it easy, Guy, and I'll handle the death certificate."

Fran moved out the side door, across the gravel of the parking lot. She could hear Guy's footsteps behind her, crunching, crunching, until finally, when they'd reached his car, she turned abruptly and walked back toward the open window. "I'm sorry," she said carefully.

"Sorry, Fran?"

"About the way I spoke to you tonight."

"Forget it."

"About Larry, too."

"Thank you, Fran."

"Guy . . ." She wanted to scream it. "Guy . . . Guy . . . *Guy!*" But the words did not come. She laughed nervously. She said, "Anyway, Parker leaves today, and that's something . . . something." Then she jerked about and hastened on toward the nurses' quarters. Behind her she could feel his eyes on her back, and the car engine did not start until she was inside the building, sitting on her bunk, thinking strangely of a green felt badge of honor and the most colossal lie of all.

The dying horse, the boy in the dust, the explosion of Guy's revolver—these had never returned. Instead, now she dreamed fitfully in quick hot fevers of a nurse with thick legs, of Paul Revere's forgotten spurs, of a Chinese family dinner and small laughter and groping hands and some great black hole through which she sometimes fell, down and down to more and more darkness and no bottom at all.

She gripped the sides of the canopied bed. Something moved in the black hole. Tires on gravel, a door closing, footsteps on the gravel, deadened as they crossed the frozen lawn, faintly now on the front steps, and now the knock, very soft, repeated three times, followed by Peter's sleepy complaints.

She sat up. Dawn was coming. It was only twenty after seven and there were no jingling milk bottles of Chet Belknap, no slap of a paper against the door. She put on the flowered robe, went out to the hall, and saw Guy's figure through the glass side panels of the door. He stood exactly as before, nights ago, and she descended the stairs as she had then, one hand trailing on the banister, the other clutching the same flowered robe about her body, her hair loose and black, falling down across her shoulders.

She opened the door and saw the mask of a face, and thought nothing at all except that he looked terribly weary and was carrying her suitcase.

"You left it in the car," he said.

"Yes . . ."

"When I brought you back from Falmouth yesterday."

"You could have returned it later." She pulled the door open wide. He walked into the hall, set the suitcase by the stairs, then moved on to the living room. She followed, clutching the robe tight, though now, of course, it was not necessary; for that groping night was gone and the black bottomless hole was there instead. "It's about Larry," she said finally.

"Yes."

"Would you like some coffee?"

"Please."

She went into the kitchen and made instant coffee. Mrs. O'Hara poked a nightcapped head from her room off the kitchen. "It's all right," Mar told her, and the head disappeared. She heard Peter say something uncouth and unintelligible, heard Guy's restless footsteps on the wide boards of the livingroom floor. Then the coffee was done, and she took it to him, and he sat and sipped it, glanced up, said, "He died last night and I need this, and I'm sorry and I love you, Mar," all in the same disconnected sentence.

Outside the limbs of the trees were frozen black in the rising day. She looked at the trees, back to Guy's trembling hands lifting the pink Limoges cup. "I didn't tell him," she said finally. "He was in a coma last night, so I couldn't have told him anyway."

"Mar . . . Mar, Mar . . ."

She saw the intense pain in his eyes and knew that he wanted to cry, and she wanted to cry, too, but could not until later, perhaps, when this final death became more definite than the slower death of the months before. "God," she said, whispering in her throat. "He answered our prayer."

"Cut it out, Mar."

She sat motionless, lit a cigarette, and heard footsteps in the hall above. Guy glanced up, shut his eyes tight, opened them again, and seemed to brace himself as the footsteps came on down the stairs and Sam appeared in the doorway from the hall. His thin hair stuck straight up above his head. There was the stubble of a red beard along his jaw, and his twitching hands fumbled with the cord of a black robe. He blinked at them in the early light. "Guy," he said, and "What the hell!" He looked at Mar, and she saw his mouth tremble and saw him sit and heard him say, "All right . . . I understand . . . All right."

"I'm sorry," Guy said.

"When was it?"

"A few hours ago, and I'm sorry."

"Yes, *you're* sorry."

"Do you want a sedative, Sam?"

"I don't want *anything* from *you.*"

Guy wet his lips. He rose and touched Sam's shoulder and moved out to the hallway. Mar followed. At the door Guy turned and looked at her. He started to speak, then touched her hand and jerked his own hand back again. She wanted him to hold her so that she could cry against him. She wanted him to say something real and personal, and say such things herself, except it was impossible, of course, because of Sam—and more than that, because death was here, and in the awe and sadness of death, each person is always entirely alone.

"I'll do what I can," he said. "But someone—you—you'll have to make the arrangements yourself."

"I understand."

"Hood and Son. Mr. Hood will take care of all the details. Get in touch with Doctor Treleaven, too."

"Yes."

"All right then?"

"All right." She stood silent a moment, staring into his bloodshot eyes. Then she touched the sleeve of his tweed coat, and he turned and went out the door across the frozen lawn.

Back in the living room Sam was mixing a drink. She knew, though, that he would not get drunk. He had to do *something,* and this was the only outlet he knew. A drink would let the explosion come. It would also remind him that someday, later on—even this early in the morning—he still had a way out of his own personal hell.

Peter swore.

Sam said, "Shut up!"

"Sam," she pleaded, and Sam turned then with the drink and said, "I should have had a specialist. I knew it all the time."

"No, Sam."

"And you're not even crying. Don't you feel anything? Not anything? Don't you even *care?*"

"I care, Sam."

"Then why aren't you crying?"

"I'm crying, Sam. You just can't hear it."

"He's *dead.* Don't you get it? Dead, dead, dead, *dead!*" Sam's voice rose and he tossed off the drink, said it again, *"Dead, dead,"* threw the glass into the fireplace, then sat on the sofa and put his head on his trembling hands and cried with great racking sobs.

She went close to him. He waved her away. "Leave me alone, leave me alone." She paused, then turned and moved back up the stairs. She sat on the bed and looked at the picture of Sam's wife in the gold frame and thought that Sam's wife was dead. She looked out the window at the black branches of the trees and thought they too were dead. She smoothed the flowered robe across her knees, felt a sudden pain in her stomach, doubled over, then straightened again and tried not to think of the pain or where she would go after this, what she would do, how it could ever possibly come right. She thought only of this, today, now, and Sam's racking sobs from the room below, and the sobs that would come finally to herself—in a moment now—as she waited for them—as she sat and waited.

Caesar barked in greeting as Guy opened the side door and went into the waiting room. He said, "Hello, boy, hello, boy," patted the brown head, set his black bag beside the desk, and moved on to the living room. He swayed, sat for a moment in a cracked leather chair, and told himself that he had a hangover. Nothing else. A hangover and nerves and lack of sleep. In a few hours now he'd be quite all right again.

He rose, went back to the office, took two Nembutals from a bottle in his desk drawer, and swallowed them with a glass of water from a vacuum pitcher. The water was stale. He felt sick, rested his head against the desk, then moved his eyes slowly to the side until they fastened on the black bag. "Over!" he said. "Over, over, over and done!" He opened the bag, took out the empty bottle of morphine and tossed it into the basket. "Over and done!"

Caesar whined. He stumbled into the kitchen and fed the animal. "If the phone rings," he said, "come upstairs and bark. You understand?" He patted the dog and climbed the narrow stairs to the room above, where he took off his clothes in the morning light through the many-paned window, then returned down the stairs in his undershorts and opened all the doors, so that if Caesar failed to bark, then perhaps he would hear the phone himself.

Upstairs again, he doused cold water in his face, glanced at his own red devil's eyes in the bathroom mirror, then lay down on the bed and stared up at the bullet hole in the ceiling. He would sleep now and he would dream now, but not that old business any more—that old, tired, worn-out stuff that had plagued him for so very long—because now, of course, he had something else to dream about. Even drunk, even stony-cold plastered, crocked, gassed, palooted, he would never see Charlie Chaplin again. He'd proved that fact already. Tonight. Drunk, and no Charlie Chaplin. The man was gone, replaced by fresher memories. And though he was glad of Charlie's passing, he wished now—he wished to God he could have him back to submerge the nightmares of the future.

He closed his eyes and tried hard now to remember what he'd done, where he'd been from that last moment when he'd gotten into his car and driven away into the cold night. Two bars . . . not Pat's . . . out of town . . . A dark road . . . almost hit a tree . . . headlights in his eyes . . . foot on the brake . . . "Look, mister, you *sure* you want another?" . . . Deceptive road . . . two-lane road that had once been single . . . Something wrong with the steering . . . pulling to the left . . . won't stay in the proper lane . . . driveway too narrow . . . garage doors too small . . . paint off the front right fender . . . need a bigger garage . . . Caesar barking . . . Let him out . . . no more drinks . . . walking walking, walking, walking . . . down to the boatyard . . . up the ladder, down into *Julia*'s cabin . . . sit on bunk . . . cold . . . Mar here once . . . warm . . . here twice . . . warm even when not touching her, still warm . . . Can't stand it now . . . cold now . . . climb to deck, down ladder . . . Caesar waiting . . . stumble, fall . . . Caesar whining . . . stagger out to night, along shore past cannery . . . past yacht club . . . past summer cottages . . . cottage where Julia lived with parents . . . boarded up now . . . parents gone . . . Julia gone . . . everyone gone . . . Nothing but dunes, cold, freezing cold . . . here, a secret place, a cave from boyhood under the dunes, hidden, protected from the wind . . . Sit, get a clear head . . . hear the surf, see the light at Keever's Point . . . sand all frozen, icy, sticky, in large lumps . . . freezing, freezing . . . Caesar there, too . . . whimpering . . . "What's the matter, old fellow, old fellow?" . . . Doze in the freezing night . . . Hat gone, lost, button off coat, shoes filled with sand . . . Wake up with bad taste . . . gray in the sky . . . still freezing . . . Caesar still whining . . . push up to knees, look over dunes . . . see house and widow's walk . . . No Charlie Chaplin . . . gone into the rocks below, blood feeding the sleeping tulips . . . See cross on St. Joseph's . . . not gold . . . black . . . evil, threatening, horrifyingly black . . . Shiver with cold, tremble with fear . . . Get up and run toward house, Caesar following . . . into waiting room . . . Phone ringing in office . . . pick it up . . . Fran . . . pull self together . . . "Hello . . . Doctor Montford."

"Guy, this is Fran."

"Oh, hello, Fran. Something wrong?"

"It's Mr. McFie. Larry."

It was Mr. McFie. Larry. Guy opened his eyes and listened

intently. The phone was not ringing. If it did ring, he prayed to God that Caesar would hear it, because he could not let a patient down. Not now or ever, he could not, he would not, he would never let a patient down.

CHAPTER SEVENTEEN

The news of Larry McFie's death spread rapidly through the town. Fran told Ida Primmer, who sighed, "He was such a *nice* man," and the fat old nurse told Parker Welk, who said, "For Christ's sake, get me my clothes!" and thought that Nancy Messner was not experienced enough to handle such a delicate story, so he'd have to get the hell down to the *Chronicle* as soon as possible.

Polly Welk called for her husband at 8:15. Parker said, "Couldn't you waddle any faster?" and "If you could squeeze behind the wheel of the car, then we wouldn't have to *walk*." He strode home four paces ahead of her, thinking he could write the story at home and telephone it to Nancy at the office.

Polly struggled hard to keep up with her husband. She slipped twice on the icy sidewalk, and was panting heavily when she climbed the steps, heaved into the hallway, thumped into a chair with her legs spread wide, and grabbed for the telephone.

Mrs. Manning said, "You're sure, Polly?" and "Oh, that poor girl. Whatever will she do now? And of course I knew it would happen sometime this week."

"How did you know?" Polly asked.

"I just—*knew*." She knew because Mrs. Manning had read it in Larry's horoscope. She would not admit it, though, as she confessed to no one that she lived entirely by the signs of the zodiac, had even married the Judge simply because their destiny had been written in the stars. "I had a *feeling*," she said secretly, then hung up and rang Mrs. Treleaven before Polly could get the line. "That poor girl," she said to Mrs. Treleaven. "Whatever will she do now? And I knew it would happen sometime this week." But Frances was the minister's wife and had known all about it for a good thirty minutes.

Frances hung up and wondered why she hadn't called a

few people herself. After all, she *had* been just about the first to find out, and even though her husband had warned her again and again that a minister's wife did *not* gossip, that some pieces of information should never leave the four walls of their house, still this *would* be public knowledge, and there was one person whom she'd love to get the better of, if only this once. She called to her husband, who was taking a shower. The running water drowned out her voice. Well, if he won't *listen*, she thought, then reached quickly for the phone.

But it rang under her hand.

"Frances," the voice said, "no time to talk now, but Larry's dead."

"I know," said Frances wearily, defeated, as Mrs. Coffin rattled on as though the news were entirely fresh. "Died in his sleep last night, and I thought you ought to know, being the minister's wife and all."

"I *do* know," said Frances in vain.

"I got it from Chet Belknap, who heard it at the hospital while he was delivering the milk. He comes almost straight to my house from there, you know. So of course I wanted you to be the *first* to know, and— Hello? . . . Hello?"

Frances hung up. The water turned off in the shower. Next time, she thought. Next time . . .

Mrs. Coffin sat laughing by the kitchen phone. "Frances is furious," she told her husband, "because *she* didn't know before *I* did."

"What's the difference?" said her husband.

"Remember, Cy, when you used to take Larry out in the boat?"

"Yeah." Cy was gnarled and weather-beaten. He sat at the oil-cloth-covered table, drinking coffee in his fish-smelling clothes.

"A long time ago." Mrs. Coffin paused and studied her husband's leathery face and wondered why she had ever married this man. She'd been very young at the time, and he'd had such wonderful corded arms and such a flat, hard belly, and he'd slept with her fiercely twice a day for twenty-eight years, until finally it had become a ritual—ten at night, five in the morning (fishermen had to get up so early), and no children in all that time. But that was all over now, so Cy was no longer the potent young adventurer, but only a smelly fisherman with a broken-down old boat. And though she still felt quite affectionate toward him, of course—still it was a crying shame. If she were young again, if she knew then what she knew now— Lord, you could *sleep* with anybody. But you couldn't *marry* just anybody. And even though Mrs. Manning, for instance, had probably never had a sexual crisis in her life, it didn't matter now, because in the long run with her money and her feeble little Justice of the Peace of a husband— Still, Mrs. Manning had won. She had wealth and social position, and she had won.

"You make my sandwiches?" Cy said.

"What happened, Cy? What happened?"

"No more sardines. Don't I see enough fish?"

"What happened to *us?*"

"We got old," Cy said.

Mrs. Coffin sighed. Someday she would open a teashop and people would come from miles around and say, "Isn't that Mrs. Coffin's place divine, in such perfect taste?" Someday . . . Someday . . .

Ruth Kiley was on her way to the cannery when she heard the news from Mr. Castner, who was opening the door of his drygoods store. He spoke carefully, in that dry, boring way of his, and Ruth merely nodded and moved on dumbly through the town. She thought only of Sam . . . poor Sam . . . Oh, God, oh, God . . . And the bottle in Sam's drawer and thirty-six years ago and what had happened then, and how, after his release from the sanitarium, she'd been able to give him some comfort during those nights of passion in the cabin on the shore. Well, she couldn't help him much in *that* way any longer, because she was a little old for sex now. But still, he'll need me, she thought. We're both old now, but he'll need me again . . . Again. And she walked a little faster then, and breathed deep, almost in relief, because now, after all this time, it was good to be needed again by someone, and especially by Sam.

Pat's opened at nine. Pat himself had heard the news through Chet Belknap, as had Mrs. Coffin and many others. Pat felt a weight of sadness as he made coffee in the shiny urn. He relayed the news to Larson Whitt, who came in for toast and coffee, and to Bert Mosley, who came in for an entire breakfast of poached eggs, sausage and toast, with clam juice on the side because he'd been constipated for the last forty-eight hours.

"He was a good guy," Larson said solemnly.

Bert belched. "I never knew him."

"Friends in high school," Pat said.

Bert belched again.

At nine thirty Stewed Schaeffer wandered in, ordered a beer and said, "Worked at the glassworks a couple of summers," then drank his beer and turned his mind to other things.

At nine thirty-five one of the leftover summer artists—bearded, long-haired, absorbed in his own thoughts—eased onto a stool, drank black coffee, smoked two filter-tip cigarettes, and said, "Who the hell is Larry McFie?"

While up at the Lincoln Hotel, Betsy pondered sentimentally over the loss of a man who, some fifteen years ago, had taken her twice within an even thirteen minutes.

CHAPTER EIGHTEEN

A thin drizzle of freezing rain began falling during the early afternoon, so that many of the men wore waterproof topcoats in place of warmer overcoats, and many of the women wore plastic raincoats over their furs.

Guy attended the funeral service alone. He came in late from a call to Seaside, and sat at the rear of the church, keeping his overcoat buttoned to hide the fact that he had not found time to change his gray suit for something more appropriate.

The church was jammed and, waiting for Doctor Treleaven, Guy scanned the mourners with a feeling of unwonted bitterness. He wondered how many of these people really missed the passing of Larry McFie. How many would be here now, on this nasty day, if Larry had been brought home from a far-off place, or had died a more common death at an older age? There had never been a case of Hodgkin's in the hospital before. And since Hodgkin's was more rare, more dramatic than cancer or heart disease, the town had felt vicariously involved in Larry's pain, so that now, with his death, they were personally involved in that too. It was much like the huge crowds that attend the funeral of a small girl, raped and throttled by a madman. Outside of the few who had actually known the child, the rest were professional mourners—people who looked for tragedy (the more gruesome the better) and mourned, perhaps sincerely, not so much for the child herself, as for the manner in which she'd died.

It was wrong to think this way. Even though Larry had

been away a long time, there were still those who remembered him, and probably most of the congregation honestly mourned the passing of any church member—regardless of how well they knew him, or how often he attended services or church social affairs.

The idea assuaged some of Guy's bitterness. He wondered if perhaps someday he might belong to this church himself, then thought that what he had done—regardless of the reasons—what he had done was as great a sin in this church as in the church that he had once claimed as his own. You could not transfer your sins; you could not go peddling them, looking for a ready buyer. Perhaps, if he could confess, he would be forgiven, except that he was not prepared to be forgiven for an act which he did not honestly believe to be a sin at all. In the eyes of the church—a sin; in the eyes of the courts—a crime. In the heart of Guy Montford—sober, clear-thinking again—a merciful act which transcended the laws of both.

Doctor Treleaven appeared among the great display of flowers which had exhausted the resources of Hill's Flower Shop, and forced Mr. Hill to make quick, profitless deals with shops in Harpswell and Hyannis. He looked solemnly, thoughtfully over the huge crowd, waited until there was complete silence, then began the short service.

Guy watched the light on Doctor Treleaven's rimless glasses. He listened to the words. ". . . Popular young man . . . athlete . . . honorable . . . brave . . . soldier . . . untimely . . . loss to all who knew him . . ." He thought that John Treleaven was not quite so naïve as he sometimes appeared. The man knew his job. He knew his congregation. He knew about death and how people in small towns felt about it, and what they wanted to hear and what they wanted to believe. He used tired old words, said tired old things, as though he had a card file of speeches prepared for any deaths that should occur—old ladies, old men; middle-aged ladies, middle-aged men; young ladies, young men; small children, and babies.

But Doctor Treleaven was no fool.

". . . his wife and father," the minister was saying, and a few heads turned surreptitiously toward the first row, where Mar sat with Sam, her head bowed, her black hair blending with her black hat, so that it was all hair, or all hat, all black, with only the white of her neck above the coat. Guy stared at the patch of white, then lowered his own head as the prayer began. And now, as he once prayed for Larry's death, he prayed fervently for Mar's life—and knew, as he had known then, that again it was up to him, and not a matter for God at all.

Outside the rain continued. It froze on the windshields of the many cars, so that before the funeral procession could get under way, the drivers had to remove the films of ice with gloved hands or plastic scrapers. It was a piece of everyday annoyance in the midst of a solemn affair, and somehow made it all wrong—even, somehow, a little indecent.

The Protestant cemetery was only a few blocks away. Guy drove alone in the second car, directly behind Mar and Sam. The windshield wipers clicked and slid over the freezing rain. He saw Mar's white neck, blurred, out of focus through the ice on the rear window. He saw the headlights of the cars behind through the ice on his own rear window. It was a slow, dreary journey, and he thought, quite sincerely, that Larry rode in more peace and comfort than those who mourned him.

Though the cemetery attendant had turned the earth frequently during the morning, the ground had frozen again around the deep hole, so that Doctor Treleaven had to scrape with his fingernails in order to get a decent handful.

"Earth to earth, ashes to ashes, dust to dust;
in sure and certain hope of the Resurrection
Into eternal life."

The frozen earth fell with a clump on the coffin below, and the people wept silently under their black umbrellas in the rain.

Ida's umbrella was large enough to protect them both. But Fran actually preferred the rain against her face. It was cold, and reminded her of popsicles and swims in a granite quarry and all the nice things in her imagined childhood. It kept her mind from the coffin and the minister's droning words, the evil black branches of the trees and the dried, frozen wreaths, and the pathetic little flags over the soldiers' graves, all stiff now, unable to wave at all.

Then suddenly it was over.

"You're getting soaked," Ida whispered.

Fran did not answer.

"Come on, walk along under my umbrella."

Fran shook her head. Melted ice slid from her forehead. She watched Sam McFie as he bent down to touch the stone next to Larry's grave. There was an inscription on the stone: *Cora McFie . . . Loving wife . . . 1895–1921*. Sam ran his hand along the inscription. The bare hand shook on the cold stone. He straightened slowly and looked at Guy

Montford. The entire left side of his face began to twitch spasmodically, and there was horrible reproach in the crying eyes. Mrs. McFie touched Sam's arm. Sam jerked his arm away, then strode off fast between all the shiny stones and all the stiff little flags. His face was still twitching hideously.

"Come *on,*" Ida said.

Fran tried to pull her eyes from where they had focused on the face of Mrs. McFie. The eyes, though, would not move. They were frozen like the rain. Everyone was leaving. But Mrs. McFie remained motionless. She looked very sad and very beautiful. She stared down at the fresh grave, then up again very slowly into the eyes of Guy Montford. Guy went close, nodded, and touched her arm, gently, the way a doctor would—except somehow, in that moment, it was not *exactly* the way a doctor would.

"All right," said Ida. "If you want to stay here all day."

Fran closed her eyes tight, jerked them open again.

"No, I'm coming."

Guy heard her voice. He glanced up and smiled faintly. It was there in his eyes. Everything—every single inch of everything—all right there, and God, what a stupid, naïve, sentimental child she had been!

She turned and walked back with Ida toward the hospital. Ida kept trying to hold the umbrella over both of them and Fran kept sidling away into the rain. Ida said, "Did you see that Mrs. McFie—that lovely sad face?"

Fran said, "Yes."

"Lord, I know how she must feel. If I'd lost *my* husband like that!"

Fran did not answer.

"So maybe I was lucky I decided to throw myself into a career of mercy. I mean, at the time Harry simply wouldn't hear of it. But I told him nursing meant more to me than any man alive—any man at *all.* And of course I still mean that too, and that's why any time a man starts getting serious, I back right away—hands off—I don't want to get involved. I was *too* involved with Harry, and suppose I *had* married him and suppose he'd died like that—horribly like that—"

"Yes," Fran said.

They walked on the wet pavements. Ida said it had broken Harry's heart. She said it must have broken Mrs. McFie's heart. Ida said nothing about her own heart, broken by Harry in Rochester, New York, and broken a dozen other times in a dozen other places by a dozen blind dates who had never called again.

They reached the hospital, walked across the frozen gravel and into the dormitory that had once slept the horses of

Mrs. Cyrus Mills. Fran sat unmoving on the bed. One of the nurses asked, "Was Doctor Kelsey at the funeral?" and Ida said, "Yes," and the fat old nurse said, "He won't be back here till eight thirty though, in case you're interested."

Fran took the kerchief from her blond hair and shook out the melted ice.

"Something wrong with you?" said Ida.

"No."

The telephone rang. Someone called, "Fran Walker!" and Fran rose and walked stiffly to the phone.

"Fran?" Bert's voice was anxious, probing. "I know you were at the funeral or I would have called earlier."

"Yes, Bert."

"I didn't go myself because I never met Larry McFie in my life."

"I know, Bert."

"Well—I was wondering—it's lousy out. I'm lonesome as hell. You've never even *seen* my place here, always refused to come up because someone might see you. But there won't be anyone on the street tonight—"

"Yes, Bert."

"And we haven't been together—not *really* together since *that* night—*you* know."

"I know," wishing he'd stop begging, stop groveling.

"So I just wondered."

"Yes, Bert."

"You mean yes, you'll come?"

"Yes . . . Yes . . . Yes . . . *Yes!*" She was almost screaming at the end.

For a moment the phone was silent. Then Bert said, "Eight thirty all right?" awed, as though he still did not quite believe it.

"Nine," she said.

"Fran—"

"I have to see Doctor Kelsey. I have—to see—Doctor—Kelsey!" She hung up. She put her forehead against the phone and said, "Oh, God, God, God!" then went into the bathroom and dashed cold water into her already freezing face.

CHAPTER NINETEEN

"Careful, Fran . . . Careful, careful." Doctor Kelsey pressed his thick thumbs together until the joints ached, then relaxed and studied the girl in the chair across his desk. She was dressed to go out, pretty, calm, but with an odd brightness in her pale eyes, a barely discernible tremble to her full lower lip. He rose and stared out the window, bracing his big hands on the sill, then turned back and said it again, "Careful, Fran . . . careful."

"I merely told you what happened, Doctor."

"What happened."

"Exactly."

"Exactly." He sat again, brushed back a lock of white hair, said, "Why *now,* Fran? Why not yesterday or the day before? Why not that same night?"

"I wasn't sure."

"Sure of what happened or sure of whether or not you should report it?"

"Both."

"Both?"

"First I thought I'd made the mistake myself. Then I realized I hadn't. But I'd already falsified the report, you see. So I let it stand, even after I knew it wasn't my error. Then at the funeral I saw Mr. McFie and Larry's wife, so terribly sad, and I—well, I knew I'd done wrong in falsifying the records, and in not saying anything after I *realized.* I'd been carried away with compassion for Doctor Montford, you see—after all these weeks—what it had been doing to him."

"Now suddenly you've lost the compassion?"

"No, sir. It's strictly a matter of right and wrong. After all, I'm admitting I falsified the records."

"So," Doctor Kelsey said wryly, "you're martyring yourself in the cause of righteousness." The heavy thumbs came together again. They formed a pyramid, then came apart and the white-haired fingers interlocked. Here's the church and here's the steeple.

"I just thought you ought to know."

Open the door and see all the people.

"I mean if I *hadn't* come to you, nobody would ever know, you see, because since *I'm* librarian—well, the other nurses never look past the report of the previous shift. Why should they? They worry about their *own* shifts, and if I simply subtract one hundred milligrams of morphine from my report, then they accept it, and don't look back at all. And in the long run, as librarian, it's my responsibility anyway."

"In the very long run," said Doctor Kelsey, "it is *my* responsibility."

"Yes, sir."

Silence. He studied Fran's bright eyes, the trembling lip. She was not acting like a nurse at all. If she'd reported all this when it had happened, then she'd have been doing her duty. Even if she'd only been trying to hide her own mistake, he could still understand it. But this right and wrong stuff—it was a lot of crap. Somehow Fran was involved with Guy Montford and the death of Larry McFie. She was acting strictly on an emotional basis with a thin layer of righteous indignation to keep it hidden. "Fran," he said finally. "Let me understand this. You didn't *see* Doctor Montford enter the utility room?"

"No, sir."

"And the relief nurse—Miss Primmer—and Doctor Bolls—neither of them actually *saw* him with the morphine?"

"No, sir."

"Yet you're positive Doctor Montford took the key from the desk, went to the utility room, took the morphine, gave it to Larry, and returned the key—all during the time you were attending Mrs. Roscoe, waiting for Doctor Bolls and Miss Primmer?"

"Yes, sir."

"And Doctor Montford called Miss Primmer himself?"

"Yes, sir. He told me to attend to Mrs. Roscoe, and he'd take care of the relief nurse. I was giving her ether, you see, because Doctor Bolls won't give spinals. He likes his patients to be conscious so they can bear down, and—"

"But nobody actually *saw* Doctor Montford?"

"No, sir. But I heard him talking in Mr. McFie's room before he came back to the desk that first time. He said, 'If you could, Larry, if you could,' and things that didn't make much sense. But then, when I found the morphine missing, then I sort of understood."

"I see."

"So—that's it."

"Yes," he said. "That's it." That was it. He rose wearily. He lit a cigar and blew a great wreath against the window.

The freezing rain rattled on the glass and the smoke bounced back from the cold pane. That was it. He did not understand it, and goddamn it, if Fran had just left it alone—simply falsified the report, and *left it alone,* then there would be no problem at all—no problem for anyone.

"What are you going to do?" Fran asked behind him.

"What?"

"What are you going to do?"

He turned, stared at her again. "What would *you* do, Fran?"

"Well, it—it *is* against the law."

"How do I know it *wasn't* your mistake, Fran? And now you're deluding yourself, or even lying?"

"Because I'm not, and you know it."

"Fran . . . Fran . . ." He sat, put his head into his hands, ran the hands through the white thicket of hair, down over his bushy eyebrows and craggy features. "Fran, did you ever see a doctor spank a baby a bit too lightly or a little too late? The child's deformed, a monster, and the doctor gives it a halfhearted whack, so it never does breathe, and the mother never knows the difference? *Nobody* ever knows."

"Yes, sir."

"Do you remember only a few years ago, Fran, when premature babies were often blind because hospitals were using the wrong oxygen proportion in the incubators? Do you remember looking down at some baby that you knew would be blind, you knew would never live anyway—not a chance, really—only a pound and a half, for instance—and the parents were going crazy, but nobody told *them* what was going to happen, so they thought everything was just dandy—just dandy—beautiful baby fighting for its life. And then one day the baby was dead. Then the parents were told, so they got over it pretty fast. They went home and had another baby."

"Yes, sir, I remember back then."

"Fran, were *you* ever negligent in caring for one of those infants? Did you ever just *happen* to cut down the oxygen or make some tiny error in the feedings?" He watched her face. She blushed. Her eyes moved away, then back again.

"Negligence," she said. "That's different."

"Is it?"

"It's not a positive act."

"Mercy killing is acceptable when it's due to deliberate negligence, but not acceptable when it's committed through an overt act? Is that correct, Fran?"

"I don't know."

"Fran . . ."

"Doctor Montford *did* it and I *know* he did, and there's no other way to explain away the morphine! And I didn't come here to *argue* about it! I came to tell you what happened, and I told you, even if it meant hurting myself, and now you want to *argue* with me!" She rose. Her eyes were blazing now, partly in guilt, he thought, and her body was tense, her words wild as she shrieked them into the room. Yes, she was emotional, all right. Something personal, all right. It was stamped all over her face as she turned abruptly and started for the door.

"Fran!' She stopped with her hand on the knob. "Thank you for telling me, Fran, and let me handle it, Fran."

"How?"

"In my *own* way, Fran. As head of this hospital, in my *own* way."

"You won't do anything. You'll let everything stay just the way it is."

"Please, Fran. I'm asking you. I'm begging you. Let *me* handle it."

She hesitated. She said, "Well," and "I don't know . . . I just *don't know."* And then she was gone through the doorway.

The sleet rattled on against the window. The cigar ash fell onto the desk, and he said, "God damn it! God damn it!" then sat there staring at the still-intact tube of gray ash, trying to see into it and behind it, as though it were gray tea leaves or a crystal ball.

Bert Mosley's apartment over YE OLDE ANTIQUE SHOPPE on the eastern edge of town consisted of a living room, bedroom, kitchenette, and bath. He rented it furnished from Mrs. Manning, who rented the shop below to Miss Edna Welles, a flighty, middle-aged spinster who hadn't the faintest idea how to distinguish between an authentic antique and a piece of junk. Her shop was littered with broken chairs that had found their way to East Norton from Grand Rapids, Michigan, pickle jugs, and prune bottles that had a "lovely purplish color," common sea shells, atrocious Victorian portraits of unknown grandparents in chipped gold-leaf frames, and anything at all that Miss Welles could pick up cheap.

Edna was a friendly character, gay, optimistic, constantly darting about town in her old Ford station wagon, returning with a moth-eaten braided rug or an old milking stool for which she had paid a dollar or two, and sold for a few cents more to the summer visitors, who knew as little about their purchases as she did. Occasionally she picked up some

Sandwich glass, usually chipped, and, "Someday," she liked to tell Bert, "someday I'll pick up a perfect treasure for nothing—and then all my troubles will be over."

Bert doubted she would recognize the supposed buried treasure in Pirate's Cove if she dug it up herself. He humored her, however, and occasionally, on lonely nights, found contentment in her frenetic rattling about in the shop below.

Tonight, though, Miss Welles had closed up early because of the funeral, and Bert would not have wanted her about in any case. The freezing rain was turning to snow, promising slush in the morning. But he was not worrying about the morning either. He'd already gone down to the liquor store for a fifth of good scotch. He'd already cleaned up the rooms which Mrs. Manning called "furnished," though everything was broken, worn, and completely nondescript. And since he had no interest in such things anyway, the apartment looked almost exactly as it had when he'd rented it two years before.

Perhaps Fran would help him redecorate. The thought of her pliant body moving about as she inspected everything, tushing and tishing and ahing and suggesting—there was something very warm and personal and comforting in the idea, and for a moment he sat motionless, savoring it, until he remembered Fran's voice saying, "Yes . . . Yes . . . *Yes!*" and then he knew, of course, that there would be no sentimental nonsense tonight. No, sir, he'd never heard Fran give in so easily, so almost eagerly. Always there'd been a bit of conversational byplay to get things going. And she'd never, *never* consented to come up to his apartment, for fear that Miss Welles might know and stay all night in the shop below, listening and giggling.

This is it, Bert thought. This—is—*it*. And a great relief it was, too. For ever since way back at the Robins Nest—weeks ago—he'd had no real experience with Fran at all—nor with anyone else, for that matter, except for that one humiliating experience with Betsy. Betsy, he thought now. You go to hell, Betsy! Asking if I'm a pansy. My God, I'll show you! Yes, sir, yes, sir! He laughed triumphantly within himself, went into the bathroom, and brushed out the wave in his blond hair. He squirted male deodorant under his arms, washed his face, squeezed out a tiny blackhead, and changed his clothes for a winter sport shirt and slacks. Casual, casual. But neat, too, and nothing rushed. Let *her* take the reins. And she would, too, and he was more sure of it now than he'd been since the day he'd first set eyes on Miss Fran Walker.

He buttoned his shirt, then pulled back the dusty chintz

curtains and peered out the living-room window at the falling sleet. The streets were empty. It was already ten after nine. But he knew she'd come. The way she'd talked—the almost frightening intensity—

He was nervous. The anticipation was unbearable. He decided to have a drink, poured himself a shot of scotch, and sat waiting, wondering whether it would be advisable to suggest the bedroom, or simply lower the lights right here in the living room. It was an odd thing, that. Here he'd known Fran, been carrying on with her over all these months, and still he didn't really know her at all. She made him excited. She made him jealous and possessive. He'd often thought seriously of proposing marriage, and yet he was still awkward in her presence. He still couldn't *suggest* the bedroom, or, for that matter, make any move at all until *she* was ready.

Tonight she was *more* than ready.

He'd finished the drink and started to pour another when the bell sounded. He was startled, then overwhelmingly relieved. He opened the outer door and called, "Hi, there," and Fran answered, "Hello, Bert," and climbed toward him in the dim light. She wore a yellow raincoat over a tweed skirt and a pink sweater. She took off the coat and shook the water from her hair and said, "So this is where you live," and stood silent a moment, appraising the room.

"I got scotch," Bert said.

"All right."

He went into the kitchenette and made them both a drink. When he returned he found Fran standing at the window, her smooth hips very rounded as she bent forward, away from him, her hair glistening yellow as it reflected in the black glass. "Your drink," he said, and she answered, "Thank you," and straightened and took the glass and sat gingerly on the broken springs of the sofa.

He sat across from her in a claw-legged chair. He wet his lips and noticed the brightness in her eyes, the moisture on her mouth, the way her breasts stood up high and firm beneath the pink sweater. "Well," he said. "Well—"

"So this is where you live?"

"You said that."

"Did I?"

"Is something the matter, Fran?"

"No."

"If you want to tell me—"

"Since when did you want to *talk*, Bert?"

She was bitter, he thought. Hurt, he thought. He said, "Now, Fran—"

"Since *when?*"

"If you want to talk—"

"No, let's get on with it, shall we? Let's just—get *on* with it." She put down her drink and rose and pulled the pink sweater over her head. She murmured something about a pink dress with a big pink bow, then dropped her skirt and bra and panties, and kicked off her shoes, but left her stockings on. Then she came to him and knelt down before him and made it all extremely wonderful and simple, so that he merely had to obey, like a young boy with his first whore . . . "on the floor . . . right on the floor," and "There now, you have a wonderful build, Bert," and "Not yet, Bert," and "Now, Bert," and "I'll help you, darling," and "There, darling," and then suddenly a terrible ferocity with her fingernails scraping the skin from his back and her teeth biting at his lip, until suddenly afterwards, she broke and cried. She rolled over on her stomach on the old flowered rug and cried while her bare shoulders shook and her bare rump quivered and her stockinged legs trembled in the yellow light.

Bert said, "Fran . . . Fran . . ." He wished she'd get up. He went into the bedroom, closed the door, and dressed. He felt weak. He sat on the bed and smoked until finally he heard her rise and move across the room. He waited another moment or two until he was certain she had dressed, then went back to the living room and freshened her drink without looking at her face.

"I'm sorry," she murmured away from him.

"About what?"

"I was using you. I was upset—using you."

"My pleasure." He laughed. But it was no joke. He strengthened his own drink and sat again, and thought that perhaps he did love her and someday, when they were married, someday he'd really get to know her.

She seemed to be reading his mind. "Bert . . . I can't come up here like this again. Tonight I used you, and sometimes I've let you use me. But I won't keep going on like that."

"I see."

"If we were engaged, Bert, then it would be different, of course. I'd come up here all you like and help straighten up the place. Maybe redecorate it a little after we were married, and then pretty soon we could move to Boston like you've always wanted."

"Fat chance," Bert said. "I talk it, but I can't *do* it."

"Don't you feel anything toward me at all?"

"You know how I feel. It's just I hate being stuck here—forcing you to be stuck here, too."

Silence. He thought that he'd always intended to ask Fran to marry him. And yet now, when he was sure she'd accept, he was being strangely hesitant. He did not want to lose her, and perhaps someday he *would* marry her. But he did not like to be rushed or pushed or compromised. He'd had a satisfying relationship with Fran, and perhaps marriage would only ruin it.

Fran lit a cigarette. Her hand shook. "I wanted to tell you something, Bert. I've got to tell *somebody.*"

"What?"

"I'd like another drink first. I'd like to know you love me first."

"I told you, didn't I?" He poured them both another drink. "So we're engaged," he said impulsively, "so what did you want to say?"

"You mean it, Bert?"

"You want it in writing?"

"No, I'm sorry, Bert." She stared into the brown liquid, then raised her eyes and smiled faintly. "Well, then—now that we're—engaged—I guess I can tell you everything. I mean I really *ought* to tell you."

"If Parker Welk's been after you—"

"No . . . No, I really need you, Bert. I guess I can say anything, can't I? *Anything?*"

"Please, Fran."

"I mean you're a lawyer, aren't you? And something happened, and—I've got to *talk,* Bert."

"You talk," he told her. "We're engaged, and no secrets," he told her, and sat drinking slowly, watching her tense face, listening to the faltering words, taking it all in with increasing awe, until after she had finished, he said, "Guy Montford. What do you know! My God, my God! The great and well-loved and honorable Doctor Guy Montford!"

"Bert—"

"So Kelsey's taking care of it, is he? *Sure,* he's taking care of it."

"That's not all, Bert."

"Sure, he is."

"Bert!" She shouted at him, and he stopped, shook his head, and looked up at her while her voice lowered, almost to a whisper now. "It wasn't a mercy killing, Bert. Not *entirely* anyway."

"What are you talking about?"

"Mrs. McFie."

"What about Mrs. McFie?"

"I've seen them together, Bert. I've seen him touch her hand and whisper to her, and—"

"You're crazy!"

"No, Bert, no," with growing intensity, bent forward as she spoke, so that now he recognized that peculiar brightness in her eyes, he understood the twitching fingers and the moist lips. The woman scorned, and here was jealousy, hurt, rage, and revenge. Blind, irrational revenge. "That time Guy went to Boston to the medical convention. It was the *same week* that she went to visit someone in New Haven."

"Fran . . . So what, Fran?"

"Don't you *see,* Bert? Don't you *see?"*

He rose and moved about the room. He said, "You can't prove any of this, Fran." And then, "Of course if you knew the dates he was in Boston—the hotel he stayed at—"

"The Statler, and I can look up the dates."

"Why are you telling me this, Fran? Why? *Why?"* though he knew, of course, and he knew why she'd been so fierce in the night's passion, and why now, suddenly, she was willing—even eager to marry him. He felt hurt, angry, even terribly let-down, until a moment later, looking back at her face, then all the possibilities, all the opportunities became horribly clear, so that they shocked even himself, and he had to sit and shake his head again before he could even say the words.

"Fran . . . You want my advice—what you should do. All right, I'll tell you." He twirled the glass between his fingers. His hands were warm despite the cold of the glass. He could scarcely believe he was saying the words—scarcely comprehend the enormity of his own intentions. "I'll tell you, Fran. Go to Larson Whitt. Straight to the sheriff. Tell him the whole story—everything—how you told Doctor Kelsey, how Kelsey said *he'd* take care of it, but you knew he wouldn't."

"The sheriff, Bert—I don't know."

"Only don't say anything about Mrs. McFie. You understand? *Nothing!"*

"But why?"

"Reasons, Fran. Reasons. And why involve her anyway? She seems like a pretty decent sort to me. So why drag her into it?"

"I don't know, Bert. I just don't know."

"Fran . . . Fran . . ." He sat beside her and slipped an arm around her shoulders in the first display of affection he had ever shown her. He patted the pink sweater and said, "Nothing will happen except what's *right,* you understand.

Only what's *just*, and you have no reason at all to cover up for anybody."

"He's covered for us, Bert. Twice."

"Different . . . Different. We were innocent victims. He was protecting us from scandal. But this is homicide, Fran . . . Homicide . . . And we *are* covering the scandal for him. No mention of Mrs. McFie. So on that score we're even. We start all over again. And we start with homicide."

Still Fran didn't know. Bert comforted her, cajoled her. He talked about marriage and going to Boston. They'd go very soon, too. Not even a year from now. Not even six months from now. He'd just remembered an old friend up there who could locate him immediately with a good firm. Everything was going to be fine, and they'd leave East Norton with a good, clean conscience.

"They'll arrest him," Fran said.

"Nothing. Manslaughter. Suspended sentence. Nothing more than he deserves."

"That's right," said Fran. "What he *deserves,*" though she meant something else, and Bert knew and it fitted beautifully. He got her raincoat and placed it around her shoulders. She turned in to him and kissed him with relief and affection and even gratitude, all different from the way it had been before. Then she went down the stairs into the rain.

Bert watched her through the window. She walked with her head lowered, slowly, rather pathetic in the yellow raincoat, until finally she'd left the light of the street lamp and disappeared into darkness.

Bert poured the last of the scotch into his glass. It was a large drink, but God he needed it, considering what he planned to do. Call the Statler in the morning—start making a few discreet inquiries. After that simply wait. And it would not be a long wait either. The Fourth Session of the Grand Jury was already meeting in the courthouse down the street.

"To Boston," he said, and raised his glass. "Mud in your eye, Guy . . . Mud in Guy's eye . . . The good guy Guy with mud in his eye . . . And in yours, Colin Eustis . . . Big-shot District Attorney . . . cock of the walk . . . snotty sonovabitch . . . This one—this one, Colin, will blow you through the roof."

CHAPTER TWENTY

Larson Whitt crossed his legs, straightened them again, then pulled up heavily from the rattan chair and stared out across the bay toward Keever's Point. He could not see the lighthouse though, because the melting snow had been falling all night, and the entire bay was concealed behind the oppressing gray. He glanced at the magazine he'd been skimming—an old copy of *The American Legion*—and remembered that Guy had been in the invasion of France, and probably figured a lot of his patients liked to relive their war experiences, even though he never spoke of his own.

From the inner office he could hear Guy's voice droning on as he spoke to a patient. "Damn it," Larson muttered, and flung down the magazine and sat brooding once more in the rattan chair. He was a tall, gray-haired, gangly man, and his legs stretched halfway across the floor. At the moment he was extremely nervous. He pulled the legs in, pushed them out again, rose again, and stood twisting his beaten gray hat between bony hands as the office door opened and Edna Welles flitted out.

Guy, in shirt sleeves, stepped out behind her. "Just take it easy," he was saying. "You've got enough antiques to last a couple of years. Give yourself and the station wagon a long rest."

"*You* never buy anything," Edna pouted.

"Oh, but I will. I noticed some lovely Sandwich glass in the window."

"It's chipped."

"Then a pickle jug."

"It's a bargain," Edna giggled. She nodded to Larson, went out the door, and tiptoed through the melting snow between the boxwood hedges.

Guy looked after her. He rolled up the shirt sleeves over his brown arms, flexing his fingers all the while. "If she weren't so *eager*," he said, and then, turning, "How are you, Larson?"

"Fine." Larson coughed in embarrassment. "Fine."

"You've got a cough there."

"Guy—this ain't a—professional visit."
"You mean from *my* point of view."
"No, I—look, Guy—I'd like you to come down to the office for a couple of minutes. Talk over a couple of things."
"Can't do it here?"
"Well—it's better at the office." Larson was acutely uncomfortable. He twisted the hat. His boots felt heavy as he moved about. "Thought maybe you knew what it was about already. If you don't, then—then that's the best news I ever heard."
"I know what it's about," Guy said.
"Oh . . . Well, I'm sorry, Guy. God, you don't know."
"Thanks, Larson." Guy went into the office and returned, slipping into his jacket and overcoat.
"It was Fran Walker," Larson said to the window.
"Yes, I thought so."
"She gets hysterical sometimes."
"She's not hysterical." He touched Larson's arm. "As they say, Larson, it's all in the line of duty."
Larson followed him out the door. He wished to God the man would ask some questions or try to explain or put up some arguments. But instead he seemed calm, withdrawn, quite sure of himself.
The windshield wipers moved very slowly over the gray slush as they drove down the winding hill. Melting chunks of ice dropped with a plopping sound from beneath the fenders. Larson watched Guy in the mirror and tried to find some emotion in his expressionless face. "Everybody's gettin' ready for Christmas," he ventured finally.
"Yes." Guy glanced out the window at the Santa Claus driving his reindeer over Main Street, at the unlit blue and red bulbs strung along the store fronts, quite ugly now in daytime, with their black cords more conspicuous than the bulbs themselves. There were Christmas decorations in all the store windows, and on the sidewalk before the supermarket a long row of tightly bound Christmas trees leaned green against a makeshift stand.
"Maybe a white Christmas," Larson tried.
"Could be."
"For Christ's sake, Guy! For Christ's sake!"
"Take it easy," Guy said. "Like Miss Welles—take it easy."
Larson gripped hard on the steering wheel. Why should *he* be upset? It didn't make sense. He'd brought in many men for questioning in his time, and some had argued and some had quivered and a few had fought. Never, though, had he done his duty so reluctantly. And never had the man

beside him seemed so completely oblivious to what might follow. He decided it was all a mistake—something to be cleared up with a few simple questions. But, "She's not hysterical," Guy had said of Fran Walker, and it worried Larson, and he did not look at the doctor's face again.

There were many cars parked along the curb by the courthouse. The Grand Jury was in session, and always then, the town seemed to spring alive for a few days before the twenty-three men got into their cars and drove off to other places. There were children on the green as usual, dressed in soggy snowsuits as they played on the Civil War cannon and tried futilely to lift the pyramid of balls.

"Finally fastened 'em down," Larson remarked. "Kept disappearing, and the Chamber of Commerce had a hell of a time finding new ones. God knows why anyone'd want a cannon ball."

"They make pretty good anchors," Guy said. "I had one myself, only I lost it in the bay."

"Well, I'll be damned!" Larson parked the car and led the way around the courthouse, through a basement entrance to his office.

Judge Manning was there, bald, wizened, hunched over with his kind but disillusioned eyes focused somewhere on the oiled floor. He glanced up, then down again. "Want some coffee, Guy?"

"Thanks."

Larson poured the coffee from an old percolator on a hot plate. He glanced at the picture of his wife and two small children on his desk and thought that Guy had delivered both of them, and what the hell *was* this anyway? What the hell was *happening?*

"I've called Colin Eustis," croaked Judge Manning. "I ought to wait for Crawford—him being County Court Judge —but he's sitting on the Grand Jury, and I guess we won't need him anyway."

"That's a new picture," said Guy, studying Larson's children.

"Taken this fall. They're growing like crazy."

"The little one needs his tonsils out."

"Well, I been meaning to—" And shut up, shut up, will you shut up!

Larson sat at his desk and sipped his bitter coffee. The Judge tapped his cane. Voices rose and fell in dull echoes from the courtroom above, until finally the door was flung open and Colin Eustis strode into the room.

Colin was young and hawk-faced—lean and intense, with thin black hair and sharp, unblinking eyes. He moved in long strides and spoke in a high, strident voice, as though even the most casual remark was of the utmost importance. Larson did not like Colin. He was too ambitious for a good district attorney. He was too sure of himself, always looking for trouble. If he couldn't find it, he made it.

"I'm supposed to be in court," Colin protested. "This hit-and-run thing over in Seaside. The guy was drunk—he ran—it's manslaughter, and the knuckle-heads up there keep right on asking questions." He looked at Guy.

"Doc Montford," said the Judge. "You and Colin know each other?"

"I've heard of him," said Colin. "Seen him around." He sat, stood up, sat down again. He was nervous, excited, trying not to show it, trying to think of exactly how to begin. "All right," he said finally. "Let's get on with it." Then, turning sharply to Guy, "The reason you're here—Miss Walker, a nurse at the Mills Hospital—she came to Larson with some pretty serious accusations. Larson checked with Doctor Kelsey. Kelsey said he was planning to look into it himself, whatever that means. Doctor Peterford'll conduct a coroner's inquest, and if we find what we think we'll find, somebody'll be in for trouble. You know what I'm talking about?"

"I know."

"Then you're the somebody?"

"Yes."

"Homicide," said Colin.

"That's your word."

"That's the *law's* word. But you don't call it that?"

"He died. But I don't call it that."

Colin fixed his unblinking eyes on Guy's face. He was trying to stare Guy down, Larson thought, but it wasn't going to work. Guy stared back at the man, easily, almost gently, and in the end it was Colin who rose and moved restlessly about the oil-smelling room.

A long silence. Colin pulled at his nose, looked out the door, across the small court to the brick wing that held the tiny jail. "You want to make a statement, Doctor? None of this double talk? Just a plain, simple statement?"

"If you like."

"I'll get a stenographer."

"Nothing in writing, because there'd be no possible way for me to honestly express it. But if you're ordering a post-mortem, yes, you'll find morphine, and yes, I injected it."

"That's all?"

"That's all."

Colin glared at him again. He was unnerved, Larson

thought, not quite sure how to handle this. He'd always been confident before. But Guy was getting under his skin and they all knew it—and worse, Colin knew that they knew.

"You knew he'd die," Colin said. "It was willful. Premeditated."

"An act of mercy."

"What's this mercy crap?"

"Don't you know?" Larson felt his temper rising. "Maybe it isn't according to law, Colin. But Larry was Guy's oldest friend, and at least you can *understand* it."

"I understand that if an act is willful and premeditated, then it's murder. *That's* what I understand." Colin swung to Guy. "I thought you were a *respectable* doctor." But then his voice trailed away. Guy had risen very slowly. He strode toward Colin and Colin backed away and squeaked, "Larson . . . Larson!"

Larson did not move. He hoped Guy would bust the bastard in the mouth. But Colin didn't give him the chance. He shrieked, "Get him in jail! Suspicion of murder!" and scurried through the inner door, where he collected his dignity and called out that he'd stick around, except they needed him on that manslaughter indictment. He hurried off down the hallway with his hard-soled shoes clicking fast on the wooden floor.

Judge Manning sighed deep within. Guy sat down again. "I'm sorry," he said, and Judge Manning said, "Pipsqueak . . . Lord, these pipsqueaks," and then, "Sorry, Guy, but Larson'll have to place you under arrest." He pulled to his feet, supporting his almost hunchbacked little body on the cane. "Colin'll go for an indictment, and you'll have to be held for the Grand Jury."

"I understand."

"So get yourself a good lawyer, Guy. Fellow in Boston by the name of Coomstock. Old friend of mine, and you'll need a criminal lawyer. The very best."

"Thanks, Judge."

"That pipsqueak's a hellion. Nothing I can do. Inferior judge, that's all, and what can I do except tell you to get the best lawyer going. And I'll call Coomstock myself." He sat down again. He was winded. He looked tired, Larson thought, and hoped the old man would take it a little easy himself. He was a good old gent, regardless of what people said about his having married his wife for all that dough. He was a kind, gentle defeated old man, and Larson wished to God that in the weeks ahead, old Judge Manning could be sitting in the chair of Judge Crawford Strike.

"Well," he said, "this way, Guy." His boots thudded

dully on the floor as they walked down the short corridor and turned right into the brick wing toward Willie Nye's desk with the two small cells beyond. Willie was sleeping. He snored, jerked upright on his one good leg, and stared at Doctor Montford. "Doc," he said, blinking. "What the hell, Doc?"

"How's the leg, Willie?"

"It's the damp weather. My wife says, 'You hadn't been a crazy fisherman, you wouldn't of jammed it against the pier. You wouldn't end up tendin' a town jail.' So I told her it wasn't *that* leg she had to worry about. Not *that* one." Willie roared at his own joke, then stopped abruptly and blinked back and forth between Guy and Larson, his thin mouth half open, his dry, bent body pivoting on the good leg. "What the hell?" he said. "What the hell?" He was still saying it as he unlocked the cell door and Guy stepped in and sat wearily on the bunk. The barred door clicked shut behind him.

"Anything he wants," Larson said.

"Sure, Larson, sure." Willie blinked again. "Maybe a game of stud—gin rummy, Doc."

"Fine," Guy said. He lay back on the bunk and stared up through the small window.

Larson led Willie down the corridor. He explained simply to the simple, uncomprehending man. "Just treat him good, Willie. He's better off with you than over in Trousdell, and the other cell doesn't get used much anyway. Drunken drivers, disturbing the peace, transient stuff."

"And Stewed Schaeffer. He practically owns that other cell."

Larson frowned. "Well," he said. Then, "God," he said, and walked back to his office. He knew all about that Stewed Schaeffer scandal. It could be a rough deal, putting those two together. But then, all that had happened a long time ago, so why should it make much difference now?

A door closed at the end of the corridor. Willie's shoes made an irregular sound as the man limped back toward his little desk. "You want to play gin, you name it, Doc." The words were forced, halting. "And there prob'ly won't be no one in the next cell to bother you. Except me, maybe. Sometimes I sleep there myself when the wife's sore at me." His chair creaked as he sat down. "Only place I can get a good sleep."

"I'd appreciate it," Guy said, "if you'd tell Larson to get in touch with Doctor Kelsey. Ask him to look after Caesar. Find someone to take over my patients."

"Sure, Doc, sure." Willie cranked at the phone above his little desk, then gave up in disgust and went back down the corridor.

The bunk was hard, but not uncomfortable. Through one of the two barred windows he could see the branches of an oak tree. The light, melting snow dripped from the branches, giving them a black shine.

He closed his eyes. And now, in the dark, the calm left him so that his entire body tensed rigid. Perspiration broke out beneath his shirt, and he knew, of course, that he'd never really been calm at all. It had all been a dull pretense, an unconscious act to prove to himself that nothing bothered him. He had done right, so there was no reason to feel guilty or fear God or the law or his own conscience. And Mar had had nothing to do with it. Mar—the unborn child—they'd merely hastened what he would have done in any case. Sooner or later it would have happened anyway. It had been right. It had been merciful—deliberately consciously merciful—and he would stamp that deep inside his mind, he would never let it go.

He thought about Mar. He thought that he loved her and if this nightmare were ever over, then he'd leave town and meet her somewhere. Perhaps Maine, perhaps New Hampshire. He had no definite plans. Even before today, everything had been vague, uncertain. Mar's love, uncertain. Where Mar was going, uncertain. Where she would meet him, when she would meet him, even *if* she would meet him—all uncertain. There'd been exactly three certainties. He loved her; she would have their child; and he would not let Larry suffer any longer. And when this was over—if it were ever over, if the uncomprehending God and the misunderstanding state would ever allow it to be over—then he would start life again, secure in the integrity of his own actions, the absolute morality of his own personal self.

"Get a good lawyer," Judge Manning had said. Well, Coomstock was supposed to be the best. It was a tricky business. But with luck, perhaps, Coomstock would handle it—force a quick trial, so that Mar would not have to appear in court after her condition became painfully obvious, perhaps keep her from having to appear at all.

He stood and called out to Willie. "Tell Judge Manning to call Boston immediately. *Immediately!*"

Willie's voice came back from the far end of the corridor. "Coming, Doc, coming!" Then Willie appeared, with Bert Mosley walking behind him.

Guy sat down again. Willie said, "Mr. Mosley here, he

wants to see you." He unlocked the door and Bert came in and motioned Willie away down the corridor, out of hearing. He sat in the straight metal chair and brushed back the damp curl in his hair, brushed drops of water from his polo coat. "Rain or snow," he said. "I wish to God it would make up its mind."

Guy studied Bert's face. He saw something confident, almost conniving that he did not like. "What do you want, Bert?"

"You need a lawyer, don't you?"

"I'm getting a lawyer."

"You never should have admitted to *anything,* Guy. Colin would've got his indictment anyway, even if you hadn't confessed. They could conduct a post-mortem, sure. They've already started proceedings. They could drag in the coroner's report and all the witnesses they liked. Still there'd have to be a burden of proof, and there wouldn't have been any burden of proof. Just circumstantial evidence. Sure, if you didn't do it, then someone else did. And after your acquittal they'd have to pretend to be looking around. But they'd never be able to prove anything against *anyone.* You didn't think of that, though. You thought, why get anyone else in trouble? And Jesus, Guy, you're making it tough as hell."

"That's not *your* problem." Guy watched the man closely. "Nothing to do with *you."*

"And considering I never handled a criminal case before."

"And you're not handling this one either."

"So all right, we'll do the best we can."

"Will you get the hell out of here!"

Bert did not move. He said, "One good case. All I want is one good criminal case. Something really controversial, like this one's going to be, and you foul me all up on the very first day." He moved to the window and looked out at the black oak tree. "Well, at least you didn't sign anything."

Guy stared at the back of Bert's polo coat. He felt sick. He said, "All right, Bert, let's have it."

"What?"

"Whatever you're not saying."

"You mean whatever I'm *never* going to say. Not to *anyone.*" Bert turned slowly and his handsome mouth broke into a tiny smile. "I called the Statler Hotel in Boston, Guy. They were very cooperative. A desk clerk who's already forgotten those two names out of the thousands that check in and out—the hundreds he has to look up every day. Doctor Guy Montford, 8B . . . Mrs. Lawrence McFie, 8W. Night of Saturday, December 7th . . ."

Guy closed his eyes.

"A woman scorned, you know. But don't you worry, fella. I'm going to marry that scorned woman, so we'll keep it all right in the family."

Guy dug his knuckles hard into the closed eyelids.

CHAPTER TWENTY-ONE

For eighteen years now, the only murder trial that could be remembered in the county of Pelham was that of one Jacob Sling, a chicken farmer whose application for a bank loan had been rejected. In a show of spite, Sling had shot the First National Bank president to death as he'd come out through the bank's revolving glass doors on his way to a Rotary Club luncheon at the Lincoln Hotel. The assassin had been arrested by Sheriff Potts and prosecuted by Crawford Strike, who had been district attorney at the time. The trial had lasted six days; and seven months after he'd been found guilty, Jacob Sling had been electrocuted in Boston's Charlestown Prison. His wife still lived on the chicken farm. She was an old woman now, who sold "fresh eggs," took in washing, and talked constantly to her dead husband as well as to herself. The children liked to believe her a witch, and stayed clear of the farm on Halloween.

Jacob's arrest had aroused great local interest. The arrest of Guy Montford was the most sensational event in the town's memory.

"If they convict him," Maidie Bolls told her husband, "then you know what *that* will mean?"

"No, what?"

"Oh, nothing—except you'll be in line to take Doctor Kelsey's place."

"I never thought of that."

"You should think of that."

"And I was there that night, too. Delivering Mrs. Roscoe. I even *saw* Guy there."

"With the morphine?" asked Maidie eagerly.

"No, but he's admitted the whole thing, hasn't he? Who had to *see* anything?"

"It would double your patients," Maidie persisted. "I'd

have to return to nursing—become your receptionist—and in another year, when the children are grown, we could take them to Europe."

"Rome," said her husband.

"Antibes. I've always dreamed of Antibes, and it's half fare until they're twelve."

Mrs. Manning coaxed the Judge into looking up Guy's birth date in the town records. Then she consulted her books of astrology and determined that Guy couldn't possibly have done it.

"But he confessed," the Judge told her wearily.

"It was someone else, and Guy's probably protecting him."

"Oh, God!" the Judge said. He went into his library and lowered his little body into a wing-back chair. There was no point in arguing with his wife. She had lived her entire life by the stars—had even married him because her horoscope had convinced her he was the right man. That had been years ago now, and he'd been the wrong man all the time. Everyone said he'd married her for her money. No one knew it had been *her* decision, and a wrong one, and someday her horoscope would prove it to her. Then she'd probably leave him penniless—a crippled old man who had been made wealthy, then poor again, all by the sign of Scorpio.

"I always thought he was such a *nice* man," Ida Primmer explained desperately to all the nurses. "I mean we *all* did."

"We all *do*," the fat nurse grumbled, "except your precious Fran Walker."

"Fran just did what she thought was right."

"Ruining the best doctor I ever worked with?"

Ida did not argue. Actually she felt the same way herself. But she had her loyalty to Fran, and now Fran was suddenly alone. The other nurses shunned her. Even some of the patients refused her attentions. Fran sat alone on her bunk for hours on end, and sometimes she wept silently.

Chet Belknap drank a beer and remarked that come spring he guessed Guy's boat wouldn't be going in the water after all.

"He ain't convicted *yet*," Bill Watts argued.

"He *admitted* it."

"You need *proof*," said Pat, leaning toward them over the bar. "He can deny anything he said once he's in court."

"It's not I ain't for him," said Chet. "Him and Larry—when they were kids, they hung around the boatyard from morning till night. So he done an act of mercy, and it ain't I approve what he done. But I sure am *for* him."

"Same here," said Pat.

"Same here," said Bill Watts.

Stewed Schaeffer came in and said, "Same here," and reminded himself that he must keep out of trouble until the trial was over. If he were drunk, feeling guilty enough, and were put in that cell adjoining Guy's, then he might blurt out what he had said only once to Father Serrano, and never to anyone else at all.

In his shabby little office at the *Chronicle,* Parker Welk worked far into the night. It was a delicate job, this turning a town against one of its most popular citizens. New Englanders—Cape Codders—they thought in terms of their own strict moralities. On the other hand, they were fiercely loyal to any of their own people, and would be especially sympathetic toward Guy Montford.

". . . the law is the law. The church is the church. Should any man take it upon himself to deliberately flout the tenets of these two sacred institutions, then he is not only placing himself superior to all men, but superior to God as well."

Parker read the editorial again. It pleased him immensely. He was writing generally now. Later, after the trial was under way, he would become more specific. He would use the word "defendant," speak outright in terms of the defendant's "admitted act." It would be ticklish, of course. But he already had more insight into the matter than the reporters from the larger cities would ever get. They'd come to *him* for their human interest material. He'd tell them what he liked, save the best parts for himself.

Bert Mosley, for instance. What the hell was Bert doing in this? And Fran Walker? Fran had always had hot pants for Guy. Maybe Guy had brushed her off. Maybe Bert had found out, and put her up to turning Guy in. But that still didn't account for Guy's having retained Bert as his lawyer. There was still something rotten in East Norton, and eventually—somehow—he would find out what it was.

Parker closed up for the night. He went out to the cold air and moved ponderously through the town, taking a long way home that brought him past the jail. There was a light in the barred window. He stood shivering in the cold, staring at the light, thinking, You burned the pictures, you stupid jerk! And what good would your word be now? So you've got nothing on me, and I owe you a little something. I owe you *plenty!* though he was vague as to exactly what harm he owed to Guy Montford, or anyone else, for that matter.

The uncertainty left him as quickly as it had come. His mind stayed on the pictures—gone, lost, never to be seen again. He had others at home, but none so exciting as those of Fran Walker. And it was a shame, even though he'd been relieved at first to know they'd been destroyed—now their loss was a dirty shame, an horrendous tragedy. And walking on in the cold, he dimly understood one particular reason why he hated Guy Montford. Guy had destroyed the pictures, and so, accordingly, had irreparably destroyed all vicarious repetitions of the most exciting few moments of Parker's life.

"Well—" Parker tried to shrug off his despondency. He stopped on a corner four blocks from home, heard the slam of a window, and glanced up at the small neat ranch house where young Nancy Messner lived with her mother and Ralph, her father, who had bought the hardware store and added power mowers and kitchen utensils, and even gifts to the former line of nothing but paints, tools, and plumbing supplies. A light shone in a rear bedroom window. Parker rounded the corner, stood motionless in the quick chilly wind, then edged up onto the rear lawn. His shoes crackled on the freezing ground. He stopped again, peered hastily about, then raised painfully on tiptoe and caught a glimpse of Nancy through the slats of the venetian blinds. She was sitting at her dressing table, putting bobby pins into her yellow hair. She wore a white bra and panties, and though he'd appraised her many times before as she moved innocently about the office, he had never seen her quite so unclothed, quite so feminine, so completely preoccupied in woman's work.

Nancy rose and went into the adjoining bath. When she returned, she had changed into white pajamas.

Parker moved on the four blocks to home.

Polly said, "I guess you heard about Guy Montford."

"I heard."

"It's a crying shame."

"A man without morals," he said. *"That's* not the crying shame!"

"Well, you're no angel, Parker."

"And how would you know *what* I am?"

As usual, she had no answer.

Parker went up to his room and took the little packet of photographs from the locked metal box in his dresser drawer. There were none to replace Fran, though thinking back to only moments before, standing tiptoe on the frozen grass, it seemed possible that someday, perhaps—someday he would find a substitute.

It was earlier, in late afternoon, when Ruth Kiley heard the news from one of the local fishermen. She was sitting at her desk in the tiny cubicle outside Sam's office. The canning machines clanked and roared, so the informing fisherman had to bend over and shout in order to make himself heard. He wagged his head, rolled his eyes, and went off into the deafening roar.

Miss Kiley sat motionless. She glanced at the frosted glass of Sam's closed door. Then, after a long time, she rose and knocked lightly.

"Come in!" Sam shouted.

She went in and closed the door behind her.

Sam looked up from a pile of papers. His jaw twitched. He said, "Yes, Miss Kiley?"

"Sam . . . Sam, Sam, Sam, Sam." She looked out the window at a black dory in the bay, then told him gently, still watching the dory, and waited, holding her breath while the machines clattered dully on beyond the door. "Sam?" she said finally in the roaring silence. "Sam?"

"Ruth . . ." The word choked from his quivering mouth. That was all he said. "Ruth . . ."

She opened the desk drawer and poured him a drink with her own hands. But he did not even want it.

Mrs. O'Hara poked her head through the kitchen doorway. "You want that blue sweater washed?" she asked. " 'Cause I'll have to stretch it overnight if you do."

"There'll be plenty of time, thanks."

"You're taking the morning train, aren't you?"

"No, the afternoon."

"All right then." Mrs. O'Hara disappeared behind the swinging door.

Margreth rose and paced slowly in the living room. She went up the stairs and sat on the bed and looked at Sam's bobbed-haired wife in the gold-leaf frame. It was twenty minutes to five. She'd called Guy twice in the last hour, but had received no answer, though his office hours were two to five. She did not know how he would react to her leaving. But whatever his feelings, she would have to talk with him before tomorrow's train. New Haven and a short stay with her Sweet Briar roommate, a visit to a good, reputable obstetrician this time, who might relieve these nighttime sweats that had seemed to be nerves, but were becoming more frequent as the days went by. Then west or east or north—anywhere but south. She had thought no further than New Haven, no further than the fact that now, with Larry gone, she could not stay in East Norton. Perhaps later she would want Guy to join her and their child, and perhaps later he would still want her, and perhaps they would have some life together after all. But not now, the day after Larry's funeral. Not for months, perhaps. Not ever until it was all completely calm within herself, until she understood how much she honestly loved Guy Montford—until he could clearly understand how he honestly felt himself—how much he would have to leave behind, what sacrifices he would have to make for a sin that had been more hers than his.

She went back down the stairs and lifted the phone once more. This time a woman answered, and she remembered that Guy had a Portuguese cleaning woman who came in two or three times a week.

The woman insisted that Guy was not there. She hesitated, said, "Who is it, please?" then spoke low to a whispering male voice that seemed to be coaching her. Finally her voice came clear again. "I don't know when Doctor Montford will be back. Shall I tell him to call?"

"Please. I'll be home the rest of the day." Mar hung up. She wondered at the strange voice that had been giving instructions. She sat in the living room and stared at the portrait of Sam's great-grandfather, a huge bearded man with bright red cheeks. Peter cackled and she started violently. She felt uneasy, as though something were wrong that she did not understand. Peter cackled again and Mrs. O'Hara called, "Having codfish balls!" and she murmured, "Fine," and thought idly that if she went somewhere into the Midwest, she would never have to eat fish again.

A car pulled into the drive. Sam, she thought. Coming home to drink his drinks and curse his curses. But tomorrow Sam would also be left behind. No more codfish, no more Sam. No more Larry either. No more Guy either, though perhaps sometime Guy, and what *was* the matter? What *was* the matter?

The bell rang.

"I'll get it." She opened the door on a strange man with an intense hawkish face and a thin, restless body.

He took off his hat. "Mrs. McFie . . . I'm Colin Eustis. District Attorney."

"Oh . . . Come in, won't you?"

He said thank you. He came in and looked at the parrot and said, "That's some bird," and Peter said, "Some bird, goddammit!" The man laughed. He twirled the hat. He glanced at Sam's red-cheeked great-grandfather, then turned abruptly and said, "You haven't heard? I was at Doctor Montford's house when you called, so I assume you haven't heard."

"What?" she said. "I'm leaving tomorrow. I wanted to say goodby. What haven't I heard?"

"I'm afraid you won't be leaving, Mrs. McFie."

"What? . . . What, *what?*"

"Doctor Montford has been arrested."

She sat shaky on the sofa. The man's voice was high, harsh, even in his attempt at gentleness. "He made a statement . . . Held for the Grand Jury . . . Thought I'd tell you myself . . . You may be called as a witness . . . Sorry . . . Sorry . . . Conducting a post-mortem . . . Coroner's inquest . . . Your approval . . . make it easier . . . Could force it, though . . . Want justice, don't you? . . . Murder . . . name of mercy . . . Understand that . . . But against the law . . . Prosecute to the fullest . . ." His voice went on, high, harsh, until finally all the words had been said except, "Thank you," and "My sympathies," and "Good night, Mrs. McFie."

She said good night. The door closed. "You think I should make a tomato sauce?" . . . "That will be fine, Mrs. O'Hara." . . . The swinging door creaked and creaked . . . slower slower . . . Peter rustled on his perch . . . The refrigerator opened and closed . . . A car door opened . . . slammed . . . She rose, looked out the window at Sam getting out of his car, shaking off the supporting hand of Ruth Kiley . . . Ruth turned, went off down the street, walking slowly . . . slowly . . . Sam shuffled slowly across the frozen ground . . . up the steps . . . into the hall . . . Standing behind her now, staring at her back . . . His voice boomed shaking in the room. "You *heard?* Have you *heard?*"

"Yes."

A squirrel crossed the lawn. It stopped, dug an acorn from a patch of ice, sat nibbling, one brown eye watching her through the window.

"My wife . . . Now my son . . . Murderers . . . *Murderers* . . . Father and son, both *murderers* . . . Why? . . . *Why?*"

"I'm going to see him."

"Why?"

"Right now."

"You crazy! . . . You stark raving *crazy!*"

"I'm going to see him."

"You don't *believe it!* You hear it and you don't *believe* it!"

"I understand it."

"Nothing to *understand.*"

"I understood Larry . . . I loved Larry . . . Guy understood Larry . . . Guy loved Larry . . . You never loved either. You *needed* your son—at the end, when it was too late . . . I *loved* and I *understand.* And I'm going to *see* him, because he's suffered as much as we have." She turned then. Sam stood quivering beneath his great-grandfather. His mouth worked. He started to speak, couldn't. She said, "Sam," gently now. "Sit down, Sam . . . Have a drink, Sam."

Still he did not move. She walked past him to the hall. She took her coat from the closet, flung it over her shoulders. She moved to the door, looked back, said, "Sam . . . Whatever this is, he's a good man, Sam . . . Whatever this is, in his own way, he cared as much as we did."

Sam sputtered.

Peter squawked.

Sam screamed, "Shut up, shut up!"

Mrs. O'Hara called, "Mashed potatoes, Mr. McFie?"

"Shut up, shut up!"

She went out and closed the door.

CHAPTER TWENTY-TWO

Six miles west of Atlanta, on a rise of ground in the town of Chiddester, there is a large brick southern colonial home called Wild Acres that was built entirely by slave labor in the year 1836. There are four white columns along the wide veranda, and huge chimneys at either end of the rectangular structure. Inside, in one of the massive, high-ceilinged rooms, in the year 1923, a second child was born to Mr. and Mrs. Winston Sloane. She arrived unexpectedly, at the very moment that the doctor was mounting the curved stairway, and was declared a "great beauty" from the moment she let out her first wail to the time, eighteen years later, when her picture appeared along with pictures of five other local girls in the Atlanta papers, announcing the coming out of the season's debutantes at the Henry Grady Hotel.

Everyone in Chiddester said that Margreth Sloane would "marry well." Her mother was so sure of this fact that she spent all her time and energy in making something attractive of her older daughter, Elizabeth Sue, who had slightly protruding upper teeth, and stood round-shouldered when she walked, though Mrs. Sloane always claimed, "She'd be a greater beauty than Margreth if she'd only *try* to hold her head up, and if we could only find a *decent* dentist." She was advised to send Elizabeth Sue to a beauty school, but refused, making her walk around the house balancing books on her head instead, as she also refused to send the child to a famous dentist in New York, maintaining that there was nothing in

New York that they didn't have right here in Chiddester—or at least Atlanta.

Margreth grew up in the shadow of her sister. At first she accepted this secondary role on the basis that Elizabeth Sue was the first-born. Later, though, she gradually understood her mother's attitude. Elizabeth *needed* the attention, whereas Margreth had all the necessary equipment to fend for herself —beauty, grace, gentleness, good teeth, and a straight slim body. Sometimes, as a growing child, Margreth wished that she were ugly. At other times she invented imaginary ailments in order to steal some attention away from her sister. And for a while, during her thirteenth year, she walked about with her head and upper lip stuck forward until her mother said, "Did you sprain your neck, dear?"

"No, this is the way I *feel* like walking."

Her mother told her to stop feeling that way, and turned her attention to Elizabeth again, who had reached the stage where she could carry three books on her head at once.

Few parties were held at Wild Acres while Grandmother Sloane was still living. The old lady did not approve of extravagant spending, and though a senile, half-crazy invalid during the last ten years of her life, she still kept a tight rein on the finances and activities of the plantation, until she died at ninety-six, urging Margreth, in her last coherent words, to always wear clean underwear in case she were hurt in an accident and had to be disrobed in the ugly reality of a hospital.

After the old lady's death, however, Wild Acres became the property of Margreth's father, who felt that the Sloanes had been frugal quite long enough. So from then on there were always a great many guests at Wild Acres, many parties, many "beaux"—always plenty of everything, even after Mr. Sloane died of a heart attack while trying to help one of the Negro servants mend a broken rail in the Virginia post fence that surrounded the entire thirty-six acres. There was a Tennessee walking horse to ride in the proper habit, and a Presbyterian church to attend in the proper hat. Boy friends were entertained in the parlor, and though there were many, Mrs. Sloane thought little of whom Margreth would eventually select from among them. He would, of course, be a "nice young man" from Atlanta or Knoxville or Montgomery or Richmond. He would have graduated from the University of Virginia or Alabama or North Carolina, and would probably have family money, and perhaps a position, too, as her husband had always had his own little business just to feel as if he were "doing something." Mrs. Sloane was always a little vague as to what a Southern gentleman was *supposed* to do—now that slavery had been abolished and the cotton fields no longer bloomed—except drink a little, fish occasionally, and pass most of his time attending to the wants of his wife.

Accordingly, she did not think too much about it.

One particularly suitable young man was courting Margreth at the time that Elizabeth Sue decided it was imperative she marry soon, before people started "talking." And since it was apparent that Mar had no interest in her suitor, no intention of being foisted on anyone, Mrs. Sloane arranged for Elizabeth to be on hand each time the young man called for Margreth, until eventually he settled for second best and took his new bride off to Chattanooga, where they lived happily and Elizabeth gave birth to three lovely children—all dark-eyed and even-teethed and straight-backed—all "Sloanes."

After Sweet Briar, Margreth fell in love with a soldier from somewhere up North. Mrs. Sloane fought the marriage, then gave in reluctantly when she realized she had no influence over her younger daughter at all. Margreth was rebelling, in her own way, quietly, without fuss, but firmly too, so all Mrs. Sloane could say was, "Well, we'll make the best of it." And after that, she always introduced Larry McFie as "Major" McFie, though he was quite obviously a second lieutenant, and even encouraged him and Margreth to live in the guest room at Wild Acres until Larry got "settled" somewhere.

He had finally "settled" at Dekker and Lobe, an Atlanta real estate firm that handled only the largest of estates. He seemed happy there, and eventually bought a house in Atlanta proper, so that he and Margreth came out to visit on weekends only, and the rest of the time Mrs. Sloane was alone in the great house, looking forward to Sunday afternoons and the occasional visits of Elizabeth Sue and her nice Southern husband and her charming children, wondering idly, a little "dirtily" she admitted, why Larry and Margreth did not have children of their own.

"Why?" she asked Margreth one Sunday afternoon over tea and oatmeal cookies. "What *is* the matter, dear?"

"Nothing. I just don't seem to get pregnant, that's all."

"Is it—" Mrs. Sloane had looked away when she asked it. "Does he use those *things*—you know?"

"We're trying, Mother."

"Well, I'm sure *you're* all right."

"Please, Mother."

"Your father used those things from the day we were married. But we had two children anyway. 'I'm playing the odds,' he used to say. 'You want two children, we try not to have any. If we didn't fight it, we'd have a dozen.' "

"Yes, Mother."

"Your father was an extremely virile man."

"Someday I'll have a child, Mother. Someday—I'll have a child."

Someday she would have a child.

She walked on through the frozen streets in the winter's early dark, and it was odd to remember that conversation now, almost amusing to imagine what her mother would say if she went home and announced that she had finally succeeded. "He's a Sloane, isn't he, Mother? A Montford and a Sloane. And who are the Montfords? Well, now that's a long story, Mother—that is a very long story."

Mr. Ralph Messner looked up as she passed the hardware store. He was bringing in the snow shovels and sleds from the sidewalk, and though she did not know him, he looked after her with intense interest. Farther along she passed Fran Walker, moving lethargically with her eyes fixed staring at the pavement. She said, "Hello, Miss Walker." But Fran only gave her a startled look and walked on faster into the shelter of the dark.

"They *know,*" she thought. "They all *know*, and they're all *wondering,* and they'll all be watching and thinking their own thoughts."

She pushed "they" from her mind—Sam and Colin Eustis and Mr. Messner and Fran Walker—and everyone else she had met before and might meet again in the days ahead. Her present concern was for Guy and her child and for no one else. She wondered why she did not feel shocked or angry, why she did not hate Guy as Sam did, despise him so that she wanted nothing more than to see him pay and pay for what he had done. But she stopped wondering in a moment, for she had known the answer all along. She knew why it had happened, and she knew, too, that the responsibility was mainly hers.

As she turned past the cannon balls and the black iron statue of the Union soldier, Bert Mosley came down the sanded cement walk from the rear of the courthouse. He walked with his head thrust forward, the polo coat flopping about his knees. He glanced at her briefly, stopped, started off, then turned back again.

"Mrs. McFie?" He wore no hat and his blond hair was uncombed, ragged curls above his handsome face. "I'm Bert Mosley . . . Remember—we've met in church."

"Oh . . . Yes, I remember."

"I'm Guy's lawyer."

"Lawyer?" She stared at the complacent eyes. "I don't understand."

"You mean this isn't my line? I'm not a criminal lawyer? Well, Guy and I have discussed the matter, and he's decided to retain me anyway."

"I see." It seemed that Bert was smiling. There was something unsaid in all this, and she felt exposed, naked under the watching eyes.

"You're going to see him?" Bert said.

"Yes."

"You're not shocked—angry?"

"I think," she said carefully, "I think I understand."

"You want him acquitted?"

"That's for the courts. I told you, Mr. Mosley, I understand."

"Fine." Bert smiled openly. "Fine. Then I think you *should* see him. To hell with what anyone thinks!"

She closed her eyes, opened them slowly on the still-smiling face. "What do you mean by that, Mr. Mosley?"

"Nothing. Except your facing him—understanding him—it's good for public sympathy. If not for acquittal, at least to help lighten the sentence." He paused. "I just thought I'd tell you—I don't intend to put Guy on the stand at all. I mean, after all—under the circumstances—"

"Circumstances?"

"His verbal confession. There's no telling what he'd say if Colin got the chance to cross-examine him—considering his attitude."

"And what is his attitude, Mr. Mosley?"

"That it was right. He'd do it again."

"Perhaps he would."

"Under the circumstances?"

"Yes—under the circumstances."

Bert drew a deep breath. "Well—I have to pick up some lawbooks at the office—be burning the midnight oil." He nodded and started off, his hands thrust deep in the pockets of his polo coat. She called him back and said, "How soon?" and Bert said, "Guy asked the same question. I don't understand the rush, but I'm pushing it as fast as I can. So if we're lucky, it'll be early in January." This time he was not smiling. Rather he looked slightly puzzled before he shrugged it off and strolled away.

Larson Whitt said she was a brave woman to come to his office like this. He said, "A lot of us understand—the way him and Larry felt about each other. But for you to understand, too. *You,* of all people."

"Guy was Larry's doctor," she explained. "And his friend. And he was my friend, too, in a strange town, when my husband was dying and I needed friendship. Whether he acted rightly or wrongly—that's a matter for the jury."

"You're a brave woman," Larson repeated. "You're a kind woman." He turned away, embarrassed at his own show of sentiment. "You can see him in here. I'll have to lock this outer door, and I'll be out there in the corridor myself. Not that he'd try to run, or even want to. But the law, you know, and—well, he's been mighty quiet all afternoon. And nothing'd cheer him up more than for you to talk to him—maybe even forgive him." He started out, stopped. "Not that he did right, you know."

"I know."

"And that's the whole trouble here. There's a lot of us that's sympathetic. But you'll go a long way in this town before you find someone who thinks he done right." Larson shook his head, said, "Well—a minute now—" and went off down the oiled floor and around a bend in the corridor.

Mar sat in the swivel chair at Larson's desk. She looked at the photo of his two grinning children. She looked at the case of rifles along the wall, and thought of those movies where the criminal smashes the glass case, grabs a gun and ties up the sheriff, then breaks out and drives off fast in a getaway car with his "moll" beside him. She was Guy's "moll." The murdered and the moll, with no getaway car and no fierce hatred of society, but only a great sadness that things should sometimes be the way they are.

The inner door opened and Guy stepped into the room. He was in shirt sleeves; he needed a shave; his eyes were black haunted holes, and he moved heavily, as though carrying a great weight. Larson shut the door behind him and after a long time Guy said, "Mar . . . Mar . . ." He moved toward her, and she rose and put her arms around him. He seemed completely helpless, a child looking for comfort. "It's all right," she told him. "All right, all right."

"You forgive me? You understand why—*why*?"

"Yes . . ."

"But I would have done it anyway." Again and again, "I would have done it anyway." He sat wearily and she gave him a cigarette. He dragged deep, blew out the smoke in a great cloud.

She sat opposite him in the swivel chair. "You mustn't blame yourself, Guy. Not yourself."

"Would have done it anyway."

"And you mustn't think of me or the baby or anything

except yourself—nothing except getting out of here and going back into practice."

"Understand, Mar. I'm tired, that's all. Deep, aching, dying tired. But it's not guilt, you understand? Not conscience, you understand?"

"Guy . . ."

"So maybe the baby made it happen quicker—maybe *you* made it happen quicker. But it would have happened if I'd never met you—never seen you before in my life! Do you understand that? Do you—*understand*?" His words were low, tense, aching to be believed. He stared at her, gripped hard at her wrist. "Mar!"

"Yes, I believe you."

"Then hate me if you want to. Why don't you hate me?" His fingers relaxed. He said, "Sorry . . . I'm tired, that's all." And then, after a long pause, "What are we going to do?"

"I told you—somehow—some way—you're going to get out of this and go back into practice."

"No, us—*us*."

"Later. I've always said that. Later."

"All right then. All right." A pause, and then he raised his head and looked deep into her eyes. He said, "Have you seen a doctor, Mar?"

"No."

"You've *got* to see a *doctor*."

"I was going to. Actually, I was leaving for New Haven tomorrow. But now I'll have to wait. I can't leave town, and I can't go to any doctor for miles around. Now—after this—even in New Haven I'd have to use a different name."

"Your eyes are too bright. You're *too* healthy. Your cheeks are *too* rosy."

"The cold air."

"No, you've got to have a check-up."

"All right, I will. Yes, I will." She watched his hands clench together, unclench as he raised the cigarette to his mouth, and she thought the guilt was still there, deep inside him, only he was fighting it hard with all the cold rationality he could summon. "Bert Mosley," she said finally. "He knows something."

"No . . ."

"Not everything, but *something*."

"No, Mar."

"I just met him, Guy. I could *tell*."

"All right, all right."

"About us. And he blackmailed his way into defending you."

"Yes. But it won't go any farther. Fran and Bert. And Bert wants desperately to win, so he wouldn't cut his own throat."

"He doesn't know about the baby?"

"No."

More silence. She rose and moved about slowly in the room. She stood behind Guy's chair and touched his bristling hair and said, "I could kill myself for having done this to you."

"I told you, I *told* you."

"Trying to run off like that. Then breaking down and saying I'd have to tell Larry about us. My own weakness. Honesty is sometimes a weakness."

"Stop it, stop it, *stop it*!"

She came around in front of him. She knelt on the oily floor and put her head in his lap and spoke into his knees. "Oh, Guy . . . dear Guy . . . dear Guy . . ." And then, after a long time, she pulled to her feet and moved aimlessly about, touching everything, the chair and desk, the Currier and Ives calendar and the photo of Larson's children and the glass case that held the row of guns. She said, "We'll crash this joint, Mac . . . We'll blow this town, Joe . . . Nobody'll take *us* alive . . ." She laughed and said, "I'd like to leave Sam's, but I can't do that . . . It wouldn't look right . . . I'll stay, try to live with him . . ."

"I love you, Mar."

"I'll have to think. I won't destroy you. I won't do that."

"I love you, Mar."

A knock on the door. She called, "Just a moment!" then turned back and said, "I won't see you for a while. I can't come here again."

"I know . . ."

"And after it's over—even then, I'll—I'll have to go away."

"I'm going with you. If they won't let me—not for a long time—then I'm coming later."

"Guy . . ."

"Anywhere you say. Anywhere on earth."

The knock again, and she said, "Good-by, Guy . . . Good-by, dear Guy," then kissed him quickly on the mouth, strode fast to the door, and opened it on Larson Whitt.

Larson was embarrassed. "Sorry, Mrs. McFie."

"Yes," and "Thank you," and "Good-by, Doctor."

"Good-by," Guy said.

She went out to the early night. She moved down the walk, and her heels crunched lightly on the sand.

CHAPTER TWENTY-THREE

December Twenty-Third, 1957, Monday, Court called at 10:00 o'clock A.M. Honorable Crawford Strike, Judge, presiding.

Eo die, the District Attorney, Colin S. Eustis, Esq., moves the court for leave to submit Bill of Indictment Number Thirteen, December Sessions, to the Grand Jury.

Eo die, Leave is granted the District Attorney to submit the above Bill of Indictment Number Thirteen, December Sessions, charging Guy Montford with Murder, to the Grand Jury.

Eo die, Court adjourned at 5:30 o'clock P.M.

> The Grand Jury of the County of Pelham, by this indictment, accuses the defendant of the crime of murder, committed as follows: The defendant on December 16, 1957, in the County of Pelham, the Commonwealth of Massachusetts, did willfully, and with premeditation, inject morphine into the body of Lawrence McFie to cause his death.

Snow fell in huge, lethargic flakes outside the barred window, and if he stood to one side, peering diagonally past the brick corner of the jail, he could see the red and green lights along the store front and the first three reindeer of Santa's sleigh riding high over Main Street. Comet and Cupid, Dunder and Blitzen. He could not remember them in proper order, though that first one leading the herd was Rudolph, of course, added two years ago at the insistence of the grammar-school children.

It was Christmas Eve. The stack of trees had all but disappeared from in front of the supermarket, leaving only a few rejected scrawny spruce for the latecomers. The town was busy despite the falling snow. Most of the stores stayed open late, and everyone wore galoshes and laughed and kicked the snow in pleasure as they walked, carrying their gay packages gingerly in both hands.

Willie limped in with an armload of mail. "Don't know where you'll keep it all," he said, and dumped the small sack on the cell floor. "You already got more cards than anyone else in town."

Guy sat on the bunk and opened the cards. He felt rather embarrassed for the senders. "Merry Christmas . . . Happy

New Year." The best of intentions. Yet there was something ironic in the greetings all the same. Most of them contained some small note of encouragement. "We're with you," or "Don't let it get you down," or "Your friends haven't forgotten you." Mrs. Coffin had written a little poem. Mrs. Manning assured him that according to his horoscope, he would enjoy a prosperous New Year. Many patients advised him of the progress of their illnesses, and added that though Doctor Bolls was taking care of them now, they would, of course, want Guy back again as soon as this business was over and done.

A few cards were unsigned. They read, "Lousy Christmas," or "I hope you hang," or "Who do you think you are—God?" There was a card from Fran Walker, too, with a brief, forlorn note: "Dear Guy . . . Please don't hate me for what I did. I don't understand it myself really, and I hope everything works out beautifully. I'm going to marry Bert and we're going to Boston, so I'll never bother you again."

There were two packages. One, a bottle of Ballantines 17-year-old scotch from the "Gang at Pat's," the other a beautifully carved clipper ship in a large bottle. There was no card attached, but Guy knew it was from Mar. He set it on the window ledge and watched the snow fall softly behind it.

At nine the church bells rang. And an hour later he heard the voices of the choir as they wound through the streets singing carols. He could imagine Mrs. Coffin leading the group. She would blow frantically on her pitch pipe and stumble slightly in her heavy overshoes. Nothing was different in the town outside. And he remembered other Christmas Eves—the very old ones when he'd gone with his father to midnight services at St. Joseph's; and the Christmas Eves with Julia, when they'd sat alone before a huge fire and drunk eggnogs (which they both detested, but drank as a kind of ritual), until after it was all gone, then they'd laughed with relief and opened a bottle of champagne and exchanged presents and made warm love on the hooked rug before the fire.

He remembered a Christmas in a farmhouse in France. Everyone had gotten very drunk, and he'd slept affectionately with a young French girl who'd kept saying, "Noël, Noël," until the final moment, when she'd closed her eyes and spoken very slowly in halting English. "Good will toward men."

A Christmas Eve three years ago at a party given by Mrs. Manning; two years ago at Doctor Kelsey's; only last year, when a Christmas tree had caught fire in a house on the road to Pirate's Cove. A child had been severely burned, and he'd stayed the entire night in the hospital until all danger had passed. Then he'd walked wearily into the reception room where the parents waited. "She'll make it," he'd said. "And Merry Christmas," he'd said, and the parents had wept openly in each other's arms.

There'd been thirty-eight Christmas Eves. He remembered a great many of them, except for those few during his teens, which he did not want to recall, so had blanked out entirely, as he'd blanked out all those aching years after his father's death, when he'd lived alone with a mother whom he'd hated —though later he'd forgiven her, so that the hatred was only a dull acceptance of this woman who had deceived his father, who had literally killed him.

The door clanked open and Willie entered with two cheese glasses. "Christmas cheer," he said. "Ain't in the rules for me to set in here and have a drink with you. But it's Christmas Eve, and I say to hell with the rules." He opened the bottle of scotch and poured them both a large one. "Merry Xmas," he said.

"Merry Christmas, Willie."

"And wait'll you set teeth in your Christmas dinner tomorrow. Pat's doing it up with all the trimmings—roast turkey, cranberry sauce, sweet potatoes, mashed potatoes, pumpkin pie, mince pie—we're having ham at my place. I hate ham, especially with pineapple. But it's turkey on Thanksgiving and ham with pineapple on Christmas, and my wife don't give a damn what I like."

They drank the entire bottle of scotch. Willie got quite drunk, and went on in long broken sentences about his wife. "It must be the change of life or menopause or whatever you call it. Starts crying all the time, and wants to go to bed all the time, and that's all right except when I'm drunk. And I don't get it, Doc. A few drinks and I'm not for anything in skirts, except my own wife. And with her I'm limp . . . plain limp. And that gets her crying all the more . . . Says I think she's old . . . I think she's a hag . . . God, God, I don't know . . . Why *is* that? . . . Have another drink . . . Merry Christmas . . . Must be the change of life . . . Happy New Year . . . Turkey and creamed onions and Indian pudding . . . God, I hate ham with pineapple! Season's cheer . . . Yuletide greetings . . . Me-r-ry Christmas!"

Willie gave out. He leaned back on the bunk with his head against the wall, and in a moment he was snoring.

Guy took the key from Willie's pocket. He unlocked the barred door, went out to the corridor, and unlocked the door to the adjoining cell. He carried Willie into the cell and laid him on the bunk. He returned the keys to Willie's pocket, started back toward his own cell, then paused and stared fascinated at the wall-box phone above Willie's desk. Outside the church bells tolled in the snowy night, and a horse-drawn sleigh, filled with laughing children, jingled merrily along the street.

He edged toward the phone, lifted the receiver, and spoke in a flat voice when the operator answered the ring. His heart beat up fast in his chest as he waited. And then in a moment he heard Mar's voice, soft, inquiring.

"Hello?"

"Mar . . . I know you can't talk."

"No . . ."

"I just wanted to say Merry Christmas."

"Merry Christmas," she said.

"I got the little ship in the bottle. I put it on the sill, and with the snow behind it, it looks like it's sailing through a storm."

"It'll make out," she said.

"Yes . . . And so will we." He wet his lips. His hand trembled on the receiver and he thought that they were only blocks apart, and if things were different they could be together now, riding in that children's sleigh or making love on a hooked rug somewhere, or simply walking through the snow in heavy boots, holding mittened hands and laughing or talking or saying nothing at all. "I love you," he said. "Merry Christmas and I love you, I love you. I love you, I love you."

Sam's voice sounded faintly, off. "Who is it, Margreth?" And Margreth said, "My mother, calling from Atlanta." Then close to the phone again, "I wish you were here . . . Lord, I wish I could see you. I wish, I wish . . ."

"I love you," he said again, then hung up slowly and stood motionless beside the desk.

Willie snored. The church bells tolled. Guy went back to his cell and closed the door. It locked shut automatically. He lay down on the bunk and watched the snow fall softly behind the tiny ship in the clear glass bottle. The bells rang on in the night air, and far off the children's choir sang, "Oh, come, all ye faithful, joyful and triumphant . . ."

On Monday, the 6th of January, afternoon court was called early at 1:00, since Judge Crawford Strike, Colin Eustis, Bert Mosley, and everyone else concerned, were anxious to get a jury empaneled as quickly as possible. Over the past three days of court, sixty-nine veniremen had been examined from the hundred-odd members of the panel that still crowded the inadequate courtroom. Judge Strike had excused twenty-eight for cause; Bert had used seventeen peremptory challenges, and Colin Eustis, eleven.

It had been obvious from the beginning that Bert was

worried about getting too many Catholics on the jury, Colin about a jury composed of those who, though they did not know Guy Montford personally, were still influenced in his favor, perhaps subconsciously, through his local reputation, or even that of his father before him.

In the end Colin settled on the fact that practically no one in Pelham County had never heard of the Montfords, and he had at least succeeded in getting a majority of Catholics empaneled—seven, plus the alternate.

It was a long, wearing afternoon. The out-of-town reporters had already arrived—nine in all: two from Boston, two from New York, one from Providence, New Haven, and Hartford each, along with a representative from both the A.P. and U.P. They sat at a long table at the left (the one normally used by members of the bar waiting to come before court), and were quite obviously bored with the town and the long afternoon proceedings. They stretched their legs and scratched their ears. They studied the prospective jurors in the ten tiers of oak seats that faced the judge's huge walnut bench; they stared at the high churchlike windows, the cream-colored walls, bare except for the pompous portraits of past judges.

One reporter was a woman, and sometimes, during a lull in the proceedings, while Colin studied the list of witnesses on the back of the bill of indictment, Bert found his own eyes wandering to this single female. She was in her late twenties or early thirties, dressed smartly in a tailored beige suit. She wore a small, tasteful hat on her short-clipped brown hair, dark-rimmed glasses across her firm, chiseled face. Her fingernails were long, painted red, and the enamel caught the sun through the tall windows as she removed her glasses, poked a stem between her teeth, took it out again, and laughed suddenly in a hoarse, almost masculine voice as the reporter beside her bent near to whisper.

A career woman, Bert decided. One of those pseudo-sophisticated, dirty-joke-telling, unshockable, martini-drinking women who live almost exclusively in a world of men. He did not like her. There was nothing soft, nothing yielding, nothing feminine about her at all. He did not like her, and yet his eyes kept turning back to the efficient fingers making notes, the tiny hat on the brown hair without a strand out of place. He imagined she bathed twice a day and spread cold cream on her face at night; she did setting-up exercises to keep in trim for herself alone. She viewed the world cynically, sexlessly, and could wither a man with a single contemptuous look or word—or could sleep with him in cold deliberation, refusing to allow herself even the slightest bit of enjoyment.

It was five o'clock. The clerk's gavel pounded three times

and Judge Strike announced that court was adjourned until 10:00 the next morning. The hard-won jury filed out a side door behind the two raised rows of chairs, and Colin Eustis strode over from the Commonwealth's table and smiled grimly. "Satisfied, Bert?"

"They'll do."

"See you in court." Colin strode away fast, his briefcase swinging in against his legs.

Bert stuffed papers into his own attaché case and started for the door. A group of reporters caught him in the hall. "Nothing to say," he told them. "No statements." He remembered seeing that kind of scene in the movies and became increasingly aware of his own sudden importance.

Parker Welk stood silent among the men from larger papers. He avoided Bert's eyes. The bastard, Bert thought. He'll try to kill us. Guy and me—he'll go after both of us. He shrugged into his polo coat and went down the steps into the January cold, then stopped when the single woman reporter approached him from a waiting position around the corner of the building.

"Mr. Mosley?"

"Nothing to say."

"About yourself, perhaps."

"Myself?"

"I'm Sylvia Stein . . . *Boston Recorder*."

"Yes?"

"I thought perhaps a feature on you. I got a story on Mr. Eustis yesterday. Now one on you, and the readers will have an inside look at both the attorneys."

"I see."

"It's important, you know. One of those controversial cases that hits every paper in the country."

"I know."

"So?" she said. "So?" She was watching him with those cynical, unblinking eyes, and he liked her even less now that he'd spoken to her. "Well?" she said. "Well, Mr. Mosley?"

"Not now."

"Tonight. If the actual trial starts tomorrow, I'd like to get it done before morning."

"All right then. Tonight. I have an office over the hardware store. The center of town. In fact you can see the doorway from here. The third street light there, past the intersection." As he pointed across the street, she moved up behind him, her eyes following the direction of his finger. She was quite close and it occurred to him that she gave off no warmth at all. "Eight o'clock," he said, and strode away fast toward Pat's.

The boys at the bar were curious. "What the hell does Guy want *you* for?" said Chet Belknap. "He's gone crazy?" said Pat. "You got something on him?" said Bill Watts.

"Now what's that supposed to mean?"

"Don't get sore," Bill said.

"I'm not sore. I'm just asking."

"Then you *do* have something." Everyone laughed and Bert left them to sit alone at a corner table. He ordered a T-bone steak and mashed potatoes. He drank a beer while he waited and remembered Guy's face that night of the arrest, when he'd mentioned the two nearby rooms at the Statler Hotel. First Guy had sat there motionless, digging his knuckles into his eyes. Then finally he'd stood up very slowly. His hand had jerked out and grabbed Bert by the coat collar. He'd said, "You sonovabitch, Bert! You lousy, sneaky, small-fry sonovabitch!" Guy was not heavy, but tall, and Bert had backed away, suddenly afraid. The man looked peaceful, tractable enough. But when he was angry, a kind of fierce, awesome strength went all through him so that he seemed almost dangerous.

Finally he'd let go of Bert's collar. He'd said, "O.K., Bert. O.K., take the case. But *win* it."

Christ, Bert thought now. Christ! Win a case with a defendant who's already made a verbal confession, and given half a chance, would make it again. Christ. He finished the beer and dug into the steak. It was tough. He started to complain, then changed his mind. Everything was tough. Colin was tough and Guy was tough and Judge Crawford Strike was honest, but tough, and that Sylvia Stein was tough. To hell with Sylvia Stein!

He finished his dinner, went out to the night, and walked slowly toward his office. He could feel the tension in the town around him—in the faces of those who passed and nodded, in the furtive glances of the people he did not know. He went up the narrow stairs to his office above the hardware, inside to the tiny cluttered room. On weekends, when the heat was turned off, it was always cold. Now it was hot, almost muggy. He took off his coat and settled down with Wills' *Principles of Circumstantial Evidence*. He'd already pored over Bishop's *Criminal Procedure* and Wharton's *Criminal Evidence,* and there were a number of other books he'd have to look into before the morning. He began doubting his own impetuous plan for a fast trip to fame and glory. Suppose he made a fool of himself? Suppose he lost out on everything, all the way down the line? He had an approach worked out, but it was quite weak and obvious, really; and though he would use it, of course, in the long run he would have to depend entirely on the inherent sympathy of the jury. Yet he did not dare put Guy on the stand in his own defense. It was a mess—an impossible rotten mess.

He read a few lines of the lawbook, closed it again. He had told Miss Stein to come at eight o'clock, and it was already five after. Funny, she didn't *look* Jewish. Yet Stein was a Jewish name, wasn't it? Once, in law school, he'd known a Jewish girl. She'd been black-haired and black-eyed with a very soft body and a beautiful complexion. Miss Stein had a nice complexion, but her eyes and hair were brown, and her body had looked firm, almost hard beneath the tailored suit. Well, all Jews didn't *have* to be dark. It wasn't a *rule,* was it?

The knock was firm, almost loud. He rose and glanced at his face in the small, cracked mirror. He brushed back his hair, wet his finger, and wiped a tiny smudge of ink from his chin before he opened the door.

Miss Stein said, "God, it's cluttered," and "God, it's hot!"

"Over the hardware," he explained. "Before Ralph Messner bought the place, it was owned by an old man who was a plumber on the side. Every time he had a spare minute, he'd stick in another radiator. But he didn't believe in thermostats."

"God," she said and took off her coat. She lit a cigarette with those long, red-tipped fingers, sat and crossed her legs. It was not sexy—just plain efficient. He imagined she would be efficient about everything—housework and sex and bearing children and raising them, and eventually dying. "Now," she said, flipping open a notebook, wetting a pencil with the tip of her tongue. "*You*—are Bertram Mosley. A native?"

"No, Boston. Belmont, actually."

"I'm Brookline," she said, not even looking up. "The Jewish bedroom."

"B.U.," he said.

"Same here." She made a note, then raised her eyes under the horn-rimmed glasses. "What in hell are you doing in this place?"

"Oh, I don't know. I came one summer on vacation and just—stayed."

"I see." Her eyes watched him, unblinking. "And now it's paying off."

"Now look, Miss Stein—"

"Oh, cut it out, fella! It's common talk around here that you've never handled a criminal case. Now every word you say in that courtroom's going to get printed across the country. Handle it right, and you've got a small name for yourself."

"Well—" He was angry. He felt uncomfortable. He said, "You jump right in, don't you?"

"But I don't print what I find at the bottom of the barrel."

"O.K.," he said. "I happen to be a friend of Doctor Montford's."

"It makes sense."

"He already made a confession—but there are certain technical points."

"I said it makes sense."

"And after it's over, if it *does* do any good, yes, I *am* getting out of here. I'm going back to Boston."

"Look me up."

"Sure—I'll look you up." He felt the glass wall between them. He was angry, saying what he shouldn't have said because of the anger. These career women! These superior, phony women, who always tried to put a man on the defensive! He stood and moved about in the hot room. "I don't think you want any more."

"We haven't even started."

"Personally, I've finished."

"O.K." Her brown eyes narrowed behind the glasses. "I wish you luck anyway. This Montford seems like a nice fellow."

"He is."

"So all right." She rose and pulled down the jacket of her suit. He noticed that her breasts were firm beneath, and wondered if she wore falsies, decided she wasn't the type.

"Funny thing," she said, groping for a cigarette, "this Parker Welk fellow—editor of the town's *own* paper. He hopes they hang the guy."

"Yeah . . ."

Bert started to laugh. He couldn't stop. Miss Stein was waving for a match, and he was still laughing when he finally found her one and lit her cigarette. He was still laughing when the light knock sounded and Fran stepped in. He shook out the match and stopped laughing.

Fran and Miss Stein appraised each other.

Bert said, "Miss Stein . . . Miss Walker . . ."

Miss Stein put out a hand and Fran took it hesitantly. "I was just leaving," said Miss Stein. She moved toward the door, stopped, said, "Miss Walker," with her eyebrows going up. *"Fran* Walker?"

"Yes."

"Aren't you the one—"

"She's the one," Bert said hastily. "A State witness, but we happen to be good friends."

There was a long, silent moment. He knew Miss Stein was trying to make something of all this, though there was nothing to find, no matter how carefully she scraped that barrel. He wasn't thinking about that anyway. Instead, he was noticing how very young and childish Fran looked and talked and acted when compared to this woman who was a match for any man.

Miss Stein said, "Well, good night," and left. Her heels sounded in the hall.

Bert sat and listened to the heels. Fran said, "Why didn't you tell her we were engaged?" and he said, "I don't know. I just didn't." He was irritated. Fran was upset, and that irritated him even more. God, she was *always* upset. One thing or another. Sad, jealous, passionate, resentful. Never without emotion of one kind or another. Now it was repentance. "I didn't *know*, Bert . . . All the trouble I'd be causing . . . I'm so *sorry* for Guy . . . I shouldn't have *done* it, Bert . . . You shouldn't have *told* me to . . . That awful Grand Jury—all those men I didn't even know except for Mr. Polk at the bank—just staring at me, and I had to answer all these questions and Doctor Kelsey was there, too, and he kept looking at me like I was a worm or something, and even the coroner, Doctor Peterford—I hardly know him because he lives in Pirate's Cove, except he's been to the hospital sometimes—*he* looked at me like I was a worm, too, and oh, Bert, oh, Bert . . . Bert . . . I don't understand. First you want me to go to Larson, and then suddenly you're Guy's lawyer, and I don't know . . . I don't *know*."

She started to cry. She sat and sobbed into her handkerchief, and Bert rose and put an arm around her shoulders. "There now . . . there now . . . Guy *wanted* me to defend him. And no matter what I think personally, it's my duty to do everything I can to get him off."

"Oh, I hope you do, Bert! I hope so! But now I'll have to say everything all over again!"

"Just the truth about what happened that night. But not a word about what we know between us."

"And we *are* going to Boston, aren't we, Bert? We *are* going to get *out* of here."

"Sure," he said. "Sure . . . sure." He kept patting her shoulder, thinking all the time that Miss Cold-fish Sylvia Stein would never cry in front of anyone.

CHAPTER TWENTY-FOUR

". . . I trust that is clear," Judge Crawford Strike was saying, "clear not only to the attorneys and jury, but to the press and every person in this courtroom. Euthanasia—mercy-killing—is *not* an issue here. The defendant is on trial for murder as set forth in the indictment. He is to be tried on that indictment and judged on that indictment. And I warn the defense attorney again—the court will not tolerate any attempt to baldly or circuitously imply that the crime in question is a matter of *malum prohibitum*—that is, wrong because it is forbidden, rather than wrong in itself.

"Now it is true—quite obviously—that in a case such as this, there will be those who feel a special sympathy for the defendant. There may be those who actually condone the act of which he stands accused. In the empaneling of the jury, certain veniremen openly stated that they could not view the act as a crime in any way. What their feelings *were*—what yours *are* on this subject—does not enter into this case. The law makes no allowance for so-called euthanasia. There are three degrees of murder, and the defendant is here on trial for having committed murder in one of those three degrees. He is guilty or he is not guilty. And I repeat again, the question 'Is there an eternal law that transcends men's best intentions and even men's laws, and if so, how are men to interpret it?'—that question will not be discussed within this courtroom . . ."

There was more. From his chair beside Bert's at the small oak table to the left, Guy heard it only dimly, as an echoing voice from another room. He knew he should concentrate on every word; he should think carefully, follow all the proceedings with the intense interest and apprehension of a man on trial. Yet his mind refused to focus on the whole, and picked out scattered details instead. He noticed that one of the women jurors wore a flowered hat—obviously an Easter hat, which she'd taken out of storage for this January occasion. Judge Strike had a thin mustache, and he wondered whether the judge had grown it to detract from his balding head or to cover an overlong upper lip—and whether, when things became abnormally dull, he ever turned off that little hearing aid behind his left ear.

Colin Eustis was speaking now. ". . . and I will prove," he was shouting, striding about on his thin, springy legs.

Bert smelled of after-shave lotion. There was something on his hair, too— *Guaranteed not greasy . . . no alcohol.* One of the reporters at the long table on the left was a woman. She had clipped brown hair and wore dark-rimmed glasses and made notes with a great flourish, as though she were playing a concert piano. The stenographer's machine was silent. The stenographer looked asleep. So did Edgar Beechum, the bailiff, leaning with his shoulders and rump against the wall behind the jury box.

Now Bert rose and talked. The smell of shaving lotion and hair tonic was gone, then strong again when Bert returned to the table.

Judge Strike said, "The prosecution may proceed with its first witness," and there was Doctor Peterford from Pirate's Cove, putting his hand on the Bible while Clerk of Court Harold Sims said, "Do you solemnly swear to tell the truth, the whole truth, and nothing but the truth, so help you God?"

"I do."

"Your name please?"

"Stephen Peterford . . . *Doctor* Stephen Peterford."

"You are the medical examiner for the County of Pelham?"

"I am."

"On the afternoon of Thursday, December 19, 1957, did you conduct a post-mortem—"

The courtroom was crowded, but silent, so Guy was scarcely aware of the rows of people behind him. If he turned his head to the left, he could see the faces of two men and a woman who had rigged some kind of ladder outside, and were peering in through one of the high windows. They looked cold. Their faces were a bright red. If he swung his head to the right, the corner of his eye picked out the long row of potential witnesses. Fran Walker looked miserable; Ida Primmer embarrassed; Doctor Bolls impatient. Sam sat with his chin dropped down to his chest. His mouth twitched; his hair looked quite red in the artificial light. When he raised his head, his face was red, too, and his eyes were staring as though he were not quite certain of what was going on.

Mar sat beyond Sam. Her forehead was white, but her cheeks were pink, her eyes very black and very bright . . . too bright . . . too bright . . . Her eyes turned slowly to his. Her face did not change expression, and he kept his own face the same and said that he loved her with his eyes across the room.

"Yes, I have a few questions." Bert rose and moved up before Doctor Peterford. "Now, Doctor, could you please tell us the exact time of Lawrence McFie's death?"

"No, of course not. My inquest was not conducted until after the deceased had been actually interred. As I previously stated, death caused by an overabundance of morphine would probably occur about twenty minutes after the morphine was injected."

"After how *much* morphine was injected?"

"You mean—how much did I find, exactly?"

"I mean, how much, exactly, caused Mr. McFie's death?"

"Well—" Doctor Peterford frowned. "In the case of morphine, an autopsy does not necessarily reveal the exact amount that is present in the body."

"Nor when the amount that *is* present was actually put there?"

"Well—in time, of course, it will diffuse through the body tissue. I mean morphine is not accumulative in the sense that arsenic is, for example."

"No, but am I correct in saying that it *is* accumulative to some degree?"

"Yes, I suppose—"

"Tell me, Doctor—if a patient is receiving morphine daily —*every* day—in gradually increasing doses—if a patient is seriously ill—his body unbalanced in all respects, so there are a thousand things that could go wrong—and you exhume the body and find morphine—how can you state as a fact that death was caused by a quarter grain of morphine, one hundred milligrams of morphine—or even by morphine at all?"

"Well—there was enough in the body to have caused death."

"Granted. But *did* the morphine kill Mr. McFie, or was he *already dead* when the defendant visited him on the night in question?"

Guy looked up slowly. Doctor Peterford was trying to explain that in a dead body the morphine would not diffuse so readily through the body tissue. He might not have found the morphine at all. But he did find it, and— No, it did not *prove* the patient had been alive at the time of injection. It did not *prove* it, as a scientific fact— Bert smiled and dismissed the coroner and turned away. Colin was calling his next witness. "Was he already dead?" Bert had asked. *Was* he? *Was* he? It was possible . . . possible. Larry *could* have been dead before the injection. He could not remember whether Larry's arm had felt cold or not. He could not remember feeling any pulse. So, yes, Larry could have been dead. And if that were the case, then he should not be here in this courtroom, accused of anything at all. He studied Bert's face, the faces of the jury, and felt a tiny touch of hope. Suppose it had been that way—just suppose—

"Your name?" Colin said.

"Mrs. Janet Columbo."

"You are the defendant's housekeeper?"

"Well, I clean for him. Twice—sometimes three times a week."

"Did you work for him on Monday, December sixteenth of last year?"

"I did."

"At that time did you empty the wastebasket in the defendant's office?"

"Yes, sir."

"And when was the next time you cleaned for him?"

"Thursday."

"The nineteenth?"

"I guess so. The day after Mr. McFie's funeral."

"And did you empty the basket that day, too?"

"I always emptied the Doctor's basket."

"Tell the court what happened on that Thursday afternoon."

"Well," Mrs. Columbo explained, "I was cleaning like always, and you came and knocked on the door, sir, and you said, did I see a little empty bottle around anywhere? And I said if there was one it would probably be in the Doctor's office basket, and I hadn't emptied it yet, so I'd go and look."

"What did you find?"

"A little bottle."

"Is this the bottle?" Colin drew a bottle from his pocket. He held it close to Mrs. Columbo's face. She nodded. Colin gave the bottle to Judge Strike, who studied it, and returned it to him. "Now," said Colin, "did the defendant *ever* empty his own office basket?"

"No, sir."

"So the bottle must have been deposited there some time between the afternoon of the sixteenth before Mr. McFie died, and the afternoon of the nineteenth, when I came to see you?"

"Yes, sir."

"That's all." He looked at Bert. Bert said, "No questions," and Mrs. Columbo waddled back to her seat. Passing Guy, she looked at him furtively with her dark old eyes. She was apologizing for what she had said. He smiled at her. It meant that she'd only told the truth. He understood.

Fran was next. She wore a dark blue conservative dress. Her yellow hair shone in the neon lights. She kept her eyes on the floor and looked more like a repentant child than a full-blown passionate woman. Yes, she had been on duty . . . Yes, she'd heard Doctor Montford talking to Larry . . . Yes, she'd left the desk because of Mrs. Roscoe, and there'd been plenty of opportunity for the defendant to have taken the key, opened the utility room door, removed the morphine, and returned the key . . . Yes, she'd noticed the morphine was missing . . . At first she hadn't been sure where it had gone . . . Then she'd thought back, and to the best of her knowledge, no one but the defendant could have taken it. The records were in order when she came on duty at eleven. They were not when she went off duty at seven . . . Yes, she'd falsified the records because she was the librarian, afraid it might be her own error, and she wanted time to check . . . Yes, she'd told Doctor Kelsey what she suspected, and he'd said that he'd take care of it . . . But then she'd become frightened, thinking *she* might be blamed, after she knew she really *wasn't* to blame, so she'd gone to Sheriff Whitt . . .

Her voice was flat, dull. The words were forced from her throat, torn out, as though they did not want to emerge at all. In the end she was crying openly.

"Now," Colin said. "Now one more question, Miss Walker . . . Is this that missing bottle?"

"Yes," in a hoarse whisper.

"How do you know?"

"The number. Everything is numbered."

"That will be all, Miss Walker."

Bert moved slowly toward the witness stand.

Bert: You say you went on duty at eleven?
Fran: Yes.
Bert: When did you first look in on Lawrence McFie?
Fran: Right away.
Bert: Shortly after eleven?
Fran: About five after.
Bert: Was he conscious?
Fran: He was in a coma.
Bert: Was he often in a coma?
Fran: Toward the end, a great deal of the time.
Bert: Did you give him morphine?
Fran: No.
Bert: Why not?
Fran: Because of the coma. Morphine's to relieve pain, and when a patient doesn't need it, it's better not to give him any.
Bert: Too much can be dangerous?
Fran: Yes, of course.
Bert: You were merely following Doctor Montford's orders?
Fran: Yes, the next injection was to be at seven when I went off duty.

Bert: At the time, when you went *on* duty, did you touch the patient in any way?
Fran: No, it was dark in the room. I just—looked in.
Bert: All right. Now—did anyone else visit Mr. McFie on that night besides yourself and Doctor Montford?
Fran: Well, I understand Mrs. McFie came in earlier—
Bert: Not what you understand. What you *know*.
Fran: During *my* duty, you mean?
Bert: After eleven o'clock, yes.
Fran: Well—there was one other visitor. The patient's father, Mr. McFie Senior.
Bert: What time did Mr. McFie visit his son?
Fran: About—quarter of twelve.
Bert: Mr. McFie went into the room?
Fran: Yes.
Bert: Did you hear him speak to his son?
Fran: Yes, I did.
Bert: Did you hear what he said?
Fran: He called his name. "Larry," he said. "Larry, are you awake, Larry?"
Bert: Did you hear his son answer?
Fran: No, I didn't.
Bert: How long was Mr. McFie there?
Fran: Just a couple of minutes.
Bert: Until about ten minutes of twelve?
Fran: Yes, about.
Bert: Then Doctor Montford arrived?
Fran: Yes, at about twelve fifteen.
Bert: The eminent District Attorney has already questioned you about both your and the defendant's actions on the night in question. But there are two points I'd like to clear up. First, you testified that when the defendant first went into the patient's room, he said, "If you could, Larry . . . if you only could . . ." You heard no more than that?
Fran: No.
Bert: It could have meant anything?
Fran: Yes, I guess so.
Bert: Did the patient say anything to prompt that speech? Did he give any answer to those words?
Fran: No, I didn't hear him say anything.
Bert: So as far as you know, from eleven, when you came on duty, until the time that Doctor Montford left the room, the patient was in a coma?
Fran: Yes.
Bert: Or dead?
Fran: I don't know.
Bert: Of course you don't. You don't know what time he actually died, and neither does *anybody else*.

There was a murmur in the courtroom. Colin crossed over

to Sam, and they conferred in low voices. Fran stepped down. The gavel sounded and Judge Strike wet his mustache and called a recess until 1:30 that same afternoon. Then he turned off his hearing aid.

Lunch consisted of beef stew, Jewish rye bread, and black coffee, all brought over to the jail from Pat's as usual. Bert had ordered fried oysters, and ate them with his fingers, dipping them in a large bowl of tartar sauce while he talked. "There's no question of whether you did it or not. Of course you *did* it, and Colin's got all the evidence he needs to prove it, even including your own confession."

"I did not confess to murder," Guy said wearily.

"No . . . Except you're not making up the rules. But if Larry was in a coma all that night—dead when you visited him—"

"He *could* have been."

"Except I can't put you on the stand to say he was. I mean if you'd known he was dead, you wouldn't have bothered with the injection."

Guy did not answer. He poked at a square cube of meat, sipped at the black coffee.

"So if we can just create a reasonable doubt—not as to whether you injected the morphine, but as to whether he was alive at the time. I understand Mrs. McFie was there earlier. I could put her on the stand, put on that other nurse that Fran relieved—prove he could have died at any time within a seven or eight hour period. Except it won't work. Eight hours isn't long enough. Kelsey's all for you, but he's no liar, and he'll go on the stand this afternoon. He examined Larry himself, and knew damn well he hadn't been dead as long as I wish he'd been." Bert ate the last of his oysters. He belched and eyed Guy from under half-closed lids. "Why did you make that verbal confession? *Why?*"

"Because it was true."

"All right, all right." Bert rose. He was tired. How could he possibly have expected this—a defendant who committed a crime, and denied there was any crime at all? "I thought it was right. I still think it was right. Under the same circumstances, I'd do it all over again." God, what a schnook! So maybe he was laying Larry's wife, but at least he could have waited for the fellow to die by himself, instead of shooting him with morphine and then taking this big integrity attitude. "I don't get it," he said finally. "I just don't get it."

"And you never will." Guy finished the stew, lit a cigarette, and drained off the coffee. Mar understood and he understood.

Bert wouldn't. The jury wouldn't. No one else could possibly understand.

1:35 P.M. Harold Sims, Clerk of Court, pounded his gavel and called, "Oyez . . . Oyez . . ." Judge Strike leaned over his bench toward the stenographer. "Note that the defendant and his counsel are in court." Then to sleepy Edgar Beechum, "The bailiff may call the jury."

1:42 P.M. The jury was seated. The courtroom doors were closed. Three red-cheeked faces appeared at one of the windows and Judge Strike turned on his hearing aid. He turned it up too loud, so the whispers in the packed courtroom became a roar. He shouted for order. But the roaring continued until he realized his error and turned down the volume.

1:52 P.M. Doctor Saul Kelsey was sworn in. He was a reluctant, a belligerent witness. He said that yes, he had signed the death certificate himself. Normally Doctor Montford would have signed it. But under the circumstances, since he was present and Doctor Montford was upset, he had not wanted to bother him with what was only a routine detail. He had written "Death by natural causes." When asked how long the deceased had been dead, he squirmed uncomfortably. "About six hours," he said finally, hating every word of it.

2:40 P.M. Defense Attorney, Bert Mosley, cross-examined the witness.

Bert: I believe you stated that the deceased had been dead about six hours?
Kelsey: Yes.
Bert: Could it have been longer?
Kelsey: Yes, it *could* have been.
Bert: I thought it was possible to establish a time of death with some certainty.
Kelsey: It is, when necessary.
Bert: You didn't consider it necessary?
Kelsey: I assumed it was a natural death. The patient was going to die anyway—
(Colin objected)
Colin: Whether the patient was near death or not has no bearing here.
(Judge Strike sustained the objection)
Strike: We all realize that the patient was seriously ill. If the court had any interest in his chances of recovery, it would call medical authorities, and we would argue the point for days.
Bert: All right. The point is, the body was cold—no corneal

reflex—no heartbeat—no pulse—dead for a number of hours. You say about six. It could have been eight.

Kelsey: Yes.

Bert: In other words, he could have died at ten o'clock in the evening, even *nine* o'clock.

Kelsey: No, I'd say eleven—that's eight hours—at the very earliest.

Bert: Doctor Kelsey . . . Please don't misconstrue the purpose of this next question. It is purely hypothetical, you understand, and is not meant to suggest any malpractices of yourself or your colleagues, nor to cast any shadow over your profession.

Kelsey: I understand.

Bert: Fine. Now here is the question. If *you* wanted to put a patient out of his misery—if you wanted to do it mercifully and safely—that is, leaving no evidence whatever of your act—*even* if the body were exhumed—just how would you go about it?

Kelsey: Well— Well, air, I think. I'd make three or four 10 cc injections of air into the patient's veins. The air bubbles would move to his heart, and he'd die quickly without pain. I would then sign his death certificate "Death by natural causes," and there'd be no evidence whatsoever of what had happened.

Bert: Has this ever been done?

Kelsey: You mean do I know of a particular case?

Bert: I mean in your long experience as a doctor, have you at any time—ever—anywhere—heard of a doctor who did just that?

Kelsey: Yes, I have.

Bert: More than one case?

Kelsey: Yes, more than one.

Bert: You mean it's a common practice?

Kelsey: I mean only that it is done occasionally in various hospitals under certain circumstances.

Bert: So—if the defendant had wanted to perform a mercy killing in this particular case, he could have used that method. Is that correct?

Kelsey: Yes.

Bert: He certainly *knew* such a method existed.

Kelsey: Of course. Doctor Montford is a highly skilled and knowledgeable physician.

Bert: Yet he deliberately used morphine instead of air—knowing it could be traced—probably would be traced. He did not even hide the bottle, merely dropped it in his office basket. How do you account for that?

Kelsey: I assume he was too emotionally upset to think about it one way or another. Doctor Montford had been under a severe strain for weeks. I insisted he go to a medical convention, merely to get him away from that strain for a few days. When he returned, he was still emotionally upset.

Bert: So—in this highly emotional state—the defendant would not necessarily think about covering his act? He would merely perform it with the purpose of putting an end to suffering?

Kelsey: Yes, I can't explain it in any other way.

Bert: Thank you, Doctor. That will be all.

3:21 P.M. The District Attorney called the Sheriff, Larson Whitt. The Sheriff repeated the defendant's verbal confession, made in the presence of the District Attorney, Judge Manning, and himself. "If you're ordering a post-mortem, yes, you'll find morphine, and yes, I gave it to him."

3:46 P.M. Ida Primmer took the stand. She was very embarrassed. She giggled a great deal. The spectators laughed openly, and Judge Strike called for order in the court. Ida stated that she had been called in as a relief nurse when Mrs. Roscoe was about to give birth. She had seen Doctor Montford. He had nodded to her. He had looked "peculiar." She'd always liked Doctor Montford, and so did everybody else, and—

The gavel went on pounding, and it was some time before she stopped her hysterical babbling and left the stand.

4:52 P.M. Bert Mosley sat brooding, his eyes narrowed, focused on Colin Eustis.

4:58 P.M. Bert Mosley's eyes turned to Sylvia Stein at the reporters' table. She smiled at him cynically. At the same table sat Parker Welk. He also smiled—not at Bert, but rather secretly and assuredly within himself.

5:04 P.M. Court adjourned until Wednesday, January 7, at 10:00 A.M.

CHAPTER TWENTY-FIVE

Colin Eustis drove on through the dirty gray morning, pulled into town, and parked behind the courthouse. He went in through the side door and climbed the stairs to the attorneys' room.

Bert Mosley sat in a wooden chair before the long, high rows of lawbooks. He was hunched forward, studying some papers intently. He looked up, and Colin said, "Morning, Bert," and "At least it's nearly over."

"Is it?"

"Oh, come on, Bert. I've got two witnesses that'll kill that dead-before-injection crap cold. And that doesn't leave you a thing. Of course *he* knows—*you know*—first degree's a bastard without malice-aforethought. So all murders are presumed to be second degree, and I'd have to *prove* first. Well, I can't, and I'm not trying. I'll settle for second. I'd like first, with a recommendation for mercy, but I know this town even better than you do. The jury'll bring in second, and it's a victory in any case."

The door opened and Edgar Beechum blinked sleepily into the room. "One minute to ten," he drawled. "Judge is in his chambers."

"O.K., Edgar." Colin started for the door. He looked back at Bert, said, "Give it up, fella. Throw in the towel and go back to income tax reports." He went out and closed the door.

The courtroom was jammed as it had been the day before. Now, though, there were chapped faces at all the windows. Judge Strike sat unmoving behind his bench while the jury filed in. Then Guy was brought in by Larson Whitt. He sat next to Bert, keeping his eyes on the cream-colored walls and the American flag and a portrait of the late Judge Adam Turner. The gavel sounded and Judge Strike turned on his hearing aid. Bert glanced at the reporters' table. Sylvia Stein wore a white blouse and gray skirt with a loose matching jacket. He glanced at Mrs. McFie, who sat next to Sam, yet miles away from him. Sam was more nervous than ever. His face twitched. His eyes moved constantly. His hands clenched and unclenched, and he continually recrossed his flannel-covered legs, so that the shine of his highly polished loafers made a faint gleam each time he raised a foot.

"The court will come to order."

Bert put his head into his hands, ran his fingers through his tonicked hair. He heard Colin call Mr. Samuel McFie. He heard Sam shuffle to the stand, heard Harold Sims swear him in, then heard all the expected questions and all the expected answers.

At about ten minutes to twelve on the night in question, Sam had spoken to his son. His son had answered. He had not been in a coma at all—at least not then, at ten minutes to twelve.

What had his son said?

He'd said he was frightened. He wanted another doctor.

What had Sam answered?

Sam had said he'd get another doctor in the morning.

"Your witness," said Colin Eustis.

Now Bert raised his head, and saw Colin smile at him, smugly, a little guiltily, he thought. "One question. One question, Mr. McFie."

Sam's eyes continued shifting. His legs continued crossing. His eyes finally settled on a spot on the far wall, far above Bert's head.

"Why?" Bert asked. "Why was your son frightened?"

"Well, it was Doctor Montford." The eyes shifted. The man was blatantly lying, but there was nothing to be done except make the most of it. "The way he'd been acting," Sam continued.

"Your son told you he was afraid of the way Doctor Montford had been acting?"

"Yes."

"Did he say *how* Doctor Montford had been acting?"

"Yes. Upset, you see— He was afraid Doctor Montford was going to kill him."

Parker Welk was next. His nose still showed signs of the break caused by the swinging chair leg. There was a livid red scar across the top of his bald head. He was slow-talking and sure, and kept his pig-eyes directly on the District Attorney's. He'd had a room across the hall from the defendant's on the night in question. Yes, he'd heard the deceased talking. Not only to his father, but calling out after Sam had gone, just before Doctor Montford had arrived. He couldn't make out any words, only a kind of frightened mumbling. But the sound itself had been very distinct, and he was absolutely positive of his testimony. After all, he'd heard the deceased's voice a number of times during the few days he'd been across the hall. So why shouldn't he have recognized it?

Colin turned to the jury. "If the deceased were already dead *before* the defendant entered the room," he said carefully, "then his death would have occurred during the short period of only a minute or two, between the time Mr. Welk heard his voice, and the time the defendant arrived. A highly remote possibility, yes. But I think you'll agree, considering the importance of that minute or two, that we'd be stretching the odds a very long way in order to give the theory any credence at all." He looked at Bert and inclined his head slightly in a nod.

"Yes," Bert said. "A question or two." He rose and moved slowly toward the bald, bloated man on the witness stand. He studied him with an open personal contempt. Parker blinked, lowered his eyes, forced them to Bert's face again.

"You were in the hospital on the night in question?" Bert said.

"Yes."

"Why?"

"You know why."

"*I* know. But do the ladies and gentlemen of the jury?"

Judge Strike said, "What difference does it make *why* the witness was in the hospital? If he had some embarrassing ailment—"

"I was attacked by a vandal," said Parker. "He hit me with a chair leg."

Bert sighed wearily. There was nothing to ask, nowhere to go. He asked Parker if he were prejudiced against the defendant, and Parker admitted that he'd written an editorial to the effect that mercy-killing was an abominable flouting of our laws and established moralities. But what difference what he thought or wrote? What difference? Right now he was only giving facts, telling what he'd *heard*.

"All right," Bert said. "All right, all right." He waved a hand, turned away, sat at the table once more.

"He's lying," Guy whispered. "So was Sam."

"You know . . . I know . . . Even Colin knows. But who can prove it?" Bert put his head into his hands again, ran his fingers through his hair once more, studied Margreth carefully from under the protection of his palm. Colin was saying that that concluded the list of witnesses for the Commonwealth. He had originally planned on calling Mrs. Margreth McFie to the stand, but thought she had suffered enough, and any testimony she might give would not contribute substantially to the Commonwealth's case.

Judge Strike commended Colin for his consideration in not causing the deceased's wife any unnecessary pain. He looked at Bert. "Mr. Mosley?"

Bert jerked his hand from his eyes, rose slowly, still thinking about Mrs. Margreth McFie. "If it please the court," he said, "I should like to request a recess until tomorrow morning. At that time I hope to produce another important witness for the defense."

"You've had plenty of time to produce any witness you require."

"I know that, your Honor. But under the circumstances—" He stopped. Judge Strike's eyes swung to Margreth, who sat motionless, staring at the floor. "I see . . . Yes, I see." He drew in his breath, spoke to the Clerk of Court, then to Bert again. "We would all like to conclude this case as soon as possible. On the other hand, we do not wish to deny the defense any legal means at its disposal which may strengthen its position. Accordingly, court is hereby recessed until ten tomorrow morning. At that time, if this—*witness*—does not take the stand, then the attorneys will make their summations immediately. I shall summarily charge the jury, and the jury will retire at once to reach its verdict. Is that clear?"

"Yes, your Honor . . . And thank you, your Honor."

The gavel sounded.

In Pat's, Bert had become quite a celebrity. He was needled, prodded, laughed at. Yet there was respect beneath the jesting, for he was the town's champion—East Norton's Don Quixote, tilting at a hawk-faced windmill from Harpswell.

"Not a chance," the regulars told him at lunch that day. "Or is there? . . . And what was this business about *why* Parker was in the hospital? . . . And oh, that sonovabitch, lying in his teeth . . . If the jury couldn't see that . . . But they don't *know* Parker . . . Well, we're for you, Bert . . . But Colin's blown your case sky-high . . . It was a good try, Bert . . . But even if it had worked, it would have been attempted murder, wouldn't it? . . . I mean the intention was still there."

Bert listened and nodded and did not commit himself.

"Who's this new witness, Bert? . . . Mrs. McFie? . . . Guy? . . . You putting Guy on the stand?"

Still Bert did not answer. He drank a beer with a hot pastrami sandwich. Then, when he was certain she'd be home, he put a quarter into the nickelodeon, got a dollar's worth of nickels and dimes from Pat, went into the phone booth, and called Mrs. McFie.

She answered.

He said, "Bert Mosley . . . Are you alone? I mean can anyone hear you?"

"No, Sam's not here. And Mrs. O'Hara's gone shopping."

"Fine . . . Shall we be frank, Mrs. McFie?"

"Frank?"

"Frank." It was warm in the booth. He ran a finger around the inside of his collar. "You're on a private line, aren't you?"

"Yes."

"All right. You were in court today. You saw what happened. They were both lying, but nobody can prove it."

"I know that."

"So I'm left with only one alternative. Put *you* on the stand and ask you a few leading questions."

"*Leading*, Mr. Mosley? With lies for answers?"

"So long as they're the *right* answers."

A long pause. The operator asked for another dime. Bert

deposited it, said, "Look—you understand why I'm his attorney, don't you?"

"Yes."

"So all right, I'm a rat, a blackmailer. You hate me. So all right. I want to get Guy off as much as you do, even though we have different reasons. And I'm assuming that he wouldn't be in this mess if it hadn't been for you—if you catch my meaning?"

"Now look here, Mr. Mosley—"

"I'm not suggesting anything. Just that there's more to this than simple mercy-killing. You know it, I know it, Guy knows it. But he can't bring himself to admit it—even to himself. He was a religious man once. He's always been an honest one—integrity—whatever you want to call it. All I'm saying is I can't put *him* on the stand, and you're the next best thing."

"I don't know . . ."

"This town, Mrs. McFie—these people—you don't know them as well as I do. They *want* him acquitted. The jury *wants* him acquitted. But they *won't* acquit him without an excuse that will salve their own consciences. Do you understand? They don't condone euthanasia. They're New Englanders, and very set in what they believe. To make it worse, there are seven Catholics on that jury. So we've got to give the jury a way out. So all right. Your husband *wanted* to die. He begged you to *help* him die. So you talked Guy into doing it for you. You're a beautiful woman, Mrs. McFie. A Southerner in a New England town, and Larry was Guy's best friend as well as your husband, so it makes good sense. Guy *would* listen to the way you felt about it . . . For all I know, maybe he *did* . . . Maybe it *was* your idea. But the point is, if you want to save him, then *you* be the villain in the piece. The jury'd love to blame you . . . Love to see Guy as a moral Cape Codder who let himself get persuaded into doing wrong by an immoral Southerner. They'd hate you all right. But he'd get off, and you wouldn't be prosecuted." A pause, and, "I'm asking you to let the town and jury blame you instead of him, and it's asking a lot, isn't it?"

"Yes, it is."

"Yeah . . . But I figured—considering what I know already—I figured maybe you *owed* him a lot."

"Did you?" There was sudden silence as the record ended on the nickelodeon and a new one slid into place. Voices murmured at the bar. Stewed Schaeffer had come in reeling, steadying himself, trying to maintain dignity as he climbed onto a stool.

"Mrs. McFie?" Bert cupped his mouth against the phone.

"I understand," her voice said finally.

"When I call you to the stand tomorrow—well, you're a smart woman. Just lower your pride a little, but don't say *too* much."

"I said I understand."

"Mrs. McFie . . . Mrs. McFie . . ." But she'd hung up.

Bert opened the booth door and stepped out into the smoky air. He breathed deep, then sat at the bar and ordered a beer. There was nothing to do now but pray and wait, pray and wait.

"Wanna tell you . . . don' unnershtan . . . don' unnershtan . . ." Stewed was very drunk.

"OK.," Bert said, "I don't understand," and thought that it wouldn't be long now before Pat called Larson Whitt, before Larson came in that tired way of so many times before, and led Stewed away to sleep it off in his own private cell.

CHAPTER TWENTY-SIX

For a long time Mar sat motionless at the phone. Then finally she rose and moved slowly into the living room. "What do you think, Peter? . . . What do you think?"

She was cold. Peter pruned his feathers. Mrs. O'Hara had laid a fire in the huge fireplace, and she thought that somehow the warmth of an open fire would get through skin and bones into the very heart of her. She could never manage the Cape Cod lighter with a single match, so she lit a section of the *Chronicle*, held it under the lighter until the kerosene-soaked stone caught fire, then pushed the burning torch under the dry logs. She pulled a footstool close to the growing flames and sat huddled with her arms about her knees.

Sam came in through the back door from across the terrace. He glanced at her sharply, then crossed into the hall and hung up his hat. He had not been drinking, and would not drink really heavily, she thought, until tomorrow when the trial ended. Then he would either quit entirely or go off on a huge bender. She felt his eyes on her back from the hall doorway. There was a long, awkward silence.

"Well?" he said finally, defiantly.

"You lied, Sam," speaking into the flames.

"You think so?"

"I know you did. I can't prove it, but I know it."

"You know a lot, don't you?"

"I know you're trying to alienate every single person who ever cared about you. You lost your wife and son, and you've got this ridiculous idea—"

"It's ridiculous, when he confessed it?"

"Even his father—"

"These Catholics . . . These Catholics . . ."

She put her face against her knees. "I know you don't want me here, Sam. I don't want to be here either. After tomorrow I'm leaving immediately."

"That's your business."

"Yes, it's *my* business."

"Anyone who feels sympathy for the murderer of her own husband—"

"Sam . . . Sam . . ."

"That's what it was—murder. Cold-blooded, deliberate murder. And that's why I lied. All right, I lied! But like you said, you can't prove it."

"Why, Sam, *why?* It's the jury's business."

"The jury," he scoffed. "The jury! They don't know what he did to me—or what his father did to me either. Sure, I got drunk one night and tried to kill Paul Montford. And I spent *two years* in a sanitarium—behind bars—because of it. And his father—did he ever pay? Not for what he did to *me,* he didn't. Just because Stewed Schaeffer was carrying on with his wife—"

"I don't want to hear about it again."

"Just because Guy caught them together."

"What are you saying, Sam?"

"Walked right in on them."

"No . . . God, no!"

"Just a kid at the time."

"No . . ."

"Well, he's not getting away with murder. He's going to pay . . . pay . . ."

"I think," she said softly, "I think he's already paid, and I think he'll go on paying—all his life." She pulled to her feet and walked slowly toward the door. Sam said, "Where are you going?" and she said, "Up to my room." Sam said, "You never loved him, you never loved him." He started shrieking at the end, as she moved wearily up the stairs. And as always, when Sam shouted, Peter began complaining and Sam turned on Peter, so the noise grew increasingly louder until she'd closed her bedroom door.

She leaned heavily against it. She thought. "That old man, and Guy *seeing* it . . . that boy actually *seeing* it . . . that poor old drunken Stewart Schaeffer . . ." Then she sat at the vanity and looked at the photograph of Sam's wife. "Why did you die? Why, *why* didn't you live?" She drew a slip of blue stationery from the drawer and wrote slowly, painfully, not knowing what to say in this most important letter she would ever write.

Doctor Treleaven led the way to his study. It was a musty room, filled with books and photographs and velvet-covered Victorian furniture that had belonged to the church for nearly a hundred years now.

Mar sat on the stiff, red, horsehair sofa. Doctor Treleaven sat behind his desk. "A letter?" he said.

"Yes, I'd—like you to deliver it to Guy."

"I see . . ." She felt his eyes watching her as he took the envelope. He cleared his throat, said, "Of course I'll deliver it. And if there's anything else—now, any time—" He coughed, looked away, then down at his own nervous white hands. "Mrs. McFie . . . I was born and raised in Pennsylvania."

"Oh?"

"Scranton, to be exact. It's a far larger town than East Norton. I went to college at Penn State and Divinity School in Washington. The point is—I'm not a New Englander. I think my own thoughts, yet at the same time, I try not to offend my parishioners."

"I understand."

"To me everything is not, as you may think, entirely black or white. I have a fierce reverence for the inviolable dignity of the human personality. That reverence tempts me to believe that a man has a right to die an honorable—a dignified death under certain proper conditions. But who decides when that moment is? God? Or man, as in the case of capital punishment? I don't know. My church does not condone Doctor Montford's act. Myself, I am more interested in human beings than in acts—fallibilities, errors in judgment, the blindness of passion—these are as human as virtues. They must be taken into account. And in the final analysis, it is not only the loss of your husband's life that matters, but the welfare of another man's soul."

He was embarrassed. He bent forward, and the steel rims of his glasses sparkled under the green glass shade of the desk lamp. "What I am trying to say—I realize where your sympathies lie. I can almost—guess—what is in this letter. I merely want you to know that you can trust me—that I am not a man to condone, forgive, or condemn. Only one who tries, in his own small way, to understand, and if at all possible—to help."

Mar wet her lips. "You'll deliver the letter right away?"

"Of course."

"No one will know why I came here? Not even Mrs. Treleaven?"

"No one."

"Doctor," she said. She closed her eyes, swayed a little, then opened her eyes very slowly and felt the great relief as the dam burst and overflowed, and the words rushed forth, quiet, husky, filling the musty little room.

There was too much noise and his hand could not seem to lift the glass. The far-off voices made no sense, and his patched elbow kept slipping, slipping from the bar . . . It had been a good suit once . . . years ago . . . years and years ago . . . repaired, woven, padded, rewoven, repadded . . . Soon it would need leather patches on the elbows, and then it would not slip so easily, though leather *was* slippery, of course . . . Who's touching my arm now? . . . Careful of my suit now . . . Coming, coming . . . Yes, sir, no trouble . . . Coming, Larson . . . Coming, Sheriff . . . across the floor through the rising, falling voices . . . out the frosted door into the freezing air . . . Jesus, Sheriff . . . Sorry, mustn't swear . . . Catholic all these years, and good Catholics don't swear ever or sin ever or lie ever or covet another man's wife, ever or ever . . . Into the car, and away we go . . . over the fields to grandmother's house . . . over the square to Stewed Schaeffer's house, warm and sleepy and cozy in the little cell in the new brick wing . . . Over the fields, over the dunes . . . in a one-horse open shay . . . in a Buick touring car . . . Esther . . . Esther . . . See how we run . . . See how we laugh, and when we are married, happy we'll be, underneath the bamboo, underneath the bamboo tree—boom, boom—underneath the canvas top of the Buick touring car—boom, boom—underneath the overhang of the dry, sun-baked dunes—boom, boom—boom, boom— And of course I'm going to stop drinking, Esther, stop—boom, boom . . . stop, boom boom . . . for a week, a month, a year, forever . . . next week, next month, next forever . . . next boom, boom . . . Oh, Esther, Esther . . . I remember, I remember . . . the first day and the middle days and the last final day of all . . . Off to drink in Falmouth, going like sixty with the top down on the touring car . . . No responsibilities, no family man, I—but a fine fellow for drinking and laughing and making false promises and making true love along the dunes . . . making love on and on, year after year in the good old doctor's house . . . Sometimes drunk and sometimes sober, saying, "It's too late, too late, and I *know* why you married him . . . What *else* could you do? . . . And

I'm no good and irresponsible and not a proper type fellow to be a woman's husband or a child's father." . . . And what else could you do but go on loving me in the afternoon with the bright eyes smiling and the bright black bun of hair against the afternoon pillow with the afternoon sun on the afternoon face, and the afternoon door swinging wide with the boy home early in the afternoon—him gaping, staring—me gaping, staring while I'm groping groping for my clothes . . . ? The boy's feet are running, running down the stairs . . . The door shuts, slams . . . I'm leaving, too . . . "Good afternoon, Esther." . . . And after that I wasn't there . . . I heard about it—what the good doctor said before he climbed to the widow's walk and leaped into eternity . . . pushed, shoved, nudged, betrayed into eternity . . . And the afternoons were never good for us again . . . Not afternoons or evenings, winters or summers, springs or falls . . . never again after the boy's wide staring eyes and the man falling black into the bed of tulips . . .

"Thank you, Sheriff . . . Hello, Willie . . . My room in order? . . . Thank you, thank you . . . Someone in the next room, looking at me through the bars . . . gaping, staring . . . Let me out of here! Esther, where are my clothes, Esther? . . . Stop staring, staring, boy . . . You hear me, boy, you stop that *staring!*"

"Sorry," Willie said. "He'll sleep it off, Doc. Every time we bring him in, he starts talking crazy. Doesn't mean anything."

"I know."

Willie was embarrassed. "Look, I'll ask Larson to move him over to Trousdell."

"Thanks, it's all right."

"No trouble."

"It's all right, Willie."

Willie left. Stewed Schaeffer snored. Guy stared through the dividing bars at the man's face, old now, remembered as young and frightened in that one terrible moment. Gone now. Gone, replaced by other, more recent memories. He turned his back on the snoring man and opened the sealed envelope that Willie had brought from Doctor Treleaven. He unfolded the note paper and wondered why it was blue and what Doctor John Treleaven could possibly have to say.

The note, though, was from Mar.

DEAREST GUY,

When I saw you—spoke to you last—days ago—it seems

years ago—I said that you *must* be a free man again—somehow—some way. Yet I see now that there is no way for you to personally fight for that freedom, nothing you can say that can counteract your own verbal confession. As an honest man, you would not deny that confession and, accordingly, Mr. Mosley is undoubtedly wise in insisting that you do not take the stand in your own defense. However, I cannot let you suffer alone for a crime which was as much mine—perhaps more mine—than yours.

Someday, yes, I think there will be a final reckoning for both of us. You are already paying, as I am now paying by loving you without being able to. Do you understand that? I love you, but am unable to love you. So we are both paying now, and will continue to pay and pay until God is through with us. But the law is not God's, and you cannot fight the law with moralities, but only with the law itself.

I am trying to say to you, Guy, dearest Guy, that though *you* cannot fight this law with truth, *I* can, and tomorrow I intend to do so, simply because I want you to be free, and then be patient. "Someday," you said, "someday you will love me freely." And I answered, "Yes, someday I believe I will," meaning that someday I will be *able* to love you, freely, openly, without the horror that now surrounds us both.

It is not right for either of us to justify sin by trying to defend it with our own convenient beliefs. We were wrong, Guy. And whether you were justified or not in the way you protected this wrong—protected Larry and myself and Sam—and your own self too—that is for God to decide. Not you and no, not even the law.

The law has its own terms. You were wrong on those terms, and there is no legal way for you to prove you were not, regardless of what you may believe. I, on the other hand, am accused of nothing, though I belong there beside you at the defendant's table. So it is only right that I should take some of your suffering upon myself, make some small effort toward insuring your freedom.

Tomorrow then, on the advice of Mr. Mosley, I shall take the stand in your behalf, because I want you to be a doctor again and a man always, above all else—with the opportunity to *be* a man in the freedom of society. I want our child, and someday I want to send for you and love you as you've loved me. I want there to be a someday. I want God to make it what it shall be, whatever He determines it ought to be. But it can never be anything at all, so long as I hide my own guilt behind yours, so long as I am too cowardly to admit at least some part of the influence I had in prompting you to act as you did.

I am saying all this because I shall not see you again. I shall do everything in my power to help you, and then, after the trial, I shall leave East Norton, not in shame, but because I have hurt you enough, and I will need time—time alone—to consider all the problems that we may someday face together. So please bear with me, dearest Guy, and please understand within your dear, wonderful self.

It was signed simply "Mar."

Guy folded the letter. He struck a match and burned the blue note paper to ashes and dropped the ashes into the tin can that served as an ash tray.

For a long time he sat quiet on the steel bunk. Darkness came outside the window. The branches of the huge tree became as black as the bars themselves, until all was black except for the single naked bulb above his head and the brighter light near the far end of the corridor.

Willie stirred in his chair at the tiny desk outside. "You want to play gin, Doc?"

"Thanks just the same, Willie."

"Blackjack?"

"No, thanks."

"My wife says I shouldn't let you beat me all the time."

"I'm only two games ahead."

"Even so—" Willie rose and stretched. "I'm going for coffee. You want some?"

"No, thanks."

"Guess I'll have to go home tonight—with Stewed here." He nodded toward the snoring old man in the adjoining cell. "If I'd known at lunch, I'd of eaten a couple dozen oysters. It's been four nights I ain't been home now, and the wife'll be a real bear for it. Well—" Willie said. "Well—well—" as he limped off down the corridor. The door opened and he disappeared from view.

Silence then, with the old man's snoring in the silence. Occasionally he sputtered and coughed. Once he rolled over on the bunk. Don't think about him, Guy told himself. Think about Mar and tomorrow and how much you love Mar and how much you want *some* tomorrow.

"Tell you shumm . . ."

Never mind the price.

"Lishen there . . . Lishen there . . . Boy . . . Boy . . ."

Don't think about him.

"Tell you, boy, tell you, boy." The bunk creaked as the old man's feet scraped along the floor. His voice was close now; his breath was hot, sour as it blew against the back of Guy's neck. "Unnershtan, boy . . . I loved her, boy . . . Going to marry her, and then I run out . . . I run an' run . . . shcared . . . shcared . . . no good . . . no good

. . . Paul Montford, boy . . . noble man, boy . . . ve-ery noble . . . unnershtood everything . . . everything . . ."

Don't listen, don't listen. But the remembered words were there all the same. "You promised," his father said behind the door. "When I married you, Esther, you promised"—

"I killed him, boy . . . Don't hate your mother, boy . . . Hate me, boy . . . Thash right . . . thash right . . ."

"And I've treated him like—" his father had said behind that door, before he'd run wildly toward the cave beneath the dunes. "I've treated him like—I've treated him like—"

"Look at me, boy . . . Pleash, boy . . . Pleash, boy, pleash, boy . . ."

"Look at me, boy."

Guy turned slowly and looked at the old man. The eyes were dark, blurred, the mouth loose, hanging open, saliva at the corners. He stared at the mouth that had once been straight, the eyes that had once been clear, the nose that had once been firm without all the tiny broken veins. "She needed me," the mouth said.

Mar needed him.

"I let her degrade herself," the mouth said.

He could not let Mar degrade herself.

"Treated him like my own—" his father had said. And then, in that moment, he knew that he could never let Mar take any of this hell—any of his guilt upon herself. Never, never, he could never let her suffer for him, nor could he leave her unprotected either, alone, so she could not call him when she needed him—so he could not go to her when she finally wanted him—so he could not be the father of his child. He must be free—on his own terms—gain freedom in his *own* way, regardless of his integrity or pride—regardless of his intellectual beliefs, which he'd been holding so close—

"I treated him like my own *son.*"

The old man wheezed and sat down. He began crying, but Guy still saw himself mirrored there in the crooked old face, in the hot wet tears, in the blurred old eyes and the working old mouth. He knew, he finally *knew*, and he said, "Oh, God, oh, God . . . No, no, *no!*" And he stood then and shouted wildly down the corridor, "I want Bert Mosley! . . . Get me Bert Mosley! . . . I've got to see Bert Mosley!" And he kept on shouting while the old man cried, until after a long time Willie came in limping and asked, frightened, what in the hell was wrong.

CHAPTER TWENTY-SEVEN

Bert had never felt better in his life. He wanted to laugh out loud, shout out the window of his car, rush up and down the streets of town, shaking everyone's hand, pounding everyone on the back. He wanted to get drunk, except that would not be enough. He wanted Fran Walker, except she would not be enough. She would cry and baby him and pamper him, and he wanted none of that now. He wanted real action—a good fight, a swim in the icy water of the bay, a ninety-mile-an-hour ride in a topless Jaguar.

"Boy! . . . Boy, boy!" He skidded to a stop before the Lincoln Hotel. There were lights in all the windows on the third floor, where the jury had slept guarded during the course of the trial. A few lights shone in the reporters' rooms on the second floor, too, and the cocktail lounge was filled with light and talk and music.

"Boy! . . . Boy!" He climbed from the old gray Plymouth coupé, almost ran up the slippery walk with his coattails flying out behind. He burst into the cocktail lounge, surveyed the room hastily, and felt a touch of disappointment that he could not quite explain.

Betsy moved toward him, thin, haggard, her tired breasts drooping beneath the pink uniform. "You want a table, Mr. Mosley?"

"Yes, sir, yes, sir." She no longer embarrassed him. To hell with her! To hell with everybody!

He sat at the table with his back to the doorway. The room was filled with hard-drinking, hard-laughing reporters, with out-of-town visitors, who had driven to the courthouse every day, and came here for drinks and dinner before going home to await the next day's developments. Well, they'd really see something tomorrow. Get their money's worth tomorrow. Step up, folks, it's all free—the greatest show on earth, presented by that brilliant, erudite, master showman, hard-fighting attorney, Mr. Bertram L. Mosley, Esq.

"A drink?" Betsy said over the noise.

"A double, Betsy. A triple." As she moved away he slapped playfully at her rear end. She started, turned back, gave him a slow, cynical smile.

"Feeling your oats?"

He roared with laughter. He roared at the bored state trooper who stood guard at the stairway, allowing only the reporters to the second floor, while another guard, further up, kept everyone from climbing to the third. He roared at the reporters and the unknown out-of-towners. And when the drink came, he took it at a gulp and told Betsy, "If you're not busy tonight, honey—"

"Remember the last time."

"To hell with you." To hell with her with her flat-on-her-back, "What are you waiting for" attitude; and to hell with Fran Walker with her "There now, there now," caressing him, helping-him-along attitude. Who needed either of them? Not Bert Mosley. Bert Mosley needed nothing from anybody.

A reporter detached himself from the group at a far table. He was a thin man with odd, staring eyes. He said, "Do you mind?" and when Bert nodded toward the chair, the reporter sat and twirled his glass and stared at Bert across the shiny formica top with the palest eyes Bert had ever seen. He was slightly drunk, and seemed to have nothing to say at all. "I've been watching you," he murmured finally. "In the courtroom."

"Yeah?"

"You give a good performance. A striking appearance. Tall, that blond curly hair, big shoulders." The eyes were very bright despite the pale color. Bert felt uncomfortable. And for no reason, he wanted to slug the man. "I got some whiskey in my room," the man was saying, and then Bert understood, and began trembling all through him.

"Get out of here! Get the hell out of here!"

"Sorry." The man rose unsteadily. "I made a mistake."

"You're goddamn right you made a mistake!"

The man kept on muttering apologies. "Made a mistake . . . You fooled me, had me fooled."

"Get out!"

The man stumbled away. Bert glared after him. He lifted his drink and his hand was shaking. He wasn't the type. Not Bert Mosley. Not the type at all.

"Good for you," a voice said behind him. It was Sylvia Stein. She still wore the skirt and blouse, the loose-hanging jacket, the horn-rimmed glasses. She was still cold and firm and completely impregnable. She sat beside him and said, "I've been watching. I wondered what would happen."

"What did you *think* would happen?"

"I didn't know." She brushed at her short, neat hair. "After all, you can't tell a book entirely by its cover."

"You're a bitch," Bert said.

"All right."

"I never had a homosexual experience in my life."

"Or any other kind either."

"Now look here—"

"Oh, I know your type. The big man—a big show."

"You get the hell out of here, too."

She ignored him. She ordered a drink. When it came, she caressed it with those long, red-tipped fingers. "What's all the exhilaration about?"

"You'll see."

"This Montford taking the stand tomorrow?"

"Guess again."

"Mrs. McFie?"

"You're so smart—you figure it."

"O.K." Then a pause, and, "Tommy tell you he had whiskey in his room?"

"Tommy?"

"The pansy from Providence."

"So what if he did?"

"I just wondered."

"Everybody's got whiskey in his room. You got whiskey in your room, I've got whiskey in my room." God, he hated her. He said, "You want to come to my room and taste my whiskey?" And after he'd said it, he kept hearing his own words floating there above the table, not sure why they had been said at all.

"You're a funny guy, Bertram Mosley."

"You can't think any worse about me than I'm thinking about you."

"Meaning?"

"I wouldn't call you exactly the feminine type."

"You like the *feminine* type? Yes, I can see you do. Someone to cling to you, only really you're clinging to her. She makes you feel like a great big boy."

"I feel," he said, "like pushing my big man's fist in your prim little face."

"Never hit a woman wearing glasses."

"Men seldom make passes—oh, nuts, nuts!" He threw a bill on the table, said, "Miss Stein, do you want to put your money where your mouth is?"

"I'll try your whiskey, if that's what you mean."

"O.K. But just shut up, will you?" He rose and walked toward the door. Miss Stein walked behind him.

In the car neither of them spoke. Miss Stein sat back against the door, and Bert bent forward over the wheel, staring fiercely at the road. The good elation of only moments before had changed subtly into anger. He still felt powerful, unconquerable. But now he wanted to destroy—and the object of destruction was Miss Sylvia Stein.

"You're a fierce man," she said mockingly. "I can see by your face."

He did not answer.

"You've got this trial licked, one way or another, and it'll be the greatest accomplishment of your life."

"Next to the greatest," he said, and again he had only a hazy suspicion of his own meaning.

He drew up before Edna Welles' antique shop. It was dark inside, and for a moment he felt a twinge of apprehension. Suppose Edna returned and saw Miss Stein leaving. Not that Edna was a gossip. But if he'd been hesitant about having Fran, his fiancée, in his rooms, wasn't it ten times as foolish to have this complete stranger? Fiancée, he thought. Fiancée? He'd almost forgotten that whole evening, when Fran had cried and they'd agreed to marry and make for Boston. It seemed months ago now—years ago—as though it had never really happened.

Miss Stein said, "Something bothering you?"

"No."

"I'm not here for romantic reasons, you know. You invited me up for a drink. I'll have it. From there on, it's every man for himself."

"Yeah . . ."

"I might scratch your eyes out. I might scream. I might slam you with an ash tray, poke a letter opener in your eye."

"I might not give you any reason." He looked straight at her in the dim light. She returned the gaze without blinking, only smiling a little, so very annoyingly hard and sophisticated and unafraid—so very able to handle herself with any man alive, and actually enjoying the opportunity to demonstrate it. He pulled his eyes away and opened the door. She followed him up the stairs, looked around the room with a touch of distaste.

"Well—you won't be here much longer anyway."

"No."

"Off to Boston—with that blond friend, I suppose."

"A friend, yes, *friend!*"

"Don't shout," she said.

He had not been aware that he was shouting. He went into the kitchenette and made them both a large drink. It was blended bourbon, and he remembered having bought scotch for that rendezvous with Fran. Sylvia Stein would get a blend, and he rather liked the idea, almost an insult to her really.

She sat on the sofa near the window, exactly where Fran had sat. But so different, so different. Challenging, waiting, and after a sip or two of his drink, he realized that he was waiting, too, that she expected him to make a pass at her, wanted him to, so she could rebuff him, make him crawl, laugh at him, and walk down the stairs, superior to the last. Well, he wouldn't give her the satisfaction. He'd have a drink or two with her, then say good night and go to bed, get a good night's sleep before the big tomorrow.

The room was quiet. Miss Stein sipped at her drink. She crossed her legs, uncrossed them again. A slight clinking sounded from below. She raised her eyebrows.

"Edna Welles," he said. "She runs the antique shop."

"Is that bad?"

"Who cares?"

She shrugged. She sipped at her drink once more. The ice rattled loud in the silence, deeper and deeper, heavier and heavier. "Well?" she said finally.

"Well, what?"

"Why don't you buy a better brand?"

"Why don't you shut up?"

"Why don't you make me?"

There was another challenge. Man to man, wife to husband, child to child. Not lover to lover at all. He put down his drink and walked toward her. She did not move, but her eyes followed him all the way, until when he was very close, then her carefully made-up mouth turned into the faintest of smiles. She put down her own drink, carefully, like a jeweler removing a diamond from a priceless ring, almost as though her fingers were delicate tweezers. He'd felt so good, so elated before he'd met her, and now that elation was oozing away. He was becoming the small, uncertain boy again, the big child crying in the wilderness. He fought against it, but it was all creeping back through her faint taunting smile, until finally he could not bear it any longer, and he reached out abruptly and jerked off her glasses.

She fought him furiously. Her fingernails raked at his face and her knee dug hard at his groin. But he paid no attention. He ripped the jacket from her shoulders, tore off the blouse and the bra beneath. He pressed anxious cold hands against her hard breasts and wedged her legs wide and when he kissed her, when she bit his lip, he actually enjoyed the taste of his own blood. And then finally, when her body arched suddenly like a quick steel spring beneath him, when she gave a little cry of sudden pain, then Joanie flashed crazily through his mind—the fierce ache inside him when he'd played with her child's breasts while she stood upside down on her head in the secret bedroom—that later night in his father's car, when her damp and goose-pimpled body had been matured and the unforgivable sin had almost been committed. Now it was being committed—the unforgivable. And yet there was no guilt now. There was only the greatest relief and pride in the certain knowledge that he, Bertram Mosley, had finally taken charge.

"I'm sorry," he gasped when it was over. "You don't know, you don't know."

"Neither do you," staring up at him with those brown eyes. But they were no longer hard or challenging. They were soft now, the eyes of a woman. And he realized slowly, looking into their soft, unexpected warmth, that Miss Sylvia Stein had been a virgin.

At quarter after ten, Fran Walker peered through the glass door of YE OLDE ANTIQUE SHOPPE and saw Edna Welles unpacking a crate of china. Edna looked up, frowned worriedly through the excelsior which clung all about her—in her hair, on her eyebrows, in patches about her clothes—then opened the door. "Well," she said, "hello, Fran."

"Hello . . ." Fran hesitated. "I came to see Bert," she explained finally, "and I saw your light."

"I was just leaving."

"Well, the point is—if you saw me going upstairs, you see, I thought you might get the wrong idea, you see."

"No . . ." Miss Welles was still frowning. Her head was cocked slightly to one side, as though she were listening, and Fran found herself listening too.

"Is something the matter?"

"No . . ."

"What I mean—Bert and I are engaged. We're going to be married very soon, you see, and we'll probably live upstairs here before we move to Boston, and I'll want to fix up the apartment a little, you see, and—well—"

"Yes, I understand." Miss Welles seemed impatient now. "*But* I think Bert's working tonight. He *told* me he was going to work—on his summation, you know, and—" Her voice drifted away, and then Fran heard it, too—the faint sound of a woman's voice from the rooms above. Bert said, "Might as well finish it," and the woman said, "Do you know what's happened here tonight? Do you know what's *happened?*" Then only murmuring again.

"I was just leaving," said Miss Welles. She turned away and put on her coat.

"Thank you for trying to send me away," said Fran.

"Fran, dear . . . dear Fran . . ."

"Who is it?"

"I don't know. A client, I guess."

"You've been here quite a while."

"Yes."

"She isn't a client."

Miss Welles shook the excelsior from her hair. "Really, Fran, I do have to go, Fran." She put out the lights and stepped into the night. "Can I give you a lift to the hospital?"

"No, thank you. I'll—walk."

"Well—" Miss Welles waved a helpless hand, then climbed into her old station wagon and rattled off down the street.

Fran watched her go. Then she turned and looked up at the lighted window on the second floor. She saw the dim silhouette of a woman behind the drawn shades. The woman held a glass in her hand. She waved the glass, and then Bert's figure moved into view, and then both figures moved out of sight across the room.

It was funny, Fran thought. She'd always been faithful in her way. Funny, too, that she didn't even care who the woman was. She should be hurt, of course, but she wasn't—only angry with Bert, and especially with herself. But it was good anger, too, because now she was finally awake to the real, honest feelings that had been buried inside her all the time.

She waited in the dark. After a while a woman came down the stairs and she saw that it was that reporter woman, that Sylvia Stein. Miss Stein disappeared in darkness and Fran rang the bell. She heard Bert call, "Sylvia?" then saw his face as he opened the door and watched her come toward him up the stairs.

"Fran," he said. "I thought—"

"I know what you thought. I know what you've been doing, too. I can see it in your face."

"No, Fran . . . You don't understand."

"Don't I?" She closed the door. "Sit down, Bert." He sat, staring at her. She smiled and opened her coat and the blouse beneath. "See me, Bert . . . Do you want me, Bert?" He only stared, and she knelt before him the same as last time. She touched him and smiled and said, "What's the matter, Bert? Don't I excite you, Bert?"

"For God's sake!"

"You had her, didn't you? So now you're completely helpless."

Bert glared at her in anger and embarrassment.

She laughed. "I'm *glad,* Bert. You *used* me, Bert. I almost *hate* you, Bert." She bent forward, exposing both naked breasts to his temporarily indifferent eyes, said, "Take a good look, Bert, because you'll never see them again, and I'll never touch you again. Never never again." She straightened and buttoned her blouse. She said, "Good night, Bert," and walked from the room, down the stairs to the street below. And walking back through the night, she thought that perhaps she should feel alone now, more alone than ever, with no red Alfred to watch leaping through the fields, no wondering, groping boy to mother in the hay of the empty stall, not even a badge of honor to hide in the garden, yet keep alive and secret inside her heart. But she did not feel alone at all. Instead she felt immensely relieved, and even a little sorry for Bertram Mosley, who did not even realize that someday, when he was a very small boy again, he would remember their final moment together—he would remember, and he would care.

Bert rose and made himself a drink. He felt drained, suddenly depressed, without knowing exactly why. Where was that old enthusiasm of only minutes before? Why did he give a goddamn whether Fran walked out or not? He hadn't really wanted to marry her anyway, so why didn't he just forget about her? Hell, he didn't *need* that kind of loving any more, did he? He had Sylvia, didn't he? He could go to Boston, couldn't he? Get the hell out of here and get really involved with Sylvia, once this trial was over. And it would be over tomorrow. Mrs. McFie would take the stand, throw herself to these small-town wolves, and he'd give the big speech about the good, honest, home-town boy, influenced by the emotional, "foreign," Godless wife of his closest friend. He wouldn't go too far, of course. Not suggest anything intimate between the two. But considering everyone had seen them sailing together—everyone, including Doctor Kelsey and even Sam McFie, knew she'd been leaning on Guy, depending on him for advice—draining him, draining him—well, if she were willing, let her be the sucker, the villain, the patsy, the fool in the thing. The jury'd acquit Guy—the town would run her out, and if she were stupid enough to go along—and she'd already *agreed* to go along—well, there was still a chance—still a faint chance—

The phone rang. Willie Nye said, "Mr. Mosley . . . You got to come down to the jail right away , . . No, I don't know what it's all about . . . Doc Montford, he got this letter from someone, and he's threatenin' to tear the place apart if you don't get down here right away . . . No, I told you, I don't *know*, Mr. Mosley . . ."

Bert hung up. He felt suddenly cold. He put on his coat and combed out his curly hair and kept telling himself that this *was* the only way, and if he wanted to put Mrs. McFie on the stand, that was *his* business, wasn't it, and what she said, that was *her* business, and he was going to win this case whether Guy Montford liked it or not. He *had* to win it, and now, with Fran gone, somehow it was more important to win than ever.

CHAPTER TWENTY-EIGHT

On the morning of Thursday, January the ninth, the courtroom in the courthouse of East Norton, Pelham County, was occupied by more people than at any time since the present courthouse had been erected in the year 1843. It was a still, cold morning, and the four hundred-odd occupants (as hastily counted by Clerk of Court Harold Sims) were still and cold as well. The women did not remove their coats, and some of the men kept their hands in their pockets during the entire morning. Judge Strike asked if it would be possible to get more steam into the hissing radiators, but was informed the heating system was inadequate (as he very well knew), and in time the room would become warmed by the body heat of its occupants.

Bert Mosley did not notice the cold. He sat dumbly beside Guy at the defense table, his elbows on the oak surface, his fingers spread wide along his forehead. He had a bad hangover, so his mind refused to work properly, and in a way he was glad, because there was nothing good to think about. He glanced at the man beside him—still, motionless, staring straight ahead, unblinking, completely unafraid; and though Guy was a crazy fool, of course, still he had to admire the raw guts of the man, the stubborn loyalty of any man who could worry so much about a woman that he'd risk prison rather than let her lower herself even temporarily—even for a few moments of time that would be soon forgotten.

He moved a hand to touch Guy's arm, then changed his mind, remembering the night before. "I'll take the stand," Guy had told him quietly, while Stewed Schaeffer snored in the adjoining cell. "Just put me on the stand and I'll tell my story, and I'll tell it in my own way."

"It's suicide, Guy. But if you'd just let Mrs. McFie—" He'd stopped then because he'd been afraid of the quiet man with the soft, determined voice. He was still afraid. He could call Mrs. McFie to the stand right now, if he liked—if he weren't so afraid. Why *was* he afraid? Why? Because Guy had said, "Don't call her, Bert. Colin's already said *he* won't. And *you* won't either." Guy's eyes had looked at him and his mouth had scarcely moved when he spoke, so he'd known then what kind of man this was—a very tough and honest man who'd take his chances with a stern New England jury, go down in honest defeat, perhaps destroy himself completely, rather than allow himself to be saved by a few repentant words from a woman he'd laid in a Boston hotel. The jerk! The tough, honorable, stupid, noble jerk! Just because he'd had a roll in the hay with her—my God, my God—

Well, it was over. He'd lost. He was frightened, awed, completely beaten, so he scarcely heard the dull echo of the gavel and Judge Strike's voice as from a long way off, saying, "You may call the first witness," scarcely heard his own hoarse voice either, saying, "I call the defendant, Guy Montford."

Guy rose slowly, walked stiffly to the stand. He heard voices whispering behind him. Harold Sims held out the Bible. He noticed a scar on Harold's cheek. It moved in little jerks as he said, "You swear to tell the truth, the whole truth, and nothing but the truth, so help you God?"

"I do." He turned and sat, and there before him were the dozens of watching faces—all one face, blurred together, out of focus so it hurt his eyes, and he tried to concentrate on any fixed, impersonal object he could find—a brass doorknob, red ear muffs on a head outside the window, Bert's gold Boston University cuff links, the multicolored feather on the hat of Polly Welk.

"Now," Bert said, softly, his voice quavering, when the courtroom was completely quiet, "now I want you to tell the court—in your own words—exactly what happened on the evening of Monday, December the sixteenth. Now and then I may interrupt in order to clear up a point or two. But otherwise I want you to tell the court in your own words."

Guy closed his eyes, opened them slowly. Mar's face swam into view. It was a beautiful face, surprised now, frightened and angry as she half rose and looked toward Bert, started to speak in protest, then caught his eye and held it for a long, hurting time before she understood and sat again, wearily, and he remembered what she would have done for him, what she was prepared to do at this very moment, and he thought, Oh, God, how much he loved her—how very much—

"Doctor Montford—if you'll please tell the court . . ."

"Yes . . ." He shut his eyes tight once more. He must not

look at Mar again. Above all, he must never look at Mar. He snapped the eyes open, focused them hard on the distant brass doorknob. "Well—that night—you must understand . . . It was only the culmination of many nights. I mean, you have to understand—the deceased—Larry McFie—Larry—he and I were childhood friends, all through grammar school, junior high, high school—close, inseparable friends. I was a year older, a year ahead of Larry in school, so naturally I was the leader, almost his protector, you might say. At least I felt that way. He wanted it that way. So that was the kind of relationship we had, for many long years, through all the fun, all the learning, all the troubles a boy has in trying to grow up, Larry without a mother, myself without a father. My father died, you see—" He stopped, closed his eyes, opened them on the bleary face of an old man, and thought, No, that is not Stewart Schaeffer—that is not my father—

"Doctor Montford?"

"Yes." He opened his eyes, avoiding Mar, avoiding Mar. "Yes, so whatever hurt one of us also hurt the other. We understood each other. Let me say this—in the true, honest sense, we loved each other, as brother loves brother. And that's the point, you see. We went our separate ways . . . college, the war, and after that I returned here and Larry married and stayed in Atlanta. I heard from him. Often I thought of him, until finally he returned, sick—dying—dying by little inches . . . little inches . . ."

"He *was* dying?" Bert said.

"Yes, of course," into the still courtroom, toward all the watching eyes.

"I mean there is no known cure for Hodgkin's disease?"

"No . . . No, I've read everything I can find on the subject. I even discussed the matter with a Doctor Jacques Pastene at a medical convention in Boston only a few weeks before. He's the recognized authority, and admitted there was no possible hope of a cure in such a case. He'd had some luck in arresting certain cases—meaning, in Larry's case, keeping him in comas, in pain—helpless, suffering, for days, weeks, months, but *no* recovery."

"And no miracle drug that might be found in those next days, weeks, months?"

"None that anyone can foresee."

"All right. Go on, Doctor."

"Well, I—I was Larry's doctor because he wanted it that way, because he depended on me, just as he always had when we were boys together. But there was nothing I could do for him—nothing *anyone* could do. I tried—everything—and I watched him dying and I felt myself dying, too. I wanted to help him, more than anything I'd ever wanted in my life, until I realized that his only comfort—ever again—his only comfort would be in death. I knew this—clearly, absolutely for certain—and I knew then that somehow I would have to do something . . . *something!*"

"What did you mean by 'something'?"

"At the time I didn't know *what* I meant. Just that—well, I had to help him—regardless of the way or the results, I had to help him. So that night, the night he—the night he died—I drove around for a while. I don't know where I went—or why—or what I planned to do. I simply—drove around, until a little after twelve. Then I went to the hospital. I went down to Larry's room. I don't know whether he was alive or dead. I don't know. I simply don't know. Anyway, I looked at him. Perhaps I spoke to him—I can't remember. Then I left the room, and as I came down the corridor, Miss Walker told me that Mrs. Roscoe was about to give birth. She was calling Doctor Bolls in Harpswell, and would need a relief nurse. I told her I'd call the relief."

"Why?"

"I don't know. It was—an impulse."

"Then?"

"Then Miss Walker took the key to the utility room from the desk drawer, got out some ether, came back, and put the key in the drawer again. The drawer was slightly open, and I—I kept staring at that key. I couldn't stop staring at it. Somehow it was as though—well, as though it could unlock all the misery, let it all out, get it all over for everyone concerned—Larry, Mr. McFie, Mrs. McFie—and myself, too. So—well, I took the key—went to the utility room and got the morphine. I remember that. I don't remember whether I called for the relief nurse before or after I went to the utility room. It doesn't matter, does it? I don't know. But I went back to Larry's room. I injected the morphine into his arm and put back the key, and—and then I left. And I don't know whether he was alive then or not. I don't know—I simply don't know."

His voice sighed away. He sat motionless, staring at the brass doorknob, the feather on Polly Welk's hat, the shine on Sam's loafers. He thought that he had told the truth. The truth, but not the whole truth. Nothing but the truth, with other bits of truth left out in the telling. It was like going to confession those years ago. You confessed only as much of your sin as was required for absolution. Sometimes the sin was greater than the way you told it, but you felt that absolution for part of the sin would automatically absolve the whole. Now he was in the confessional booth again, only it was light now instead of dark, and Father Serrano's hidden voice had been replaced by the dozens of sharply held breaths and hoarse whispers and rising falling murmurs in the room before him.

Bert looked sick. He shook his head ever so slightly, meaning, "You fool, you crazy fool." He muttered under his breath, pulled down his cuffs, wiped his forehead with a handkerchief. "All right," he said finally. "Now—you heard Doctor Kelsey's testimony that an air injection could bring death to a man without being detected in an autopsy."

"Yes."

"You knew Miss Walker would discover the missing morphine?"

"Yes, I suppose I knew."

"But you did not consider using an air injection?"

"No."

"Why not?"

"I don't know. I didn't think about it. It just happened. It—just—happened." He waved a hand. "It just—happened."

"I see," Bert said. And then, after a long moment, "I want you to tell the court why you admitted your act to Sheriff Larson Whitt and District Attorney Colin Eustis, yet refused to sign a written confession."

"Why? . . . Why? . . . Because the act—Larry's death—I didn't mean it as murder. I was *helping* him, you see, and the District Attorney, Mr. Eustis—he called it murder, and anything I signed, that would *state* murder or imply murder, and I—I couldn't confess to murder, you see—" He closed his eyes, opened them halfway and spoke in a low, hoarse whisper. "The point is, at first I—I thought that what I'd done was right. I wanted to believe it was right. I wanted to believe it was a deliberate, willful, premeditated act that had nothing to do with murder. I didn't want to be guilty of a sin—either moral or legal."

"You say at *first*. You felt this way at *first?*"

"Yes, because I realize now—finally—I realize that it *was* a sin. It *was* wrong. Morally, legally. It was wrong. I was confused, upset, unstable. Larry—he'd been my closest friend. I was his doctor simply because it was felt by his previous physicians—by his wife—that he would die more peacefully in his home town, with an old friend attending him . . . I couldn't tolerate thinking I'd killed—murdered my closest friend. But I *did* kill him. I actually *murdered* him. I understand that now. I don't know—I—I wasn't being an objective doctor. I didn't know *what* I was doing. I should have refused to attend him. I hope someday Mr. McFie, Mrs. McFie—I hope someday they'll forgive me—God will forgive me.

I hope someday I'll forgive myself. No man has the right to decide when another man should die. I—I know that now. I—"

He could not go on. His eyes burned from staring at the bright feather on Polly Welk's hat. He put his hand over his eyes and could say no more.

"That's all," Bert said, his voice whispering as from a long way off.

Still he sat there, his hand across his eyes. He heard Colin Eustis say, "No questions," and he knew why, of course—because a few women were blubbering in the audience—one woman sobbing outright in the jury box. And of course Colin would not think it wise to ask pointless questions of a poor, downtrodden fellow, would not want to turn public feeling against himself, destroy his own sure facts by encouraging a lot of hysterical emotion.

Bert was quiet now, thinking, thinking, putting it all together, and Guy understood exactly what was going on in Bert's mind, exactly what Bert was mouthing over and over to himself—the key words, figuring exactly how to use them. "I didn't know *what* I was doing . . . I didn't know *what* I was doing." And why had he said them? . . . Why? . . . Because they were true words, of course, and of course he *had* murdered Larry—blindly, drunk, overcome with emotion. He had not been the thinking, merciful doctor that he'd pretended to be—to Mar, to Bert, to Larson Whitt, to himself—not merciful at all, but rather an unthinking man in love—passionately, hopelessly, sinfully in love—who had committed unforgivable murder in a moment of violent irrationality.

"You may step down," said Judge Strike.

He stepped numbly from the stand. Judge Strike said the court would adjourn until after lunch. A woman on the jury still sniffled into her handkerchief. Polly Welk cried openly with huge glistening drops running down her fat cheeks. Mrs. Coffin wept in short, erratic bursts; Ida Primmer wept slobbering between her prominent teeth.

Only Mar did not weep, except somewhere deep, so deep inside that her tears would never come at all.

Willie Nye was nearly mobbed as he fought his way back from Pat's with the covered dish held carefully between his hands. "He don't say nothing," he kept insisting to his excited questioners. "It's corned beef hash with an egg—fried— No, he didn't ask for it, but it's the blue-plate special, and Pat says if he'll eat anything, it'll be the hash."

"He must say *something*."

"No, he's just settin' there on the bunk."

"Not a word?"

"Oh, we played a hand of gin rummy. But he wasn't payin' attention, so I ginned in the first six draws."

Willie fought on through the pressing throng. As he approached Larson's office, the door swung open and Larson stepped out to address the crowd. He said something about everybody calming down. He said there was a good fair jury and the jury would make its own decisions. Willie did not hear the rest. He limped down the corridor to the cell where Guy sat motionless on the bunk. The adjoining cell was empty now. Stewed Schaeffer had been released this morning.

"Still not hungry?" Willie said.

"No, thanks."

"Corned beef hash, fried egg, rye bread, coffee."

"Just the coffee, thanks."

Willie gave him the coffee. "You're sure about that hash, Doc?"

"Go on and eat it."

"Well—if you don't want it."

"Go on and eat it."

"I should have brought some catsup," Willie said, and poked his fork into the yellow eye of the fried egg.

Bert's summing up began at one twenty-six. His oratory was impassioned, full of gestures, full of sound and fury, signifying many things that had no bearing on the case, signifying others that came dangerously close to encroaching on the prerogatives of Judge Strike's coming charge to the jury.

"In any crime," Bert insisted, "there must be the presence of moral guilt on the part of the accused. Accordingly, we must discriminate between acts which externally seem alike, and of which the consequences to the victim of the act are the same. And how clearly—how clearly must those consequences be in the heart—in the very soul of a man—before we can judge that he is guilty of them, whether it was an intentional act or not?"

Bert said that it was not the law that made murder an offense that must be eliminated, but rather the community desire to eliminate murder which had created the laws to punish it. "Is it," he asked, "is it social desire to keep suffering humanity alive at all costs? Since the law springs from social desire—since the law is the result of social desire, and accordingly is—and must be—always behind social desire—"

Judge Strike interrupted. He asked Bert to confine himself to the facts of the case. Bert argued that these *were* the facts—that there was a famous remark made by an ancient Roman lawyer, to wit: "Law is the art of equity." All he was discussing here was equity.

Judge Strike nodded and stroked his mustache.

Bert turned back to the jury. "Each case," he said, "is distinctive and separate within itself. Are there not," he asked, "particular cases in which deliberate volition of murder may be present, but in which there is no moral guilt whatsoever? Can moral right and legal right *always* be completely coexistent?" He swung sharply toward Judge Strike. He said he was aware that the honorable Judge was about to reprimand him. Yes, he remembered the Judge's warning when this case had first opened. There would be no discussion of euthanasia here—no moral discussions, no religious discussions. The attorneys would confine themselves to legal facts, and the jury would consider legal facts alone. Well, technically, Doctor Montford was *physically* responsible for the death of Lawrence McFie. Was it, however, willful? Was it premeditated? Certainly it was not done with malice aforethought. In other words, was the Doctor sane at the time the act was committed? Remember his own confession this very morning—the confession of a man who acted in temporary insanity—did not even think to hide his crime—even *believed* in his crime. But with a clear mind again, that same man then realized that he'd been wrong, and could not bear to face the fact that he had ever succumbed to such a moment of emotional weakness.

There was more. Twenty minutes more in all, until finally, when Bert felt quite certain that all the quiet, brooding people in the jury box had seen their way to condoning a crime without destroying their own personal beliefs, then he turned abruptly and sat down.

Colin's face had not changed expression since the moment Bert had first begun his summing up. Now, too, it remained firm and gaunt, like an anemic Dick Tracy as he rose slowly, folded his hands behind his back, and stared fixedly at the jury. His eyes traveled over each member in turn. Then he stepped back a pace and surveyed them altogether.

"You have just heard," he said, "an act designed specifically to play upon your emotions. I will not degrade the Commonwealth's case by referring to it in any part, since the defense's summation, when stripped to the *facts* instead of fancies, expresses the Commonwealth's position as clearly as I could express it myself." He managed a tight smile, pulled at his ear, then suddenly thrust his finger toward the foreman. "I say simply this: A murder has been committed. The defendant has confessed to that murder, and even without his confession, there is more than sufficient proof that he *did* commit it beyond any reasonable doubt. The honorable Judge, in his charge, will detail for you the various degrees of murder. I do not ask you to bring in a verdict of murder in the first degree—simply a verdict of guilty—in whichever degree you good people see fit. And if, for one moment, you are tempted to believe the defendant might have been insane at the time the murder was committed, then I ask you why he did not plead insanity in the beginning—why he waited until the case was all against him before putting on that simpering display of 'I'm sorry, and I didn't mean it, and I'll never do it again,' and *why*—most important—if he were temporarily insane—why he *remembers* having committed the crime at all?

"You are New Englanders, ladies and gentlemen. As such, you *are* not—you *will* not be fooled by the histrionics of either the defendant or his attorney. You were raised in a heritage of clear, uncompromising justice. I ask you not to cast aside the law, your own moral beliefs, or your own New England sense of what is right and what is wrong—who should be punished, and how severe that punishment should be. I ask you to examine your own consciences, and bring in the only verdict possible under the overwhelming lot of proof of guilt which you have heard in this courtroom—a verdict of guilty."

Judge Strike played nervously with his thin mustache. He turned up his hearing aid, then turned it down again, and stared through half-lowered lids at the silent jury.

"Members of the jury . . ." He coughed, started again. "Members of the jury, in this bill of indictment the defendant on trial before you is charged with murder. It is averred that he did kill and murder within this county one Lawrence McFie . . ."

Guy stared at the portrait of the deceased Judge Adam Turner. The eyes stared back. He looked at the desk while Judge Strike reviewed the evidence, but he felt the painted eyes on the top of his head, and thought that in some strange way, thinking back on this courtroom, he would remember the dead Judge Turner more clearly than any living member present.

Judge Strike said, "The distinguishing mark of murder is malice aforethought. 'Malice' in a legal sense means cruelty, wickedness, carelessness of consequence, and is present in all murders of the first degree—that is, murder which is perpetrated by means of poison, or by lying in wait, or by any other kind of willful, deliberate and premeditated killing, or which is committed in the perpetration of, or in attempting to perpetrate any arson, rape, robbery, burglary, or kidnaping . . ."

Guy felt Judge Strike's eyes on the top of his head, replacing those of Judge Turner. He ran a hand over his bristling hair as though to wipe the living eyes away.

"Clearly, we are not dealing here with murder in the first degree, since, in this unusual case, malice aforethought has been replaced by mercy aforethought. I do not think anyone in this courtroom will question the intentions of the defendant, regardless of whether he acted with premeditation or not."

No one in the courtroom, Guy thought, while Judge Strike's voice droned on. No one but himself and Mar. And to them the intention was quite clear, of course. To gain another man's wife. As simple as that, forgetting all that rationalizing crap about how he'd have done it anyway. He *wouldn't* have done it. He knew that now. Not in a thousand years. Not if he hadn't taken Larry's wife—not if she weren't going to have his child. He'd kept claiming otherwise, believing otherwise. But he'd been lying in his teeth. It never would have happened.

"On the matter of premeditation," continued Judge Strike, "the law fixes no particular period of time. That is, the defendant could have devised his murder plan in terms of weeks, days, minutes, or possibly even seconds. There has been some discussion here as to how much premeditation *did* go into this confessed crime. And that, you understand, is a point which you must consider most carefully, since, if the defendant acted with even the slightest premeditation, had even the slightest *awareness* of his act, then he is guilty of murder in the second degree—whereas, on the other hand, if you find he committed murder with *no* premeditation, *no* malice aforethought, *no* willful design to take a man's life, then you will find him not guilty at all, by reason of temporary insanity. A person who is temporarily insane at the time he commits a crime is one who cannot, at that time, distinguish between right and wrong, and accordingly does not know the nature or quality of his own act . . ."

Guy glanced up from beneath his arm. He saw the scar on Harold Sims' cheek. That and Judge Turner's painted eyes, the Easter bonnet and the feather on Polly Welk's hat, the accusing eyes of Sam McFie and the blurred eyes of an old man who looked like another man he'd seen only hours before through the bars of a cell. Those images before him were real; those behind him remembered—like the brass doorknob and the gun on Larson Whitt's hip and a pair of highly polished shoes. Yet all were more real than the words being said, more a part of this courtroom than anything that had gone before or could possibly come after.

"In the case of murder in the second degree," Judge Strike went on, "the court will impose the penalty. You, however, must decide if, in your considered opinion, the defendant is guilty of the crime with which he is charged. In this connection, you should make careful note of the fact that it has never been held that a man cannot act deliberately, with premeditation, simply because he was upset at the time, nor is a man entitled to an assumption of temporary insanity. The State does not have to prove the defendant sane. Rather the defense must prove him *insane,* and your duty is to determine whether he was sane or not, guilty or not, and to bring in a verdict commensurate with all the admissible evidence which you have heard in this courtroom." He stared hard at each member of the jury, then swung his eyes to the front and down at Harold Sims. "Swear the officers," he said.

Harold rose and said, "You do swear that you will well and truly keep this jury in some private and convenient place until they have agreed upon their verdict; and that you will not suffer any person to speak to them, nor speak to them yourselves, without the leave of the court, except it be to ask them if they have agreed on their verdict. So help you God."

He closed the Bible. He picked up the gavel and pounded twice. Court adjourned until 8:00 P.M.

CHAPTER TWENTY-NINE

The bread was slightly stale, the chicken dry, the lettuce wilted. There was too much mayonnaise on the sandwich and the coffee tasted bitter, so that she could not finish either. The clerk—one of those bewildered men who innocently starts jerking sodas in his teens, and finds he is still doing it some twenty years later—moved over hesitantly to her table. "Is the sandwich all right?" he asked.

"Yes, it's fine. It's just that I'm—not very hungry."

"If there's too much mayonnaise—"

"No, really it's fine." Mar lit a cigarette, dragged deep, took a small bite of the sandwich in order to please the anxious clerk, then rose from the wire-backed chair just as Nancy Messner turned from the toiletries counter, where she was inspecting a row of toothbrushes.

Nancy hesitated, then moved awkwardly toward the marble-topped table. "Mrs. McFie?"

"Yes?" She sat down again.

"I'm Nancy Messner. You know—I met you at church."

"Yes. Hello, Nancy."

"I just wanted to tell you—I think you've been so brave and all." Nancy's corn-yellow hair swung over her forehead as she dropped her head in embarrassment. "I mean so *kind*, the way you haven't *blamed* Doctor Montford and everything —well, I just wanted to tell you."

"Thank you, Nancy."

"Everybody feels that way, and just because I work on the *Chronicle*—well, I want you to know that I don't approve of those awful editorials Mr. Welk's been writing at all. I mean that's editorial policy or something, and *he's* the editor, so—"

"I understand."

"I'd stop working there right now if there were somewhere else to get my reporter training."

"Now don't you worry, Nancy." Margreth smiled and pulled to her feet. She felt dizzy and thought she would have to eat more in the future, though tonight she couldn't have borne eating frankfurters and beans at the table with Sam—tonight of all nights—so she'd come here to the drugstore instead. "Eating for two," they called it. Eating for two.

"Do you feel all right?" Nancy asked.

"Yes, thank you, Nancy. I'm fine."

"Well—we'll know in another hour or so."

"Yes, we'll know." She smiled warmly at the girl, paid the worrying clerk, then moved out to the street. A big storm was expected to blow in from the north sometime during the next few days. But tonight the air was unusually clear—very cold with the stars close and bright in a black sky. She pulled her coat collar high about her ears and walked slowly under the street lights, passing time, waiting. And wasn't walking good for you? Isn't that what doctors recommended for pregnant women? Walk, walk. So she walked, going nowhere, simply avoiding Sam's house and everything that was in it. She would not ever go back there again—not tonight or ever again. She would write him a polite thank-you note for his "kind hospitality." She would send a little gift to Mrs. O'Hara. Both would be mailed to New Haven, from which point they could be forwarded to East Norton, so the postmark of her actual whereabouts would not appear on either.

She kept her face toward the ground as she moved along. Still, two or three church members and one of the nurses recognized her. They said, "Hello, Mrs. McFie," in strange, awkward voices, and she did not feel quite free again until she'd gained the outskirts of the lighted town, busier this evening than it had been since Christmas Eve.

Before her, Guy's house sat dark upon the hill. She moved toward it slowly, watching the black shape loom above her, watching her own steam of breath against the dark, until finally the house was left behind and she was walking around and down, past the curve where the red-haired, sports-loving Julia had been stabbed to death by a steering wheel, on toward the high, awkward shape of Chet Belknap's boathouse. She noticed that the broken door had been repaired, and thought, If it had only been repaired earlier—two months ago—then none of this would be happening at all. If I had never entered that dark shed, never climbed into *Julia*'s cockpit, never gone down the ladder to her cabin— She said, "Guy, dear God, dear Guy," and tried vainly not to remember that night or the other on the canopied bed, where Sam's wife had smilingly watched them from the goldleaf frame. Not even that glorious sin-free night in Boston; not anything about Guy at all, because there would be time later to remember—and perhaps time later to forget.

The cannery was lighted. The machines clanked dully behind the yellow windows. The fishing boats rubbed and squeaked against the pier, and the smell of fish was everywhere. Sam was not there, of course. Sam was home eating, drinking, waiting, as the whole town waited, as people all across the country waited—waited—her mother, who had written four times (she'd insisted her mother should *not* come to the funeral); her sister, Elizabeth Sue, who had written twice from Chattanooga. (She'd written a short note in polite reply.) Both wanted her to come visit immediately. "It will do you so much good," her mother had written. "First that terrible tragedy, and now this dreadful Doctor Montford—" She could not go home, of course, nor to Elizabeth Sue's either, of course—and now, with her name in newspapers everywhere—not even to New Haven.

The Portuguese section was quiet, with comfortable homemade lamps glowing warm in the cottage windows. Row on row of low picket fences, and there beyond, the narrow wooden spire of St. Joseph's. She found the black cross against the black sky, and thought that this had once been Guy's church, then turned and walked on up the hill behind the Congregational Church and Doctor Treleaven's small frame house, three blocks on to the frozen cemetery with the stiff little flags and the leaning old stones, and the few ones that shone in the bright half-moon. She stopped at the newest, the shiniest stone of all. It was simple, half-rounded on top, a graceful stone of Vermont marble. *Lawrence McFie—1921–1957*. She had not wanted any inscription because such words as "loving wife" would only degrade their own meaning. She had been a loving wife. She had loved Larry passionately, with every part of her body and soul, and she'd been faithful, too, until the end, when it mattered the least—when it mattered the very most.

She placed her hand on the stone, dropped her forehead against the hand. The cold of the stone seemed to go through the flesh of her hand, into her forehead, on through, till there was ice in her brain. She shivered, tried to lift her head that was sealed against the cold hand. To this moment the crying had all been hidden inside. But now it came rushing to the surface, and she wept openly against the marble, until finally it was all out of her and she pulled to her feet once more and walked back through the town and the knots of waiting, whispering people, up the steps of the courthouse, down the aisle past all the turning heads to the empty place on the cold oak bench.

Beside her, Sam was bent forward, his elbows on his knees, his chin cupped tight between his hands. He did not look up. She stared straight ahead, waiting, waiting, until finally the side door opened and Guy walked in with Larson Whitt. He looked tired, dead, his eyes unseeing. She thought how much he must love her—how much of a man he was—and could not bear to see so much hurt in such a being. She turned her eyes toward the opposite doorway, through which the jury was now filing in—the small doorway to the rear from which Judge Crawford Strike emerged. She rose as the gavel sounded, "All rise, the court is now in session," and sat with the rustle of those behind her. The room was very still. The windows cracked in the cold. Judge Strike's voice echoed back and forth, seeming to repeat itself over and over.

"Mr. Foreman, have you agreed upon a verdict?"

"We have, your Honor." The foreman was large, pompous. She understood that he dealt in feed and grain, and lived in a place called Seaside. His eyes looked at Judge Strike. His face gave away nothing.

"Prisoner, you will rise and look upon the jury . . . The jury will look upon the prisoner."

Guy rose. He stood erect, staring straight at the jury, pinning them there in their wooden stall.

"How say you? Guilty or Not Guilty?"

The large foreman cleared his throat. He coughed, and could not stop. He wiped his mouth with a handkerchief, said, "Sorry, your Honor."

Mar closed her eyes.

Judge Strike said, "What is your verdict, Mr. Foreman?"

"We, the jury, find the defendant Not Guilty."

Then, in that moment, the room exploded. Men yelled. Women wept. The gavel pounded and the clerk of court shouted for order. Judge Strike, his face shocked in disbelief, tried to reprimand the jury for its complete disregard of everything he had said in his charge. But he could not make himself heard. He could not clear the courtroom or bring about any order whatsoever. He could do nothing but nod to the clerk, shrug his berobed shoulders, and turn off his hearing aid.

The bailiff and Larson Whitt tried vainly to restore order, then finally gave up, too, and joined the celebration—the handshaking, back-slapping, cheering crowd that surged around Guy, carrying him with them toward the side exit behind the jury box.

Mar looked after them. She moved impulsively forward and saw Guy's face through the sea of heads for the barest fraction of a second. His eyes touched her own, and she saw love there and relief there, but no happiness there at all.

She turned and pushed her way toward the rear of the courtroom, past Bert who was grinning triumphantly, his arm thrown casually around the shoulders of that mannishly dressed woman reporter; past Doctor Kelsey who stood frowning, hesitant, looking after Guy as though uncertain whether to follow him or not; past Fran Walker. who wept in open relief; on out to the small hall and down the steps into the night.

The crowd was all around her. Nancy Messner rushed up to say, "I'm so glad, I'm so glad," then off again, while Parker Welk scowled deeply before he shuffled after Nancy with his bald head taut and gleaming beneath the lights. Chet Belknap and Bill Watts; Judge Manning and Edna Welles; Mrs. Coffin and Maidie Bolls and that pathetic waitress from the Lincoln Hotel. Some she knew by name, others by sight, still others not at all. They moved around her, hemming her in, until finally she had fought clear and was striding fast away up the street.

She rounded the corner and saw Sam's car screech past her toward the cannery, slipping, roaring, as though some hidden demon raced close behind. And then in a moment she had reached the waiting sedan.

She climbed in beside the driver. The motor started and the car swung out through the town and the milling throngs, through the intersection on the road to Falmouth—and the sounds of celebration were not entirely gone until she'd passed the lighted hospital and was swallowed finally in the dark.

Ruth Kiley expected Sam to be shut away in his office, as she expected him to be drunk. Still she was shocked, a little frightened, by the wild-eyed man who stared at her from across the desk. The thin red strands of his hair stuck out in all directions. His hand shook violently when he raised the bottle, and his voice was hoarse, strange, a ghostly voice she remembered from a long time back.

"Ruthie," and a leering wink, and "Been waiting, Ruthie . . ."

She closed the frosted door. The clanking machines were muffled and his voice was louder. "Let's go now, let's go, Ruthie."

"Sam . . ."

"Been waiting, Ruthie, waiting, Ruthie . . ." He screwed the cap on the bottle, rose, stumbled, and braced himself against the desk. "Killed my wife," he mumbled. "That sonovabitch . . . big-shot doctor . . . and all the time Stewed Schaeffer's been laying his wife all over the place, and he doesn't even *know* it . . . sonovabitch . . . But you understand, Ruthie . . . *You* understand . . ." He flung an arm around Ruth's shoulder, and she half-supported him as they went out the door, down the corridor, down the wooden steps to the dock alongside the building. From the distance she heard the sounds of shouting, the honking of horns. Lights appeared in the windows of Guy Montford's house, and a procession of cars drove up the winding hill in a honking parade.

"Where are we going, Sam? You can't drive, Sam."

"Where we going, Ruthie? . . . Don't play it coy, Ruthie . . . As if *you* don't know . . . *You* don't know . . ." He laughed aloud, squeezed her arm, then climbed behind the wheel and put the bottle of whiskey on the seat between them. He started to sing, "Yes, sir, she's my baby . . . No, sir, don't mean maybe . . ." He was still singing as they wound east along the shore.

Ruth held tight to the door handle. She watched Sam's face and realized that he was drunk, yes, but more than that. Something had cracked inside him, and she was not sure what it meant or how she should handle it. A few minutes later he turned off on a rutted sand road and the car bounced toward a small cottage that hugged the shore. "Sam," she said then. "Where are we *going*, Sam?"

"Now Ruthie . . . Ruthie, Ruthie, she's my baby . . . Don't be coy, baby . . . Don't be coy . . ." He stopped at the cottage, got out and tried the wooden door. It was locked.

"Sam, you don't *own* this cottage any more."

"Where's the key? . . . Ruthie, you got the key?"

"You sold it twenty-five years ago."

"Where's the key?" He screamed the words over and over, then, in sudden fury, grabbed up a piece of driftwood and smashed at the padlock, smashed and smashed, until finally the screws worked loose and the door swung open. "I'll bet it was that Paul Montford—that's who—stole the key—goddamn Catholic—Doctor Paul Montford!" He laughed, stumbled through the doorway, and began throwing wood from an orange crate into the potbellied stove. He stuffed in some old newspapers and lit the fire, found two tumblers in the cupboards over the icebox, and made them both a drink.

Ruth was cold. She sat shivering near the stove. "I don't want a drink, Sam," and "What's the matter, Sam?"

"A toast to us . . . Sammy and Ruthie . . ." He pushed the glass into her hand and she sipped at the liquor slowly, not liking the taste, but enjoying the warmth that was beginning to seep in through the chill.

"Don't you worry," he said, sitting beside her. "Depression's not going to lick us. No, sir, that Roosevelt's got some fine ideas . . . fine ideas . . . Get that cannery on its feet, all right."

"Sam . . . Sam . . ."

"And thanks for the parrot, Ruthie . . . Going to name him Peter . . . When I was a kid, had a pigeon named Peter, so I'll name him after the pigeon . . ."

"Sam—that was a long time ago."

"Been thinking about marriage, Ruthie . . . No good, all this being sorry for myself . . . Cora's been dead eight, nine years now . . . Not fair to you . . . Making a whore out of you . . . Never marrying you . . ."

"Sam," she pleaded. "Please, Sam, *please!*" She was cold again. She was frightened. She began to cry and Sam rose and put an arm around her and led her to the bunk. She protested, but he kept comforting her drunkenly, talking crazily about his beautiful little Ruthie. She closed her eyes and thought, Oh, God, oh, dear God, we're old, we're old . . . And she kept her eyes squeezed tight, crying behind the closed lids while his hands fumbled at her dress and his voice said, "Beautiful Ruthie . . . You're good for me, Ruthie . . . Please, Ruthie . . . Help me, Ruthie . . ." And she helped him as she had on occasion in those long years ago—except he was too drunk now, he was too old now . . . They were both too old, and she felt it all in the fact that she still wore her rimless glasses.

Finally, when he stopped trying and fell heavily beside her, snoring, mumbling intermittently, "Paul Montford . . . God-damned Catholic . . . Killed my wife . . ." then she moved his hand gently from her breast and sat upright and straightened all her spinster's clothes.

She poured the whiskey down the tin sink, dropped more wood in the stove, then found some blankets and covered Sam's sleeping body. She went out the door and trudged back up the rutted road in her sensible shoes, along the macadam highway the two long miles to town. Her feet were cold. The night air stung her nose and ears. She heard the cars still honking in the distance, but had no clear thoughts at all—only the fierce aching prayer that when Sam finally awoke, it would be 1958 and he would not remember anything.

CHAPTER THIRTY

The crowd had been milling around for nearly an hour now. Someone had brought up a case of beer, and some of the men sat drinking in their cars, while others staggered up the walk, trampling the boxwood hedges, shouting and cheering, until now that the party had gotten slightly out of hand, they had forgotten exactly what it was they were celebrating.

Guy moved about restlessly in the living room. The house was cold, having been vacant for more than three weeks, and the oil burner had not yet brought the heat back up to room temperature. He lit a fire in the great brick fireplace, then sat before it rubbing his hands until the first chill was gone from the room. Outside he heard the drunken voices singing, "For he's a jolly good fellow, for he's a jolly good fellow . . ."

"A damn fine jolly good fellow," he said into the fire, then went into the kitchen and made himself a drink.

Someone knocked lightly on the back door. The knock became louder and Doctor Saul Kelsey's voice called, "Guy . . . Open up, Guy!"

He unbolted the door. Caesar leaped forward on his leash and Guy stooped and held the squirming, hysterically happy dog while Saul bolted the door behind him.

"Missed you," Saul said. "God, how that mutt missed you!" And Guy laughed for the first time in days. He poured Saul a drink and led him to the living room. The crowd still surged outside. The drunken voices still sang on.

"Why in hell don't they go home?" Guy said.

"They want you to come out and say something."

"What? . . . I've said everything. What have I got to say?"

" 'I appreciate your loyalty . . . Thanks, boys.' You know. And if you don't, they'll stay all night."

"All right, all right!" He slammed down his glass, went through the office and opened the waiting-room door. The men broke into a cheer. Then everyone started shouting at once. He recognized Chet Belknap and Bill Watts; a few men from the cannery, a number of fishermen; some old patients, old friends, old high-school classmates, and some men he scarcely knew at all, who had tagged along for the beer and singing. There was a scattering of women, too, most of them trying to get their husbands home to bed. And there was Fran Walker. She looked up at him from beneath a plaid scarf wrapped across her head to cover her ears. Her face was white, without expression. She merely stared at him for a long, unspeaking moment, then suddenly broke and rushed forward, crying, "Guy, I'm sorry, Guy . . . Forgive me, forgive me," before the shouting voices drowned her out and she turned and rushed off sobbing in the night.

Guy looked after her. He looked at the laughing, cheering men. "You don't *know,*" he shouted. "Thank you, thank you, but you don't *know,* you don't *know!*" Then he turned and went back into the house as Larson Whitt appeared to disperse the crowd.

Back in the living room Guy finished his drink at a single swallow. He sat with Caesar's head against his knee. He said, "*You* don't know either, Saul. The whole town—I've betrayed every goddamn one of you!"

Saul said, "God, how that dog missed you!" and then after an awkward pause, "Guy . . ."

"What?"

"You got a letter a few days ago. I knew what it was and took the liberty of opening it. I did what I could about it, made phone calls, even took a day off and flew to Boston. But—I'm sorry."

"I know, Saul."

"The State Board—they've revoked your license."

"Violating medical ethics." Guy laughed shortly, went into the kitchen and poured another drink.

From the living room Saul said, "They'll reinstate it—two, three months—six at the most. It wasn't a question of whether the jury found you guilty or not."

"They have their own little jury."

"I said they'd reinstate it."

"Yes, and thanks, Saul. Thanks for everything."

"Take a trip," Saul said. "Go off for a while."

"Maybe I'll do just that."

"When you come back—license restored—everything'll be just like before."

"Just like before." He waved the glass and Saul said, "Well, the crowd's gone. Go along myself, I guess."

"Good night, Saul, and thanks, Saul."

"Not all personal, you know. I need you at the hospital—we need you in this town. If you don't know that by now—" Saul waved and went out through the kitchen. His car started up and wound slowly down the hill.

The silence was long and empty. Caesar whined with delight, and the clocks all ticked at once in different rhythms. The grandfather clock in the hall, the banjo clock in the living room; even his own watch seemed to tick audibly, louder than ever before. He moved absently about the familiar room. Finally he went into the office and lifted the phone. "Go away," Saul had said. "Come back and it'll be the same." Well, he'd go away, all right, but not alone.

And he would never come back at all.

"Hello . . ." The voice was Mrs. O'Hara's.

"Hello, Mrs. O'Hara. Is Mrs. McFie there?"

"No, sir . . . Is this Doctor Montford?"

"Yes."

"Congratulations, Doctor."

"Thank you. Do you know where Mrs. McFie's gone?"

"No, sir. She's just gone. Bag and baggage."

And now the chill came, creeping slowly, beginning at his knees, up, up through his entire body. She'd written that she was leaving, but why so soon? . . . Why so *soon?* His hand shook on the receiver. His voice broke. "You mean she's—already left for good?"

"Yes, sir. But she left a message for you to call Doctor Treleaven."

"Oh . . . Thank you, Mrs. O'Hara."

"Good night, Doctor."

"Good night," he said. "Good night, Mrs. O'Hara." He hung up. He stood leaning against the wall, feeling the terrible cold, though the house was warm by now. The phone rang while the receiver was still in his trembling hand, resting firmly on the hook.

It was Doctor Treleaven. He said Margreth had told him everything—*everything*. He'd driven her to Falmouth right after the trial. She was going away for a while. She would not write. But after she'd thought it all out, when she was absolutely certain of the way she felt, then she'd let him know where she was—if he still cared.

"If I still care—" Guy said dumbly.

"What?"
"I suppose *you* know."
"Yes."
"New Haven?"
"No, and there's no point in asking and no point in looking for her."
"I see."
"Guy . . . Guy . . . It's for *you*. Don't you understand that? She has to be sure, absolutely *sure*, before she'll obligate you in any way."
"I'm sure," Guy said simply. "I love her and I'm sure."
"You'll be hearing, Guy."
"I'm sure," he said again, and hung up and had four more drinks before he climbed the stairs to the bedroom, undressed, and crawled between the sheets in striped pajamas. Caesar laid his head on the blanket. He fondled the dog's ears. He said, "You won't run away, will you, boy? You won't ever run away."
Caesar whined.

The first shot had waked him immediately. It had smashed through the window and embedded itself in the ceiling. The second had followed close on the first. Then he'd heard the cursing in the yard below, before his mother had come in to comfort him, and Sheriff Potts had arrived to lead Mr. McFie away to jail, and eventually to a sanitarium.

He threw off the blankets as the third shot crashed in the night. He yelled, "Mother!" and peered quickly out the window. The fourth bullet whined up at the house and smashed the pane only inches above his head. He jerked back, shouted, "Mother! . . . Mother!" But there were no footsteps on the stairs, and Sheriff Potts was nowhere in sight. Instead Caesar barked and growled, and turning sharply, he caught a shadowy glimpse of his own face in the bedroom mirror. Guy Montford, thirty-eight years old.

Caesar went on growling as he raced down the stairs. He threw on a coat, slipped his bare feet into boots. The fifth bullet slammed into the side of the house; the sixth whined through the living-room window and ricocheted off the brick fireplace.

He opened the back door.

Sam stood some yards away, frantically trying to reload the rifle. His legs were spread wide to keep him steady. His hair flopped in the slight breeze. "Paul!" he screamed. "You sonovabitch!" he screamed. "Killed my wife, you killed my wife!" He'd managed to reload the rifle by now, and as Guy moved toward him, the barrel swung up, aimed directly at his chest.

He was going to die now, and he was not afraid. Some part of him was almost relieved, waiting, almost anxious for the bullet to smash him into oblivion. Gently he said. "Sam . . . It's Guy, Sam . . . It's Guy." And perhaps those few words stopped the bullet—and perhaps he should not have said them.

Sam lowered the rifle. He began trembling all through him.

"Guy," he said, "I wouldn't hurt you, Guy . . . Where's your father, Guy?"

His father was in bed probably, drunk probably.

"I wouldn't hurt his child."

Doctor Paul Montford was childless. He had no child.

"I'm sorry, Guy, sorry . . ." Sam began to weep. His entire body trembled. He dropped the rifle and kept on trembling and sobbing about how Larry and Guy were such good friends, and he'd never held it against Guy—never—never—and he'd never never hurt Doctor Montford's child.

Doctor Montford, of course, had never had a child. Stewed Schaeffer, but not Doctor Paul Montford. And the thought stayed planted ironically in Guy's mind as he took Sam's arm and led him to his car.

The motor was still running. He helped Sam into the front seat, then climbed in beside him and drove down the hill, through the quiet town to the big colonial house on Elm Street. He parked the car in the drive, then supported the still-sobbing man up the steps and into the house.

Mrs. O'Hara looked out from her room off the kitchen. Her face was dark beneath the white nightcap. "Drunk again," she complained. "I'm leaving," she declared.

Guy told her to wait a minute. He took Sam up the stairs to his bedroom, eased him down to the bed, pulled off his shoes, and covered him with a blanket. The man was still mumbling, weeping, "Sonovabitch . . . I wouldn't hurt a child," until finally he closed those red wild eyes, and the sputtered words gave way to heavy, rhythmic breathing.

Guy locked the door from the outside. He left the key in the lock, started for the stairs, then paused a moment before the empty bedroom at the top of the landing. He stared at the big canopied bed and the embroidered spread and the new cold emptiness of the remembered room. Then he turned and went on down the stairs.

Mrs. O'Hara waited in the living room. "I'm leaving," she stated. "I got relatives in Harpswell."

"No . . . Mrs. O'Hara . . . I've locked him in. When he

wakes up either he'll be all right or he won't. You understand. If he's all right, leave him alone and you won't have to leave. If he screams or yells or acts difficult in any way at all, then keep him locked in and call Doctor Kelsey immediately. You understand? *Immediately!*"

"He was in a sanitarium once."

"And he doesn't want to go back again. So if he's all right tomorrow, he'll be scared enough to lay off."

Peter complained at being wakened in the middle of the night. Mrs. O'Hara said, "Well—all right. I been trying to give him a chance." She glanced at Guy's boots pulled over his bare feet, the striped pajama bottoms that dropped below his coat. She started to smile, became aware of her own flannel nightdress, murmured an embarrassed "Good night, Doctor Montford," and scurried toward the kitchen in her pink woolen slippers.

Guy left the house and walked slowly through the town. It was dark except for the street lights and the blinking red light at the only stop sign and the row of lights along the second floor of the hospital. He stood motionless a long moment, staring at that row of lights. He located Room 2B, and remembered Larry there and Mar there—and remembered himself there last fall. He jerked his eyes away, jerked his memories away. He looked up at the sky and noticed that clouds had moved in from the north, which meant a storm was coming, then turned up his collar and moved on alone and cold through the empty town.

PART THREE

CHAPTER THIRTY-ONE

The first heavy snow fell in late January, throwing a white blanket over the town of East Norton, smothering the Montford affair as well. Snowplows rumbled through the night, followed by other trucks that blinked their red taillights as they spilled yellow sand over the freshly plowed roads.

The next morning children coasted on the steep hill behind the glassworks, and days later, after the snow had turned gray and melted, after the first zero weather of the season had stabbed into town, they abandoned their sleds for ice skates, and skimmed happily between the blades of grass that still poked up through the thick layer of ice along the marshes.

Edna Welles drove frantically about in her old station wagon, one broken chain clanking merrily on the bare spots of the roads as she searched and appraised and bargained in preparation for the official opening of YE OLDE ANTIQUE SHOPPE only short months away.

Edna saw little of Bert Mosley now. Early each Friday morning, Bert drove his old Plymouth coupé the hundred-odd miles to Boston, where he passed the day making frantic bargains in the inner and outer offices of various law firms. Saturdays and Sundays he lolled in the Charles Street basement apartment of Miss Sylvia Stein. It was a small, Bohemian place, cluttered with unframed Daumier and Dégas prints that were Scotch-taped to the ochre painted walls, with Honduran straw mats on the cement floor and one large folding studio couch on which Bert and Sylvia slept frequently and ferociously, in a sometimes successful attempt to find some identity within themselves.

Edna saw little of Bert, and Ruth Kiley saw little of Sam.

He scarcely ever went to the cannery now, but phoned in each day instead. He seemed embarrassed over the half-remembered night in the cottage on the dunes, and once, when Ruth managed a few face-to-face words with Mrs. O'Hara, she was told how Sam was brought home that same night by Doctor Montford. "Wearing his pajamas under his coat," Mrs. O'Hara explained in feigned modesty. "And Mr. McFie didn't wake up till four o'clock the next afternoon and wouldn't leave his room till suppertime. He didn't say a word either, not even when Peter began raising the devil on his perch. Just sat there eating kippered herring. In a daze, he was—scared to death, you know. So I left him alone, I did."

Ruth asked if she'd heard from Mrs. McFie, and Mrs. O'Hara showed her a beautiful bag of black top-grain leather. "Came from a department store in New Haven," she boasted, then added wisely, "but that don't prove she's *in* New Haven. I mean it wasn't *her* writing on the card, and if you ask me, *nobody* knows where Mrs. McFie is. And if you ask me, she's just gone off somewhere to forget the whole nasty business. But I wish her luck, wherever she is, because I liked the lady . . . I liked the lady . . ."

Ida Primmer liked a boy from Hyannis. He was a tall, freckled pharmacist named Patrick Starkey, whom she'd met through a nurse at the hospital in Falmouth. On their first date Patrick had kissed her with his mouth open, and a week later he'd left the motor running, the heater on, while he'd undressed her to the waist in the back of his Ford sedan. Ida had always been rather ashamed of her tiny, uptilted breasts. But Patrick had been fascinated by them, and had kissed her rigid nipples with such reverence that she'd fallen in love with him at that exact brief, shivering moment.

"Of course he lives with his family now," she explained to Fran. "But he owns a half interest in the pharmacy"—she refused to call it a drugstore—"and he's already saved over two thousand dollars. So if I keep on working—well, I wouldn't mind living in Hyannis. And of course I'd quit nursing after I became pregnant, you know."

Fran reminded her of a certain Harry from Rochester, whom she'd thrown over in order to dedicate her life to nursing. Ida protested that she'd been younger then, not quite so mature as now, yet did not bother to mention that Harry had never undressed her, had never kissed her with his mouth open—in fact, had never made a pass at her at all, only frequent retreats to her own advances.

Parker Welk, though, was not retreating, in fact had already started his first slow advance on Nancy Messner. Now that winter was here, Nancy wore few dresses which allowed him a glimpse of young flesh beneath a careless neckline. Even so, she looked fresh and virginal and terribly exciting in her standard winter uniform of white cardigan sweater and brown woolen skirt. And accordingly, Parker's strategy called for time, perhaps months, before he could possibly make the final proposal. First he tried to get close to Nancy in a warm, fatherly way, and since she responded with childish innocence, though she still resented him for having written those editorials against Doctor Montford, he decided he could now risk the next decisive step of confiding his interest in photographic art. He showed Nancy some impersonal nudes which he'd found in a magazine, and carefully—very professionally—explained to her why each one was good or bad, depending on the lighting, the pose, the creative imagination of the photographer, along with the special qualities of the model herself.

Nancy showed interest and admiration for Parker's knowledge of art. "There's just no real *culture* in a small town," she complained. And Parker sadly agreed, and sighed deeply and remarked that if he could ever find time to leave the prudery of East Norton for the more cosmopolitan atmosphere of Boston, he'd certainly like to attend one of those photographer's classes, where a man could work with a real live model.

Though the Montford affair was officially over, though the doctor no longer practiced and was no longer a familiar sight as he bumped over the rutted roads of town to call on an out-of-the-way patient, still he was seen now and then on those rare occasions when he left his weathered house on the rocky hill.

Chet Belknap saw more of him than anyone else in town. "Spends four, five hours a day at the boatyard," he reported. "Used to paint above the rail at night when his wife was alive. But now he's doin' the whole thing. Woodin' down, refinishin' bright work, scrapin', caulkin', paintin' the bottom and topsides, varnishin' spars and dinghy, workin' on the runnin' riggin', puttin' in new moorin' warp, new fenders, doin' all the whippin' and splicin' himself. Better job than I could do. Most of your sailors around here get by on a short splice and an eye splice. But Doc knows 'em all: Flemish, grommet, chain splice. You name it . . . You name it . . ."

Mr. Castner reported that the doctor had bought four new Hudson Bay blankets from his drygoods store, and the hardware's Ralph Messner remembered selling him a new pair of canvas gloves, a deck mop, a flashlight, and a refill for a fire extinguisher.

"Saw him over in Falmouth," Cy Coffin told his wife. "Tyler's marine store, picking up some spare rope, gear, battens, an anchor key, some sail slides, and twine and lacing line."

"Where's he going?" Clara asked.

"Couple of monkey blocks and a sister block—"

"Where's he *going*?"

"His own business."

"Didn't you *ask* him?"

"When was it *my* business?"

"He can't go anywhere in February."

"That Friendship of his'll go anywhere, any time, and there's no one alive can handle it better."

Some of the townspeople spoke to Doctor Montford when they met him on the street, embarrassed for themselves as well as for him, and some actually knocked on his door, despite the knowledge that he much preferred to be left alone.

Mrs. Columbo saw him three days a week when she came to clean his house. She was still apologetic for having "betrayed" him on the witness stand, but eventually consoled herself with the fact that he *had* been acquitted, and perhaps, in some obscure legal way that she did not understand, her own damning testimony had actually contributed toward his present freedom.

Guy was always polite and considerate, she thought, "Wrapped in himself," she explained to others. And sometimes, vacuuming the living room, she'd find him sitting motionless in a leather chair, staring off into space as though he were completely unaware of her presence.

Bill Watts, too, saw Guy three times each week when he delivered the milk. Although he reached the doctor's house in the darkness of winter's six o'clock, there was always a light in the kitchen, and Guy was always up, drinking black coffee and smoking his first cigarette while Caesar buried his snub nose in a green plastic bowl. Bill always knocked, opened the door, and put the milk away in the refrigerator. "Freeze up solid if you leave it out ten minutes," he ventured as a ritual remark. And Guy always nodded and said, "Have a cup of coffee, Bill." Usually Bill refused. But occasionally he did accept, to find himself doing most of the talking, while Guy merely nodded politely as he smoked another cigarette.

Larson Whitt saw Guy's lights burning in the late of night. Once he stopped in to ask if anything was wrong. Guy said everything was fine. He gave Larson a drink and asked after his children. Larson said he'd waited too long about having the younger one's tonsils out, so Doctor Bolls was doing it this very week. "I would've waited for you," he apologized, "but you know how it is, Guy."

"I know. And besides, I probably won't be here."

Larson did not want to probe. He finished his drink and continued his slow rounds of the quiet, freezing town.

A female member of the jury met Guy on the street, stopped him, started to explain what had gone on in the jury room that night, then decided against it, and scurried away in her fur-topped overshoes, while Father Serrano called on him one Sunday evening, said useless words, drank three cups of coffee, and left with the certainty that they would never speak again unless Guy finally came to him.

Mrs. Manning encountered Guy in the supermarket, where he was buying cases of canned beef stew, corned beef hash, and chili con carne. She said, "Remember what I wrote on my Christmas card? According to your horoscope, everything'll work out fine. That's because you're a Sagittarius. I wish I were, but I'm just an old Scorpio, and I don't expect anything to work out fine at all."

Doctor Kelsey met him in the drugstore, and Stewed Schaeffer ran into him in the liquor store, where Guy was buying a case of bonded bourbon. Stewed, sober at the time, with only vague memories of that drunken night in the town jail, said, "Looks like you're getting ready to hole up for the winter."

"In the boat," Guy said.

"A little early for sailing, isn't it, son?" He meant the "son" innocently, to denote their difference in age, but realized too late that he could not explain his own intentions. He bought a gallon of cheap Italian wine and passed that entire day in his room drinking, until he forgot everything there was left to remember.

The sun was bright on that February afternoon. It reflected off the hard crust of snow and burned Fran's eyes so that she stopped in at the drugstore and bought a cheap pair of sunglasses. It felt odd, wearing sunglasses with woolen slacks and a heavy toggle coat. But with the hood pulled over her head, scarcely anyone recognized her as she moved past Pat's and down the winding hill toward Chet Belknap's boatyard.

She had no idea what she was going to say. Rumors had reached her from various merchants and patients, even from Doctor Bolls, so that she knew for certain that Guy was leaving town. Many times, in the weeks before, she'd been tempted to call him or make some plan to meet him as though by accident. Each time, though, her courage had failed at the last, until now, when it was too late for scheming, she would have to face him outright. "Good-by," she practiced, and "I'm sorry," she practiced, and even "I love you," though none seemed quite right, and she was not exactly sure of her own real feelings anyway.

She first saw him as she came down the long wooden dock that extended out beyond the low-water mark. He stood at the far end, bent over as he lowered a large cardboard carton into *Julia*'s cockpit. The hull of the boat was hidden below the dock but the mast loomed high above it, and the rakish bowsprit poked up from one corner while the tip of the boom extended beyond the other. For a moment Guy disappeared down the ladder. Then he reappeared again, heaved another case to his shoulder, lowered it carefully over the edge of the pier, and disappeared once more.

Fran moved forward until she stood looking down into *Julia*'s cockpit. The sun was warm against her face, though the wind off the water knifed through her slacks so she was cold and warm at the same time—a strange, rather sensual feeling that she had never experienced until coming East to a Cape Cod water front. She breathed deep and felt the air freeze in her nostrils, then breathed out again through her mouth, watching the quick steam blow fast away.

Guy came out of the cabin. He wore boots and dungarees and a heavy mackinaw, leather mittens, and on his head a blue hunting cap with the ear flaps down. He looked up at her slowly, as though he did not quite recognize her.

She took off the glasses. "Hello, Guy . . ."

"Oh . . . Fran."

"What am I doing out in the cold?"

"Something like that."

"Can I come in?"

"Down—and you may." He smiled quickly, held up a mittened hand, and helped her down the ladder to the cockpit. "It's warm below," he said, and slid open the hatch, then waited while she preceded him to the cabin.

She sat on a bunk, dropped the hood, and shook out her hair while he watched her closely, his tall frame bent slightly forward to avoid bumping his forehead on the overhead. "Coffee?" he said finally.

"No, thank you."

"A drink maybe?"

"No, I don't intend to stay. I know you're busy. Leaving tomorrow."

"Yes."

"So I—well, nobody seems to know when you're coming back."

"Including me."
"So I thought—well, I'd say good-by."
"Thank you, Fran." He poured himself a drink, a rather large one, she thought, considering that everyone knew he seldom ever drank before Larry McFie had returned to town. He swallowed half the whiskey at a gulp, made a face, said, "Don't say anything you don't really want to say."
"You told me that before. In your car, remember?"
"Yes."
"Only I said it anyway. I was impulsive then. I was impulsive when I falsified the drug records, impulsive when I went to Larson Whitt. I guess I'm still impulsive."
He took off his mittens, gave her a cigarette, and lit it for her. She looked at the black hairs on the back of his hand, remembered doing the same thing on a ride back from the Robins Nest Motel, said, "Thank you," inhaled the smoke, then added, "I'm not marrying Bert Mosley, you know."
"Yes, I heard."
"I walked out on him, and now he's all involved with that girl reporter from Boston. It was Bert who made me go to Larson. I didn't understand what he was planning to do. Then, when I did, I wanted to die. I thought I hated you, but I don't hate you at all. I was jealous, you see, and I guess I still am. So—that was the reason I was going to marry Bert until I understood my own feelings."
Guy did not answer. He swallowed the rest of the drink, and she went on deliberately, straight out because she had to know. "You're going to Mrs. McFie, aren't you?"
"No, Fran, I'm not."
"You're in love with her though."
"Yes . . ."
"Of course I won't ever tell anyone. I've already made things hard enough for you. So I won't tell."
"I know you won't, Fran."
"You're never coming back here again."
"Not if I can help it."
"Well—" She put out the cigarette and rose and laughed and said, "If you ever do come back—if everything goes wrong for you and you feel very lonesome—I mean I know you're lonesome now, but you're trying to do something about it. And I'm lonesome, too, you see, because everybody resents me, and—well, if you'd forgive me—that's all I really mean—if you'd forgive me, then I wouldn't care whether anyone else did or not."
"I forgive you," he said. And then, "Why don't you leave town, Fran? Go to another hospital?"
"Because it's always the same. Always trouble, always trou-

ble. I don't know—it seems to follow me everywhere. I'm always lonesome, so I start doing terribly immoral things, but it never helps really, and I can't go home. I have no home. A house in a town in Indiana. But everything I ever told you about it was a lie—just what I've always pretended it was, when I really hated it, and I can't go back."

"Fran," he said. "Fran . . . Fran . . ."

"Oh, God, oh, God!" And she could do nothing then but cry, until finally there were no tears left and she blew her nose and climbed the smooth ladder to the cockpit, the rough wooden ladder to the pier, and strode fast down the pier in the hot sun and the cold wind, until she'd reached the frozen ground again, where she put on the sunglasses so that no one could tell she'd been crying.

CHAPTER THIRTY-TWO

Darkness still lay over the bay; the lights still winked in the town behind. But this was the way to go—early in darkness—the escaping fugitive, the banished exile, the guilty man fleeing his potential accusers and the condemnation of his own conscience.

Guy climbed down the ladder to *Julia*'s cockpit, started for the cabin, and only then recognized the dark figure that leaned against the wheel—John Treleaven in a black hat and black ear muffs and black gloves, bundled tight in a great black overcoat that made him nearly invisible except for the quick shine on his rimless glasses.

"Guy . . ." John's teeth chattered audibly. "Before you leave . . . I heard you were leaving, but first, it's very important—"

"Important?"

"I'm going to Nantucket, you understand. Next week. Tuesday—and now you're going off yourself—without warning—" He paused. His body shivered beneath the coat. Guy suggested they go below. But the minister declined; he had only a few words to say. ". . . Siasconset, to be exact . . . a six-month exchange with a minister at the Congregational Church . . . Coming back at the end of summer . . . Want you to know . . . No, can't tell you where Margreth is . . . Gave my word to her and can't break my word . . . But I'll keep in touch with you . . . After next Tuesday, perhaps I'll have heard from her . . . Perhaps she'll want to see you . . . Understand . . . Mustn't get out of touch . . ." He talked on in broken sentences that snapped chattering from between his teeth. "That's all . . . But important . . . It's cold . . . I'll be there for six months . . . write you if there's anything important. So keep in touch with the post office . . . Understand . . . Keep in touch, and good-by, good luck, good-by . . . too cold to be a minister and give any personal advice or consolation . . . Too *goddamned cold!*"

The voice stopped. John shook his head in horror at his own oath, then turned abruptly in embarrassment and hastily climbed the ladder. The last Guy saw he was a black shadow walking fast, almost running down the pier, as though the cold, or perhaps an avenging devil, were running close behind.

He turned to the business of getting under way. He started the two-cylinder engine, cast off, and chugged out into the bay. Daylight was breaking now. The wind was from the south, which meant he'd have to sail close-hauled and make at least one tack in order to clear Keever's Point. He was heading for New Bedford, though he had no particular reason to select that town over any other. It was off the Cape, however, a town in which he would probably not be recognized, a lazy day's sail around Woods Hole and across Buzzard's Bay, as reasonable a destination as any. And he thought no more about it as he checked the metal hawk at the masthead, then ran free across the southerly wind past Poponesset Beach and Cape Beach, Falmouth Heights and Nobska Point, with Long Neck to starboard and the Elizabeth Islands to port, until he'd rounded the heel of the Cape, he steered a northwesterly course for New Bedford. The wind had shifted slightly to the east, so *Julia* ran dead before it now, and he liked the danger of the sailing position, though regretted that it was not the fastest.

The day was gray and cold, the water choppy, throwing spray against the sails. Twice he had to knock ice from the running rigging and backstays, and twice more he set the wheel and went below for hot coffee in the warmth of the cabin, where Caesar lay snoring on a bunk. He sat across from the dog and watched it closely, trying to find an almost human contact with the animal, since he had deliberately broken off all relationships with every person he knew. He tried not to think of anyone, especially not of Mar. She would send for him; she would not send for him. Whatever her feelings, he could not change them, and he did not want her to falsely return his love through guilt or obligation. He was free now—free of all those good people he'd betrayed, those honest friends who believed in him more than he could ever possibly believe in himself again—completely free, with only one objective: to find Mar, somehow to find her, and then to watch over her and their unborn child and do what little he could in this time of need.

The day was fading fast when he made the first landfall at Sconticut Point, followed by another at Clarks Point. Moments later he lowered sail outside the New Bedford harbor at the mouth of the Acushnet, started the sputtering engine, and steered for a known Marina along the water front near the center of town.

"Guy Schaeffer," he told the dock attendant, finding grim humor in the pseudonym, then walked up the pier to a diner, where he had two frankfurters and bought some ground beef for Caesar. He drank coffee in the cabin while the sloop bumped gently against the tire fenders and then later, before bed, he had three straight shots of bourbon. He dropped into the bunk and lay there staring at the dull red glow of the kerosene heater. He thought that he'd gotten through the first of a series of searching, lonely days. Beginning tomorrow he would telephone the East Norton post office every morning. He wondered how many calls he would have to make before word came from Mar. Or would he never hear from her at all?

The following morning was damp, ugly with a dirty gray sky. He ate breakfast in the cabin, then telephoned the postmaster, fat little Clem Doudy, from a phone booth in a bar at the end of the dock.

Clem answered with his sharp New England accent. "Couple of bills; bulletin from Harvard University; Abercrombie and Fitch catalogue, and some medical journals, along with a bunch of *Lifes* and *American Legions*."

"Save the journals and catalogue, throw away the bulletin, and keep the rest for yourself."

"When you come back, Guy, why don't you start taking *Esquire*? Or maybe *Playboy*?" Clem chuckled over the phone. "They got a lot of girlie magazines out these days, and even though they can't get most of 'em through the mails, at least you could subscribe to *Playboy*."

"You're talking 'ifs,' Clem." Guy hung up. He felt restless. When he'd first decided to leave East Norton, he'd thought he'd find peace in being alone. Actually, yesterday on the open bay, he had found some of that wanted peace. But it had worn off overnight. For a man could not sail about endlessly in a small boat. There had to be some focal point, some purpose to his life. He could not face East Norton, and yet that was exactly where he belonged—facing it—until he was allowed to practice again and the town finally forgot, or until he found Mar and left forever to be with her and their child. One way or another, he should be facing *something*. And he deplored his own inability to stand up to a trusting society, to a distrusting self, to come to some solid, constructive decision, and stand on it regardless of any hardships and any end results.

"You bastard," he told himself. "Figurative, amoral, irreligious, murdering bastard. Literal, weak, sniveling, running-away bastard!" as he strode restlessly around the streets of this town that had once been the world's greatest whaling port, but was now just another manufacturing town—cotton and tools and electrical equipment and aircraft parts.

He went back to the sloop. He fed Caesar and ate a can of chili con carne. It was seven o'clock. The evening lay long ahead, with no relief from this self-hatred, this building tension that was accented by the maddening thump of *Julia*'s hull against the rubber fenders and the small sleepy whines of a dog who could not understand. He poured a drink, sat on a bunk, and watched the dog in the bunk across the narrow deck. After the third drink it occurred to him that Caesar was defiling that bunk, for it was there that he had first made love to Mar. He ordered Caesar down, then sat motionless, trying to remember exactly how Mar had looked in the yellow light of the swinging lantern. Slender, black-haired, her skin very clear and taut and white, her legs long, her mouth red, the lips moist, parted, the eyes black and oriental and a little wild then, her breasts round and soft in firmness, her thighs firm too, soft too, and—

No, it had been *this* bunk, the one he was sitting on himself. Caesar could go back to bed once more. Mar's body was gone, perhaps forever, and a mongrel dog again replaced her.

It was 9:36. He'd had four drinks, but they'd only increased his restlessness. He rose, bumped his skull on an overhead, swore, stumbled slightly, then forced himself out of the quick dizziness. He would find Mar. He would not sail helplessly about, getting nowhere, only hurting and remembering—somehow he would find Mar. He would *find* her!

The phone booth was warm and smelled of stale beer. The information operator claimed there was no such town as Chiddersburg.

"Chiddersville . . . Chitterton . . . Chiddester . . . Yes, that's it—Chiddester. Right near Atlanta . . . And the name is Sloane . . . No, I don't know the first name, but it's a small town, so if you could get the local operator—"

"One moment, please."

He waited. He lit a cigarette and prayed and wondered why he had not thought of this before. The Chiddester operator said that yes, there was a Mrs. Sloane in town, and yes, she lived in a large colonial house called Wild Acres. She would call Mrs. Sloane immediately.

More waiting, and then the Southern voice, high, cultured, a little vague, Guy thought. He said, "Mrs. Sloane?"

"Yes . . ."

"This is Doctor Montford. Guy Montford." Silence. He rushed on. "I've been trying to locate your daughter—Mrs. McFie."

"I read all about you, *Mr.* Montford."

"Yes, I understand. But this is very important, you see. Mrs. McFie left quite hurriedly after the trial, and—well, it's to her own advantage for me to get in touch with her as soon as possible."

Mrs. Sloane hesitated, indignant, uncertain, then abruptly dissolved into tears. She said she didn't really blame him, not really, because after all, Larry had been in an Atlanta hospital for a while, and she knew firsthand how hopeless it had all been—but no, she didn't know where her daughter was at all. She'd received one letter, forwarded from New Haven, from Margreth's college roommate probably, a girl named Susan Leister, except Susan was married now, and she didn't have the faintest idea what her married name was, nor could she think of any way to find it out.

"Who were Miss Leister's parents, Mrs. Sloane?"

"I don't know. She came from Chicago. That's all I know, and I'm so sorry I can't help, because I'm so worried that something's happened to Margreth—I mean she's always been so headstrong, you know—stubborn, you know—and I mean maybe she's had a breakdown or something."

"No, Mrs. Sloane, not a breakdown." He dropped the cigarette, stepped on it, said, "No hint in her letter to you . . . Nothing?"

"Well, she did mention a harbor. She lives in a cottage that overlooks a harbor."

"That's all—just a harbor?"

That was all. He started to tell her not to worry, that a Doctor Treleaven knew where Mar was, then decided against it, since there was no reasonable explanation as to why the minister was keeping it such a tight secret. He said good-by and hung up and thought Mar must be near anyway—somewhere on the Cape, probably, except there were hundreds of harbors . . . hundreds of them . . .

CHAPTER THIRTY-THREE

The next morning he called Clem Doudy from a bar, forgetting that the post office was closed on Sundays. Angry, impatient, he called John Treleaven. No answer. Still at church, of course, bidding a final good-by to all the good people of East Norton: Fran Walker and Mrs. Coffin; Mrs. Manning and Saul Kelsey; Ida Primmer and Sam and Ruth Kiley and Bert Mosley and Parker Welk and all the rest of them.

He drank a beer, then tried again, and this time John's wife answered.

"Oh, Guy!" Frances exclaimed. And "Where *are* you?" she asked. Then, after he told her briefly with no elaboration, her voice echoed off as she called her husband.

No, John had nothing to report. He was leaving Tuesday as planned. "Just keep in touch with the post office . . . Keep in *touch!*"

"I've got to know, John . . . Where is she, John? . . . I swear if you don't tell me, I'll find her . . . Somehow I'll *find* her" . . . John did not answer. "All right, John . . . All right."

Guy hung up, drank a second beer, then went back to the Marina. It was early afternoon, but he could still make Woods Hole before dark. Why Woods Hole? Because Woods Hole was on the Cape and Mar was somewhere on the Cape, in a cottage that overlooked a harbor, one of a thousand cottages that overlooked one of a hundred harbors, and somehow he would find her.

The wind was strong from the northeast. All the way he remembered how he and Julia had sailed like this, fast off the wind, and how sometimes she'd held the wheel herself and laughed into that wind with her red hair in tangles, the freckles dotting her childish, impish face, and how sometimes, on summer days, she'd lain completely naked in the sun on the cabin's roof, her firm athletic body stretched out in sacrifice to the wind and sun and weather that she loved.

The winter dark had already descended when he chugged into Woods Hole. He tied up at the public dock, then went into a small water-front bar and restaurant for his first meal of the day—fried clams and french fries, eaten ravenously after two glasses of beer.

It was after that, during coffee, that the weathered old man appeared in the doorway, searching for the fellow who owned the black Friendship. He was a Mainer by birth. Retired lobsterman. Had his own boat, then a lobster pound. He'd made money and retired to Woods Hole here, where he lived with his married daughter. For three years now he'd been looking for an authentic Friendship in sound condition. *Julia* was authentic. She looked sound. He wanted her.

"Not *entirely* authentic," Guy told him. "I had the builder extend the cabin aft a couple of feet, and there's one other catch—she's not for sale."

The old man left his name and phone number. Price no consideration. "I can smell a boat. She smells good. I'd take real care of her. You wouldn't have to worry. Any time you want to sell. Only make it reasonable soon, 'cause I ain't gettin' any younger." He put out a strong, gnarled hand, touched his stained yachting cap, and left.

On the way back to the boat, Guy met an automobile salesman from Falmouth. The salesman, a casual friend, nodded and hedged and tried not to ask questions. Guy said he was just taking a vacation.

"Yeah," the salesman said, and walked off in an awkward hurry.

John said he was leaving for Nantucket tomorrow. His voice was gentle, sympathetic. "So don't call me here again, Guy. And take care of yourself," he said, "but keep in touch with the post office because any letter from me will concern Margreth . . . You understand? . . . I will not write *unless it's about* Margreth." A pause, and then, "Stop running," he added. "Sit down and think awhile. Get yoga about it. Contemplate your navel. Struggle with it, wrestle it, but don't run from it." Words to live by—Teddy Roosevelt or *The Reader's Digest* or Rudyard Kipling or Norman Vincent Peale. John knew and coughed in embarrassment and hung up.

Back in *Julia*'s cabin, Guy studied the chart of Nantucket Sound. He could sail along the southern side of the Cape, put in at one harbor after another, make inquiries about a beautiful dark-haired woman who lived in a cottage above the bay. But the chances were one in a thousand that he'd ever find her.

He decided to try the larger harbors east of East Norton. The retired lobsterman was there to see him off. "You got my name, my number?" the old man asked anxiously, and "It breaks my heart to see her leave." He stared at the boat for a long hesitant moment, then said, "Your name's Montford, ain't it?"

"No . . ."

"That place you ate at last night—I just had a beer there, and they said this Montford fellow had a black Friendship."

"Did they?"

"Said it was funny both of you come in there to eat."

"Both of us?"

"First that Mrs. McFie . . . Same night the trial ended. They recognized her from the pictures in the paper. Had dinner there with a minister just before the ferry left."

"The ferry?" Guy said. He wet his lips, studied the old man's wrinkled face. "Did she take the ferry?"

The old man shrugged. "She ate there just before the ferry left, and that's all they know, and last night you ate in the same place, and they thought that was kind of funny, wasn't it?"

"Yes . . . Funny." He started the engine and thought that the ferry went to Martha's Vineyard, and from there to Nantucket. There were harbors on Martha's Vineyard. There was a large harbor on Nantucket. If Mar had taken the ferry, then he'd find her after all—now he was sure, absolutely sure he'd find her.

It was late afternoon when he dropped anchor at Edgartown on Martha's Vineyard. He'd decided on Edgartown because it was more remote than either Vineyard Haven or Oak Bluffs, and if Mar were here at all, she had probably settled in the most secluded place she could find. He stood on the deck in the red sunlight and studied the rows of cottages along the shore of this island of inland ponds and crashing surf, of fat gulls and slender terns, of pine and scrub oak and Indian names. He wondered if Mar was there in any of those tiny houses, and if so, which one—which one? Well, he would find out tomorrow. Tomorrow he would row ashore in the dinghy, make his ritual phone call to Clem Doudy, and inquire after a beautiful woman who stayed alone in a rented cottage. But tonight he would have six or eight drinks, get tight enough to see everything optimistically, fancy happy fancies and dream pleasant dreams.

Clem Doudy reported no mail at all. John Treleaven was on his way to Nantucket.

Three cups of black coffee in a luncheonette. A stroll along the harbor front. Nine, eight, seven—even six years ago, he and Julia had sailed frequently to Martha's Vineyard in their proud new Friendship, *Tinker Bell*. They'd strolled the open land, smelled the huckleberry and blackberry and bayberry, gone swimming in the surf, watched the swordfishermen bring in their catch, and spent an entire day in the near-carnival town of Oak Bluffs, where Julia had caught four rings on the carousel, and they'd taken a ride in a ridiculous paddle boat.

Here, in quiet Edgartown, they had walked these streets and eaten in these restaurants and made love in these hotels. All the hotels and most of the restaurants were closed now, boarded up against the winter, cold, empty, leaving no trace of last season's laughter. Still, he and Julia had shared Martha's Vineyard together, as they'd shared Nantucket and Block Island, and practically every harbor, large or small, along both sides of the Cape.

He and Mar had shared one innocent night in Boston. He wondered if they'd ever discover another town together (for though he'd known Boston well, still it had all been rediscovered in the company of Mar). He wondered if they'd ever share another Chinese family dinner, another sail in Indian summer, another drink—another bed. He wondered why he did not resent Mar—for having left him—for having existed in this world at all. Why not defend himself? Why not actually blame her—save his own integrity with ridiculous rationalities? "If you'd never come to town—if you'd never visited *Julia*'s cabin—if you'd never called me over for a game of chess—if you'd never found me in Boston—?" If, if, if. But "ifs" were no good; reason would not help. These things had happened. He'd fallen in love with Margreth McFie. He loved her; he was *in* love with her. He would find her. *Finis.*

A whistle sounded to the north as the New Bedford ferry rounded Cape Page on its way to Nantucket. Perhaps John Treleaven had boarded that very steamer at Woods Hole; or perhaps he'd taken the ferry from Hyannis. It was shorter from Hyannis. John was going to Nantucket on a six-month exchange with a minister in 'Sconset. John knew exactly where Mar was, and Nantucket had a large harbor and—

Caesar barked.

"All right, you want to run?" He circled the town in the rising wind, warmed his face and hands in a waterfront bar and grill, much like Pat's with its painted wooden walls and wooden stools, its garish nickelodeon and the modern phone booth in the corner. At the bar he ate clam chowder and made guarded inquiries about a strange woman. No one had seen a strange woman in months. Perhaps Oak Bluffs or Vineyard Haven—perhaps Nantucket. Yes, perhaps Nantucket.

His eyes kept turning to the telephone. The wind howled outside. The window snapped in the cold. The phone was silent. The wind should not howl; the window should not snap; the phone should ring. Mar was near and something was wrong. Watching the ferry as it rounded Cape Page, all during the cold walk around the town while Caesar ran and barked before him—all during the short long winter day—he had known it. He still knew it. Mar was near and something was *wrong*.

"How's the chowder?" asked the proprietor.

"Fine," staring blankly at the phone booth.

"You want to use the phone?"

"No . . ." He crumbled crackers into the chowder and found his hand was shaking.

Someone said, "We're in for a real nor'easter!"

Someone else said, "The chowder's too thin today," and a discussion began among the bored men at the bar. They dismissed Manhattan chowder as being tomato soup made with water, into which a clam had been lowered briefly on a string. Rhode Island chowder was better, since it contained milk; but still the tomatoes were there, and you should *never* put tomatoes into clam chowder. This was New England chowder, made thick with cream and potatoes and plenty of clams. "Now there's a chowder I had in Maine," a voice said. "Sort of like this, but made with clam juice—but *no* milk. Sort of a cross between them all, you see, but good—very good."

The phone rang and Guy dropped his spoon, jerked upright, started toward the booth, then stopped and moved aside to let the proprietor answer.

"Look, Milly, I told you over and over, order your *own* milk. I know we got six kids, but still I can't go lugging a big milk can home every night, even if I do get it a little cheaper here. And you better close the shutters, 'cause we're in for a blow."

What was wrong? What in the hell was wrong that he felt, but could not touch, that he *knew*, but could not explain?

He finished the chowder. The talk was now of the relative merits of ketches as opposed to yawls in heavy weather. He joined in, talking very fast, keeping his mind on boats and chowders . . . on "shoes and ships and sealing wax . . ."

"Yep, Nantucket all right." Clem's voice rasped over the phone in a nasal twang. "Postmark clear as a bell. Three thirty yesterday afternoon. 'Sconset, Nantucket. Doctor John Treleaven."

"Clem . . ." Guy ran a shaking hand over the black mouthpiece. "Listen, Clem—"

"You want me to forward it?"

"No, I—"

"Open it and read it to you? 'Course it ain't legal, but if it's important, like you say, I could do a little winkin' at the government."

"Yes, Clem," and then, "No, Clem . . . No . . . *No!*" He

pounded his fist against the phone-booth wall. Why hadn't he *thought* of this? Of course the letter concerned Mar; but there was no telling *what* John had written, so of course he could not let Clem open it. He said, "Hold it, Clem . . . You better just—hold it."

He hung up, leaned against the tin wall of the booth. It was quarter after nine. He forced himself to stop shivering, then rang the Nantucket operator and tried to find John Treleaven's phone number. It was not listed, and he did not know the name of the minister John was replacing. "The Congregational Church in 'Sconset. Certainly you can locate—"

Yes, she could. But the lines to 'Sconset were down. Well, it wasn't her fault they were having a big gale on Nantucket. The lines would be repaired as soon as possible. An hour, two hours, eight hours, tomorrow.

He swore and hung up.

The wind had reached gale force, threatening to smash the window of the bar, tear down the TV antenna on the roof.

The proprietor said, "Told you last night it was goin' to blow," and "I made the chowder a little thicker today."

"Thanks, but I'm leaving."

"Not in this, you ain't."

"Nantucket."

"You crazy?"

"Maybe. I don't know. Maybe."

Crazy? Maybe. Crazy? Maybe, as he rowed the dinghy out to *Julia*'s mooring. He hoisted a double-reefed mainsail and storm jib so they flapped harmlessly, started the engine, and crept forward toward the buoy. He hauled in the buoy and dropped it to port on the windward side of his first tack, then went back to the wheel and sailed close on the wind, still using the engine until he'd cleared the harbor. Then he cut the engine and swung the boat to starboard. She heeled badly as he came about, then righted again as he eased the mainsail so that she spilled more wind. The boat moved slower now, but at least she stayed upright on course. That was more than some boats would do. Old slow-and-steady with her clipper bow and her heavy keel and squat grace—thirty-two feet with an eight-foot beam, a full quarter of the over-all length. But she'd make it.

The spray whipped stinging across his face. It froze to ice on his unprotected eyebrows, grew dangerously heavy in the rigging. But he did not feel the cold. He thought that John Treleaven had arrived on Nantucket only yesterday, and had sent the letter immediately on arrival. A letter from Mar must have been waiting for John . . . Or Mar was there herself—actually right there on Nantucket, right there beyond the blowing spray and the heavy waves. Yes, she *was* there . . . He knew it now. He was sure of it now. Except something was *wrong* . . . something was *wrong*. Or no, she wanted to see him. That was all. She wanted to see him. So let the wind blow . . . let the waves roll high and the ice freeze solid. He was going to Mar . . . going to Mar. And he sailed on into the howling gale—seeing Mar's face before him—laughing into the storm because he would see her soon—he would see her soon—and no storm on earth, nothing God could possibly devise could stop him now.

CHAPTER THIRTY-FOUR

Through the small window in the "wart" of the old "lean-to" house, Doctor John Treleaven could see the blinking light at Sankaty Head, and beyond that and below, the white foam of winter waves as they crashed up on the dark of 'Sconset Beach. The wind howled about the eaves, and the panes of the window rattled, promising to crack at any moment.

He went down the small flight of stairs to the living room with its exposed joints and stiff mahogany furniture, where Frances sat reading an historical novel by the light of a sperm-oil lamp. She looked up from the book—brown-haired, pleasant-looking, genial Frances, who had dedicated her married life to his parish and parishioners. No, he could not complain about Frances. If they had no children, that was not her fault. She'd always wanted children—as he had, too—and perhaps that was why he felt so protective toward Mrs. Margreth McFie. She, too, had always wanted a child. And though he could hardly condone the circumstances through which she had conceived one, at least he could understand her desire to have it.

Frances said, "Stop worrying."

"You don't understand."

"Oh, I understand all right." She always said that to him, the way she said it to anyone who wanted to find solace by exposing his problems to the minister's wife. "Of course I understand," though she never did, as she had never understood the least thing about her own husband. He was, always had been, a liberal, earthy man. So long as he did nothing to offend the church or town—nothing to offend his own moral beliefs—he saw no reason why he should conduct himself any differently than other men. He liked to swim and fish; he enjoyed poker and wrestling and baseball and the cartoons in *The New Yorker*. Or rather he had. Somehow, to Frances, these were not proper recreations for a minister. She'd even been a little scandalized on their honeymoon, when she'd found he was a man of great sexual appetite, and had immediately made a difficult compromise with him. They would have sex on Tuesdays, Thursdays and Saturdays, so long as the activities never left the realm of propriety (though she had not been—was still not quite sure what exactly constituted "propriety" in marital relations). That, of course, had been twelve years ago, when they had first married. Now Saturday's sex had been dropped completely, and John felt certain that Tuesday's would follow shortly, since he stayed late in the church on Tuesday nights, Frances was usually asleep when he came to bed, and did not like to be awakened simply to satisfy his appetite.

Tonight was Wednesday. John studied his wife across the room where she sat engrossed in that novel of unreal men and women, who lived romantic lives that had no bearing on her own. He had been rather surprised that she'd accepted Margreth's pregnancy so casually. But then, Margreth, like the characters in the novel, had nothing to do with the life of Frances Treleaven. She was simply another church member in trouble, and all Frances had said on hearing about it, all she ever would say, was "Of course I understand."

He wondered if she might have conceived on a Monday or a Wednesday night. He wondered how she'd react now if he suddenly said, "I simply won't wait till Thursday. You're my wife, Frances, and I've been reading a book about the twenty-seven different positions—"

John shook his head. No . . . No. He would think about Guy Montford and this storm, and whether he had played the right part in this or not, and whether he was continuing to play it right and honestly, as dictated by his own conscience. He said, "It's Guy I'm worrying about. If he got my letter this morning. Well—the phone lines are down, and the planes aren't in service, and since he wasn't on the last ferry—"

"He's waiting out the storm," Frances said into her book.

"You don't know him, Frances, any more than you know me really."

She tossed him an amused glance of tolerant affection. He sat wearily and lit a pipe, took a few puffs, then jerked upright, listening intently. "I thought I heard something." He tried to relax again. Frances continued reading.

"Frances . . ."

"I made you a promise, didn't I? I won't ever tell a soul."

"I made *her* a promise too, Frances."

"A minister's wife should be his right hand."

John bit his lip, started to reply, then decided against it. He continued sucking the pipe, and Frances remarked that if he were expecting a visitor, perhaps he ought to get out of that dirty old gray sweat shirt. John did not answer, but listened to the storm instead, until finally, minutes later, a car door slammed in the street outside. He rose swiftly and looked out the window. "It's him," he said over his sweat-shirted shoulder.

"The coffee's all ready."

"And I'm simply going to tell him, that's all. The rest of it's none of our business."

Then the knock sounded and he opened the door on Guy Montford. The man's face was red from the cold and wind. He needed a haircut, and his jaw bristled with a two-day beard. He wore a mackinaw over a checkered lumber shirt, a blue hunting cap and heavy woolen trousers tucked into leather boots. His eyes were bright, a little wild, John thought, like his first remark, "In like a lion, all right . . ."

"Come in, Guy."

"But it means an early spring." Guy nodded to Frances. "Hello, Frances."

She said, "Hello," and "I'll get some coffee," and left.

John said, "When did you get the letter?"

"I didn't. I just know you sent one, and it had to be important."

"Yes."

"It *is* important."

"Yes."

"Something's wrong."

"Yes."

Frances returned with the coffee. She poured out three cups and they sat and sipped it black while John scratched his armpit through the sweat shirt and said, "Of course Frances knows all about it, Guy, because Margreth's right here on Nantucket."

Guy did not answer. He sipped at his coffee. Finally he said, "I knew it. Toward the end, somehow I knew it."

"When she first told me everything—wanted to be alone, unknown somewhere—I found her a winterized cottage about half-way between here and town. Overlooking the harbor, you know."

"Yes."

"I knew I'd be coming here on an exchange, and thought it might be helpful if I were close by."

"Please, John, go on, please."

"Well, I knew she'd been going to the Cottage Hospital regularly, because she wrote occasional letters. They all sounded cheerful enough. Then, yesterday, when I arrived here and went to call on her, then I realized she was trying to hide something. So I called the hospital—her obstetrician, a Doctor Stafinos."

"And?"

Doctor Treleaven sucked hard on his pipe. It had gone out. He sipped at his coffee. "And?" Guy was saying intently. "And? And?"

He put down the cup and struck a match and sucked on the pipe again and said everything very slowly and carefully.

Frances said, "More coffee, Guy?"

"No, thank you."

"She didn't want me to tell you."

"Funny—I knew something—bright eyes, that healthy look. I should have guessed it."

"I insisted I'd have to break my promise to her."

"Why?" Guy said.

"I thought you ought to know."

"Why didn't *she* want me to know?" And then, "Of course, of course . . ." He rose and buttoned the mackinaw, put on the blue hunting cap. "About halfway to town?" he asked.

"Listen to me, Guy—"

"I told the cab driver to wait."

"The name 'T. Lewis' in gold on a black sign. But you have to understand, Guy—"

"I understand."

"She's using her maiden name. Mrs. Margreth Sloane. At the hospital, they think she's a divorcée. I told Stafinos that myself. I also told him her ex-husband might drop by to see him."

Guy said, "Thank you," and "Thanks for the coffee, Frances," then went out to the storm and closed the door. Through the window, John saw him get into the cab and drive off in the wind.

He shut the door.

"More coffee, John?"

He started an angry retort, then changed his mind, sat, relit his pipe, and said, "All right, more coffee."

She'd been tense all evening. The wind roared outside, and even the normally calm harbor was dotted with whitecaps. Now and then she glanced out at the storm; now and then she busied herself with practical things. She refilled the emergency kerosene lamps (the power line had gone down during the afternoon), and washed the few dishes and fluffed up the pillows on the redwood cushioned sofa. All the furniture was redwood, the walls bare knotty pine, sporting mounted trout and prints of sailfish and model hulls of famous racing boats. It was a small, a plain yet comfortable place—the private retreat of a sports-loving bachelor.

She had never seen Mr. T. Lewis in person, though there was a photo of him in the bedroom, which showed a large, suntanned man standing proudly beside a swordfish. "Mr. T. Lewis," she said aloud. "Theodore Lewis," named after Teddy Roosevelt probably. She wondered if Mr. Lewis ever said "Bully" or "Carry a big stick" or "Hit the line hard." She wondered if she would ever actually meet him.

She wondered if Guy would come.

The lamp smoked and she turned down the wick. She went into the bedroom and appraised her black slacks and red, loosefitting jacket in the full-length mirror on the inside of the closet door. She brushed out her hair and thought that John Treleaven had written to Guy against her express wishes. She should be very angry with him. Yet somehow she wasn't. Guy was coming, and she felt a strange relief, a fierce, aching desire.

She went back to the living room, where she sat and waited until the car door slammed and the knock sounded. She closed her eyes, let it sound three times, let his voice call "Mar . . . Mar . . ." twice over the wind. Then she rose and opened the door.

He closed it fast behind him, stood looking at her for a long, unspeaking moment. "Hello, Mar," he said finally, and she answered, "Hello, Guy," then clung hard to his wet mackinaw while his arms went around her and he said, "Getting plumper, aren't we?" and she said, "Yes," and he said, "I love you," and Caesar barked behind them.

She drew back and studied his face—the beard, the wild hair, the wilder eyes. "Guy . . . I love you, Guy . . . Guy, I love you," then patting the dog, "and you, too, Caesar, I love you too."

Guy made them drinks. They sat on the redwood sofa, and he drank slowly and wet his lips and said, "We won't talk about it. Tomorrow I'm going to the hospital and find out everything for myself. I'll tell them my name is Sloane. I'll say I was stupid enough to divorce you before I knew about the baby—before I knew about *anything*. I'll say we're going to marry again."

"Guy—"

"On Friday afternoon. John will make the arrangements. We'll have a wedding dinner in town, then come back here for our wedding night. I know it's March now. But if the honeymoon is long enough, then spring will come, and we'll still be here to see it."

She curled her legs beneath her and laid her head in his lap, ran a hand slowly along the rough wool of the trousers across his knees. There was a long silence, until finally she said, "You can't change my mind, you know."

"Tomorrow I'll see this Doctor Stafinos, find out everything. Then we'll talk about it later."

"It won't do any good."

"Later . . . later . . ."

They sat quiet again. Time passed. She said. "Of course I've loved you all along. But I could never say it, you see. Everything was too confused, and I felt so very much to blame. But now we're far away and time has passed, and I told you 'sometime' and 'sometime' is now. Now is the sometime for all true lovers to come to the aid of each other."

She kissed him, long and passionately, and felt the desire rising sharp inside her, but fought it down and laughed and said, "Not till our wedding night. I won't spoil our wedding night. I'm going to be a virgin for you. The pregnant virgin." She laughed gaily and then wildly, and after a moment he joined in with her.

He could not get back to town until morning, so that night he would sleep on the redwood sofa. She undressed behind the bedroom door, then got into bed and called him to her. "You can kiss me good night if you like."

He sat on the bed. His hand played with her face, traced circles along her throat. She reached up and took the hand and held it there against her throat. "No further tonight, mister. So far and no further, because I have a surprise for you, except I'm saving it for our wedding night."

"A surprise?" Guy said.

"You'll see, you'll see."

He kissed her very gently, then looked into her eyes for a long, searching moment. He started to speak, but couldn't.

She said, "Good night, my love."

"Good night, good night." He rose and left abruptly. For a moment she felt terribly young again, the way she'd felt when she'd first become engaged to Larry. "Larry," she whispered softly to the darkness. "Larry . . . Larry . . ."

"Did you call me?" from the living room.

"No, and good night, Guy." And "Guy . . . Guy . . ." and she closed her eyes and listened as he moved about in the other room. She knew he was thinking about tomorrow, going to the hospital, and what the doctor would say to him and what he would say to her.

But the wind was dying and Guy was near, and tomorrow was still a far time off.

CHAPTER THIRTY-FIVE

Doctor Stafinos was young with a narrow white face and a black, pencil-thin mustache. On the little finger of his left hand he displayed a red signet ring, which he had a habit of turning round and round, studying it intently as he talked. "Well," he said finally, raising his sharp eyes to meet Guy's, "considering you're a doctor yourself . . ."

"General practitioner. A New Englander, but I practice in Atlanta."

"I see." Doctor Stafinos pulled the sleeves of his neat black flannel suit over his white starched cuffs. He looked like a college boy, Guy thought. Not much younger than himself, but still a precious college boy. "If you'd like to see the X-rays . . ." Doctor Stafinos rose, drew a series of negatives from a metal file cabinet, inserted one in the viewer, and switched on the light behind it. "Quite obvious," he said.

"Yes . . ." His voice broke. "I—I didn't realize it was that bad."

"Lesion in the right upper lobe. A two-centimeter cavity." The young doctor ran a finger along his thin mustache. "Of course she was more than two months along before she came to me—or was examined by anyone, for that matter."

"We were divorced in December," Guy explained carefully. "She was pregnant at the time, of course, but didn't tell me. When I found out, I—naturally I came here immediately."

"Naturally."

"I happened to be on a sailing trip, rather close by, when I heard."

"Oh?"

"We're getting married again tomorrow. That is if you could rush through our Wassermanns."

"Tomorrow," the doctor said, and "Yes, it can be arranged." He stared hard at the X-ray, "So after tomorrow the decision will be yours to a large extent—" He removed the X-ray negative and inserted another. "If she'd been examined earlier, of course, or if I'd taken X-rays immediately—but she wasn't, and I didn't, so let's go on from there. I've been giving her streptomycin and P.A.S., and they seem to be doing some good." He pointed at the lighted screen. "You can see here—the lesions are beginning to close. Very slowly though." He switched off the light, sat once more behind the desk and twirled the signet ring. "You know a Doctor Malcomb Prince in Boston?"

"No."

"Well, a couple of weeks ago he came over to see about having his summer place renovated. He stopped in to say hello, and I showed him the X-rays. He suggested Mrs. Sloane fly to Boston immediately for a chest operation. It could be done here, of course, though Boston would be advisable. But the point is—Mrs. Sloane refused to go, and we knew of no friend or relative who might persuade her."

"You explained exactly what the operation would mean?"

"As precisely as possible. She understood there was a strong chance the baby might abort during surgery. That was two weeks ego, and now—the way I feel now—well, the lesions *are* closing, though we can't be sure she'll continue to improve."

"So," Guy said, "you don't think the surgery is necessary any longer. But you're recommending an abortion, aren't you?"

"Not recommending. Saying it's a way to settle the matter once and for all. The other alternative, of course, is to wait and see what happens. If she keeps improving—fine. If not, there's still time for the vaginal operation."

"I understand." The young doctor was studying him closely. Guy rose and said, "Thank you," and Doctor Stafinos said, "You look very familiar, Doctor, though I can't place your name," and Guy said, "She's never had a child. After this, I doubt she could have another."

"I agree. One reason why I'm tempted to wait a bit. As a last measure—at twenty-six weeks, we could still play it safe—a hysterotomy, and three weeks later a pneumonectomy."

Guy drew in a breath, let it out slowly, said, "I can tell you right now, Doctor, she'll insist on waiting the full twenty-six weeks. The trouble will start when—if and when—it becomes necessary—"

"Let's not worry about that now."

"Fine. We won't worry now." He nodded good-by and left.

Outside the sun was shining. The phone lines had been repaired, so he went into a drugstore and called John Treleaven. He told John about the wedding plans, and John said he would cooperate to the fullest. The clerk in the town hall was a member of his temporary parish, and would very likely agree not to disclose their correct legal names, which would have to appear on the marriage license. Perhaps if the clerk were invited to the wedding—if the wedding were held right here in John's own living room, and the clerk acted as best man—

"Tomorrow afternoon," Guy said. "I'll get the license today, and Stafinos promised to rush through the Wassermanns. He doesn't have to know who we really are, so long as the clerk will cooperate."

John said he'd get right to work on it, and Guy went out to the cold and walked slowly in the winter air beneath the wineglass elms along Main Street, past the horse trough and the empty benches where old men sat smoking and sunning and playing checkers and cribbage in the summertime, past the Old Rotch Market, now the Pacific Club, with the names of those three famous ships painted large on the outside walls—*Dartmouth, Eleanor,* and *Beaver,* boarded by "Indians" in 1772, when their cargoes of tea had been dumped overboard into Boston Harbor.

He decided to rent a jeep so he could take Mar on a honeymoon ride, and wandered the streets making inquiries in bars and luncheonettes and drugstores. He was shuffled about the town from one possibility to another, down Centre Street, known once as "Petticoat Row" for the many Quaker women who ran shops there, along Quince Street and dark India Street and Orange Street, where one hundred and twenty-six whaling captains had lived in a row, past the Ships Inn near Fair and School Streets, and back to Main Street past the old Pacific Bank, its red bricks now a faded pink, until he finally located a service station near the rows of docks, where a stubborn young man offered to rent him a muddy jeep for the sum of ten dollars a week. Guy paid him two weeks in advance, then drove the rattling car across the moors to the cottage of Mr. T. Lewis.

Mar said that Frances Treleaven had already called. John had persuaded the town clerk to keep their secret, and the wedding would be held at four tomorrow, Friday, in Frances' living room. The clerk (his name was Judson Blassinghame) would be the only person present besides Frances, of course, and John, who would perform the ceremony. On the other hand, if Guy felt they should be married in a Catholic church—

"No," he said. And, "My God, imagine what a priest would

say! That's all gone now . . . all gone," and he was still saying it as he led Mar out to the jeep and drove her slowly over the uneven road to town.

"You don't have to crawl," she laughed. "I'm not that far along."

He did not answer.

"I see . . . You talked with Doctor Stafinos."

"Naturally. And I should have known. Right from the beginning. Your healthy look, bright eyes, those quick night fevers. I should have *known.*"

"Now you know—and you agree with him about what should be done."

"I agree that there's still time."

"Fine. So we won't talk about it. The day after tomorrow, but not today before the happiest day of my life."

"The second happiest."

She studied him carefully, almost angry. "Guy, we're old people in our thirties. There was once a Julia and once a Larry. But now they're both gone, like *all* the past is gone. So tomorrow *will* be the happiest day of our lives." She was silent awhile. The air was cold through the open sides of the hard-riding jeep. "You have to understand," she said finally to his eyes in the dirty mirror. "I wondered—all this time before I saw you again—I wondered if we could ever stop feeling guilty—either of us. I wondered if that guilt would prevent us from ever being honestly in love—from ever being happy together. I thought that it would. We didn't have a chance. So it was wrong to marry and destroy each other with our common guilt. Then yesterday you walked through my door, and suddenly it didn't matter. I saw you and nothing else mattered at all." She touched his arm, and he said, "I felt that long ago," and drove on over the cobblestoned streets beneath the leafless elms.

Doctor Stafinos took their blood tests immediately. He said, "Good luck to both of you," stroked his mustache and studied his ring. "Atlanta?" he said carefully to Guy.

"Yes, and I'm sure we've never met." He took Mar's arm and led her quickly from the hospital.

Judson Blassinghame was a merry little man with an avocado-shaped head. He winked slyly as they signed the marriage license, then leaned confidentially across his desk. "Four o'clock tomorrow." He put his finger alongside of his nose, like Santa Claus about to rise up the chimney. "Mum's the word." He winked again, and was still winking furiously as they left the town hall and drove back to the cottage in the afternoon dusk.

Mar said good-by at the doorway. "You'll have to sleep on

the boat tonight, and you can't even come in for a drink. It'll be our honeymoon suite, you see, and I want to make everything ready and make myself as attractive as I can, too, despite this lovely lump in my stomach. And you mustn't see me again until the wedding."

"Mar, we're not children, Mar."

"Yes, we're children." She said it simply, like a child, then kissed him lightly and went into the cottage.

He left Caesar with her and drove back to town in the March night. He thought how much Mar had changed since only months ago, when she'd been a tired, mature woman—even a rather aloof woman. Now she was a young girl, ingenuous, rather pathetic, he thought, without the slightest concern or understanding of her own condition. And he loved her all the more for it. But there was something frightening about all this too, as though she were only pretending gaiety, covering up some terrible fear that went deeper than the medical problems—as though there really were no time at all, and if they were not young, not gay and reckless now, if they did not make the very most of today and tomorrow and the day after that, then there would never be another chance at all.

He parked the jeep at the end of one of the five big wharfs, then walked over the wooden planks past the few fishing smacks, and the little artists' studios with names like "Bideawhile" and "Water's Edge." He climbed down to the dinghy and rowed out to *Julia*'s mooring across the horseshoe-shaped harbor with Nantucket to starboard and Coatue to port, and dead ahead the summer-resort village of Wauwinet, which translates freely into "Lucky Boy."

Lucky Boy. Guy Montford was a lucky boy. He tied up the dinghy, went down to the cabin and lit the kerosene stove. He poured himself a large drink and sat on a bunk and said, "I am a lucky boy," and reminded himself that tuberculosis was nowhere near as serious a problem as it used to be.

Tomorrow was his wedding day; tomorrow night he would lie close with Mar. And tonight, alone, he would drink very slowly and think about exactly that and nothing else.

CHAPTER THIRTY-SIX

As a rule, Frances Treleaven felt little sentimentality over anyone's wedding, since she'd attended so many over the years of her marriage that they'd all blurred together into one hazy image of yellow flowers and white dresses and purple orchids, organ music and tears and John's quiet, monotonous words. Even her own wedding in Reading, Pennsylvania, had long since lost all individuality, so there were times when she could not remember exactly how her wedding gown had looked, or how she had felt inside herself on that most important day of her life.

Today, however, Frances felt anxious, inexplicably nervous. She was dressed by three, primping her hair for the third time by three thirty, and by quarter to four, had begun to feel as if she were flying all apart.

"Relax," John told her. "You've been to hundreds of weddings." He was in his undershirt then, his arms white and flabby, his stomach slightly protruding—not the way he'd looked on their wedding night at all, or any of the Tuesday, Thursday, or Saturday sex nights that had followed down through the early years.

She could not relax. She said, "I still don't approve. I mean there's nothing *wrong* with drinking champagne, I suppose. But having it right here in our *own house*—everyone getting drunk in the minister's living room in the middle of a Friday afternoon."

"Nobody's going to get drunk," John assured her. He slipped into his shirt, and she said, "John, I wish you could understand. It's as though we were in a conspiracy against God or something."

"Let me worry about God."

"But sometimes you think He's so *lenient*."

"Sometimes He is."

John patted her arm, and then the jeep pulled up and she fluttered down from the bedroom to open the door.

Guy was dressed in a dark flannel suit. He seemed uneasy, Frances thought, not at all like a man who'd been married before, like a man who'd already slept with his pregnant bride. John had told her not to think that way. But she couldn't help herself. She'd always *liked* Guy Montford, though she'd never really approved of him from the first day they had met. Guy was a sort of Catholic atheist, it seemed, which was bad enough, not even counting the fact that he'd committed a crime of which he'd been acquitted simply because the jury hadn't known the real *reason* for that crime, and—

No, she did not approve. She could not even sympathize. She said, "Would you care for some coffee?" and Guy said, "No, thanks," and she thought that he probably knew about the champagne John had bought and was saving himself for all he could drink.

John came down from the "wart" and shook Guy's hand. Then, in a moment, another car drove up and Margreth entered with Judson Blassinghame. Margreth wore a dark blue woolen suit that displayed a white orchid on the collar. Judson Blassinghame was dressed in a faded black old-fashioned suit with a high-starched collar and high shoes that squeaked when he walked. He was terribly excited about the whole thing, and insisted on shaking hands all around twice, dancing about in the squeaky shoes, his bald head glistening beneath the lights as he laughed in that squeaky voice and winked in a manner that seemed to squeak also.

The ceremony started immediately. John took his place by the window. Guy stood facing him, while Frances sat at the old upright piano and began the "Wedding March."

Margreth stepped forward on the arm of Judson Blassinghame. She was taller than he, and had to stoop slightly in order to hold his bony arm in the proper manner. Frances let the last chord fade away, then turned on the piano bench and watched the ceremony through slowly misting eyes. No, she did *not* approve, she did *not*, she did *not*. Yet the tears squeezed out regardless, and for a moment there she hated herself for being more emotionally disturbed by a secret sinful ceremony than she had ever been by one of proper dignity.

". . . in richness and poorness, in sickness and health, till death do you part . . ."

Margreth was in sickness. She was pregnant and she had tuberculosis and it was a terrible thing. Frances watched Guy kiss his bride gently, then buried her head in her hands until John's hand touched her shoulder and his voice said, "All right, dear, all right . . . We'll serve the champagne now."

She forced a smile. She rose and kissed the groom, and was horrified to discover that sinful as the man might be, he was certainly most attractive.

Judson had kissed Margreth four times, rising on tiptoe in order to reach her cheek. He looked like a small boy kissing his mother good night. When the champagne corks popped and the yellow liquid bubbled into the glasses, then he drank eagerly, also like a small boy, drinking ginger ale on a hot summer's afternoon.

Guy had three glasses of champagne, Margreth two. John drank two also, and Frances one, though she detested the way the bubbles irritated her nose. Nearly all the rest was consumed by Mr. Blassinghame, who became drunker with every sip, and began loudly extolling the virtues of his beloved Nantucket, the "Little Gray Lady of the Sea." He clutched at Margreth's arm, spilling champagne onto his sleeve as he rattled on, explaining that Nantucket was a Natick Indian word meaning "Land far out to sea," that tourists were properly called "trippers," that an off-islander was "from off," and a Nantucketer was not a "native," because natives were savages in the South Seas, visited by whaling captains in the years gone by. He giggled into his champagne. "Some of the goings on," he hinted. "More'n one skipper had himself a dusky little maiden, I can tell you. Yes, sir, considering back in them Quaker days, a man never even saw his own *wife* naked. So you can imagine, what with suddenly comin' on a girl wearin' nothin' but a grass skirt—well, now—" And more giggling, and then embarrassment, followed by coughing and a hasty explanation that a widow's walk was properly a "walk," that women were bad luck to sailing ships, and that many Nantucket houses had hidden rooms and stairways used to conceal spies and contraband during the Revolution, when the island had remained neutral. He ended by clapping everyone on the back and shouting, "Butter on the pie . . . Butter on the pie!" after which he danced a shaky hornpipe, then fell to the floor in a wriggling black heap.

Guy lifted the little man to the sofa, where he lay squinting up at the ceiling. "Kiss the bride," he mumbled. "Kiss her again . . ."

Margreth bent and kissed the domelike forehead.

"Hope you have butter on the pie," Mr. Blassinghame mumbled in appreciation.

"And I hope," said Margreth, "that you always eat high on the hog."

Mr. Blassinghame closed his eyes. "Butter on the pie," he sputtered twice more, then sat up abruptly and gave one tremendous wink and a long gurgling belch before he fell back and lay completely still.

It was twenty minutes to six. Guy helped Margreth into her coat. He put on his own coat and shook hands with John, said, "Good-by, Frances, and thank you, Frances," then took Margreth's arm and led her out the door to the winter dark.

The jeep coughed and sputtered, then bounced away down the rutted road.

Everything was very still. John stood at the window, staring out at the night. Judson Blassinghame snored. Frances sat on the piano stool and studied her husband's back. From this angle she could not see his paunch. He looked quite strong and tall, and she found herself remembering her own wedding night, the awful shock she'd experienced in discovering the animal instincts in this otherwise delicate man. She rose and poured herself a second glass of champagne.

"Well," John said, "it's over."

"Over, over." He turned, and she saw the paunch now, and closed her eyes and remembered how he'd looked before he'd gained weight and started wearing glasses. "I suppose they'll stay at the cottage tonight."

"Yes."

"I suppose Mr. Blassinghame will sleep for a long time."

"I expect so."

"How long?"

"A few hours at least. Why?"

"No reason. I was just thinking."

"What?"

"Nothing . . . *Nothing.*" She was irritated, with him and with herself. "I hate people who get drunk. I hate them!" She finished the champagne at a gulp, then rose quickly, felt suddenly dizzy, grabbed up the champagne bottle, and climbed the little stairs to their bedroom in the "wart," where she sat on the bed and stared disconsolately at her own face in the dresser mirror. She was thirty-five. Her hair was a dirty brown in color, her chin a little too narrow, her lips too thin, her eyes a shallow muddy brown. She was the wife of the Reverend John Treleaven, and all during her marriage she had stood by his side through thick and thin; she had cleaned his house and comforted his parishioners; she had nursed his colds and cooked his meals and discouraged his tendency toward worldliness. Now suddenly she was tired. She had never had any real *fun*. Other people had real fun, but not she. Other people, like Guy and Margreth, lived exciting, romantic lives. Immoral lives, shoddy lives, disgusting lives, yet romantic all the same. And why was it that the good people found nothing to be thankful for but their own goodness? Why did the *nice* people like herself go childless while the sinners conceived at the drop of a— She was ashamed of the implication. Even out of wedlock was what she meant, and it was not fair. It was not fair at *all*.

She rose and felt dizzy again. She poured out another glass

of champagne, held it up to the mirror and toasted herself silently, wishing there were something daring and exciting to make a toast to and a fireplace behind her in which to throw the glass. She took off her dress, reached for a plain house dress, then stopped to appraise herself in the mirror. She decided she was too bony. She removed the white slip, then the bra, and studied her thin, angular figure, the narrow hips, the small, large-nippled breasts, remembering that the old whaling captains took plump, dusky mistresses in the South Sea islands, simply because they had never seen their own wives naked—thinking that tonight Guy Montford would take beautiful, naked Margreth in their cottage that looked out across the harbor. She started to put on the dress, changed her mind, and lay on the bed with a pillow propped against her back, while she listened to the windows creak and snap in the cold air and felt the goose-pimples rising on her nude body. "I am a plump dusky maiden, drinking coconut milk on a South Sea island . . ."

John knocked on the door. "Are you all right, Frances?"

"I hate people who get drunk."

"What did you say?"

"You may enter, Captain Ahab."

John came in. His mouth dropped open. His eyes widened in surprise, then narrowed slowly to desire. "I'm sorry," he said, wetting his lips. "I didn't realize . . ."

"I am at your pleasure, Captain Ahab."

"What did you say, Frances?"

"You may ravish me, if you so desire."

"Ravish you?"

"Lay me then, if you prefer your white man's tongue."

"You're drunk, Frances."

"Mere coconut milk, marvelous for my dusky complexion." A drop of champagne fell to her breast. She flicked it away, feeling the nipple become rigid, feeling John's eyes focused on it, his mouth open, his tongue still running slowly around his lips.

"You may kiss my dusky breasts, oh Captain."

"It's only six o'clock," John blurted stupidly, "and—well, it's Friday, you know. I mean you never *wanted* me on Friday. I mean, I always thought it was silly, of course, but just the same, it *is* Friday."

"To hell with that!" She heaved the glass against the wall.

"Frances!"

"I said come to my straw mat, oh white man Ahab, and to hell with everything else in the whole goddamned world!"

There were no side curtains on the jeep, so the air blew cold against their faces. Mar huddled against him, rested her head on Guy's shoulder, put both hands into his overcoat pocket. He liked her warm nearness, and drove slowly to keep her there, near and warm and all his own, until finally they reached the cobblestoned streets of town, the small lighted bar and grill where they would have their wedding dinner.

There was frost on the window and sawdust on the floor. The mahogany-stained booths were chipped, the tables scarred with innumerable initials of summer visitors. They ordered whiskey sours and toasted each other silently.

Mar sipped at her drink, put it down carefully, said, "Remember the Lincoln Hotel?"

"I remember."

"Remember a lounge in Boston and a Chinese restaurant on Route 128?"

"Yes."

"You always said you loved me. Sometimes aloud and sometimes with your eyes, and sometimes with nothing but your presence. But I always knew."

"I still—" he started, but her fingers quickly brushed his lips.

"No . . . Now it's my turn. Now I say *I love you.* I say it with words and with my eyes and soon now, I'll say it with my body. I—love—you—Guy—Montford."

Then, for a long time, they sat motionless, unspeaking, looking at each other and into each other, and Guy thought of Doctor Stafinos and thought, There's still plenty of time, and heard the quick laughter of men at the bar, the thud of restless boots on the sawdust floor, the sizzling of fat from the kitchen beyond—all the small sounds of the present now—and he thought this was now and he loved this woman, his wife, and he said the words very slowly, "We were born today, at four o'clock this afternoon. I'm less than four hours old, and there's so very much farther to go."

Mar did not answer. She smiled with her eyes only, and he thought again how very young and eager she was now, how different from the months before.

She said, "What are you thinking?"

"A long time ahead."

"And baby makes three."

"Oh, Mar . . . Oh, God, Mar!" But he would think of that tomorrow.

They had bluefish and hashed brown potatoes. The bartender located a dusty bottle of Liebfraumilch, which they drank slowly with dinner. Then, after coffee, they went out to the cold and drove all the way around the island, along the shore where the surf pounded up white in the fierce March, across the moors where an occasional rabbit raced ahead down the road, and the wild hawthorn trees—the spirits of mateless old maids—were twisted silhouettes against the clear dark sky.

Back at the cottage, Mar made him a tall drink, then went into the bedroom and closed the door. He sat on the redwood sofa and played with Caesar's ears. He rose, looked out the window and saw the blinking light at Brant's Point across the harbor. He sat on the sofa once more, listened to the tiny rustle of clothing in the room beyond, until finally Mar appeared in the bedroom doorway. She wore a soft white negligee, and laughed in quick modesty, the embarrassed young bride, as she sat away from him across the room.

"You remember that story of Dorothy Parker's about the young couple on their wedding night?"

"Yes."

"Well— 'Here we are.' "

"Here we are," he said.

"Do you want to put on your pajamas?"

"My bag's still in the jeep." He started for the door. She said, "Don't be long," and he said, "No, I'll be right back." He pulled the bag from the rear of the jeep, then drew a long breath of the cold air. His heart was pounding hard inside him. He told himself, "We're married. She's my wife. Mar is *my* wife . . . *my* wife," and could not quite believe it when he entered the cottage once more and saw her still there in the white negligee, watching him fondly across the room.

"Here we are," he said, and then, "I'll get into my pajamas, I guess." He went into the bedroom, put on the new blue pajamas, and noticed the clean fresh sheets and the two pillows on the bed, the two night tables with an ash tray on each. He went into the bathroom and brushed his teeth, then hung his brush alongside Mar's on the tiny rack, and knew then, seeing the brushes side by side, that they were finally married.

Back in the living room, they sat apart once more, sipping slow drinks, not touching, speaking very little until it was twelve o'clock and Mar said, "Well, here we are, and are you getting sleepy?"

"Yes, I'm pretty sleepy."

"I guess it's kind of crazy."

"What?"

"Nothing."

"What?"

"After all this—I feel as though tonight—this night—we're going to make love for the very first time."

"So do I."

"I'm glad." She put down her glass and rose and went into the bedroom and closed the door.

He finished his drink, rinsed the glasses in the sink, then put out the lights and followed after her. He found her under the covers with her hands behind her head. She did not speak, but only watched him with her black warm eyes while he slipped in beside her and lay there quietly, until finally, after a long time, he raised on an elbow and looked down into those bottomless eyes and said, "Here we are, and I love you," and ran a gentle hand along her smooth forehead, along the white oval cheek and the smooth round chin, along her bare throat and shoulders while she smiled and said, "You remember, I promised you a surprise," and he said, "Yes," and she said, "Undress me, darling," and he did, and saw her white breasts, full and round, and she said, "Do you like the surprise? I mean my bosoms have grown, you see, what with our baby, and I'm so very proud of them, you see."

He said they were beautiful. He kissed them both, then her throat and mouth, and she clung to him, hard, then lightly again, and after that it was all light, caressing, easy, easy, for a very long time, until finally, at the last, she said, "I'm a virgin, you know," and then the moist warmth and the parted lips and the pounding hearts in the fierce ecstasy—the breathless climax—the slow relaxing into each other's arms, and her voice in his ear whispering, "Butter on the pie, darling, butter on the pie . . ."

CHAPTER THIRTY-SEVEN

"Try to understand," Guy explained patiently. "It's natural for you to feel good, and you'll feel even better as time goes on."

"Then the drugs must be working."

"Yes, they are. Except some of the way you feel is because of the baby. As the baby develops, it keeps pushing harder against your lungs, you see, and gives you relief in that way. But then, when it's born, then the pressure is removed all at once, and if the cavity hasn't healed sufficiently by then, it could break down and—" He stopped, turned away from her and stared out at *Julia*'s black hull in the bay below.

"What?" Mar said, behind him. "And what?"

"For God's sake, don't argue!" He scratched a fingernail on the pane of glass. It made a harsh, squeaking sound.

"Don't do that, darling."

"For God's sake, I'm a doctor, Mar. A doctor!"

"And I'm a woman, darling. A woman." She said it simply, quietly, sprawled on the redwood sofa before the sputtering fire. She said, "I'm sorry, darling, I did promise to be reasonable, didn't I?"

"Yes, you did." He turned back from the window and stared into the fire. "You promised."

"All right then, I'll be reasonable."

"Well, then"—pacing now, up and down before the fireplace—"you should have gone to Boston for chest surgery as Doctor Prince recommended. But you didn't, and perhaps it's all for the best really, considering your latest X-rays do show some improvement. But all the same, Stafinos feels that you're not improving fast enough, and only this morning he recommended an immediate vaginal operation."

"A week ago he thought it was perfectly safe to wait awhile."

"He still does. But why go through more weeks of pregnancy for nothing?"

"Because. Just *because*."

"I thought you were going to be *reasonable!*" He said the words violently, continued pacing until finally she called him softly, and he sat beside her on the sofa. She laid her head against his chest and said, "You want to destroy our baby—deliberately—*kill* our baby?"

"Listen, Mar—"

"Oh, I know it's perfectly ethical, and *you* wouldn't be doing the operation anyway."

"What difference—"

"Because you don't *believe* in abortion, even for a good legal, medical reason. Not for any reason at all."

"Mar—you know how long it's been since I've had anything at all to do with the Catholic church?"

"But it's still there inside you. I know, darling, I know. All during the trial—all that fighting with yourself to try and believe in euthanasia—your conscience finally won over your rationalities, because you don't believe in taking any life, no matter what the reason. An abortion means taking life, too, so you don't believe in that either."

"It's not true, Mar."

"Yes, it's true. Be honest, darling. It's true. Larry's death was illegal, and the death of my baby would be legal. But all the same, you don't really see any difference at all."

Silence then. She reached up a hand and played with his ear. "You have the loveliest ears, darling."

"There is a difference, Mar."

"They're beautiful."

"There *is*, Mar."

"Remember, darling, you were so shocked when I considered having an abortion in New Haven. You wouldn't *let* me have an abortion."

"It's different now."

"You mean it's different for *me* now. But it's no different for our baby. Everything you did—not letting me see the doctor in New Haven, what happened to Larry, what you said in the courtroom—every word of it was said and done to protect me and our child. And now, after all the hells we've both suffered, you're willing to kill again—this time to make things easier for me—protect me by destroying what we've both been suffering *for*."

"I love you," he said. "That's all the difference. I love you."

"Darling, darling"—her fingers still playing with his ears—"you loved me when Larry died. But loving me wasn't enough. Because look what Larry's death did to you—inside—what it's still doing to you. You know it and I know—you were selfish once—so was I—but we can't ever be selfish again."

"For God's sake, Mar—"

"All right, *tell me! Say it!*" She sat up abruptly, spoke the words straight to his face. "Say, 'I want this child killed. I killed once because I wanted this woman, and now I'll kill again because I still want her.' "

"No, that's not the point." He rose and shouted at her. "It's not the *point!*" And now she was shouting, too, the words high and loud, her eyes bright and angrily defiant, "Say it, say it, *say it!*"

"All right," speaking softly now. "I'll say exactly what I think. No, I don't believe anything has to be done at the moment. After all, Doctor Prince was wrong. A specialist, and he didn't expect you'd improve, and you *are* improving, so all right, we can wait a bit. But after your twenty-sixth week, unless you've improved more—*much more*—then you should definitely have a hysterotomy at six and a half months."

"The same thing. You'd kill the baby."

"No, a hysterotomy is actually a Caesarian. The baby has a chance—"

"A strong chance?"

"I said a *chance* of surviving."

"A six-and-a-half-month baby?"

"It still has a *chance*—so small that it's not worth waiting for. And that's Stafinos' point—why go through all this waiting and hoping when you'll end up having a hysterotomy and losing the baby anyway."

"By then I might be completely well."

"Dreams, Mar, dreams . . ."

"We'll wait," she said.

"All right, we'll wait. As long as the medical treatments seem to work, we'll wait. But when the time comes, if it's the safest thing, you're going to have that hysterotomy, three weeks later a pneumonectomy—lung surgery, because we're playing this safe—absolutely safe, and I want that understood —*now*—right *now*."

"Of course, darling, of course." She pulled him back against her on the sofa again and whispered, "You see, darling, you see. And I tell you what—I *know* it's going to work out. I'm going to get completely well. I know I am. But just to make sure, we'll go to Arizona and I'll have my baby in the finest hospital there, and I'll rest and breathe the right air and take the right drugs, and everything *will* work out, and then we'll buy a small ranch and soon you'll be able to practice again and I'll raise horses and we'll have a glorious life."

"Mar," he said. "Mar, Mar—yes, Arizona's fine. Yes, we'll go there anyway, whether you're completely well or not. We'll play it safe all the way. Plan on leaving in May, at six months, and either you'll be well and we'll wait out the three last months in Arizona, and you'll have a normal child, or else—"

"No, darling, there's no 'or else,' no 'or else.' "

"Or else you'll have that hysterotomy right after we get there."

"I'll get well," she said. "You'll see, darling . . . we'll wait, darling . . . All we have to do is wait."

They waited.

March went out in its lamb's way, and April blew in with sun and rain and daffodils behind picket fences, promising later roses and hollyhocks and cobalt-blue hydrangeas in the cottage yards.

"It's all butter on the pie," Mar said. "Butter on the pie," as she laughed into the ocean spray or walked beside him over the moors as spring bloomed in, bringing green to the bayberries and heather, the mealy plum, and the Scotch broom. "Butter on the pie," while they waited, waited, and Mar seemed to bloom like the spring flowers themselves, so that he felt this was paradise here and now. And the here would stay forever, the now would remain for all time. They would make love and go sailing; they would sit close in the spring nights—in the here and the now—with nothing to disrupt this idyl in the wilderness.

Doctor Stafinos was the single note of hard reality. "I know who you are," he told Guy in privacy. "I knew after your second visit. Doctor Guy Montford, and your wife is the former Mrs. McFie. Obviously it goes no further, and I wouldn't mention it now except that I'm Mrs. Montford's physician and I realize, of course, that the McFie case has a direct bearing on the fact that you refuse to persuade your wife to undergo an operation."

"I can't *persuade* her," Guy told him.

"You could *insist*. And if you insisted, she'd go along." The young man stroked his mustache, twisted his ring, placed his elbows neatly on the desk. "On the one hand, an illegal act of euthanasia. But this is legal. Even moral, depending on where you go to church."

"You said it yourself—it's perfectly safe to wait till May."

"You're a Catholic, aren't you?"

"No, I'm nothing."

"You *were* a Catholic."

"I *was* a lot of things."

Doctor Stafinos sighed his young sigh and gave it up. He said Mar had mentioned Arizona.

"We'll fly out in May," Guy told him. "I'm contacting a hospital near Phoenix. And the lesions *are* closing."

"Yes, but slowly, slowly. A hysterotomy's inevitable. She'll lose the baby in any case."

"I know that. And she's agreed to give up hoping after twenty-six weeks. So all right, we're praying for a miracle. In the meantime I'll make plans for going to Arizona. Barring a miracle, she'll have the hysterotomy there, followed by a pneumonectomy."

The doctor said nothing, only turned his ring and very gently shook his head.

So they made definite plans. Guy wrote Bert Mosley that he was never returning to East Norton, and would like to sell his house at the earliest convenience. He wrote another letter to the retired lobsterman in Woods Hole, offering to sell *Julia* in May, sail her to Woods Hole himself. Mar said she'd sail there with him. Anywhere he went, she would go, too. He told her no. He would deliver *Julia* alone; she would fly to New York; he would meet her there and they'd fly on together to Phoenix.

"I'm sailing *with* you," Mar persisted.

"I'm sailing *alone*."

Mar argued no further. She did not want to argue about

anything, not worry about anything, not be upset by anything. The weather was warm now, and soon, perhaps even before they left, the Madonna lilies would bloom among the black-eyed Susans. "We're still on our honeymoon," she said, "and there's still so much to say and so much to do that we can't waste a single, single minute. We'll do everything and we'll say everything, and we'll learn everything there is to know about each other . . ."

They learned to know each other: the mole beneath Mar's left breast, the callus on the bottom of Guy's foot; her addiction to sauerkraut juice, his insistence on strong coffee; where to touch each other, how to kiss each other, when to speak and when to be silent.

They learned to know each other. And they did things.

Each morning they were awakened by the bell in the Unitarian Church, which struck its sweet notes fifty-two times each sunrise. They lay there counting the strokes, then made love in the morning and slept late, sometimes till noon, when the bell tolled fifty-two more times, as it did again each sunset.

They had "brunch" in their pajamas. And afternoons they inspected every corner of the town that had already shaken off the long winter and the late spring and was now getting ready for summer and the coming flood of "trippers" from "off," the women having given up their bridge clubs and sewing clubs, their book clubs and quilting clubs for spring cleaning and gardening, while the men no longer went scalloping, no longer drove out to the town dump on a dull night to amuse themselves by shooting rats in the glare of their headlights. They learned to know the people, the places, the things: the walking sticks and the crochet needles, the toy parasols and whale-tooth "scrimshaws," the ships' models that still adorned the bornin' rooms and the keepin' rooms of the stately mansions on stately Main Street, and the little gray house at the corner of York and Orange Streets, where old Captain Owen Chase lived after his retirement, when he was remembered mainly for having resorted to cannibalism while marooned once in the South Pacific in an open whaleboat—remembered now, years later, for Chase's own favorite story—how, as a bent old man, in constant terror of starvation, keeping bits of food in his pockets and secret places about the house, he was once visited by a reporter, who said, "By the way, sir, perhaps you knew one of my great-uncles. His name was Isaac Cole, and I understand he died in a whaleboat in the Pacific," to which the old captain replied, "Know him, son? I *et* him."

They drove the jeep across the moors through the sand and beach grass to visit the Old Grist Mill, whose vanes were once a secret signal to whaling ships, informing them whether or not British frigates were near the harbor—and the Athenaeum Library, where they saw a painting of Abram Quary, the last man of Indian blood on Nantucket, who died in 1854 at the age of eighty-two—another portrait, this of Maria Mitchell, a white-haired spinster who became world-famous in 1847, when she discovered a comet and was subsequently presented with a gold medal by King Frederick VI of Denmark. They saw every movie at the Dreamland Theatre, watched every incoming steamer from their house above the bay, and occasionally, on sunny days, took *Julia* beyond the harbor for a quick sail in the spring wind.

It was all their town: the long white beach at 'Sconset and the calm water of the harbor: the surf on the South Shore, where they fished for bass and bluefish; the sand at Monomoy, where they hunted futilely for arrowheads and had "squantum" beach picnics and once a Nantucket clambake—lobsters and clams and corn-on-the-cob buried deep in seaweed and steamed over hissing coals in a great pit lined with red-hot rocks. It was theirs: the sun, the grass and twisted hawthorn trees, the elms and the cold blue water and the crying gulls dropping conch shells in the sand before the cottage. It was theirs, and they lived there and they made love there. They did things there.

And said things there.

Guy told her about Stewart Schaeffer. "When I first realized he was my father—in the next cell, just staring into his face—then at first I was horribly shocked, and then I realized that I couldn't hurt you the way he'd hurt my mother—I couldn't let you hurt yourself."

"Darling . . ."

"So he did serve some purpose—some purpose. And it doesn't bother me now because I'll never see him again. We'll never go back there, so I'll try to forget it, go on pretending it isn't so—it never happened."

And she told him about her batty old grandmother, who ran the Wild Acres estate from a private room on the second floor. "She claimed to have been a mistress of Robert E. Lee, and when I was in the third grade I told the whole class that my grandmother knew General Lee. Everyone laughed, and even the teacher smiled. So the next day I brought a little boy home to prove it. I remember how I opened the door to Grandmother's room, and there she was, ninety-odd years old, a dried little stick in that old rocking chair. And I said, 'Grandmother, there's someone here to see you.' She squinted and said, 'Who is it, child?' And I pushed the boy toward her, and Grandmother pulled upright and put out her old hand and tried very hard to curtsy. 'After all these years,' she said finally. 'After all this time, it's so good to see you, General Lee.' "

They talked about tomorrow and next month and Arizona. She taught him about horses, because they would own at least two, of course, so he should know *something* about horses. And he said all right, if she'd learn to sail, then he'd learn to ride. So they quizzed each other endlessly, until Mar knew that a "bight" was the double part of a rope, a "bush" was the centerpiece of a wooden sheave in a block, a "marlin" was fine two-stranded small stuff, usually tarred, a "nip" was a short turn in a rope, a "sheave" was a wheel within a block, a "shell" an outside casing—while Guy learned how he must sit in the middle of the saddle instead of back on the "cantle," how he must carry his heels lower than his toes, how he must hold his hands close together with the second knuckles facing, the thumbs topmost, the little finger lowest; why a Baucher snaffle is better than a ring snaffle; all the nine rein positions; the three gaits—walk, trot, and canter—and why a horse should be taught to go from a walk to a canter and never from a trot to a canter; and how a horse canters with the right foot as well as the left leading, and the reasons for making him canter on both feet alternately.

Mar talked very fast and laughed very often, and Guy laughed with her in the warm sun, until finally with mid-May only a few days off, they went to Stafinos together, and he said it all very carefully, enunciating each word as he twisted the signet ring.

"I'm sorry, Mrs. Sloane—Mrs. Montford. Yes, you have improved. But not enough, and your husband is quite right—a hysterotomy, yes, and the baby will have a chance— Yes, only one in a thousand, but a *chance,* and after all, it's *your* life that matters most."

"It's the baby that matters most."

"No . . . No . . ."

"You agreed," Guy told her. "You said wait and we waited, and now we can't wait any longer. I'm contacting Phoenix immediately, making arrangements for a hysterotomy the moment we arrive. We're leaving here on the sixteenth. I'll meet you in New York and we'll fly on together."

"I want my baby," Mar said.

"And you *may* have it."

"One chance in a thousand . . . One in a thousand . . ."

They drove home in the spring evening. Mar said, "You chose the child over Larry, and now you're choosing me over the child."

"It isn't a matter of choice."

"Isn't it?" She looked squarely at him in the dusty mirror. "If I went the whole nine months, then the baby would probably be born normally, healthy, only *I'd* be in danger."

"Yes . . ."

"This way I'll be all right, but the baby's almost certain to die."

"Mar . . ."

"So isn't that a matter of choice, and aren't you a Catholic, darling? Aren't you supposed to sacrifice the mother for the child?"

"Nobody's *sacrificing* anything. You'll have a Caesarian, and everything on earth will be done to save the child. I'm *not* Catholic, and if I were, I'd *still* be acting in good faith, because nobody's going to *destroy* the child—simply make sure we *save* the mother."

"Semantics, darling."

"Sense," he told her. "Plain, medical sense. And we won't discuss it again!"

On the last night of all, they lay still beside each other in the half-dark. Caesar scratched on the door. Guy let the dog in to lie beside the bed on the straw mat.

Mar said, "You're going to take Caesar with you on the boat?"

"Yes, of course."

"I'll take him on the plane with me, if you like."

"No, he likes to sail."

"So do I."

"We've gone through that, Mar."

"I know. But I've felt—all day—I don't know why, but I've felt that once you leave tomorrow, I'm never going to see you again."

"I'll be in New York by tomorrow night."

"No, I won't ever see you." She rolled over toward him and he felt the child stir against him. He said, "There's nothing to worry about. I've made all the arrangements for when we get to Phoenix. They already know what to expect. They've already studied your history. I've got the top T.B. men, the best obstetrician."

"I won't see you," she said simply. "If I take that plane to New York, then I'll never see you again."

The fog was thick over La Guardia, so the plane could not land for over an hour. When it did, a wheel rolled off and the plane crashed into the terminal building, killing scores of people. She was unhurt, though, and took an immediate limousine to Manhattan. The limousine went through the

Mid-town Tunnel, which collapsed, killing everyone but herself. She swam up through tons of rushing water and was rescued from the East River by a tugboat, which promptly struck a piling and sank. Again she swam, climbed onto a pier, found a cab which was struck by an oil truck, walked away unhurt, and finally reached the hotel elevator. The elevator fell fourteen floors. She walked painfully up the fourteen flights of stairs. She was extremely tired. Inside the room, she sat wearily in a chair and waited as time passed and passed and the long night wore on, until morning broke and the news came with it: One Doctor Guy Montford, sailing from Nantucket to Woods Hole, had slipped on the wet deck of his Friendship sloop. He'd been killed instantly when his head struck a chock.

Mar awoke and stared into the darkness. Guy stirred beside her. She said, "Darling, that thing that's a metal casting used as a fair-lead for a mooring line or anchor chain—that's a chock, isn't it?"

"Yes."

"Be careful of that old chock, won't you, darling?"

"Sure."

"Don't fall, darling. Don't fall."

She lay a long time awake, thinking hard, sensing what women do, then fell finally asleep with her arm across Guy's chest while the baby moved and she knew, despite the dream, that tomorrow night they'd be together after all.

CHAPTER THIRTY-EIGHT

At five o'clock that morning the moon was still round and full in its losing struggle against the day. Mar cooked a large breakfast of sausage and eggs, and they ate together silently, Mar in a housecoat, her hair loose so that it fell long around her shoulders. She wore no make-up, and Guy thought, watching her over his eggs, that she was two people really: in the evening cool and lovely; the rather distant woman with her hair done up neatly, her lips bright red with lipstick; in the morning a warm woman, casual and childish and very close and very much his own.

She said, "What are you thinking?"

"About tonight, in that hotel room. A strange place, a second honeymoon."

"Do you think," she asked, "that it's safe to sleep with me any more?"

"There's a variety of opinions on that. Some doctors recommend it right up to the end, and others claim there should be no sex at all for the full nine months."

"What does Doctor Montford think?"

"He thinks, considering you'll be having a—" He stopped, smiled at her. "He thinks you burned the sausages."

He had two cups of coffee. It was twenty after five. "I'm driving to 'Sconset first," he said. "John wants to say good-by. He said to wake him before I left."

"He's going to see me off on the plane this afternoon." A pause, and then, "How long will you be in 'Sconset?"

"Not long. I'll stop by here on my way to town."

"No, don't stop by." Then hastily, "I only want to say good-by once. Just once."

"Good-by then." He rose and went into the living room. Mar followed. He picked up his bag and put it down again. She moved against him and he said, "I'll see you tonight, if I have to take a cab all the way from Woods Hole."

"I'll see you," she said.

"I love you," he said.

"Same here. All of me. Both of us. We both love you."

He kissed her and called Caesar and went out to the jeep. She watched him from the doorway. He looked back at her and wondered at the strange calm of her this morning, when for days now, right up until last night, she'd kept insisting that she go with him on the boat, that if she didn't, something was going to happen and they would never meet again. He thought she was sometimes an enigma, reasonable at one moment, superstitious the next. He thought that he loved her, and wondered if their love would be as full, as complete, if there had never been a Julia, never a Larry, so that they'd met while much younger and made love and married in the conventional way that they had both experienced in the past. He decided they would feel exactly the same.

John Treleaven was waiting in the living room. He wore a flowered robe over white pajamas. He said, "Haven't seen much of you, and I suppose we'll never meet again."

"Of course we will."

"Here again, perhaps—some summer, perhaps."

"Yes."

"But not in East Norton."

"No."

"They'll never find out. Change your name legally to Sloane. It'll save you both a lot of heartaches."

"Yes."

"Well, then—" A pause, and, "I'm sorry about the child, though I understand there *is* a chance."

"Medically, yes—practically, no."

"Margreth knows this?"

"Yes . . ."

"She'd prefer taking a long chance on herself?"

"Yes, but I won't let her."

"You could have lied to her."

"No, I never have—I never will."

Frances brought in coffee from the kitchen. She looked different somehow, as though in the past weeks she'd become more of a woman and less of a wife. Guy had seen this same quick blossoming in many girls during the month or so after their marriage. Suddenly, with all their frustrations gone, they gained weight and relaxed into an entirely different being. Frances, though, had been married for years. Yet something had changed in her relationship with John—something good, Guy thought, as he watched her pour the coffee and run an affectionate hand along the back of her husband's neck.

Well, they deserved the best. He would miss them. They had done more for himself and Mar than anyone else on earth.

It was ten after seven. He finished the coffee, rose, said, "Good-by, and thank you. Both of you. Thank you, thank you."

"If there's ever anything I can do," John said.

"Just pray for a miracle, I guess."

"I'll pray," said John. "And someday, perhaps, you'll trust in your own prayers as well."

"Perhaps," Guy said, and went out to the rising sun.

The day was clear with puffs of clouds and a rare strong wind from the west. Guy decided to sail northwest across it, then make one tack on a southwesterly course, another northwest again to Woods Hole. He checked the hawk on the masthead, hoisted the sails, slipped out smoothly past Coatue Point, swung a few points to the east, then sat in the cockpit making small adjustments until the feel was exactly right and *Julia* moved forward easily in her squat grace.

Caesar lay on the clean-scrubbed deck of the cockpit. Occasionally the dog rose and scratched at the hatchway, whined softly, then lay down again, his paws stretched out, his nose touching the mahogany hatch.

"You've already eaten," Guy told him. "But if you're still

hungry—" He went below and opened a can of hash left over from his lonesome winter sail. The dog refused the food, but continued to whine, scratching now at the hatch to the tiny "head." Guy laughed. "You'll just have to wait," he said, and returned to the cockpit, thinking this was the first time Caesar had ever associated the "head" with his own needs to find a tree or a hydrant.

The sun climbed higher over his left shoulder. The spray was cold and pleasant, the strong wind quite warm against his face. This was his last sail of all. In the months ahead he would learn to ride a horse, and it would be a long time before he felt the special thrill of sailing again. He was assuming, of course, that there were no permanent problems. They would simply go to Arizona, he and Mar, and Mar would have a hysterotomy, followed by a pneumonectomy, and everything would be perfectly fine again, except the child would die, of course, though someday she might have another. Someday, God willing, someday . . .

Caesar still persisted in climbing the ladder, whining, then going below again, over and over, until finally he stayed in the cabin completely and the low whines turned abruptly to erratic barks. It was late morning then, and Guy had come to the end of the first tack. He shouted for Caesar to shut up, then came about sharply into the wind as the dog's barking reached a point of hysteria. The boom began its long swing across the boat, and it was then, as the boom passed amidships over his lowered head, that he saw Mar's face in the open hatchway. She was smiling gently. Her hair blew lightly in the wind. She started to speak, then looked up, startled, as the boom swung all the way and the wind caught quickly at the sails and the boat heeled obediently to port. She gasped. She said something small, incomprehensible, groped frantically to regain her balance, then fell out of sight into the cabin below.

For the fraction of a second Guy did not move. He still saw Mar's face, first smiling, then startled—there in the hatchway, then gone, yet still there inside his mind. He said, "Mar . . . What in the hell!" then secured the wheel and leaped forward all in one continuous movement.

Mar lay moaning softly between the bunks. Her pained eyes were open, looking up at him. She said, "I wanted to come with you . . . I had to come with you, and I'm such a nuisance, darling . . . such a bad old nuisance."

He lifted her to the bunk. He said, "Never mind that. How do you feel?"

"I have a cramp, darling, only it's not bad, and I'm sure it will go away."

"Oh, God!" he said. "Mar . . . Mar . . ." and then, "Lie still, don't move, and let me know exactly how you feel, every minute, even the smallest change."

He kissed her, and climbed back to the cockpit. Mar was here. Mar had a cramp. It had happened so fast, he had acted so automatically that he could still not quite believe it. He checked his course and the direction of the hawk, then went below again and spread the chart of the Sound out hastily on the other bunk. Mar was there behind him, and he could still not quite believe it. He was still acting automatically, doing everything the way he had once done things in the war, mind working, hands working, with no real awareness of the enormity of a situation, only the blind knowledge that something must be done about it. He had no radio equipment, and had not plotted his course, since he knew these waters too well to bother with little more than a compass and sight bearings. Even so, he figured he was now at roughly 70° 20′ longitude, 41° 35′ latitude, which placed him near the center of a line between Oak Bluffs on Martha's Vineyard and Hyannis on the Cape, with Hyannis slightly closer—approximately twelve miles to the northeast. The wind was now from the northwest, which meant that on a time basis, sailing on an angle of about 45° across the wind, he'd probably reach Hyannis a fraction sooner than Martha's Vineyard. Also, it would be a smoother sail, which might, in the long run, prove more important than actual sailing time.

Behind him Mar said, "I'm sorry, darling, I'm so terribly sorry." But he did not hear. His mind was turning fast, thinking a thousand thoughts as he raced back to the cockpit, brought the boat to starboard into the wind, then set off on a new tack to the northeast. With luck he could make the mouth of Hyannis harbor on a single tack. He started the engine, secured the wheel on the new course, making the best adjustment to give him both speed and direction, then went below again, where Mar lay motionless, her damp eyes staring upward at the overhead.

All this time he had thought nothing except that Mar was here and Mar had cramps and should be gotten to the nearest hospital as soon as possible. Now, with this decision made and acted upon, he knelt beside her and watched her face and tear-filled eyes and the little lines of pain along her mouth. He said, "Are you all right? . . . How do you feel?"

"I told you, darling. Cramps, darling."

"I've changed course. We're heading for Hyannis."

"You're angry because I was a bad girl, wasn't I? I hid in the toilet—the 'head'—and that was bad, wasn't it?"

"Don't talk about it."

"I dreamed you'd fall and bump your head on one of those chock things. But then I had to be stupid, so I fell myself, and do you think I'll have my baby right here—I mean, right in the boat?"

"No, of course not." He brushed the hair from her forehead, said it again, "Of course not," then climbed the ladder and stared across the bow at the shape of blue land ahead. He thought that yes, she might have the baby right here in *Julia*'s cabin. He thought that six months' pregnancy plus T.B. precluded a short fast labor, and it could happen right here in the boat except it must not happen here, it must *not* because there was a chance she might hemorrhage, and if she did hemorrhage, there'd be nothing in the world that he could do about it.

"Think like a doctor," he told himself. "Clear, cold, unemotional, like a doctor . . . like a *doctor!*" He went back to the cabin and asked again how she felt. "I'm getting pains," she winced, "but they're quite far apart."

"Tell me when you get the next one."

They sat and waited. They did not speak. He watched her closely, like a doctor . . . like a doctor. Caesar whined. Mar said, "You're so professional, darling. Such a marvelous bunkside manner." Then suddenly she winced sharply and said, "Now, darling," and he looked at his watch and saw that it was ten after ten.

At twenty-two after she had another pain, and he knew then that soon the pains would start coming very fast, and Hyannis was still a long ways off.

In the cockpit again he noted that the wind had shifted once more, slowing him down somewhat unless he tacked off to the northwest toward Oyster Harbor, then came about sharply and made a fast run for Hyannis. Oyster Harbor, though, was still closer than Hyannis—actually the nearest landfall of all, except there was no hospital there. Mar would have to be taken by car to the hospital at Hyannis—unless, of course, she were taken the much shorter distance to the hospital that was actually the closest of all—there beyond Oyster Harbor, there beyond the familiar lighthouse at the end of Keever's Point.

Mar watched him as he came slowly down the ladder. She said, "I've been timing the cramps myself, darling. Seven minutes apart now, getting closer all the time."

"Yes."

"What are you thinking, darling?"

"Nothing."

"That it'll happen in the boat?"

"No."

"That the baby will be born dead? I mean because it's only six months—"

"No, that's not what I was thinking." He closed his eyes, pressed hard knuckles into his forehead, opened his eyes slowly and knelt before her on the deck. "Mar," he said softly, stroking her forehead, "I'm changing course again."

"Oh?"

"For the nearest hospital."

"Hyannis, you said."

"I was pretending to myself. Lying to myself."

"East Norton," she said slowly. Then whispering, "East Norton," and then, "No, Guy . . . No . . . *No!*"

"It's much closer."

"Oh, Guy . . . No, darling, *no!* . . . I don't *care* about myself. I don't *care*. But it isn't fair to you—it isn't *fair*—"

"Mar . . . Darling, listen, darling . . . I know what this will mean—going back—*I* know, *you* know . . . But I won't take chances now, and there's nothing else we can do."

Mar's pains were coming one on top of another as *Julia* swung past Keever's Point and edged in past the breakwater. The sun was high, a familiar gold on the windows of the hospital, on the tiny panes of glass in Guy's own house, on the cross atop St. Joseph's.

Chet Belknap waited at the end of the dock. Other watchers appeared from nowhere—Bill Watts and the Clerk of Court, Harold Sims, and the banker Mr. Polk, who owned the largest boat in East Norton, and now stood paint-spattered in old working clothes, wearing a hat that advertised Ralph Messner's Hardware.

Chet caught the line and made the boat fast. "Guy," he said. "Good to see you, Guy."

"Get your car, Chet!"

"What are you talking—"

"Get your car!" He shouted it, over and over, while Chet gaped, then scurried back down the dock as Guy went below to the cabin.

Mar's face was white, pinched in pain. "We're here," she said.

"Yes . . . I'm going to carry you now. Close your eyes. Don't look at anyone."

"I was bad . . . I was foolish . . . I should have taken the plane."

"No . . . No, no . . ." He lifted her in his arms, took a step toward the ladder, then stopped and kissed her gravely, because this, perhaps, would be their last moment alone together for a very long time.

He said, "I love you. Close your eyes. Don't think about the pain. Don't think about the people. Think about how I love you and how we're going to Arizona, and don't think about anything else." He kissed her again and carried her up the ladder.

There were perhaps a dozen townspeople on the dock, standing motionless, waiting curiously. They looked at Mar in his arms. They did not move. They did not speak. Chet's car edged in among them, and Guy said, "You take her, Chet, and be gentle, Chet . . . Very gentle."

Chet lifted Mar in his big arms and placed her in the rear of his car. Guy climbed the ladder and stood now in the center of the little crowd. Still no one spoke. He said, "It's Mrs. McFie," then staring at them all, one by one and all together, not seeing any of them, "It's Mrs. Guy Montford . . . You understand? . . . Mrs. Guy Montford."

He got into the car. The knot of people parted as Chet started the engine. Guy saw the paint on Mr. Polk's nose, the scar on Harold Sims' cheek. Larson Whitt was there now, too, and Nancy Messner, whose mouth remained half open, and old Mr. Castner, who was partly deaf and kept repeating, "What'd he say, what'd he say?"

"He said it was Mrs. Montford," said Larson.

"What?"

"Shut up!" said Larson. "Shut up, shut up!"

Then the car moved off down the dock. Guy cradled Mar in his arms. He said, "It's all right. We're flying over Arizona now. I see herds of cattle and lots of cactus and some bad men riding like hell toward the canyon. There's tumbleweed, and there's a lovely ranch down there, and a stream where a small boy's catching trout. And there's the hospital now. It's a beautiful place, and the doctors will all be waiting, just like I promised," while his dumb eyes saw his own barren house with the spring flowers dying in the early summer, then the Civil War monument and the black cannon balls and the black cannon, the Congregational Church and the Lincoln Hotel, the liquor store and Pat's and Castner's Drygoods and Stewed Schaeffer sitting drunk on the steps of the courthouse—all the old familiar places, all the betrayed people—as they passed down Main Street, while heads turned and saw him there in the rear of Chet's car, and the sun was bright against his face.

"Put in parking meters," Chet said embarrassed into the windshield.

"Did they?"

"Planning another traffic light—corner of Main and Water."

"Are they? . . . Are they?"

Mar groaned. He said, "We're taking that short cut through the pass." Chet grunted and swung the car into the gravel drive of the Mills Memorial Hospital.

Ida Primmer stood waiting at the emergency entrance. Her mouth opened, displaying protruding teeth. Doctor Kelsey appeared behind her. His hair was winter-white. He glanced at Mar in Guy's arms. His sharp eyes crossed Guy's face. He swung to Ida, said, "For Christ's sake, get a stretcher!"

Mar lay motionless, eyes closed, unspeaking, as she was carried into the delivery room. Guy followed. Saul Kelsey said, "How long?"

"Six months." Then, "Look, Saul—"

"Don't tell me about your personal life. Tell me about *her*. Six months, and anything else?"

"T.B."

The man's bushy eyebrows rose and dropped. He brushed a big-veined hand through his mop of hair. "Go down to my office."

"Listen, Saul—"

"Get the hell out of here!" He slammed the door.

Guy walked down to the elevator. The fat old nurse sat motionless at the desk. She said, "It's good to see you again, Doctor Montford."

"Thank you." He went down in the elevator, crossed the reception hall, and entered Doctor Kelsey's office. He closed the door, sat in a leather chair, and waited. There was whiskey in a cupboard. He had two straight shots. From two doors down, he heard the squeal of a baby, and wondered whose it was. He had another drink, then sat with his head in his hands, and waited, waited, until finally the door opened and Fran Walker stood there, quiet, calm in her starched white uniform.

Fran shut the door. "It's a boy," she said with no expression whatever. "Two pounds, thirteen ounces. Dark, of course, and so far he's doing fine."

He raised his head. "Mar?" he said.

"Mrs. McFie . . . Mrs. Montford . . . She's all right." Fran moved across the room, poured him another drink, pushed the glass into his hand.

"Fran . . ."

"Don't say anything. Not *anything*."

He swallowed the third drink while Fran stood close, looking down, wetting her moist lips. Her hand shook when she took the empty glass from between his fingers. "You're married and it's your child, and it was that way all along."

"Yes."

"I knew you loved her. But I didn't know everything. Now I do—everything—*everything.*"

"So does everyone." He closed his eyes tight, opened them again when Saul Kelsey's voice said, "All right, you can see her now."

He followed the doctor up in the elevator, down the green-walled corridor to Room 4B. Right next door, he thought. 2B for Larry, and now 4B for Mar, and—

Saul opened the door. Mar lay still, her eyes closed. She opened them slowly. They were bright and black. "It's a boy," she said.

"Yes."

"He's fine and I'm fine. You see God cared. He *cared.*"

"Mar . . ."

"We'll get him a Shetland pony. I'll teach you both how to ride." She smiled and closed her eyes.

He kissed her and left the room. In the corridor Doctor Kelsey said, "I'll want her history."

"Doctor Stafinos. Nantucket Cottage Hospital."

"I'll take my own X-rays immediately. She's been getting treatments, of course."

"Streptomycin and P.A.S."

"Fine. But don't count on the baby, Guy. It *could* live—except they never do."

"I know."

"Of course." He swung and started for the elevator, turned abruptly, said, "Oh, by the way, your license to practice was restored a couple of weeks ago—in case it matters."

"It doesn't." He went down in the elevator. Passing the big glass window which fronted the row of incubators, he saw Ida Primmer adjusting the oxygen for an extremely tiny, red-faced baby. She glanced up in embarrassment. He stared at the new-born child. He'd seen a thousand, all the same. Yet this one looked entirely different. Smaller, of course, but still different because it was Mar's and it was his, and soon now it would die.

CHAPTER THIRTY-NINE

The town was angry—shocked, indignant—hurt, confused.

Clara Coffin said, "I might have known—her with those big black innocent eyes, looking so beautiful and sad. And all the time she was laying that man."

"Clara!" boomed Cy.

"That's what she was doing, wasn't it?"

"Clara, it's the *man* who lays the *woman*."

"Not in *this* case," Clara insisted. "If anyone was pulling his pants down, it was certainly her."

"Clara—the woman is sick—maybe even dying."

"God's will be done," said Clara Coffin.

Doctor Bolls assured his wife that Guy's return to East Norton would not affect their own status in any way at all. "Oh, he's already got his license back. But where's he going to get any patients? In a town like this, you just can't get away with that kind of thing," while Mrs. Manning sadly admitted to the Judge that Guy's horoscope had not foretold this new development at all, and, accordingly, she was going to give up all this foolishness and study yoga instead. Of course she was too old now to stand on her head or stick pins through her nose or lie on a bed of nails or anything like that. But there were other less painful, more dignified yoga exercises, and from now on she would spend forty-five minutes in contemplation and self-examination each and every day of the week.

The old judge nodded approval. He was immensely relieved. For now there was no longer any danger that she might discover some shocking truth through the movement of the stars, which would jeopardize his marital and financial comfort. Mrs. Manning could spend the rest of her days sitting cross-legged on the living-room floor, searching herself—searching, searching—and she would never discover anything at all.

Ida Primmer, who was to marry her Hyannis "pharmacist" in July, thought the Montford affair was the saddest thing she'd ever heard in her whole life. "You see, it's not really

Guy's child at all," she explained dramatically. "I take care of the baby, you know, and you ought to see that chin. The spitting image of Larry McFie's. So you see what really happened is that Larry slept with his wife (oh, he had moments when he was quite strong, you know), and then Mrs. McFie became pregnant, but Doctor Montford didn't *know* about it. He put poor Larry out of his misery, and Mrs. McFie was so afraid it would *look* all wrong that she ran away—I mean, considering nobody *thought* Larry was up to that kind of exercise, you know. So then Doctor Montford discovered she had T.B., and being an ex-Catholic, he talked her out of an immediate abortion. Then he got so sorry for her that he married her so the baby would have a father, just in case it did live after her hysterotomy. So that's what really happened, but how can he *tell* anyone, when the town's so narrow-minded that no one would believe him anyway, and it's all so terribly, awfully sad."

Mr. J. L. Crooks, feed and grain dealer, foreman of the jury that had tried Guy Montford, did not think it sad at all. Considering the jury had bent over backwards to be sympathetic and understanding, just as the entire town had been on Guy's side all during the course of the whole filthy business, it was a disgrace to East Norton, an insult to the law, a deliberate flouting of morality. He called the jury together for coffee and ginger-bread in the parlor of his house in Seaside, where the twelve men and women soberly discussed the matter, and decided that even though they had disregarded Judge Crawford Strike's charge—even though the verdict should have been guilty, even first degree murder, for that matter—it was still better that ten guilty men should go free than that one innocent man should be punished.

"That," raged Colin Eustis, "is the trouble with our entire judicial system! A man's *presumed* to be innocent! A man can't be placed in double jeopardy! The jury can bring in any verdict it wants, for any reason at all—just because the man looks like Uncle Joe or has a tick in one eye or parts his hair on the left side, and my God, it's a wonder anybody's ever convicted of anything."

"You're bitter," his wife said, "because now you look like an awful fool."

Colin did not answer. He was thinking about Bert Mosley. Why had Guy retained Bert anyway? How much of all this had Bert really known from the beginning? Of course he'd have a hell of a time proving anything, but all the same—"That sonovabitch," he said.

"*Not* in front of the children."

"I'm talking about Bert Mosley."

"I don't care who you're talking about. *Whom* you're talking about."

"He's through in this town," said Colin. "People hate to be made fools of. They'll snub Guy Montford, resent him, even hate him when they get to thinking about it. But it's Bert Mosley who'll get run out on a rail."

The antagonism was everywhere. Bert felt it immediately in the sudden loss of his few important clients. He felt it in the shops and on the streets, and thought bitterly that that bastard Guy Montford had held out on him. If Guy had only told him the truth—the whole truth—if he'd only been a little wiser himself—seen past the two rooms in the Statler Hotel, figured out *why* Guy'd wanted such a quick trial, *why* Mrs. McFie had disappeared so quickly, *why* Guy had left a few weeks later himself, leaving no forwarding address, *why* he'd suddenly wanted to sell his house without coming back to East Norton . . .

Guy had cheated him. Guy was ruining him in East Norton. Thank God he'd already cemented a good offer from a Boston law firm to begin work in September. Yes, sir, he'd already found an apartment on Beacon Hill, available after Labor Day, already made final arrangements to marry Sylvia Stein immediately after starting in on his new job. Add it all up and things weren't too bad after all. So maybe he wouldn't spend the summer here. Maybe he'd leave next week, or maybe right after the Fourth of July, when the summer people started their big invasion, even though he had counted on them for a few extra dollars to cover a honeymoon trip to Canada. So there was no problem really, except that for some odd reason he'd really *wanted* to stay on in East Norton until the last possible moment. Oh, he'd always wanted to go back to Boston, of course, and still did, of course, and of course Sylvia *was* the most satisfactory girl he'd ever met, even though she *was* Jewish. But all the same, he was used to East Norton—to being a bachelor—and after the hectic searching days in Boston's twisted streets, the frantic searching nights in Sylvia's bed, he was not quite sure now what he wanted at all, except a little time to think it over.

Now in summer, Pat's boasted a screen door. The windows were open, and early bugs thumped pleasantly against the screen. The men at the bar turned slowly as Bert entered. They stared at him, turned back to their beers.

To hell with them! Bert sat at a table and called for a

it . . . So please, please—" And he was begging now, for a place to go, someone to listen, someone to hold onto, someone who would *understand*.

She said, "All right, Bert . . . Come along, come along." But her voice was weary. It was flat.

He hung up before she could change her mind, rushed down the stairs and climbed into the old Plymouth coupé. Miss Welles still watched him through the prune bottles in the lighted shop.

"Good-by, Miss Welles!" he shouted out the window. "Good-by, good-by!" as he stepped hard on the accelerator and headed toward Route 128 and a brand-new life.

Behind him, through the car's mirror, he saw a great red glow above the town. The brass bell rang atop the firehouse and sirens wailed in the summer night.

Let the whole town burn, for all he cared. He was going to Boston, going to Sylvia . . . Sylvia . . . Sylvia . . . She would hold him, caress him, talk sweet talk to him and make sweet love to him, and everything would be all right again. But after a while, as he drove on toward Falmouth, he pictured Sylvia's hard eyes and Sylvia's hard breasts, her glasses and her stiff hair and her mannish clothes, and he realized then that she would never understand, never sympathize at all.

Only Fran Walker—rejected in his own wild search for manhood—only gentle Fran, immoral Fran, affectionate Fran and yielding Fran—only Fran could help him now.

Parker could not stop laughing. He placed his fat hands on the cluttered desk and laughed until the tears rolled down his cheeks and sweat broke out on his bald head and on the flesh beneath his summer shirt and on his back and thighs, running down beneath his trousers until the felt pad on the swivel chair was damp with perspiration.

Nancy Messner poked her blond head through the office door. "What's funny, Mr. Welk?"

"Bert Mosley," sputtered Parker, still choking with laughter. "Did you see him—Lord, did you see him?"

Nancy had not seen him.

"Running down the street, tripping, falling—Lord, Lord, just a second ago. They beat him up. Beat the hell out of him. Lord, Lord!" Parker roared, shook, perspired with laughter.

Nancy thought it a disgrace. Of course Mr. Mosley had been wrong to withhold information, just like Doctor Montford had been wrong to be so immoral and fool everybody like that. "But all the same—"

"All the same, what?" Parker wiped the tears from his eyes, pulled the sticky trousers from his sweating rump. "What, what? And when are you going to grow up, Nancy?"

"I'm eighteen."

"Yes, but—yes, but—" There were no words to say. He closed his eyes. The laughter was gone. Nancy was eighteen. She was here beside him in his warm office on this summer night. She wore shorts and a loose shirt and stood with her weight on one bare leg, her hip thrown innocently to one side, her straight legs tanned and hairless, her arms the same. The sun had bleached her hair almost white and there was a pink birth-mark above her knee and her mouth was red-moist in the heat and she was eighteen years old.

Parker opened his little eyes, focused them hard on a spot above Nancy's head. "Everyone," he said soberly. "In the long run, all sinners must face the consequences—the law—public opinion—God—and when a sinner avoids all these—there's still his own conscience."

"Oh, I'm sure Doctor Montford's just *dying* inside. I mean what with the baby going to die probably, and Mrs. McFie—Mrs. Montford—so sick and all."

"A sinner, Nancy. And I tried to tell everyone. I wrote editorials during the trial. Nobody listened. Well, now it's too late. But God is still listening." His eyes dropped back to Nancy's face and a tremble started all through his body. He jerked his eyes to the desk, fumbled with a pile of papers, drew out the latest issue of *Art Photography*. He stared at the shadowed nude on the cover, flipped the pages one by one, aware of Nancy's hip on a level with his face, her eyes looking down over his shoulder.

"That's a new issue," she said.

"Yes."

"You never did go to those photography classes in Boston."

"I never will," Parker said wearily, and pointed to a reclining nude. "You see, Nancy, there's no beauty—no grace, no symmetry, no poetry like the female body—the most beautiful thing on earth."

"I suppose," Nancy agreed. "Except I guess a man has to be a real artist to see a woman that way—without thinking —well, you know what I mean."

"I know," said Parker, and sighed, and said, "You know, when Mrs. Welk was younger, I used to take nude pictures of her all the time."

"Mrs. Welk?"

"Oh, she wasn't always so heavy, you know," though she always had been, of course, beginning immediately after pregnancy, weeks before their marriage. "Well, that was long ago . . . long ago." He closed the magazine, put his head down on the desk. "Long ago . . . long ago," while he forced his mind from nudes and Nancy, and thought that Bert Mosley had finally got what he deserved, and perhaps Guy and his wife would also get what they deserved. Perhaps righteousness would prevail after all.

Behind him Nancy said, "Mr. Welk—"

The sinners would be paid in kind.

"I don't want to say the wrong thing, Mr. Welk. I mean I don't want to give you the wrong impression, you see—"

God was in his heaven.

"But I know how really *interested* you are in photography—how nudes are so *impersonal* to you—"

The Lord would strike.

"So what I mean is—I don't have any *false* modesty, you know—I mean, I'm *not* a small-town girl really, and I understand how you feel about art and all. So if you think I'd make a good enough model, well Mr. Welk, what I mean is—"

There was still a man's own conscience.

Parker placed his hands on top of his bald head. Perspiration ran down his arms, dripped off his elbows onto the green blotter. He squeezed his eyes shut tight, said, "Nancy . . . Nancy . . ." almost sobbing.

"Don't you feel good, Mr. Welk?"

"Yes, it's just—you're the only one, Nancy—you're the only one who ever *really* understood me."

Nancy went up the wooden ladder to the dark loft. Parker locked the doors, pulled the blinds, and inserted a film in his Polaroid camera. He heard squeaks and rustles from above. He stood at the bottom of the ladder and waited, trembling, perspiring, until finally Nancy's voice said, "All right, Mr. Welk," and he heaved up to the loft and saw her there on one corner of the army blanket, the opposite corner pulled high across her breasts. Parker coughed. He was very professional. He examined the yellow bulb above her head; he selected the proper angle, aimed his camera experimentally from all directions. "All right," he coughed finally from a dark corner. "If you'll just—drop the blanket, Nancy, and then keep your eyes straight ahead on that far wall—that far wall—"

Nancy dropped the blanket. Her body was brown from the sun, except for the white strip across her pointed breasts and solid thighs. She looked where he'd directed, and he thought that she was very moist and soft and young, and he took a picture, waited the minute for it to be developed, then took another.

"All right, Mr. Welk?"

"No . . . Another minute, Nancy." He put down the camera. "No, keep looking at the wall—the far wall . . . Don't turn your head . . . *Don't—turn—your—head.*"

"I'm getting tired, Mr. Welk. The light hurts my eyes."

"One minute . . . Don't turn your head . . . One minute . . ." He was panting now. It was hot and his voice choked and he thought, Oh, God, oh, my God! He thought, Nancy, Nancy, eighteen and moist and oh, my God!

Then Nancy turned and saw him.

He could never remember exactly what happened next. She gasped. Perhaps she screamed. She kept on babbling hysterically all during the time she grabbed for her clothes, all during the time she dressed and rushed stumbling for the ladder. "I quit my job . . . I'm never coming back . . . I'll tell my father . . . You'll be arrested . . ." She stopped, rushed back at him, snatched the two pictures from his numb hand and tore them to bits, smashed the camera against the floor, screamed, "Dirty old man! Filthy old man!" then rushed on down the open stairs and across the big ink-smelling room, out the door to the warm night.

It was a long time before Parker moved. He looked at the broken camera. He was very tired. Of course Nancy would not dare tell her father or anyone else, for that matter. But he was very sad all the same. The camera was broken. The pictures were torn. Nancy was to be the last of all. He was getting old now, and it would have been so perfect if she had just not *turned around.*

He put out the light and went down the ladder. He walked across the room, past the idle presses, out into the night, and down the street toward home. The bell sounded from the firehouse. Sirens wailed, and he thought about Nero and how he'd fiddled while Rome burned. He moved on down Main Street, a block over to Elm. The fire trucks roared past him and someone shouted. He turned and saw a red glow against the sky and thought that he was the editor of the *Chronicle* and he should go to the fire, except he didn't care—he didn't *care.* "I don't care, I don't *care,*" as he moved ponderously up the walk, up the steps to his dark, depressing house.

Polly sat in the living room, her fat legs spread wide as usual. She said, "Where's the fire?"

"Who cares?"

"*Now* what's the matter?"

"Nothing . . . Nothing." He went on up to his room. He opened the small steel box and looked at all the photographs and thought there were none of Fran Walker and none of Nancy Messner—only that old saggy waitress Betsy from the Lincoln, only a couple of skinny schoolteachers from the summers past, all yellow now, so familiar as to be repulsive. What was the use? Whatever was the use? "Filthy old man!" Nancy had screamed. "Dirty old man!" He dropped the photographs in an ash tray, touched a match to them, and watched all the faces and breasts and legs and thighs, all curl sensuously and burn, until there was nothing left but a terrible stench and ashes, ashes.

He went down to the living room.

Polly said, "I got a letter from Alice today."

"Oh . . ."

"She's coming from Pittsburgh to spend two weeks with us in August. Robert can't come. But she'll bring the baby, and considering it's so long since we've seen our own daughter—"

"Years," said Parker.

"Not since her marriage." Polly handed him a photograph. "She sent this picture along. The baby certainly has grown up."

Parker looked idly at the snapshot. Alice, in a summer dress, sat next to a plump baby boy on a wooden bench. Yes, the baby certainly had grown. And so had Alice, he thought. She was plumpish, too—almost voluptuous, he thought—almost voluptuous. She would be here for two weeks. He could always buy another camera, of course, and if one's own daughter could not understand her own father's interest in photographic art—

Polly said, "For heaven's sake, Parker, you're sweating like a pig." She took the snapshot from his shaking hand. "And you're trembling all over. What's the matter, Parker? What in God's name is the matter?"

"Polly . . ." It came out a whimper. "Oh, Polly, Polly . . . Help me, Polly . . . Please help me . . . Help me, help me." And he was on his knees then, his face in her enormous lap, while her fat hand caressed his glistening head and she whispered, "Parker . . . Parker, I've never seen you cry, and I've waited so terribly long . . ." while the sirens wailed and the brass bell tolled and the telephone rang—rang and rang—unanswered—and Parker sobbed into Polly's huge lap and thought that Polly was not really so fat—not really—and God was in his heaven—the Lord would strike—the sinners would be paid in kind—always a man's conscience—and next Sunday Mrs. Manning was having a buffet supper—creamed chicken on patty shells, green peas and a fruit salad, and he would go, of course . . . he would go . . . he would go . . .

Now, sitting here in the still still dark of the quiet house, Sam McFie had only the vaguest understanding of his own recent actions, his own confused emotions which had motivated them. Outside the living-room window the sky glowed red against the dark. Sirens wailed. Bells clanged. The telephone rang, but he did not answer. It rang again and then again. Still he did not answer.

Peter squawked, "Let us pray, goddammit, let us pray," and Sam said, "Shut up, Peter. Shut up!"

When had it started? Yesterday? The day before? He'd lost all sense of time. Guy Montford had come back, bringing Larry's pregnant wife, and of course it had started exactly then. Ruth Kiley had told him about it—gently, touching his arm. And at first he'd laughed, and then somehow he'd had a drink and another and then a lot more. Where had all this happened? Here in his own house? At the cannery? The Lincoln? Pat's? Somewhere anyway. And in the end it had been dark and he'd thought, Now I will kill Guy Montford. Now I will kill him dead. Except he hadn't. He was afraid. Larson Whitt would know who'd done it, and they'd send him back to that place with the barred windows, where he had to stand all day and watch the old men sitting motionless in the sun and the young men playing volley ball beneath the shade of the trees.

He'd gone to the cannery. He'd sat in his office and listened to the dull clanking of the canning machines until he could not bear to hear them any longer. He'd had three more drinks and Ruth Kiley had come in and said, "You've got to stop it, Sam." He'd said, "I hope she dies. She helped murder Larry and I hope she hemorrhages like my wife did, and she dies like my wife did, and *that* would be justice for you." His own words had fed his anger. Ruth had said, "You don't mean that, Sam," and he'd answered, "Don't tell me what *I* mean," and shouted, "Get out of here, Ruth! . . . We're too old and it's all over, and get the hell out of here!"

She'd left, weeping. He'd wanted to be alone. But still, with those clanking machines, he was not alone. He'd put his hands over his ears, and then abruptly everything had exploded all at once, so he'd rushed out among the machines, slipping on the wet floor, screaming and screaming, "Stop them, stop them! Go home, go home! . . . Leave me alone! . . . Leave me *alone!*"

Silently, one by one, the men had left. The machines stood motionless. He'd been alone among a thousand fish heads, two thousand eyes, wet and cold, staring at him from a great wooden barrel. Still, with those eyes, still he was not quite alone. He'd tried to move the barrel, but it was too heavy. He'd put a cover over it, but still the eyes could see him through the wooden staves. So that was when the plan had formed. "All right, all right. I'm leaving now. Good-by, fish heads, good-by, good-by. I'm putting out the lights. There's nobody here but you—just you."

He'd crept silent through the dark, careful to keep far from the watchful eyes inside the barrel. He'd found the kerosene and poured it slowly, soundlessly, all down the long corridor where he could not be seen. He'd touched some excelsior with a match and waited, listened while the flames licked at the wooden walls—listened, listened, until finally he'd heard the high horrible screams of the fish heads in the wooden barrel. Then he'd laughed. He'd stumbled out to his car, roaring with laughter. He'd driven home while the flames grew high behind him and the bell tolled atop the firehouse, and he'd laughed, "That'll teach you," and he'd screamed, "Leave me alone, leave me *alone!*"

Mrs. O'Hara had been cleaning up in the kitchen. He'd said, "You're fired! Get out, get out!"

"You're drunk, Mr. McFie."

"Leave me *alone!*"

"This time is the last time." Mrs. O'Hara had packed hastily and left for her relatives' in Harpswell. The phone had rung. The sirens had wailed. The fish heads had kept on screaming. From his perch Peter had said "Let us pray, goddammit, let us pray."

"Let us pray," Peter said now, again. "Let us pray."

Sam turned his head slowly. Peter stared down at him with those evil round eyes—fish eyes in a green head. "Leave me alone," he said, and Peter cackled and Sam said, "The fish are dead, and leave me alone, and stop looking at me . . . *Stop looking at me!*"

Peter did not move except to lower his head farther, so that now he seemed to be hovering over Sam like some monstrous bird of prey. Sam tried to stare the bird down, but the bright, evil eyes remained fixed unblinking on his own. Finally he turned his back, pretended to ignore the bird. The eyes, though, were still there behind him, staring, staring. He poured a drink, spilled half of it. He swore violently. He was drunk and he knew it. Crazy drunk and he knew that too, and to hell with it! To hell with all of them—Guy and Margreth and Ruth Kiley and Mrs. O'Hara—to hell with all those screaming fish heads, and to hell with you too, Peter!

"Get out!" He swung sharply, trying to catch the bird unawares. "Leave me alone!"

The bird kept staring.

"Get—out—of—my—house!"

The eyes, the eyes, smirking, unblinking, reminding him of Ruth Kiley and things gone by and things destroyed, bringing the rage up high within him so that suddenly he screamed, and when the bird still stared and smirked, then finally he charged.

Peter made the stairs in short, flurried hops, while Sam crashed into the perch and went down in a litter of sand and droppings. Peter squawked in terror and half hopped, half flew up the stairs to the landing. Sam pulled upright, swore violently and followed—up the stairs to his own bedroom, where he tripped and fell against the dresser, bringing down brushes and shaving lotions, cuff links and hair tonics—into the guest room where Peter sought refuge on the vanity behind the gold-framed picture of the dead young wife, where Sam lunged again and brought the photo smashing to the floor—down the stairs again, through the hallway to the kitchen, back into the dining room, the living room once more, back again to the hall. All the time Peter squawked and beat his useless wings; all the time Sam stumbled and fell, pulled down curtains, broke plates and furniture, tripped on rugs and swept pictures from walls and bric-a-brac from shelves with no thought in his head at all except that Peter was the last remaining link, and Peter, too, would have to go.

He caught the bird in the living room. Peter screamed and pecked viciously with his curved beak, tearing bloody pieces from Sam's hand. But Sam held him firm in drunken strength, then slowly, slowly twisted the bird's head, round and round while the screams went on and his own blood ran down his hand until finally the screams died in gurgling squawks, so that all was silent now, completely still now. And there Sam sat on the braided rug with his seafaring great-grandfather's face looking down from above the mantel. There he sat among all the family heirlooms—the sea shells and the Revere silver and the bits of ivory and the torn Chinese tapestry. There he sat with the green bird in his gray-flanneled lap, dead, though the eyes were still open—the eyes still watched him.

He was alone now, finally alone. And now alone, he was suddenly afraid. "Peter," he whispered into the silence. "Peter? . . . Peter?"

The bird did not answer. Sam straightened the twisted neck. He cradled the bird in his arms. He rocked it gently, his head lowered against the still-warm body, the bright green feathers, splotched red now with his own blood. "Let us pray," he cried softly to the dead bird and the dead past. "Let us pray, goddammit, let us pray . . ."

CHAPTER FORTY

During the first three days Mar was coherent, optimistic, full of plans for the near future. The only apparent sign of illness was her slightly increased temperature. By the fourth day, however, her temperature had still not gone down to normal, but stayed close to 103 in the afternoon, and rose high again at night, when she awoke in a hot sweat.

"I started her on a gram of streptomycin four times a day," Doctor Kelsey explained, "and I've been increasing it steadily. She's already got a ringing in her ears."

"Four days now," Guy said.

"Yes . . ." And a pause and, "The cavity's broken down, Guy. It was farther along than the X-rays indicated, and the bacilli's growing despite the streptomycin and P.A.S.—spreading to the other lung—getting into the blood stream—"

"She'll be all right," Guy told him.

Doctor Kelsey pulled at his shaggy eyebrows. "And the baby's doing fine, when by all rights, it should have died by now. Of course it'll be three months before we can be sure it'll live. But I don't know—everything seems reversed—it gives me a weird feeling, Guy, as though—well, as though you, myself, medicine—nothing has any control over this at all."

"She'll pull through. They both will."

"Guy . . ."

"And don't *ever* suggest they won't!"

But Mar would not pull through. He knew that. A few more days, another week. In the meantime more X-rays were taken that promised nothing. She had started coughing, getting pains in her chest. And now the morphine again, the quarter grain every eight hours, every six hours, every four hours . . .

"Tell me about posting," she whispered while Guy sat close beside the bed, avoiding her eyes, looking over her head toward Keever's Point and the bay and *Julia,* who would not go to Woods Hole after all. "Tell me . . . tell me . . ."

"You should never rise or post when a horse is trotting. You should sit close and firm—"

"And flexible, darling."

"Yes, and flexible until posting is a normal procedure, not a calculated one."

"Remember, darling."
"Yes."
"Everything I've taught you."
"Yes."
"We'll be leaving in another week . . . another month . . ."
"Yes."
"Oh, Guy . . . Oh, darling, Guy. I was so bad, wasn't I? If I hadn't gone on the boat—if I'd had a hysterotomy instead of a normal birth like that, then I'd probably be all right, wouldn't I, except the baby—maybe this is the *only* way the baby has a chance to live, you see . . . I don't know . . . I don't know . . . I'm praying for our baby and I'm so sorry for me. But we *will* go to Arizona . . . We will . . . we will . . ." The tears ran slowly down her cheeks, because she knew then that they would not go to Arizona after all—they would not go anywhere again.

Guy lived in numb shock. Sometimes he drove—sometimes he walked—from his house to the hospital, back to his house again, twice, three times a day. He did not see the people who passed him on the street. He looked straight ahead through the windshield—or straight down at the sidewalk—and knew that of course they all resented him, even hated him. He had duped them all, played on their sympathies with lies and half-truths, so could expect no sympathy now—not for himself, not even for Mar—no sympathy from anyone.

Occasionally someone spoke to him—or he spoke to someone. Once he passed Nancy Messner, who seemed to have grown up suddenly in the short time he'd been away. She'd quit her job on the *Chronicle*, and there was a hard, cynical gleam in her once childish eyes. He said, "Hello, Nancy," and Nancy stopped abruptly. She swung and glared at him. "Men—pigs, pigs—you're all alike," and she strode off fast without another word.

Maidie Bolls snubbed him completely; Edna Welles was too embarrassed to look him in the eye. Even the old gang in Pat's was cold, distant. Backs were turned. Lowered voices excluded him from all conversation. He would never go to Pat's again. Afterwards—when the end finally came—he would leave this town, and this time he would not return.

There were touches, though, of warmth and understanding. At the Lincoln, Betsy bent low across his table to say, "If I could just tell you—if I could only *tell* you—" And Parker Welk, of all people, walking along with his fat wife and his full-blown visiting daughter, seemed to have lost all former bitterness. "Like you to meet my daughter, Guy . . . Alice from Pittsburgh," talking slowly, an old man, tired, inexplicably worn-out, no longer interested in the sins of others.

Judge Manning, though, had not changed at all. Dignified, friendly, his old voice cracked as he leaned on his cane in the summer sun. "Got to be objective, Guy. Certainly you fooled the town. Fooled me, too. But when a man's on trial in a court of law—fighting for his very life—I suppose just about everything's fair. And you never lied outright because Colin never *asked* about Larry's wife . . . He never even *asked*." The Judge teetered away, laughing openly for his own benefit.

On the whole, though, the townspeople *were* against him. He knew and did not blame them, but actually sympathized with the way they felt. He avoided everyone possible, and thought of nothing—day and night—thought of nothing, dreamed of nothing except that Mar was dying, and why was Mar dying? Because he had not insisted on an abortion in the very beginning? Because he'd put his faith in both God and science, and now, it seemed, they would both betray him —again—for the second time? Why? . . . Why did he destroy everyone he loved—first Larry and now Mar? Everyone he loved, and even everyone he touched—

Bert Mosley, for instance. Bert had been beaten up, run out of town. And it was actually *he* who had run Bert out of town, just as it was *he* who had made Sam get drunk, burn the cannery, and drive everyone from his life, even Mrs. O'Hara, so that Sam had been all alone that night when Larson Whitt had walked in and found him there in the living room, sitting crosslegged on the floor as he sobbed hysterically into the feathers of a dead parrot. They'd taken Sam away on the following morning. He'd gone quietly, and no one expected to see him again.

Larry—Mar—Bert—Sam. There was no one he had not hurt in one way or another—even Fran Walker, who did not seem to understand what he'd done to her, who spent hours of her off-duty time looking out for Mar as she had once looked out for Larry, who brought him coffee and said kind words and cared for the child as though it were her own, and never once reproached him for anything.

He did not understand her. Sometimes, sitting beside the bed where Mar lay white, semiconscious, he looked up to find Fran watching him from the doorway. Her yellow hair dropped low to touch her shoulders; her blue eyes reflected sunlight; her white starched uniform was health and cleanliness itself. He stared back at her, unspeaking, and thought what a strange thing—how very odd it was that this girl of a thousand confused emotions, a hundred admitted sins, should appear now to be the most innocent person in town, completely guiltless of anything.

Then Fran would be gone and there'd be only the white

sheet and Mar's white face, and sometimes Mar's whispered words, "Remember, darling, when you teach our son to ride—Larry—you must have him christened 'Larry'—remember, darling, he must never let the horse go from a trot to a canter . . . never, darling, never." And he would say, "No, never, never," for it was all never now, and sometimes he put his face against the warm white of hers, and sometimes then, he cried.

In the late afternoon of the day that Larry Montford was eleven days old, Margreth opened her eyes and spoke clearly for the first time in a week. "Hello," she said softly. "Hello there, darling."

"Hello, darling." He bent forward and kissed her. He looked into the deep black eyes and said, "Feeling better?"

"Feeling beautiful, darling. Remembering everything lovely. Nothing but the lovely."

"You're lovely," he said.

"And how's our lovely son?"

"Gained a few ounces now."

"Do you think he'll be an athlete?"

"The greatest."

"Handsome?"

"A matinee idol."

"Good and marvelous like his father?"

"Brave and beautiful like his mother."

She smiled a little. "All that's lovely," she said. "A Chinese dinner and going sailing and going to bed with you—how to steam clams in seaweed, and where to look for arrowheads . . . And our wedding, darling, with Frances Treleaven banging all those awful notes on the piano and you looking so terribly serious and little Mr. Blassinghame jumping about all over the place . . . Butter on the pie, darling . . . Butter on the pie."

She began to laugh. It was high, good laughter, until then, after a moment, it turned to coughing. She tried to sit upright, but did not have the strength. Her eyes stared at him as the coughing went on, weaker now, weaker and weaker, while her eyes became more bright, seeing into him and beyond him, beyond them both, without fear and without resentment and without regret. "Butter on the pie, darling," in a last coughing whisper, and then finally, very gently—almost deliberately—she closed her eyes.

The afternoon sun was bright red on the waters of the bay. Guy stood and looked out the window at the red sails on the red boats that bobbed on the red water.

Doctor Kelsey came in behind him. His feet thumped on

the linoleum. He said something to Fran Walker. The rustle of starched sheets. "Guy . . ."

"Have you noticed the sun?"

"Shall I take you home?"

"No, I'll walk. Thank you, I'll walk." He turned and went out of the room. He did not look at the bed, but went on down the corridor past Ida Primmer at the little desk.

Ida said, "I'm glad to see Mrs. Montford's feeling better today," and he said, "Yes, she's resting peacefully now," and went down in the elevator.

The great elms were full in the late warm sun. The summer visitors had been arriving for a week. They wore Bermuda shorts and gay shirts and they laughed and jostled each other along the pavements. He did not see them. He thought, Julia died, and Mr. Hood called from the funeral parlor and asked on which side she parted her hair, only I couldn't remember. He asked me to pick out her favorite dress, only she always preferred a shirt and slacks. But he said that simply wouldn't do. Mar did not part her hair at all. He was quite sure of that. But she must have a favorite dress . . . If only he could *remember* . . .

A man jostled against him. "Where you going?"

"Home. I'm going home." He had gone home from Julia's funeral, and all the way he had planned how he would tell her about it—who was there and what they'd all said and exactly how he'd felt—except when he'd entered the house, Julia had not been there, and he could not understand it. He'd called her name three times in the empty rooms before he'd finally realized that there was no one to tell anything to at all.

The sun blinded his eyes. Mar would not be waiting. No one would be waiting. He could not go home. He could go to the Lincoln and get drunk. He could go to *Julia* and get under way and sail over the horizon into darkness. But tomorrow he would be sober again. Tomorrow he would sail back to port once more.

He walked on into the blinding sun. He stumbled, leaned against a lamppost in front of Castner's. Old Mr. Castner peered out at him over the bolts of bright cloth that lined his window. The summer people passed and a woman giggled and said, "He's drunk. Lord, isn't that man drunk!"

He was not drunk. He straightened and his eyes caught the gold cross on the steeple of St. Joseph's. It was a hot, bright gold that burned through his eyes into his brain, pulled and burned, seeming to suck him toward it so that suddenly he started running, faster and faster, stumbling, falling, rushing on through the afternoon streets, past the supermarket and the liquor store, the black cannon balls and the curious, watching people, running blindly into the sun toward the bright gold cross, until finally, exhausted, he reached the iron gate before St. Joseph's. He leaned against the gate, clutching the iron pickets, breathing heavily while the sun dropped fast to let in the darkness.

"Oh, God . . . Oh, dear God, dear God!" He pushed open the gate. It squeaked. He dragged himself up the steps and heaved open the heavy oak door. For a long moment he stood motionless in the silent church. Then finally he moved forward toward the altar and the great crucifix that shimmered in blurring lights through the stained windows. He knelt and groped hard in memory for the proper words, the correct ritual, forgotten, all lost, so that he could only say what came to him, proper or not, true or not, making sense or not making sense. "Dear God . . . Please, God . . . Why? . . . Why did You let her die? . . . Why? . . . Why, when I loved her so much? . . . So much . . . Oh, God, I loved her . . . I loved her . . . I loved her . . ."

For a moment he sobbed silently into his hands. Then finally, slowly, he raised his head once more, and he understood now, and he said, "Yes, the child . . . the child . . . In the beginning, the child, and now in the end, now still the child . . . And the sins of the fathers . . . the sins of the mothers . . . I understand now . . . I understand, and I promise You . . . I swear to You . . . If You'll let him live . . . Please let him live . . . I swear the sins will never touch this child of innocence . . . I swear, I swear, if only You'll let him live, and if only You'll help me, dear God . . . Understand *me* . . . I prayed once for death and now I'm praying for life . . . Understand *me,* and forgive me my sins, and help me, help me . . ." on and on, more and more, until it was all out of him, gone, and he rose and turned blindly in uncertain peace toward the white-haired old man, who waited in his black frock, waited, leaning on his twisted cane.

"Father Serrano," Guy said. "Father . . . I am *not* God after all."

"Made in His image," the old man said, and touched his arm.

It was dark now. Caesar whined. Fran switched on the kitchen light, poured kibble and ground meat into the dog's bowl. She looked out the back door, returned to the living room and sat waiting while the June bugs thumped against the screens. Outside a car passed in the night; a child laughed; the gulls called across the bay, until finally the footsteps sounded, the door opened, and Guy moved toward her across the room.

He looked tired, yet strangely peaceful too, and not surprised to find her here. She said, "Guy . . . Sit down, Guy."

He sat on the sofa, stared straight ahead.

"The door was unlocked, so I just—came in."

He nodded.

"About the baby, Guy. About Larry. He's going to live . . . I *know* it . . . I *feel* it, and when he leaves the hospital you'll need someone to take care of him."

"I'm going away," he said. "I'm never coming back."

"No."

"The town will never forgive me."

"Yes, they'll forgive you. They won't forget, but they *will* forgive." She sat beside him. She said, "Listen, Guy . . . I want to live here and take care of Larry . . . I want to be his nurse." He shook his head. She placed a hand on his arm, said, "Listen . . . Please understand . . . Yes, I love you . . . Always I've loved you . . . Always I will love you . . . But I know what you're feeling now . . . I know how much *you* loved, and how much you've lost . . . So I promise you, I won't push my love at you, I won't hurt you, I won't stand in your way. But you need someone, Guy . . . Larry will need someone . . ."

He did not answer. She touched his hand, said, "He *will* live, Guy, he *will* . . . And don't you see—we'll be all that's left—and I feel—loving you—loving him, too—I feel almost as though he's partly mine."

Still he did not answer. A knock at the door. She hesitated, then rose and opened it on Stewart Schaeffer. He was dressed immaculately in his old, outdated clothes—spats and a high, stiff collar, a flowing tie, and a large stickpin. He'd shaved, and his hair was combed, and he was almost sober, and frightened, too—for some reason, very frightened.

"Yes, Mr. Schaeffer?" But the old man did not answer. He stepped past her into the room. He looked at Guy and Guy stared back at the wrinkled, twitching face, then rose hesitantly while the old man moved toward him, mumbling on in his hoarse, whiskey voice. "I'm sorry . . . Sorry, and I understand, and for what it's worth, I'm with you and you can count on me, and—" He started to say more, but could not go on.

Guy said, "Thank you . . . You don't know . . . Thank you." Then suddenly the old man began to cry. He turned abruptly, tried to laugh. "Need a drink . . . Not one all day . . . Not one, and God, do I need a drink!" He laughed; he cried. He put out a hand and touched Guy's sleeve, then turned and stumbled out the door and disappeared in darkness.

Fran closed the door. She said, "Guy?" frowning, puzzled. "Guy?"

He did not answer.

She sat once more and watched him from across the room. His eyes were fixed on the floor. He looked tired, yet somehow at ease, as though he'd fought a long fight, and it was over now, and in time, with rest, he would rise and fight again.

The bugs still thumped against the screens. The gulls still cried across the bay. Caesar whined and rubbed his head against her knees. She nuzzled the dog's head, said, "Don't worry, boy," then, "Guy, would you like some coffee?"

"Yes . . . Thank you, Fran."

She rose and moved into the kitchen. She found the coffee, but it was a long time before she located the percolator. "Cream or sugar?" she called back to the living room.

"Black, please."

"From now on, I'll remember," as she stood there watching the bubbling water, thinking there was so much to learn and so much to remember. But time would pass . . . it would . . . it *would*, and Larry would live . . . he would, he *would*, and she would wait . . . wait and wait . . . as she waited now, motionless by the stove, watching the slow-perking coffee, praying and waiting in the summer night.